The Battle ɪoɪ Allegra

The Complete Season One Omnibus

Episodes One to Ten

CHECK OUT OUR FREE CONTENT!

BE THE FIRST

To see anything from The Limit of Infinity Universe!

That means you'll see all sorts of content

before anyone else!

Check us out at:

http://calebfast.com/

The Battle for Allegra

The Complete
Season One Omnibus

Episodes 1-10

Caleb Fast

www.calebfast.com

First Published in 2021 by the Author on Amazon

Copyright © 2021 by Caleb Fast

ISBN-13: 979-8517084842

This edition: First Edition, First Printing, June 2021

CONTENTS

Conscripted

Chapter One   1

Chapter Two   21

Chapter Three   39

First Kill

Chapter One   69

Chapter Two   81

Chapter Three   107

The Hunt

Chapter One   124

Chapter Two   155

Chapter Three   174

Relegated

Chapter One   182

Chapter Two   205

Chapter Three   227

Retrieval

Chapter One   240

Chapter Two   264

Chapter Three   298

Sanctuary

Chapter One   306

Chapter Two   329

Chapter Three   366

Secured

Chapter One   396

Chapter Two   419

Chapter Three   431

Harborage

Chapter One   470

Chapter Two   491

Chapter Three   500

Chapter Four   504

Revelations

Chapter One   524

Chapter Two   536

Chapter Three   554

Promotion

Chapter One   593

Chapter Two   603

Chapter Three   619

Chapter Four   654

Conscripted

The Battle for Allegra

Episode One

Chapter One

Crail, Sinclair

"There's nothing like it," Matthew Campbell whispers in awe as he stares at the coastal cliffs that hem in his hometown of Crail. As usual, the sun is just beginning to set, and it is gently slipping behind the island. A fiery red sunset seemingly highlights the dark cliffs.

Crail is a small fishing village situated on one of the few islands that dot the vast oceans of Matthew's homeworld of Sinclair. The hundred or so buildings that the village is comprised of are all built of the same monotone grey shale that the island is made of.

1

Sun-bleached wooden roofs lighten the scene, albeit only slightly. The only color that graces Crail comes from a handful of homes painted with various shades of green. That green paint was made from a seaweed that only the most patient and resourceful people dared to make a paint from, which coincidentally described a fair portion of Crail's population. Matthew didn't see why someone would put in the effort to paint a house green, but he had to admit that the splash of color did make his homecoming more pleasant.

The harbor of Crail is bustling with other ships that make up the town's meager fishing fleet. Matthew sighs as he realizes that once again, he is on the last ship to return home for the day. That means that the food waiting for him and the others would be cold by now—if there was even any left.

"And there's nothing better than it," Matthew's dad, Heron Campbell, says as he comes up behind Matthew and clasps his shoulder.

Heron had been raised up to be a fisherman and sailor since the day he was born. For generations, the family business had been fishing, and Heron wasn't about to let that change.

The problem is that Matthew has no intention to follow in his father's footsteps.

"Dad, I can't stay here forever," Matthew starts without turning to face his father. They had had this same conversation countless times before, and the answer always remained the same.

"And who would bring in the fish to feed the village?" Heron repeats the same exact argument he always used.

"You've got a whole crew. And besides that, Mark can take over for me," Matthew volunteers his younger brother. Oddly enough, he had never tried telling his father to try recruiting his other siblings to sail in his place.

"Mark is too young to work the nets," Heron replies. Matthew can hear him turn and march back across the deck of their small fishing ship toward the rear of the vessel.

"So was I when you first began teaching me! I can't just stay here and fish for the rest of my life!"

"What else would you do?"

"I've got a bit of an idea," Matthew replies as he turns and walks toward his father who is now at the ship's helm. Matthew skirts around several members of his father's crew as he makes his way across the now-crowded

3

deck. Once he passes the ship's sole mast, Matthew continues, "I was actually thinking I'd become a pilot or something. You taught me to navigate by the stars, so I'd never get lost. Besides, no one else would be able to do the same, they'd all depend on their computers to get around."

"There's already plenty of pilots out there, son," Heron shakes his head, "You can ask any of the spacers when the next shipment comes."

"But the next shipment isn't due for another month!" Matthew whines as he starts tugging on a nearby rope to help draw in the sails.

Heron remains silent for several beats before he eventually says, "Tell them that," Heron proceeds to point behind Matthew toward Crail. Sure enough, a space shuttle is slowly descending from the overcast skies above their home.

For as long as Matthew can remember, the Coalition had sent shipments of supplies and medicine to Crail once a year. Shipments usually were comprised of just a few large crates, many of which were already half-empty. But, the thrill of goods from alien planets made up for all they lacked--both in quantity and in usefulness.

In return for the measly shipments, the fishermen of Crail would fill up the freighter with most of their recent catch. Matthew was told that this was to meet a Coalition edict. Said edict dictated exactly how much fish had to be handed over and failure to do so was punishable by imprisonment.

Every year, the required amount of fish increased, which was always met with the same moaning and groaning from sailors like Matthew's dad. Despite the countless complaints from the fishermen, the increased quotas remained, and threats of a greater increases loomed. The workload on the fishermen increased to keep the pace as each man slowly was worked to death.

Frowning, Matthew mutters, "Oh joy, more useless junk."

"At least we get something in exchange for our work," Heron points out optimistically as the wind slowly carries them toward Crail's harbor.

"I wonder why they're early," Matthew muses as he finishes up his work with the sails, "I hope they haven't come for this year's collection."

"Indeed," Heron agrees with a slow nod.

For one reason or another, the Coalition Overseers who presided over the loading of fish insisted that all the fish be fresh. This meant that the people of Crail went hungry the weeks leading up to the Coalition's arrival. Such measures were necessary to ensure only the freshest fish were stockpiled for the exchange. Every single fish that was caught for nearly a whole month went directly into cold storage to ensure that they were as fresh as possible.

Matthew makes his way to the bow of his family's quaint boat as he scans the docks for his lifelong love, Dixie McNeil, who always welcomed him back ashore. Without much effort, he quickly picks her out of the crowd of people dockside, and he can't help but smile. Even at this distance Matthew can't help but admire her beauty.

"What's going on?" Matthew shouts as he cups his hands over his mouth to ensure his voice carries over the choppy waters in the harbor.

Dixie cups her own hands over her mouth, and after a short moment, her faint reply is carried over the water, "Something happened!"

Matthew raises his right fist for Dixie to

indicate that he had heard her. After a beat, he whispers to himself, "What could have happened to make them come all the way out here?"

"What's the news?" Heron calls from the helm.

"Dix says something happened," Matthew responds as he weaves his way back to his father.

"Why would they come all the way out here?" Heron wonders aloud.

"That's what I was thinking," Matthew concurs as Heron skillfully guides their fishing vessel alongside the dock where they eventually slow to a stop.

Matthew sees Dixie frantically waving him over and he quickly rushes over to the ship's starboard railing. He pauses a beat as the crew catches some lines which are thrown to them by those on the docks. Once the lines are caught, the crew starts pulling their modest vessel closer to the dockside to unload the day's bountiful catch.

Dixie works her way past the dozens of dockhands who are itching to finish unloading their final ship before they finally get to head home. Once she is near, she calls out, "They've called for us to meet in the workshop!"

"Just us?" Matthew inquires with a curious look.

"Everyone ages sixteen to twenty," Dixie answers dutifully as she returns Matthew's look. She glances around at everyone else before continuing in a concerned voice, "What do you think they want?"

"Your guess is as good as mine," Matthew shrugs as the crew lashes the ship alongside the dock. Once the ship is secure, he climbs over the worn wood rail and drops down to the stone dock below.

Matthew looks over to the space freighter which has since landed atop of the cliffs which overlook the town. He can't help but stare as people dressed in strange dark blue uniforms disembark. Customarily crates were the cargo that was being unloaded, not soldiers. One of them pulls another aside and points around the town, assumedly telling their companion everything about Crail.

"What is it?" Dixie inquires as she cocks her head at Matthew. She eventually follows his stare and whispers, "Who are they?"

"They look like soldiers," Matthew replies absently.

"What are soldiers doing here?" Dixie

wonders aloud.

"I don't know," Matthew shrugs dismissively. Looking back to his father who is still aboard their ship, he calls out, "Dad, I'm going to the workshop with Dix!"

"You're going to miss supper," Heron warns.

Matthew simply nods that he heard his father before turning and leading Dixie through the crowd of people on the dock. Several people glare at him accusingly, since he isn't helping to unload the ship, but he could care less.

"Are the others there yet?" Matthew asks Dixie once they've freed themselves from the crowd.

"Yes, I only left in order to get you," Dixie replies.

"What do they think is happening?" Matthew inquires as he and Dixie make their way down the cobbled streets of Crail toward the workshop.

"Maveric said that he only heard some of what the freighter's captain said when they were calling ahead," Dixie starts as she purses her lips. She sighs before continuing, "He said he didn't like the sounds of it, but that's all he would tell us."

Matthew silently nods for a few moments before he eventually mutters loud enough for Dixie to hear, "Something isn't right, that's for sure."

Dixie and Matthew continue the rest of the way to the workshop in an uneasy silence. Several people greet Matthew warmly as he walks by, which helps to slightly ease his worry. Thanks to his father's reputation as the town's premier fisherman, Matthew is also very well-known and respected.

The walk across town to the workshop isn't too long, since Crail was so small. As Matthew and Dixie near the large structure, they can just make out several impassioned voices arguing just outside the building.

"They can't take our boys!" Dixie's aunt, Mrs. McNeil, argues, "They've got no right!"

"They don't need a right, they're doing it anyway," seeing Matthew and Dixie approaching, Matthew's mom, Ophelia, quickly whispers her response. It is clear that she doesn't want the two of them overhearing anything.

"What's going on, Auntie?" Dixie asks worriedly.

"We don't know for sure, honey," Mrs. McNeil replies softly, "But you and Matthew need to go inside."

"But you said—" Dixie starts to protest.

"Thank you, Mrs. McNeil," Matthew interrupts Dixie as he shepherds her through the workshop's massive doors, which, as always, are wide open.

"Didn't you hear what they were saying?" Dixie demands in a hurried whisper.

"I did," Matthew nods as he looks around the workshop.

Crail's workshop is one of the few buildings in town that has electricity. The power is used to operate all the various tools which the townsfolk use from time to time. The workshop serves as a place for everyone to build and fix whatever they need whenever they needed. All the tools are lined along the exterior walls, leaving a large area in the center of the structure that can accommodate a group of nearly fifty people.

"Matthew!" Tiana Halladay waves to him. She is standing in a group of twenty-three of Matthew's friends who are aged sixteen to twenty—as per the bracket Dixie had passed along to Matthew.

"What's going on?" Matthew asks as he looks at all his friends. They had all grown up together, so they knew each other well enough to not lie.

"It would seem that they think Allegra may be under attack," Maveric replies in a serious tone. Maveric McCoy always had a serious tone, and Matthew couldn't help but think it was because Maveric didn't spare the time to joke like everyone else. Everything was so serious in his world, not to mention very black and white. Nodding Maveric looks to Matthew and continues, "I wanted to await your arrival before I told everyone."

"Allegra?" Matthew asks in surprise.

The Allegra system is the nearest populated system to Sinclair. It is much more populous than Sinclair, boasting nearly ten million people across its sole habitable planet. That isn't even to mention the additional two million living on its five moons. Much of the supplies delivered to Crail comes directly from Allegra, which is the Coalition's seat of power for the sector.

"But who would attack them?" Dixie eventually asks.

Allegra, like Sinclair, is far from what had been established as no-man's-land a little over forty years ago. Matthew had been born on the anniversary of this historic treaty that promised peace in their time. The armistice which the Alexandrians and Coalition signed established a boundary which ensured that the Alexandrians couldn't rekindle the civil war they started.

In addition to being far from the front, Allegra and Sinclair are far from the core worlds as well. They don't have much to offer in terms of resources either. Allegra and Sinclair are some of the outmost holds that humanity has in the Milky Way.

"I don't know," Maveric admits, "All I can say for sure is that the local garrison there is not faring too well."

"Do you think they are going to send us in to help?" Matthew asks, his pulse quickening. This may just be his chance to get offworld.

Maveric purses his lips as he nods slowly. He frowns and replies, "I believe so."

"But I can't leave my brother," Dixie protests helplessly, "It's all Auntie can do to feed us, she can't take care of him too!"

"I am sure they'll make exceptions," Maveric assures her, "After all, they likely didn't come here expecting too many people, so they likely won't miss you."

"Where are they?" a voice demands loudly just outside, causing Matthew and the others to jump.

"They're inside," someone replies. There is a brief pause before they continue in a softer voice, "What do you want with them?"

A moment later, Matthew sees a column of soldiers march through the workshop's doors. At the head of the group is a scowling man who appears to be in charge. His cold eyes tear through the room before coming to a rest on Matthew and the others.

Scowling, the man demands, "Is this it?"

"Yes, sir," Maveric replies as he inclines his head slightly.

"So, they do teach respect on this lousy planet," the man nods approvingly at Maveric. After what feels like an eternity, the man continues, "I am Master Sergeant Nelson. You will address me as 'Master Sergeant', or 'sir.' Any questions?"

Matthew and the others nod and a few of them go as far as to say, "Yes, sir,"

"We were told this was a sizable settlement," a nearby soldier sounds as they look at Matthew and the others accusingly.

"This is one of the larger villages on Sinclair, yes," Matthew affirms as he looks at the faces of his friends. He continues, careful to use 'sir' in order to please the man who calls himself Nelson, "But this is everyone you called for, sir."

"This is not enough," another soldier grumbles, their concern evident.

Nelson scoffs as he makes his way to a nearby worktable. He swipes all the various works in progress off its surface, sending them clattering to the ground. He positions himself behind it before he responds to the soldier, "It is all we have."

"Line up, all of you," a soldier instructs as he motions to the table, "Line up youngest to oldest."

Matthew and the others quickly line up as they were told, exchanging the occasional anxious glance with one another. Matthew takes his spot near the end of the line, just ahead of Maveric, who is the eldest.

"You, step forward," the solder instructs as he points to Emily, who, being the youngest, is at the forefront of the line. Once Emily steps forward, the man in charge looks her over.

Pulling out a handheld computer of sorts, Nelson slowly instructs, "State your name, date and place of birth, and any skills you have."

"Emily Gordon, born July twenty-second, twenty-two sixty-eight," Emily starts listing her name and birthdate.

"You just turned sixteen I see," Nelson nods.

"Yes," Emily replies with a quiver in her voice. Nelson gives her a passive look, which prods her to continue, "I was born here in Crail and I work with my parents who are the town's healers."

"Good," Nelson nods, "You'll be my new medic."

Things continue smoothly for the next five people, who seamlessly pass along their information and are given different jobs by Nelson. The soldiers, Nelson included, appear to be satisfied by how skilled the youth of Crail are, which Matthew finds encouraging.

"Next," Nelson waves Dixie up.

"I can't leave here," Dixie blurts out, "I have to attend to my brother. You see, he is ill—"

"Are you of age?" Nelson cuts her off.

"Yes, but—" Dixie starts.

"Are you able-bodied?" Nelson interrupts her once more. He continues as he stands from his table, "Every able-bodied citizen who is of age is required to serve."

"Yes, but my brother—"

"This town is full of people who can

stand in for you."

"I—"

"Come with me," Nelson instructs Dixie as he steps around the table.

Nelson nods to his soldiers who quickly make a line between the queue of teens and the table. He guides Dixie over to a nearby line of tools without uttering a word.

"What are you doing?" Matthew demands, worrying for Dixie.

"I am allowing her to stay," Nelson replies as he stops at a line of the heavy equipment. Without wasting any time, he takes Dixie's arm and forces it onto a nearby drill press.

"What are you doing?" Dixie cries, repeating Matthew's question as she jerks her arm away and tries to flee. Nelson quickly catches her and waves a few soldiers over to help him.

"Leave her alone!" Matthew shouts as he breaks from his line and takes a step toward Dixie and Nelson.

"Get back in line," Nelson warns him as Dixie struggles against his grip.

One of the soldiers between Matthew and Dixie raises their hand and orders, "Stop right there."

"You can't do that!" Matthew maintains as he continues forward, ignoring Nelson and the soldier.

The soldier nearest Matthew proceeds to hit Matthew in the gut with the butt of their rifle, stopping him dead in his tracks. Matthew collapses as the wind is knocked out of his lungs and he gasps on the floor, helplessly watching the scene unfold before him. Realizing that he won't be able to help Dixie, Matthew looks to his friends who are all frozen with fear.

"No!" Dixie screams causing a commotion outside. She kicks at a nearby soldier who catches her foot and then flips her over.

"Let her be!" Maveric speaks up. Maveric, like the others, has yet to move.

Nelson forces Dixie's hand onto the drill press once more as his soldiers struggle to immobilize her. Nelson then turns the drill on, and the drill's bit starts lowering toward Dixie's hand.

"Stop it," Matthew wheezes weakly as he tries to rise back to his feet. A foot finds its way onto his back, forcing him back to the ground.

Dixie's scream resounds throughout the

workshop, muting the screech of the drill as it digs into the metal table that Dixie's hand is placed on. The drill suddenly stops, but Dixie's cries continue on, echoing off of the cool stone walls.

"No…" Matthew chokes as he continues gasping for breath.

"Congratulations, you may now stay at home," Nelson declares as he throws Dixie to the ground.

Dixie continues crying as she clutches her right hand. Blood is streaming out from between the fingers of her left hand, which she is trying to slow the bleeding with. She curls up into a ball, doing her best to hide herself from any additional punishment that Nelson may dish out.

"Dix!" Matthew whispers hoarsely as he helplessly looks to the girl who is his everything.

"Next!" Nelson shouts to the line as he returns to his table. Once he is back behind his table, he pulls out a handkerchief and wipes some blood off his face. He looks up to the line of youth and repeats himself, "Next!"

The rest of the line cycles through, providing their various details, this time with a lot less gusto. Before long, Matthew catches his breath, but the soldiers keep him from rejoining the line. After a few minutes, all of his friends have fed their information to Nelson, leaving just Matthew.

"Now, how is my little fighter?" Nelson inquires mockingly as he gives Matthew a cruel grin.

"Go to Hell," Matthew seethes, using the most vile utterance he can think of.

"Maybe someday," Nelson nods slowly as he looks Matthew up and down. He stares at Matthew for several minutes before he eventually continues, "If you were more obedient, I would have had you by my side. I need fighters like you. Well-built, protective, brave... Instead, you'll be one of the Mudders."

Several soldiers chuckle with low voices, which sends a chill down Matthew's spine. Whatever a 'Mudder' is, it can't be good.

"Mudder?" Matthew inquires.
"You'll be on the front lines, in the mud," Nelson declares, "Alongside everyone else who is too dumb to obey their superiors."

Chapter Two

Crail, Sinclair

"Move, Mudder!" a soldier shouts at Matthew immediately after Nelson gave the order for everyone to board the freighter.

Matthew lets his head drop slightly as he follows the line of his friends up the steel ramp into the underbelly of the space freighter he had seen so many times before.

The smell of fish is thick in the air, and Matthew can see a few of his friends nearly gag at the overpowering scent. Sure, the smell of old fish is bad, but Matthew had long since grown used to it. Years of fishing trained him to ignore his sense of smell.

As Matthew and the others are guided out of the freighter's cargo area, Maveric catches up to him and whispers, "I'm sorry about what happened to Dixie."

"At least she won't have to leave her brother," Matthew shrugs, unable to shake a sinking feeling in his gut. The feeling in the pit of his stomach is just as cold and weighty as one of the weights from the drag nets he had used for years.

"Not you, Mudder," a soldier warns as he takes a hold of Matthew's shoulder to stop him.

Partially out of instinct, and partially out of defiance, Matthew jumps out of the soldier's reach. Figuring that things couldn't get worse; Matthew decides it is time to return the favor of what the soldiers did to him when he tried to save Dixie. More importantly, he wanted to avenge Dixie in whatever way he could.

"You little—" The soldier seethes before Matthew delivers a mighty blow to the base of the man's chest, knocking the wind out of him.

"We got a runner!" one of the soldiers calls out when he sees his friend squirming on the ground.

"I'm not going anywhere," Matthew mutters as he raises his fists and approaches the next nearest soldier up the line.

"Oh, so you think you can fight?" the soldier laughs mockingly, "We'll see about that."

Matthew stands idle as the soldier slowly unclasps his belt. He tosses the piece of leather behind him, sending his knife and sidearm along with it. Half of the soldiers gather behind their comrade to watch the fight while the other half herd the rest of Matthew's friends on ahead.

"You should be thanking us for letting your girlfriend get off easy," one of the soldiers warns Matthew.

"You should have picked a fight with someone who could have defended themselves," Matthew counters before he turns his full attention back to the soldier before him.

"What do you guys say, should I go easy on him?" the man asks as he eyes Matthew.

"Take him out quick before Nelson gets back," one of the soldiers offers.

"That doesn't sound—" The soldier starts before Matthew lunges at him and delivers a light punch to his gut. Matthew decided it would be better if he hid his true strength until the time was right.

"Come on," Matthew taunts.

"That was a poor excuse for a hit," the soldier mocks as he positions his arms to defend against another punch to the gut.

Matthew locks his jaw as he eyes the soldier before him. If he had learned anything from years of fighting on his dad's boat, he knew to test his adversary for weaknesses. He takes a step toward the man, his arms still raised to deflect a hit.

The soldier catches Matthew by surprise as he suddenly sends a kick directly into Matthew's ribs, just under his outstretched arms. The force of the kick makes Matthew stumble off to the side, and the soldier advances, trying to make the most of Matthew's loss of balance.

Matthew swings at the soldier with his left arm as the man prepares to deliver another hit. Luck on his side, Matthew quickly makes contact with the side of the man's head. The soldier stumbles backwards a few steps in a daze, he was clearly not ready for Matthew's quick recovery.

Matthew charges the soldier, who is holding the side of his head where he had just been hit. Several other soldiers cry out, trying to warn their friend to no avail. Matthew slams into the soldier, his shoulder hits just below the man's ribs. Wrapping his arms around the soldier's thick torso, Matthew picks the man up and throws him with all his might into a nearby stack of crates.

The crates topple atop of the soldier who assumedly had been knocked out at some point during the fight. Emboldened by the quick victory, Matthew swaggers back to the line of soldiers and gives them a cocky smile.

Narrowing his eyes at them, he challenges, "Anyone else want a try?"

"Easy lad, you don't want to get in any more trouble," one of the soldiers mutters a quick warning. Matthew looks at this soldier and notes that he is dressed in a uniform that doesn't match the others.

"I'll take you," a soldier announces as he peels off his shirt and hands off his weapons to another soldier. Matthew chuckles when he sees several bystanders exchanging bets, which they collect in a hat.

Matthew eyes the man as he approaches, and he feels a slight tinge of nervousness. This man is easily twice Matthew's weight and is also a head and shoulders taller than him as well.

At this realization, Matthew changes gears, and he decides to use his own speed to his advantage. Matthew quickly darts around the soldier and delivers two quick punches to the man's kidneys as he dances in a circle around the man.

The man brings both fists down toward Matthew who quickly retreats, unscathed. From a safe distance, Matthew sees that his two hits didn't seem to faze the massive soldier, which worries him.

"Too afraid to take me head-on?" the soldier mocks as he places his hands on his hips and lets out a booming laugh. The man looks up to the ceiling of the cargo area as he continues laughing, leaving his entire torso undefended.

Matthew briefly considers charging once more, but he can tell that doing so would be his own undoing. The laughing soldier clearly is trying to bait Matthew into coming within range. Unwilling to enter the line of fire, Matthew tries to figure out another way to attack the man.

"Go on, fight already!" one of the soldiers on the sidelines urges Matthew and his opponent after a few still moments.

The large soldier makes the first move, and he charges Matthew. Matthew freezes for a moment as he decides what to do next. After the briefest moment of thought, he opts to charge toward the man as well.

Just a meter away from smashing into the soldier headlong, Matthew drops backwards, kicking both of his legs out toward the soldier's head. Both his feet make contact with the man's chin and the soldier's head snaps upwards.

The soldier's momentum carries him forward, and he collapses on top of Matthew who quickly shoves him off. Matthew scrambles to his feet and he raises his arms once more in order to repel any further attacks.

The attacks don't come, and after a brief moment which feels like several minutes, Matthew lowers his hands and looks down to the soldier who still hadn't moved. He pokes at the man with his foot and realizes that the man is covered in blood.

Worried, Matthew drops to his knees and rolls the large soldier onto his back. He looks at the man's bloodied face, and he catches his breath when the man still doesn't move. For a split second, he wonders if he had caused more harm than he intended to.

"Get a doctor!" Matthew calls as he reaches to the man's throat and clumsily checks for a pulse.

"Moon!" the soldier in the special uniform calls out as they race over to Matthew's side.

Matthew flinches as the man reaches him, but he quickly sees that the man is more interested in his friend. The man swats Matthew's hand away from the large soldier's throat and he replaces it with his own. He holds it there for a moment before he lifts the soldier's eyelid and peers at the man's still eye.

"Is he alright?" Matthew asks, his worry evident.

"He's unconscious," the man informs him after a beat. He eventually looks up to Matthew and asks, "What were you doing? Why didn't you just run?"

"I'm no coward," Matthew shrugs as he lets the soldier take over for him.

"I can see that," the soldier chuckles. He looks up to the handful of spectators who are still watching them and calls out, "Get me a stretcher!"

Worried, Matthew quietly inquires, "Is he going to be okay?"

The man rubs his knuckles up and down the large soldier's sternum steadily increasing pressure for a few moments. Frowning, the man eventually announces, "I think you might have just put him in a coma."

"Is that bad?" Matthew asks as he looks at the unmoving man.

"It's not good, but he's not dead," the man informs Matthew as he slowly rises to his feet. Nodding approvingly, he continues, "Where did you learn to fight, kid?"

"We got bored sometimes on my dad's fishing ship," Matthew offers with a shrug.

"Well, you just beat the best soldier we

had in hand to hand combat," the man continues with a proud nod. After a beat, he continues, "I'm Captain Johnson."

"I'm Matthew Campbell," Matthew offers.

"Ah, so you're my new Mudder," Johnson smiles proudly. He offers Matthew a hand as he continues, "Welcome aboard."

"Thanks," Matthew smiles as he takes Johnson's hand and rises to his feet. Once standing, he asks, "So are you in charge of the Mudders then?"

"Yes, but I won't be in the trenches with the rest of you," Johnson frowns, "They won't let officers on the front lines since they've already lost too many of us."

"Oh," Matthew nods, crestfallen. He had hoped that he had won himself a friend.

"Campbell!" Nelson beckons with a shout from the doorway leading out of the cargo area.

"You had best get over there," Johnson advises, "After a show like this, insubordination is ill-advised."

Matthew nods to Johnson as he starts for Nelson. He isn't sure what fate lay ahead of him now, but he doubts it can be good. After the short time Matthew had known Nelson, he knew enough to be worried.

The group of soldiers who are still standing around part before Matthew. He can't tell if this is out of their fear of him, or fear of Nelson, but he doesn't care. He closes the remaining distance between him and Nelson before the man eventually shows some sign of life.

"I saw what you did back there," Nelson nods as he waves for Matthew to follow him. He then guides Matthew down several different hallways before ushering Matthew into what appears to be a meeting room. Nelson motions for Matthew to take a seat before he asks, "Where'd you learn to fight like that?"

"I picked up a thing or two over the years," Matthew replies numbly.

"That's more than a thing or two," Nelson chuckles with a half grin, "Go on, tell me more."

"Am I in trouble?" Matthew inquires as he scans Nelson's face for any clues.

"No, no," Nelson shakes his head, "No more than you were already in, at least."

"Alright," Matthew frowns, unsure how he feels about the answer. Nelson had already ruined any chance he had at gaining Matthew's trust, thanks to what he did to Dixie. After a beat, Matthew resigns himself to his fate and he starts, "Sometimes the crew got bored on my dad's fishing ship and they would fight. They'd wager their rations or things like that. After a while, I figured I'd joined in."

"Your father owns a ship?" Nelson asks, seemingly for his own sake. After a beat, he continues, "Has he ever left you in charge of things aboard his ship?"

"Well sure—" Matthew starts.

"That settles it," Nelson declares, "You're back on my good side."

"Does that mean I don't need to be a Mudder anymore?" Matthew inquires hopefully once the shock of Nelson's declaration wears off. A moment later, he frowns, knowing that he doesn't want to be on Nelson's good side for Dixie's sake.

"Oh, you'll be a Mudder alright," Nelson nods slowly, "I can't change your assignment. But I can give you a promotion. You'll be a stand-in captain down there once you're ready. You'll be training under Johnson, who I know you met."

"But he said he doesn't spend time on the front," Matthew reminds Nelson.

"We'll figure something out for that," Nelson assures Matthew as he stands, "Now I'm going to leave you in here for the remainder of the flight to ensure that you don't incapacitate any more of my people."

Nelson nods and Matthew can see by his expression that he is tickled by his fighting prowess. Nelson promptly nods and then stalks out of the room.

Nelson's infatuation with Matthew only serves to make him nervous. *What if he tries to have me join his core team?* Matthew wonders to himself with a twinge of disgust, *I'd kill him at the first chance I got! …And then I would be in real trouble.*

Matthew slowly rises from his seat and he makes for the door, which he absently tries to open. After waving over several sensors and pressing more buttons than he could keep track of, Matthew shrugs, figuring that Nelson locked him in. Frowning Matthew then walks to the far corner of the room and sits on the cold steel floor. After a few minutes, Matthew draws his knees up to his chest and he closes his eyes. Trying to get a little more comfortable, he rests his chin on his knees as well.

Dixie is lucky that she still has a hand after that stunt Nelson pulled, Matthew thinks bitterly as he scowls at the seat Nelson had been sitting in. He shakes his head, trying his best to forget Dixie's screams.

The only thing more heartbreaking than hearing Dix's cries of pain was leaving her behind on the ground in a growing pool of her own blood. Matthew had tried time and time again to break free from the grip of the soldiers Nelson had escorting him out of the city. As he was torn away from Dixie in her moment of need, Matthew felt like something was getting killed inside of him.

And then he saw his mother's face as she watched him nearly getting carried out of the workshop. All he could see in her eyes was fear and disappointment. That's what really finished off whatever it was within him that was getting killed by leaving Dixie.

Once he was escorted to the edge of the city, Nelson had the soldiers release Matthew, who, by then, had substantially calmed down. He knew he was defeated, and every step he took away from his home echoed with failure.

In Matthew's mind, his lashing out at those three soldiers was the least he could do to avenge what they did to Dixie. That, and the fact that fighting had become a great way for him to let loose. When he got mad enough, pain felt good. *Causing* pain felt even better at times like that as well.

•••••••••••••

"You made a great impression on Nelson!" Johnson declares as he enters the meeting room Matthew is in.

Matthew jumps to his feet, his eyes wide open and arms raised defensively after being awakened from the light nap he had been taking. He blinks a few times as he focuses on Johnson, who is still standing at the open doorway.

"That guy makes me sick," Matthew scowls once more at the empty seat Nelson had sat in.

"I heard about what he did," Johnson nods as he enters the room, the door sliding shut behind him. He continues after a thoughtful beat, "I'm sorry he did that. He has a thing for people trying to get out of their responsibilities."

"Dixie had a responsibility—and it was to her brother," Matthew informs Johnson who sets two trays of food on the table.

"Well, Nelson didn't see it that way," Johnson tells Matthew as he takes a seat in front of one of the trays of food.

"I don't care what he thinks," Matthew

shakes his head in disgust.

"Well, you should," Johnson advises as he takes a hold of his table utensils, "Because he's got the power to keep you alive or kill you."

"I'd love to see him try," Matthew chuckles as he looks down at his knuckles. He wiggles his fingers about before clenching them into fists.

"Keep a cap on your emotions, they haven't done well for you thus far."

"It's a little late for that, wouldn't you think?"

"It's never too late to start afresh," Johnson shrugs as he takes a bite of his food. Matthew watches him for a moment as he realizes how young Johnson is. He had to of been no more than eighteen. Johnson swallows before he continues, "Are you interested in eating, or not?"

Matthew takes a seat across from Johnson and he stares expectantly at the food for a few moments before diving in. His plate is nearly empty before he eventually asks, through mouthfuls, "So… what are… we looking at when we get… to Allegra?"

"One of the biggest bloodbaths of the century," Johnson frowns as he sets down his fork and leans back in his chair. Stroking his chin, he continues, "I've never seen anything like this. The creatures we're up against— they're not from this galaxy."

"So, where are they from?" Matthew asks before he finishes clearing his plate. Part of him longs for some more food, but he had learned how to get by with less than enough.

"We don't know yet, but I guess there are teams working on figuring that out all across Coalition space."

"How long has it been since they arrived?"

"Nearly a month now,"

"And they're just now trying to get help?"

"The local garrison was able to hold off what turned out to be the first wave. Then the second wave hit. And the third. Now we're facing the eleventh wave, and they're fiercer than ever. We lost contact with the last member of the original garrison two weeks ago."

"How many soldiers were in the garrison?"

"Five thousand."

"Five thousand?" Matthew asks incredulously, "There aren't even that many people in all of Crail!"

"And there won't be anyone left there if we don't deal with this threat," Johnson says flatly as he rises from his seat and starts pacing the length of the room.

"I was wondering one more thing," Matthew starts, hoping Johnson would bite.

"What is it?" Johnson absently asks as he paces.

"How bad is it on the front lines where I'll be going?"

"It's the worse of the war."

"Well isn't that great," Matthew mutters sarcastically with a frown as he slouches in his seat.

Johnson examines Matthew for a few silent moments before he frowns and adds, "And I won't be allowed to train you to become a captain until you've survived down there for a while."

"Well, it sounds like you'll need a new trainee then," Matthew moans as he covers his face with his hands.

"I'm sure you'll pull through," Johnson nods with an assuring smile. He returns to his seat across from Matthew before he continues, "But I have one last bit of bad news."

"More bad news?"

"You won't receive any training, other

than a quick shooting crash course."

"Why is that all I'm getting?"

"The Coalition doesn't believe that training those on the frontmost lines is worthwhile. The casualty rate is too high, so they decided to just throw people that they think are expendable up there."

"So, I'm expendable then?"

"You're the one who got on Nelson's bad side," Johnson reminds Matthew with a shrug.

"Anything else?" Matthew asks, feeling defeated.

"You'll be fighting alongside more aliens than you knew existed," Johnson chuckles, "And most of them hate humans."

Chapter Three

Spartan Fort, Allegra

"Welcome to Hell!" Nelson calls out joyously to Matthew and the dozens of other people they picked up to serve as cannon fodder.

Matthew had just been let out of his 'cage' just a few minutes before they landed. Looking around, he notes that he doesn't recognize anyone. Fortunately, Maveric had tracked down Matthew and filled him in on everything. From what he had gathered, everyone else is also from outlying systems and planets like Sinclair.

Chuckling, Maveric glances over to Matthew, "Great pep talk."

"I don't think either of us want to see his other techniques to get people involved again," Matthew winces.

The large ramp at the rear of the massive freighter eases open, and Matthew is immediately hit with a smell that is worse than dead fish. He manages to not react, unlike nearly everyone else. Many cover their noses, while others both cough, and vomit.

"What *is* that?" someone asks in horror.

"That, my friends, is the smell of war," Nelson announces joyously, "You've got a bit of burning bodies, rotting corpses, and good old gunpowder. Best part is, that's just the smell of Spartan Fort, the front lines are much worse. Now get a move on!"

Nelson charges down the freighter's ramp and all his soldiers-to-be surge out closely behind him. Once they are out in the open, the groups start splitting up according to their assigned positions.

"Come with me," Johnson orders from behind Matthew.

"Am I the only Mudder?" Matthew asks with a pang of fear.

"Only out of this group," Johnson assures him, "As I said, most of the other Mudders are all alien races that the Coalition doesn't care for."

"Where are we off to?" Matthew asks as he follows Johnson away from the others.

"Address me as 'sir' or 'Captain' when we're out here," Johnson instructs. After a few more steps, he continues, "And I'm taking you to our lookout tower. Thought I'd show you the lay of the land."

"That'd be nice, sir," Matthew nods as he steps over a puddle of what appears to be either vomit or blood. For one reason or another, he can't distinguish what it was.

From what Matthew had been told, he assumed that the planet would be very wet. After all, where did the term Mudder come from then, if not from the mud? As far as Matthew can tell, he appears to be in a desert. For the most part, the dirt underfoot is dry and cracked and there isn't a tree in sight.

Matthew tries to look around in search of mountains, or anything of that sort, but comes up emptyhanded. The countless tents and the hastily erected buildings all around obscure most of the world around him.

"It's not as nice as you'd think," Johnson frowns.

"Why do you say that, Captain?" Matthew inquires, doing his best to address Johnson correctly.

"You'll see soon enough," Johnson replies simply as he leads Matthew around a corner.

"—dead... he's dead... she's dead... that's dead—whatever it is," a doctor walks down a line of cots where various beings are laid out. Following close behind the man is a

41

team of nurses who do their best to pull a sheet over all the beings that the doctor says are dead.

"Can I have some water?" one of the patients begs a nurse with a weak voice.

Matthew looks at the man and sees a poor soul who is covered with severe burns. None of his wounds are dressed, and dirt, likely kicked up by people walking by, is caked inside of his exposed burns.

"Sir, is this what it's like on the front?" Matthew whispers, terror coursing through his veins. He can't help but shudder slightly as a rickety wagon full of dismembered body parts is carted by.

"They don't collect the bodies on the front," Johnson replies in a solemn voice, "That's where most of the '*mud*' comes from."

"Oh," Matthew whimpers, sure that his bone-quaking fear is evident in his voice.

Alright, it's just up there," Johnson informs Matthew as he points down a narrow alleyway between two of the larger temporary structures. At the end of the alleyway is a ladder that ascends several stories to a crude observation area.

"Are you going to come up with me, sir?" Matthew asks curiously without moving.

"Not today," Johnson shakes his head, "I got a thing for heights."

Matthew nods in response to Johnson's excuse and he trudges down the alley alone. At the base of the tower, Matthew looks up and nods approvingly at the structure. He then races up the ladder, oblivious to the height.

For years, Matthew had been afraid of heights. If it weren't for all his father's efforts, Matthew was sure he would still hate heights. But, out of necessity, Matthew learned to get over his fear. This was achieved by countless days ascending and descending the mast of his father's fishing boat.

"Welcome to the clouds," someone calls to Matthew when he emerges into the observation area.

"Thanks," Matthew nods as he looks to the man who hadn't turned.

"You new here?" the man inquires, "I don't recognize your voice."

"Yeah, I'm new, but I won't be here long," Matthew replies as he looks past the man to the world beyond.

The horizon is lined with mountains that dwarf the cliffs Matthew remembers from Sinclair. Between the mountains and the small fort that Matthew is in is a vast desert. As far as Matthew can see in every direction, everything appears to be dry. And not just a little dry. Matthew can't help but wonder if this part of the planet had ever seen even a single drop of rain.

"Why do you say that?" the man asks still forward-facing.

"I'm supposed to be a Mudder," Matthew replies as he continues staring at his bleak surroundings.

"You don't sound like an alien to me…" The man starts in a confused tone as he finally turns. Matthew can now see that the man has bandages over his eyes. From what he can tell, they had been there for quite some time. The man cocks his head as he asks, "So who's bad side did you get on? Henderson? Cortes? Jenniston?"

"Nelson,"

"Now that's really unfortunate."

"Well, he says I made it off of his hate list not too long after," Matthew offers optimistically.

"Really?" the man asks with a curious grin, "How?"

"I got in a fight with some of his men and put one of them in a coma," Matthew brags.

"Well, that sounds exactly like

something Nelson would enjoy," the man nods. He returns to facing the console before him and he presses a comm piece into his ear. After a brief moment, he calls back to Matthew, "You're welcome to stay up here as long as you like. It isn't often someone ventures all the way up here."

"I actually need to go now," Matthew informs the man once he sees Johnson motioning for him to come down.

"Good talking with you," the man sounds before Matthew climbs onto the ladder. He loosens his grip and pulls his feet away from the rungs and he allows himself to slide down.

Matthew catches himself several meters before hitting the ground, and he eases himself the rest of the way down. Spinning around, he quickly returns to Johnson who looks at him in surprise.

"I've never seen anyone do that before," Johnson breathes.

"Where to, Captain?" Matthew inquires.

"The firing range," Johnson replies as he starts off down the way he and Matthew had just come through.

•••••••••••••

"Well, you're the best shot I've ever seen," Johnson compliments Matthew as he stares through a set of binoculars at all the targets that Matthew had ripped through.

"I had to shoot a lot of the flying lizards back home," Matthew replies simply as he silently thanks his dad for all the shooting lessons he gave.

"Flying lizards, eh?" Johnson asks as he continues staring at the targets, "How small were they?"

"No larger than your hand," Matthew replies, "We had to keep them away from our sails and our fish."

"Shooting like that and I can assume they never came close," Johnson chuckles as he continues staring at the targets. After a few moments, he requests, "Go get those targets for me. I want to hang on to them."

"Yes, sir," Matthew nods as he rises from the kneeling position he had been shooting from behind a small pile of dirt.

Matthew jogs toward the targets and collects them from their varying distances. After several minutes Matthew reaches the furthest target at five hundred meters and he peels the paper bullseye from the dirt pile it is attached to.

On his return trip, Matthew looks down and admires his handiwork. Sure enough, every target has a hole straight through the center, in addition to every other location Captain Johnson had requested. After his examination, Matthew runs all the way back to Johnson, who likely had better things to do than just sit around.

"Let's have a look at this," Johnson mutters as he takes the sheets from Matthew. He whistles in admiration before continuing, "I'm going to show these to Nelson to see if I can work something out for you…"

"What should I do in the meantime?" Matthew asks anxiously as he scours his surroundings in search of the hostile aliens that he had heard so much about.

"I've pulled someone from the front to show you the ropes," Johnson replies as he continues scanning the targets. Matthew can't help but wonder what the man is still looking at the targets for—since nothing has changed—but he shrugs off the thought. After a beat, Johnson continues, "He should be here any moment. He'll tell you everything you need to know as he accompanies you to the front."

"So, this is it, then?" Matthew inquires as he swallows a lump in his throat.

"You'll be fine up there," Johnson assures Matthew as he stands and makes for the truck they had taken to the range. He continues as he opens the truck's door, which causes all the electronics to whirl to life, "There isn't a lot going on where you're going, so you should be pretty safe. And the man I am entrusting you with is one of the best guys I have up there. He's also one of the few humans."

"Thanks for everything," Matthew nods appreciatively to Johnson.

"Don't make me regret it," Johnson advises as he reaches into the truck and pulls out a large backpack with a rifle and several other odds and ends hanging from it. He holds it out for Matthew as he continues, "I pulled some strings to get you a full set of gear. Guard it with your life, because there isn't much in the ways of supplies at the front."

"Thanks," Matthew nods as he takes the heavy bag and places it on the ground beside himself.

Johnson looks at Matthew for several moments as he idly plays with the paper targets in his hands. After what feels like an eternity, he announces, "Your starting rank will be Private, but if you play your card right, you'll quickly rise through the ranks. Before too long, you might even be able to get off the front."

"Got it," Matthew acknowledges as he nods his head. He pushes down the urge to ask what he needs to do to get promoted off the front, knowing that Johnson had already done so much for him.

"Do me a favor and stay alive," Johnson nods to Matthew as he enters the truck and slams the door shut behind himself. A moment later, the truck is taking off back to base, leaving Matthew alone.

At least Dixie doesn't have to be here, Matthew tells himself once more as he kneels in front of his pack and unzips it. Peering inside he is immediately greeted with a dark brown uniform, which he quickly sets aside. Looking further, he sees a plethora of gear. Matthew lets out an involuntary sigh when he notes that he is at least somewhat familiar with most of the gear. Closing his eyes, he thinks, *At least that's some sense of normalcy.*

"Let's have a look at these," Matthew mutters to himself as he unrolls the tight cylinder of cloth that is his uniform.

He is soon greeted with an underwhelming uniform that doesn't seem to boast any of the flare that the dark blue uniforms he had seen thus far had. Instead, the cloth is very plain, and Matthew is surprised when he finds a name badge sewn over his breast pocket. Turning the fabric over, he finds a triangular emblem that he reasons must represent his rank.

"Yeah, they don't give us the best uniforms, that's for sure," a man declares with a chuckle from behind Matthew, startling him.

"Who are you?" Matthew demands as he spins around and prepares for a fight.

"James Robinson," the man offers as he extends a dirt-stained and heavily scarred hand to Matthew, "My friends on the front call me Robinhood."

Matthew quickly takes the man's hand with his own calloused one as he chuckles, "Robinhood, really?"

"We Mudders are the poor, so we have to steal from the rich to get by," James shrugs, "I'm just a little more skilled at this than the others."

"I see," Matthew nods slowly as he examines James.

"Nice hands, by the way, I take it you were a laborer like me?" James inquires as he drops his pack on the ground and takes a seat on top of it.

"I worked on my father's ship for several years," Matthew answers as he slowly zips his bag back up. Johnson had warned Matthew about how Mudders were apt to steal, and he wasn't about to lose his brand-new gear to James.

"I haven't seen many spacers who had working hands like that," James frowns as he cocks his head.

"It was a sailing ship," Matthew amends, "We fished for a living."

"That makes more sense," James nods. After a beat, he points at Matthew's bag, "Go ahead and check out your stuff. I saw you close it back up. We don't steal from each other—at least most of us don't. We just take what we need from those who have the posh jobs."

"Oh, alright," Matthew blushes, feeling guilty for his lack of trust.

"Johnson and the others don't understand what it's like up there because they've never been up there," James continues, "They think we're all just savages. In reality, we just aren't like the rest. So, what did you do to get stuck up here? It isn't often a human gets stuck as a Mudder right off the bat."

"Nelson drilled a hole through my girlfriend's hand," Matthew frowns as the vivid images flash before his eyes, "I tried to stop him."

"He drilled a hole—" James starts as his eyes grow wide, "What could she have done to warrant that?"

"She tried to explain that she couldn't serve because her brother is ill," Matthew explains as he dumps his gear out on the dirt before him.

"That's pretty extreme, I would have done the same thing you did," James nods approvingly, "So, did she get to stay home then?"

"Fortunately, yes," Matthew nods.

"That's good," James concurs. He scans Matthew's equipment for a few moments before he continues, "Go ahead and get your uniform on, we really should get back to the front before nightfall."

Matthew grabs his uniform and he quickly puts it on. Once he's suited up, Matthew asks, "So, what did *you* do to get stuck on the front?"

"Let's just say the Coalition and I have never been on good terms, and this is my best bet to get out," James replies mystically.

"Alright…" Matthew frowns as he gives James a skeptical look.

James rises to his feet and subsequently announces, "Let's get moving, we've got a lot of ground to cover."

"How far is it to the front?" Matthew inquires as James starts toward the mountains in the distance.

"We've got to go a ways past the mountains," James replies with a nod as he shoulders his bag.

"On foot?" Matthew asks nervously as he throws his gear back into his pack.

"We'll hitch a ride with the ammo truck," James assures Matthew, "But it's quite the walk to where we'll meet them."

"Lead the way," Matthew nods as he rises to his feet. He approaches James as he carefully adjusts his backpack until it is comfortable.

"Alright, this way," James instructs as he takes off heading due east. He continues for several minutes before he finally asks, "So, what would you like to know first?"

"What are the aliens we're up against like?" Matthew asks in a quiet voice. Part of him fears that mentioning the invaders too loud may summon them, hence his whispering.

"They're as tall as they are ugly," James starts at his usual volume, "They've got tough outer shells—like a bug—and they are blacker than death. We call them 'Beetles' and 'Beets' for short on the front. If you're ever around for one of the seldom debriefs that we give though, be sure to call them something along the lines of 'the invaders' or something like that because that's what the upper brass calls them."

Matthew nods dumbly, unsure just what to say. Part of him wonders what part he could play in such a massive war, but he didn't want to risk whining about that just yet. He wanted to make the best impression he could on James.

Likely seeing Matthew's expression, James sighs and continues with the details of how to get along on the front, "Killing the Beets is something of an art form. You've got to shoot them in the soft parts of their shell, or in any of their joints. Their soft spots are directly beneath their heads, on their sides where their arms and legs connect to their thorax-like bodies, and their butts. They bleed blue, so if you don't see any light blue fluid seeping out of them then you haven't scored a worthwhile hit.

"If a Beet notices you, it'll charge you— so make sure that that never happens. They run faster than the Devil and will rip you apart if you let them get close. They can also spit some sort of acid-venom, which kills whoever it hits within a few minutes. Don't let them spit on you or rip into you and you'll be fine."

"They sound lovely," Matthew mutters weakly as he tries his best not to shudder in fear. Whatever these 'Beets' were, they were not something he wanted to spend any time around.

"That's not the half of it," James shakes his head without turning around, "I don't even know how to describe it."

"What else should I know," Matthew asks, knowing that he stood a better chance of survival if he knew everything that James knew.

"The Beets seem to come during the heat of the day, and they rest at night. That's when some of us do our offensives. The Beets seem to enter some sort of hibernation when it gets cold. That reminds me, keep away from any holes you see. That's where the things sleep.

"If you're lucky, you won't go up against the real big Beetles. I've only seen a few of them in the two weeks I've been here. I call them the 'Biggies' and they are really hard to take down. Not only are their shells thicker, but they've got some actual armor on them as well. They've also got guns, which are some of the most frightening things I ever did see."

"Why's that?" Matthew inquires.

"I don't want to say," James shakes his head slowly. He sounds like he is struggling to hold back tears.

"Well, what are living conditions like at the front?" Matthew asks once James fails to further explain the weapons the Biggies had.

"Those of us who have been alive for a while make ourselves little bunkers which we have to dig ourselves," James replies, "We don't let the newcomers stay with us for the first few nights for our own sakes. There's nothing more painful than getting to know someone one night and then watching them get killed the next morning. We find that those who survive a couple days tend to stay alive the longest.

"The newcomers either sleep in the trenches we've got dug, in some of the craters from artillery, or anywhere else that gets them out of the line of fire for the night."

"Out of the line of fire?" Matthew asks, his interest piqued. James had only mentioned that the Biggies had weapons.

"Ah yes," James nods, realizing the information he glossed over, "The Beets have some strange energy weapons which will shoot a hole straight through even a Frazian. They must have sniper teams set up all over because they're always picking people off.

"And they've got some crazy artillery too. They send stuff that's about two meters across hurtling toward us. Sometimes it blows up on impact, sometimes it waits for people to get too close. When it blows, run. Run as fast and as far as you can. They seem to put off some gas that drives everyone in the vicinity nuts. If they don't kill themselves first, they'll hunt down and kill us."

"First off, what's a Frazian?" Matthew asks, "And second off, you're telling me that they turn our own people against us?"

"Frazians are one of the alien races we'll be fighting alongside," James reports, "That's why you need to be sure to call the aliens we're up against something other than aliens. The Frazians, and all the other alien races take offense to that, they don't like us calling them the same thing."

"And the gas that makes our people kill each other?" Matthew prods after a beat.

"Yeah, it's some nasty stuff," James

nods absently, "We caught a guy once after he was gassed and locked him up for a few days. He went silent one day, so we figured he was dead. As it turns out, he was lying in wait for us. As best as I can tell, the gas makes you think like the Beets."

"Can you tell if someone has been gassed?" Matthew asks helplessly.

"Other than having them try to kill you?" James laughs aloud. He turns and sees that Matthew isn't amused, so he continues in a more serious tone, "Their eyes go blank—like they do when someone dies. Their skin also gets either really dark, or really pale. They walk funny as well… It's a lot more ridged. Basically, if they look like dead men walking."

"Got it," Matthew nods, unsure if James is actually telling the truth.

James continues walking for several moments before he finally announces, "I just lost a Frazian who shared my bunker with me, so I worked something out with the others. They'll let you in after just one long night—so long as you kill a Beet first."

"That sounds simple enough," Matthew nods, "Thank you."

"It should be pretty easy for you as well," James continues, "Since they are rather inanimate at night. For proof, bring us the thing's head. You'll see why once we get to the front."

"Got it," Matthew responds after a moment. Part of him knows that he can trust James, but another part is screaming in his head that the man is hiding something big.

"Here comes the truck," James announces as he stops. Looking at the truck, he holds his arm out, his thumb pointing toward the mountains.

"What are you doing?" Matthew asks after examining James for a moment.

"Hitchhiking," James replies simply. When he sees that Matthew doesn't understand, he continues, "This is how people flag down a ride. Are you really from that small of a town?"

"There are a lot more people back at Spartan Fort than there are back at home," Matthew responds simply, "That and no one ever needs a ride anywhere since we're the only town on our island."

Matthew examines the large truck for several moments, trying to take everything in. The truck appears to have five axles which support its huge mass. The truck has a short windscreen which gives way to its heavily armored body. Several ladders extend up the transport's sides, leading to its roof which is bursting with both soldiers and large guns.

"Interesting," James nods as he turns back to the large truck which is still barreling towards him and Matthew.

"Are they going to stop?" Matthew asks as the vehicle continues speeding closer to them.

"No, they'll just slow down a bit," James replies after the truck flashes its lights at them. Smiling, James turns to face Matthew and he announces, "They see us, get ready!"

"Get ready for what?" Matthew asks with more than a little worry.

"It's simple enough to climb on once you've gotten a hold of one of the ladders that go up the side," James instructs, "You'll have to time everything perfectly. There are no do-overs!"

"What if I miss?" Matthew demands as he looks at the truck which has only slowed down marginally.

"Then you'll either get killed, or you'll have to walk!" James announces excitedly as he starts jogging away from Matthew. After a short while, he calls back, "Get moving, it makes it a bit easier this way."

Matthew silently follows, pushing down all the bad thoughts that are rising in his head. He matches James's ever-increasing speed until he too is at full sprint.

A moment later, the truck is shooting by, and Matthew watches as James leaps and takes a hold of one of the ladders on the truck which lead to its roof. Matthew looks over his shoulder and picks the ladder he intends to climb and then follows James's suit. Leaping, he mirrors James's moves exactly and finds himself latched onto the hull of the large armored vehicle.

"See? It wasn't too hard!" James calls to him as he scurries up the ladder to the roof of the truck.

Forcing himself to reach one hand over the other, Matthew eventually scales his own ladder. As he climbs, Matthew realizes that the truck is accelerating once more to a breakneck pace.

Before long, Matthew's uniform is whipping against his skin in the strong winds caused by the truck's swift pace. Anxious to make the stinging from the slapping of his clothes stop, he rushes up the rest of the ladder. Once at the top, he rolls over the rail and falls at the feet of those who are standing atop the transport.

"So, you're the new Mudder we heard so much about," one of the soldiers announces as they take a hold of Matthew's shirt and hoist him to his feet. Nodding, they continue, "I hear you're quite the tough little guy."

"I bet he could even take you, Leeds," another soldier calls out from the rear of the large transport.

"I'd believe it," the man, Leeds, nods as he examines Matthew, "Anyone who could drop Moon like that probably could."

"I don't care how well he can fight," a man who dwarfs every other soldier announces, "He put Moon in a coma, and I'm obliged to do the same."

"Don't, he's a Mudder, he's going to die soon enough anyway," someone warns.

"Then no one will miss him," the large man smiles as he pushes his way through the crowd toward Matthew.

"I see you've made yourself a friend already," James whispers after jockeying his own way through to Matthew.

"What should I do?" Matthew whispers back to James as he locks eyes with the man who wants to kill him.

"Do what you did to the others," James

advises before he starts to push the other soldiers back to make room for the fight.

"I'm dead," Matthew breathes as he watches the large man crack his neck.

"My money is on the Mudder!" James calls out as he throws a handful of cash into his helmet, which he is holding out in front of himself.

"No way, Walskie all the way," someone else challenges. Several other soldiers throw in their own money as they name their champions.

Matthew shrugs his backpack off and he tosses it to James's feet so he can guard it for him. Sighing, he raises his fists for yet another fight.

"You're not about to get lucky this time," the large man, Walskie, booms.

"I don't need to get lucky," Matthew shoots back as he examines his opponent.

Walskie frowns and he spits to the side. He stares back at Matthew for a beat before taking a step forward. Matthew loosens up his joints a few times as he prepares to make this fight look good.

Matthew draws near to Walskie and allows him to throw the first punch, which he deflects without much difficulty. While the man's arm is fully extended, Matthew delivers a quick punch to Walskie's elbow just hard enough to serve as a bit of a warning.

Walskie quickly pulls back and takes a step away from Matthew who shoots him a pompous smile. Walskie scowls and makes another advance, this time with more caution.

Walskie advances and he and Matthew exchange several dozen hits. Matthew allows a few strikes through in order to test Walskie for his weaknesses, which he quickly finds.

Grabbing Walskie's right hand, which is his dominant one, Matthew pulls the man close and then gifts him with a headbutt. Matthew quickly releases the man and pushes him back. Dazed, Walskie stumbles backwards further than expected before coming to a stop and shaking his head slightly.

Walskie advances yet again, and Matthew sees that Walskie is about to throw the first punch yet again. Matthew decides to mix things up, and he swings his left forearm toward the man as a distraction while also delivering a few punches to Walskie's gut with his right.

Walskie takes a hold of Matthew's forearm before he can pull away to a safe distance, and he grins cruelly. He then lifts

Matthew by his forearm for everyone to see. Matthew flails around like a fish as he tries to free himself from Walskie's firm grip.

Matthew summons all of his strength and he pulls himself up with his left arm and then he brings a crushing blow to the man's trapeziuses with his right. Walskie immediately lets Matthew go, and Matthew drops to the ground only to bounce right back up and deliver a mighty hit to the man's chin.

Walskie stumbles back a few steps as the crowd fills with a cacophony of cheers and jeers. Walskie raises his hand to his mouth and pulls it away bloody. After looking at the blood for a brief moment, he looks up to Matthew with a spark of rage in his eye.

"I'm going to wring your scrawny neck…" Walskie seethes.

Matthew simply adjusts his stance in response as he raises his fists once more. Oddly enough, his silence seems to only further enrage Walskie, who immediately charges at him once more, this time his arms fully extended and his hands grasping for Matthew's neck.

Matthew remains still as Walskie charges him up until the last moment when he dives beneath Walskie's arms and ramrods directly into the man's legs. He can feel bones cracking as the combined force of his and Walskie's charge is absorbed by the man's legs.

Walskie flies over Matthew's head and his head smashes against the steel barrier that ensures no one falls off the transport. Matthew promptly rolls over and scrambles to his feet as he looks at where Walskie is still laying.

Walskie's leg is bent at an unnatural angle and several trails of blood are seeping from the man's head. Matthew takes a step forward to see if the man is alright when he is suddenly rushed by a group of soldiers.

"Calm down there, the fight's done," one of them says as they step between Matthew and Walskie.

"No, I just—" Matthew starts.

"I knew you could do it!" one of them calls excitedly, cutting Matthew off.

"Not bad for a Mudder," one of them smiles as they take their winnings from James, who is handing out wads of cash.

"Is he ok?" Matthew asks loud enough to be heard over the commotion.

"Walskie's fine!" someone calls out in response, "But his ego's hurt."

"Give him some air," James calls out

once he finishes distributing the winnings between all the soldiers who bet on Matthew.

"Thanks," Matthew nods to James as the man hands him his pack and then ushers him to the rear of the transport.

Several soldiers clap Matthew on the back as they congratulate him on the fight. James continues pushing past the group until they eventually reach the rear of the transport. Here, boxes of supplies are stacked high and several large machineguns sit idle on their mounts.

"This is your cut," James whispers once he is confident that they are alone.

"My cut?" Matthew inquires curiously as James shoves a wad of bills into his hands.

"Yeah, half for you and half for me," James nods as he takes a seat on a nearby crate.

"Half—wait what did you do to deserve half?" Matthew demands with a laugh.

"It's the fee for collecting bets," James shrugs as he pulls quite a few bills from his long sleeves.

"Something tells me that no one else knows about said fee," Matthew chuckles as he looks down at the bills that are clenched in his fist.

"You going to count it?" James asks as he lays his own bills out before him. He doesn't wait for a response as he starts counting his winnings.

Matthew sighs as he tries to get a hold of his thoughts, which was always difficult to do after a fight. After a few beats, he decides to take a deep breath and then he holds it for a solid two minutes before slowly exhaling.

"You did not just hold your breath that long," James says flatly as he looks up from his money counting.

"It helps me get a hold of my nerves," Matthew shrugs as he slowly sits down. He starts straightening out and counting his bills without explaining himself further.

"I'll add that to the list of profitable skills you have then," James muses after a few moments.

"Profitable?" Matthew asks, bemused. There were a lot of things he would call his ability to hold his breath, and profitable didn't make the list.

James gives Matthew a serious look before he explains himself, "You'd be surprised what people would bet on."

"I'll try to keep that in mind," Matthew chuckles as he finishes counting his wad. *Two hundred dollars*, He thinks with a smile, *That's four months' wages! At this rate, I'll be able to buy Dix the best ring in the galaxy!*

"Be sure to keep some of that moolah on hand so you can bet on yourself next time," James advises, "There's a lot more money to be had if you play it smart."

First Kill

The Battle for Allegra

Episode Two

Chapter One

Camp Spenser, Allegra

"This is our stop," James's voice rouses Matthew from his sleep with a light kick to his foot.

Matthew opens his eyes slowly and he looks up to the silhouette that had awakened him. Blinking a few times, Matthew sees that night had fallen and everything is dark. It's much darker here on Allegra than it ever got back home on Sinclair.

Matthew slowly rises to his feet as he listens intently for any sounds of conflict. After a beat, he points out, "I don't hear any fighting."

When Matthew had fallen asleep, he had assured himself that he would simply wake up back at home. He hoped that he was just having a terrible nightmare. Now that he is awake, he realizes that was not the case.

"Well, it's night," James informs him with a shrug, "I told you the Beets hibernate at night."

Matthew yawns as he looks around, sure enough, night had fallen. After a moment, Matthew asks, "How long was I out?"

The world has been overshadowed with a deep darkness which makes Matthew nervous. Not only is he on a new world, but Matthew is also in a war against a race no one has ever seen before. As far as Matthew is concerned, he has every right to be scared right now. Regardless of how he feels, Matthew doesn't let the fear that has been nagging at him show itself.

A cool breeze wafts over him, reminding him of home, and the cool morning breeze which journeyed in from the ocean. Being this close to where the fighting is, Matthew can't help but wish he was home right now. He would gladly exchange the cold morning and the smell of bad fish for his current setting.

Countless pinpricks of light are scattered across the land like the stars of the sky. In some areas, there are dense blobs of radiant light while others stretch outward in haphazard patterns, much like the constellations Matthew sailed by.

"Long enough that you missed the worst part of the trip," James chuckles, "Now we've just got a few more kilometers to hike."

"How many is a few?" Matthew asks, picking up his large backpack.

"Do you see those lights way over there?" James's silhouette asks as it motions toward a few dim and lonely lights far in the distance.

Matthew's legs grow a little sore at the thought of walking so far, but he figures that he doesn't have much of an option. Doing his best to sound neutral, Matthew simply replies, "Yes."

"Well, that's not even halfway," James informs him with a chuckle.

"I'm sorry, what?" Matthew demands, his eyes wide with surprise.

"We're on the front lines," James answers with a glum voice, "This is just a forward camp. They call it Camp Spenser."

Matthew sighs in defeat as he resigns himself to a very long hike. Hoping to see where he is going, he reaches into his pack and produces a flashlight. He is about to flick it on when he says, "Well, I'll follow you then."

"Don't use that," James snaps when he notices Matthew fumbling around in search for the switch, "Save your battery for when your life depends on it. We're hiking in the dark."

"I can't see anything though!" Matthew counters in distress.

"Your eyes will get used to it," James assures him. He pauses as he looks up to the sky and he quickly adds, "The moons will be rising soon anyways. You should see how bright it gets when all five are visible.

Sighing once more, Matthew puts away his flashlight and cedes, "Fine, lead the way."

•••••••••••••

"See that ridge over there?" James asks as he suddenly stops.

"Yeah, I see it," Matthew sounds, thankful for the break.

Matthew had been following James in the dark for nearly eight hours. Sure enough, two moons have risen shedding some light on the weary world below. After such a long night, Matthew can't help but wonder when the sun would rise again.

On their trek, Matthew and James had

seen a plethora of other soldiers, all of whom weren't Mudders like them. They all boasted their sharp navy-blue Coalition uniforms which appeared to be as clean as the day they got them.

Not only that, but the other soldiers were using their flashlights like there was no tomorrow. They were using all their gear with reckless abandon. James said that this was because everyone else got everything they needed to fight. That was his way of saying they got all the food, clean water, and munitions they needed.

Mudders, on the other hand, were expected to die. They—Matthew, James, and everyone else on the frontmost lines—were simply cannon fodder until the upper brass figured out their master plan to take back Allegra.

Said plan had been in the works for over a month now. A month, and countless thousands of ill-equipped civilians.

"The front is just over that ridge," James nods confidently.

"And then I'm off to my first hunt?" Matthew inquires.

"Exactly," James nods, "If you would like, I can pair you up with some of the other greenhorns on the hunt, or you can go on your own."

"What would you recommend?" Matthew asks after several moments of thought.

"I'd go solo," James advises, "The Mud Pups may just get you killed."

"'Mud Pups?'" Matthew chuckles awkwardly as he cocks his head.

"That's what we call the greenhorns who have yet to become fully-fledged Mudders," James replies simply.

"Interesting," Matthew nods slowly, worrying for his own sanity at this point. Hanging out with James too long couldn't be good for him.

Finished talking, James marches on toward the ridge he had pointed out with Matthew in tow. Matthew looks around frantically, searching for any signs of the Beets that James had warned him about. Part of him doubts the fact that such creatures would be so vicious and still need to hunker down for the night.

Before long, Matthew and James reach the ridge and they pause to take in the view. Ravines are carved into the ground, crisscrossing the earth like cracks in broken glass. A handful of wayward lights cast an eerie glow on the landscape.

Craters mar the landscape like scars on a sailor's beaten hands, reminding those all around that they are in the middle of a warzone. Beyond the trenches, Matthew can see hundreds of still forms which he soon realizes are the bodies of fallen soldiers. After a beat, his eyes lock onto a handful of non-human figures which are moving through the field of bodies.

"Home sweet home," James sounds after a few silent moments.

"What are those?" Matthew asks as he points at the moving lifeforms.

"They're friendlies," James assures him with a nod once he's scanned the warzone, "As I said, the Beets don't come out at night."

"However, they do emerge at night on the rare occasion," a phlegmy guttural voice amends from behind Matthew.

Startled, Matthew jumps as he quickly spins around. Ready for a fight, he raises his fists before he eventually pauses long enough to take in the being who had spoken.

The creature before Matthew is about his height, but it looks nothing like anything he had ever seen before. Beneath an immensely long forehead is a comparatively very small face. Said face has a large fish-like eye on each side and its mouth is bordered with a handful of pincer-like teeth that wave in and out as the creature breathes. The creature's skin appears to be soft, much like his own, but it glistens with moisture and is a dark reddish-brown.

To Matthew's dismay, the creature's body is about as alien as its face. An ample neck gives way to a wide body that boasts six insect-like arms, all of which are moving about, which makes Matthew nervous. The alien being stands on four powerful legs that lead up to a horse-like body. In many ways, the creature looks like a centaur. Only, instead of being half man and half horse, it is half horse and half bug.

"Rooch," James calls out welcomingly to the creature.

"Welcome back, Thief," the creature returns as it bobs its head up and down.

"Rooch, this is Matthew," James makes the introduction, "He's the new one we've been hearing about."

"Anyone who harms Moon like you did is a friend of mine," Rooch sounds as he approaches Matthew.

Matthew quickly retreats several steps

before James laughs and informs Matthew, "It is customary for his kind to press their foreheads together when welcoming their friends."

"Oh," Matthew breathes as he stops. A moment later he approaches the large creature and touches foreheads with it.

They remain in that position long enough that Matthew can't help but inhale, which he quickly regrets. Rooch's breath is far fouler than he ever could have anticipated. Resisting his urge to gag and doing his best to also quell his sense of smell, Matthew remains perfectly still. After a few long and uncomfortable beats, Rooch pulls away, leaving a light film of moisture on Matthew's forehead.

"Today was unexpectedly silent," Rooch tells James before they exchange the strange forehead-greeting.

"Did any Beets show up?" James inquires as they pull away from one another.

"The invaders remained at a great distance," Rooch replies, "Their nearest burrows were all found to be empty as well."

"Interesting," James nods as he strokes his chin. He doesn't say anything else, instead, he looks out over the trenches.

"I must go," Rooch announces after a beat, "I require rest for the new day."

"Go ahead Rooch, I'll catch up to you later," James excuses the alien.

Matthew waits for Rooch to disappear into a nearby trench before he whispers to James, "What was that thing?"

"Don't call him a thing," James chides, "And Rooch is an Arrandorran, their homeworld isn't too far from here."

"I've never seen one of them," Matthew admits as he follows James who has started off after Rooch.

"Not a lot of people do," James informs him, "The Coalition keeps a lot of alien races hidden from the general population. They like using them as slaves instead."

"Slaves, really?" Matthew asks in concern.

"Yeah, they've got a lot of slaves," James chuckles, "More than you'll ever know."

"But we're supposed to have freedom here," Matthew protests.

"You don't look too free to me," James retorts as he looks back to Matthew and points at his uniform. Shaking his head, he continues, "They just tell you that you're free, so you don't join the fight to overthrow them."

"Wait so you're—" Matthew starts, his interest piqued.

"It looks like the other Mud Pups have already taken off, so you had better join them," James interrupts, "You heard what Rooch said, all the closest burrows are empty, so you'll have to go a ways to find a Beet."

"Where will you be once I get one?" Matthew inquires, shrugging off the question he was trying to ask earlier.

"I'll be in my bunker asleep over there," James replies as he points toward a small hill in the midst of the trenches.

"Alright," Matthew nods as he looks at one of the largest hills in the valley. He turns to ask James a few more questions but quickly finds himself alone.

Matthew trudges on toward the massive maze of trenches before him unaccompanied. As he draws near to them, his feet start sticking in the mud. Sighing, he now realizes that Allegra may be a lot wetter than he had initially thought. The mud quickly seeps through his old shoes and he feels the mud squish between his toes. Matthew continues slogging along for several minutes, wishing the whole way that he had waterproof boots.

Before long, Matthew finds himself

overlooking his first trench, which appears to be even more miserable than the ground he is currently standing on. The trench's floor is covered in dark puddles, and in some areas, small streams have formed.

Shaking his head, Matthew drops down into the trench where his feet land with a loud splash. The water, if he could call it that, splashes onto his uniform which quickly absorbs all the mud. With that, Matthew realizes that the Coalition truly did expect the Mudders to die early on. If he was fortunate enough to survive the first few days, the moisture was sure to kill him.

Chapter Two

The Bulwark, Allegra

"You're the new guy, aren't you?" Matthew hears a feminine inquire from nearby.

Stopping, he looks up and scans the narrow gully he is currently traversing. The hairs on the back of his neck rise when he doesn't see the speaker.

"Where are you?" Matthew demands, hoping that he isn't in the middle of some kind of hazing ritual.

"Right here," the speaker replies as a form emerges from the muddy wall.

"What were you doing in there?" Matthew inquires with an awkward chuckle. *And why would you ever want to cover yourself in mud?* He wonders as he scans the figure.

"Sleeping, at least I was until you came along," the voice continues. The form that had emerged from the wall quickly wipes the mud from its face, and Matthew realizes he isn't speaking to a human.

"What are you?" Matthew blurts out as he stares the scaled creature in her reptilian eyes.

In many ways, the being in front of him looks like a human. She stands like a human, her body is very human-like, and even her speech sounds human. Only, she isn't. She is covered in what appears to be dark-blue scales and Matthew now sees that she doesn't have ears either.

"I am a Toaz," the form replies with a toothy grin.

Matthew pauses as he can't help but stare at the Toaz's countless teeth. The Toaz has several rows of razor-sharp teeth that Matthew can't help but admire and fear simultaneously.

"My name is Rav'ian Chekkier," the Toaz, Rav'ian, continues as she stops smiling. She takes a step toward Matthew, her eyes roving across his body.

"I am Matthew, Matthew Campbell," Matthew sounds as he eyes the Toaz in return.

"Greetings, Matthew," Rav'ian nods as she circles behind him. Once she completes her circuit about him, she nods and says, "I believe you are the fighter I have heard so much about, is this correct?"

"Yes," Matthew nods slowly as he stares Rav'ian in the eyes. The 'whites' of her reptilian eyes are a pale blue which shine at a stark contrast against her black pupil-slits.

Rav'ian stares a few moments before she presses, "And I trust you are going out to collect your first kill?"

"Yes, just as soon as I get out of these trenches," Matthew affirms as he looks up to the stars to ensure that he is still heading in the right direction.

The stars aren't quite where he remembered them on his home planet, but many of them are not too far from where they ought to be. Matthew noticed this when he first saw the stars, but he reasoned that the differences were negligible.

"Would you appreciate my company?" Rav'ian asks as she looks more intently into Matthew's eyes. After a moment, she continues with a tone that portrays a sense of deep yearning, "I desire to witness your first kill."

"Is that allowed?" Matthew whispers.

"This is war, everything is permitted," Rav'ian laughs. Her laugh is oddly humanlike, which Matthew finds relieving. After a few moments, Rav'ian regains her very proper composure, and she continues, "Follow me."

"Umm, I was wondering something," Matthew sounds as he starts after Rav'ian.

"What do you desire to know?"

"How many different kinds of aliens will I be meeting?" Matthew asks, unsure how else to phrase his question.

"There are several different races that you may come into contact with and even fight alongside. However, the dominant portion of soldiers here are all Toaz and Frazian."

"What are Frazians like?"

"They are much like you and I. By this, I mean they have just four appendages. They are softskins—like you—but their stature and presence is much greater."

"Thanks, James didn't tell me a lot about them," Matthew nods, thankful for the crash course. James had told him a lot, but he failed to mention quite a few details which Matthew thought were important.

Rav'ian slows down slightly and she looks over to Matthew before whispering, "I recommend that you be wary about the Thief."

"Wary? Of what?" Matthew inquires as he cocks his head.

"He and his companions are members of a terrorist organization. They call themselves the Fulcrum."

"The Fulcrum?"

"They believe they have the means to

shift the balance of power in the galaxy," Rav'ian reports as she glances up and down the trench they are in, "You would be wise if you avoided them from now on."

"But James said he already had a cot waiting for me," Matthew protests.

"Beds are easy to come by, morals are not. Proceed carefully."

"If beds are so easy to come by, why were you sleeping in the mud?"

"This is how my people rest,"

"It doesn't sound too comfortable,"

"For your kind, no. However, those from my tribe find great comfort in the soil. It brings us memories of our homeworld."

"What is your homeworld like?" Matthew asks as he follows the Toaz to one of the largest trenches he had been in thus far.

"It is nothing like it once was," Rav'ian replies after several moments of thoughtful silence. She stops beside a ladder and motions for Matthew to climb up it, "This way."

Matthew nods and quickly scurries up the ladder. Climbing out of the trench, he scans the barren landscape. The countless bodies which litter the battlefield are even more imposing up close. The nearest corpse appears to be on the verge of bursting, which makes Matthew queasy.

"How far will we be going?" Matthew asks as Rav'ian joins him.

"Our quest will take us to the far side of the valley," Rav'ian replies as she points toward some of the stout hills ahead of them.

"Will we have enough time before daybreak?" Matthew inquires.

"Indeed," Rav'ian affirms, "Allegrian nights are exceedingly long. Another twelve hours will pass before first light."

"Twelve hours," Matthew breathes, struggling to believe his companion's words. Rav'ian marches past him, and he dutifully follows her, thankful for her guidance.

Matthew can't help but wonder if Rav'ian's words were true. *What if James really is a terrorist and is just trying to recruit me?* Matthew finds himself wondering, *I can't just join a terrorist group. But, I can't just ignore him after everything he's done for me either. Besides, we humans have to stick together up here at the front, right?*

Matthew feels a pang of guilt at his last thought as he looks to the Toaz who had taken to him. Rav'ian not only welcomed him, but she also filled in a lot of the blanks that James had left.

"Greetings, I see you have finally taken your first trophy," Rav'ian nods to a handful of beings who are heading back to the trenches.

Several members of the group are touting dark objects which Matthew quickly realizes must be the heads of the Beets. The same heads that Matthew is on the hunt for. Matthew takes in one of the heads, doing his best to commit it to memory.

"It was a long hunt," one of the beings notes. Matthew looks to the speaker and after a quick moment, he realizes it is another Toaz, like Rav'ian, only its scales are a deep bronze.

"Indeed," another Toaz agrees. Matthew now realizes that the entire group is made up of Toaz.

"It is a shame that we must resort to such primitive practices," the Toaz at the front of the group sounds. Matthew stares at the Toaz, seeing something out of the ordinary—if he could call any of this ordinary. Upon further examination, Matthew realizes that the Toaz is wearing one of the Beetle's heads as a helmet.

"Indeed," Rav'ian agrees as she nods to the Toaz at the head of the line.

"Do hurry back once you have assisted…" The Toaz at the front of the group pauses as they stare at Matthew. After several long moments, they look back to Rav'ian and ask, "Why are you assisting one of the softskins?"

"He is unlike the others, Trellik," Rav'ian replies.

"All of his kind are of one mind," the lead Toaz, Trellik, counters as he stares at Matthew with cold eyes.

"This is untrue," Rav'ian maintains before she raises a hand and continues, "This is all I wish to say on the matter."

"Raz, Riaan, accompany Rav'ian on her venture," Trellik orders. A moment later, two Toaz approach Matthew and Rav'ian.

"Thank you, Trellik," Rav'ian sounds before she starts walking toward the hills which she had pointed out earlier.

"I'm Matthew," Matthew introduces himself to the two Toaz as they follow him and Rav'ian.

"Pay them no heed," Rav'ian tells Matthew after the two Toaz ignore him, "They do not trust your kind."

"Why not?" Matthew asks as he looks at the two Toaz, "I never did anything to them."

"But other humans did," Rav'ian informs him, "Humans, directed by the Coalition, are the ones who destroyed our cities."

"How did they destroy your cities?"

"They unleashed every weapon they had on our people in an effort to subdue us," Rav'ian reports without turning back to face Matthew, "They have done so many times in the past as well."

"I'm sorry, but *I* wasn't a part of any of that," Matthew sounds as he looks to the two Toaz who are closely following him, "I had no part in any of their ac—"

Matthew is cut off as one of the Toaz takes hold of his throat. The Toaz's sharp claws dig into his skin, drawing blood. Panicking, Matthew hits the Toaz in the stomach with all his might.

The Toaz releases Matthew's throat as he stumbles back a few steps. He hisses at Matthew before making another run at him. Matthew ducks beneath the Toaz's first punch but is caught by its claws on its second swing.

"Riaan, stop!" Rav'ian demands from a distance. Matthew glances at her and sees that she is standing beside the other Toaz. To his dismay, the extent of her plea for peace seems to only be vocal.

"You are guilty by association," the Toaz, Riaan, seethes as he and Matthew lock arms.

Riaan bites at Matthew's face a few times but is just out of range. Strangely enough, his teeth are much smaller than Rav'ian's, which Matthew finds somewhat comforting. Instead of razor-sharp fangs, Riaan has much more human-like teeth.

After several attempted bites, Riaan sees that he isn't getting any closer to Matthew. Riaan then turns and clamps his teeth down on Matthew's right wrist.

Blood immediately starts pouring from Matthew's wrist, which prompts Matthew to headbutt Riaan with all he had. When Riaan doesn't react, Matthew breaks his left arm free from the Toaz's grip, and he starts smashing his fist down on the back of Riaan's head.

After several strikes, Matthew hears, and feels, something in Riaan's head crack. At that, the Toaz quickly releases Matthew's wrist from his mouth. Riaan takes a few steps away from Matthew and stares at him with glossy eyes.

Matthew makes the most of Riaan's brief exit, and he reaches into his backpack and pulls out his old shirt. Ripping a long strip of fabric from the garment, he makes himself a quick bandage and then prepares himself for another charge.

"Riaan?" Rav'ian questions after a beat.

Riaan does reply, and instead, he continues staring at Matthew. After a few moments, the Toaz shakes his head and takes a step forward. The momentum of Riaan's step somehow sends him careening to the ground. He lands face first in the soft mud and there, he remains, unmoving.

"What's wrong?" Matthew asks without moving. He isn't sure if the Toaz is simply acting and waiting for Matthew to let his guard down.

"Riaan?" Rav'ian repeats herself as she quickly closes the distance between her and the figure on the ground.

Matthew watches as Rav'ian turns Riaan onto his side. The Toaz is limp in her arms, which worries Matthew. Rav'ian feels several different places on Riaan's body before looking up to Matthew with a look that he thinks he recognizes as surprise.

"What is it?" Matthew asks, fearing the worse.

"You have fractured his skull," Rav'ian replies slowly, "The stories of your strength are true."

"Is he alright?" Matthew asks, ignoring what he thinks was a compliment.

"We must to return him to the others so our healers might assist him," Rav'ian announces as she slowly lowers Riaan's head.

"No," Raz, the other Toaz, disagrees.

"Riaan will die if we fail to bring him to the healers," Rav'ian snaps as she looks up to Raz, who is still standing at a distance.

"He would rather die on the battlefield than in the hands of a healer," Raz maintains.

"Raz, we can still save him," Rav'ian argues.

"Proceed with your companion," Raz orders as he pulls out a long blade from its scabbard on his back. Matthew stares at the sword which hadn't noticed before and he swallows a lump in his throat.

"Matthew, we must leave," Rav'ian instructs as she looks up to Matthew with fear in her eyes.

"I'm s—" Matthew starts.

"Without a word," Rav'ian cuts him off as she brushes past him. She grabs his good arm and drags him after her.

Matthew follows Rav'ian and can't help but feel a little thankful that it is just the two of them once again. Part of him is happy that Rav'ian took him away from Riaan before he died because he wasn't sure what he would have done if he had to watch the Toaz die.

Several times, Matthew tries to look back to where Riaan and Raz are, but Rav'ian catches him by the chin each time and she tells him to keep his eyes forward. After his last attempt, she explains that it is against the Toaz custom to allow onlookers when a Toaz warrior dies.

"I'm sorry," Matthew eventually sounds once Riaan and Raz are out of sight.

"Never apologize for the death of a Toaz," Rav'ian instructs, "To us, apologizing for the passing of a Toaz is reserved solely for those who are not welcomed into the afterlife. It is a custom reserved only for those who betray the Toa people.

"Oh," Matthew frowns, realizing the implications of Rav'ian's words.

"Riaan fought you to defend the honor of those who were killed by your people," Rav'ian nods, seeing the realization in Matthew's eyes, "Now he dies with his own honor."

"Is there anything else I should know about your people?" Matthew queries after a beat. Part of him is surprised that Rav'ian hadn't warned him of some of their strange customs beforehand.

"We do not interrupt a quarrel where

one's honor is on the line," Rav'ian replies, "This is why we stood idle as you and Riaan fought."

"Is it usual for your people to bite during a fight?" Matthew asks with a soft chuckle as he motions toward his battered right arm.

Rav'ian remains silent, and instead continues plodding through the mud which covers the battlefield. Matthew sighs, figuring that he must have broken another Toaz custom. This one likely revolved around poking fun at a fallen combatant's fighting style.

"Your arm requires further medical attention," Rav'ian points out after a seemingly eternal silence.

"I know. It hurts a lot." Matthew agrees, hugging his battered arm close to his chest.

"Is it still bleeding?" Rav'ian inquires.

"I think it has mostly stopped," Matthew reports after peeking beneath his crude bandaging.

"This is good," Rav'ian nods. She reaches into a small pouch she has on her hip and produces a small sealed bag. She searches in it for a few moments and eventually produces a small spray bottle. Handing it to Matthew, she instructs, "Remove your bandages and apply this to your wounds.

Once you've finished, rebandage your arm so it can heal properly."

"Thank you," Matthew nods as he unwraps his arm. He scans the countless teeth marks which mar his flesh for several beats before he finally begins spraying Rav'ian's stuff onto his arm.

The substance in the bottle burns Matthew's flesh the moment it meets it, and it causes the dried blood to bubble. Matthew lets out a moan of pain before the apparent ointment grows very cold.

"You can replace your bandages now," Rav'ian nods as she looks back to Matthew who is staring at his arm.

"What is this stuff?" Matthew asks as he examines the small bottle.

"It is some kind of salve that the Coalition gives their soldiers," Rav'ian replies, "They claim that it heals one's wounds much faster than they would on their own."

"Oh, thanks," Matthew nods before using another piece of his old shirt to cover his wrist and forearm.

●●●●●●●●●●●●●●

"Stop," Rav'ian orders Matthew as she

abruptly halts. She stoops down to the ground and pokes around in the dirt for a few beats before she takes a hold of what appears to be a small string.

"What is that?" Matthew inquires.

Rav'ian doesn't reply, and instead, she follows the tendril for nearly a meter before she stops at the base of a small mound.

Rav'ian draws a knife from her belt which she then drives into the muddy mound. A brief squeal sounds as the mound quivers before falling silent.

"What was that?" Matthew asks.

"The invaders utilize these small creatures as traps of sorts," Rav'ian replies as she reaches into the heap of mud and produces a small critter that reminds Matthew of the starfish population which is native to his homeworld. Rav'ian continues as she wraps the creature's many tendrils around its body, "We utilize them to make our stay here more… acceptable."

"James didn't tell me anything about those, what are they?" Matthew asks as he examines Rav'ian's specimen.

"My people call these creatures 'Latchers,' as they latch onto their prey and subsequently drain the life from them."

"I wonder why he didn't mention them,"

"One must actually fight their adversary in order to truly know them."

"What do you mean by that?"

"The Thief, alongside his companions, do not fight. They remain in the relative safety of their holes as my people win the war."

"Oh," Matthew mutters. He can't help but wonder who is lying to him now. Either James had led him on, or Rav'ian is trying to turn him against his own people. Either way, this seems to be some kind of race war in the makings.

"I believe your prize is near," Rav'ian sounds as she scans their surroundings.

"How near?" Matthew asks nervously.

"You are the hunter," Rav'ian nods to Matthew before she lowers herself to the ground where she takes a seat.

"So, I'm on my own now?" Matthew presses.

"Claim your prize," Rav'ian replies simply as she idly watches him.

"Alright then," Matthew mutters as he starts scanning his surroundings in search of the Beet he was tasked with killing.

Chuckling, Matthew soon notices a hole in the ground not too far from him which is large enough for a person to fall into. He quickly makes his way over to the hole and he pauses a few paces away from it. He sighs as he musters the courage to enter the lair of the evil just a stone's throw away.

Matthew looks back to Rav'ian, who is watching him with avid interest. Oddly enough, he feels slightly encouraged and closes the remaining distance between him and the 'prize' Rav'ian desired him to claim.

"H-hello?" Matthew stutters as he peers into the hole. He doesn't expect a response, but he still felt obliged to announce his arrival.

After a long pause, Matthew fumbles around with his backpack and produces a flashlight, which he points down the hole in order to see into its dark depths. He shines it around the small cavern beneath him as he searches for any sign of one of the Beetles. A worried sound comes from Rav'ian, who is still well behind Matthew.

Matthew goes to turn off his flashlight, assuming this is what Rav'ian had taken issue with when the ground suddenly shakes slightly. Startled, Matthew continues shining his light into the hole, knowing in his heart of hearts that he had awakened the beast inside.

"They are vulnerable when they

awaken!" Rav'ian's voice calls from behind him with a tone of desperation.

Not about to wait around for the Beet to fully wake up, Matthew hops into the hole, anticipating the fight of his life. For a brief moment, he considers besting the beast with just his fists, but his brain immediately vetoes the idea. Grabbing the rifle from its spot on his backpack, he prepares to shoot the first thing that moves.

To Matthew's surprise, and horror, the entire ground seemingly leaps all at once. A massive black creature leaps up in a thick spray of mud.

The Beetle, which Matthew now realizes is more of an understatement than an actual description, stares at Matthew with its three large black eyes.

The 'Beetle' looks a lot more like the scorpions from his school's textbooks than actual beetles, in Matthew's opinion. Everything about the creature looks very much like a black scorpion, save the tail, which it is fortunately lacking.

The Beet has two eyes on the right side of its oblong 'face' and just one on the other, which adds an additional sense of otherworldly-ness to it. It also has two antennae which quiver in the cool of the night, making Matthew even more nervous. The most terrify part of the Beet's head by far though is its mouth. Not only is its mouth flanked with two terrifyingly large pincers, but the mouth itself has countless tentacles writhing about as a dark drool drips down them.

The Beet has a segmented neck that leads down to a fearsome shell-clad body. Ten legs protrude out of the monster's shell, the foremost two legs boast claws with three threatening pincers while the remaining eight look very much like a spider's legs.

Matthew stares back at the Beet, taking an inventory of the many gaps between where its shell segments meet. He slowly swallows a lump in his throat as he cautiously turns off the safety on his rifle, training it on the beast's face as he does so.

The moment Matthew's shot is lined up, he fires, only to discover that his target had moved. He lets off a few more rounds before the Beet smashes him against the slick wall of the cavern.

Matthew's weapon goes flying, and he watches in dismay as it sinks into the mud. Thinking fast, Matthew rolls away from where he had slid down the wall, pulling out his knife in the process.

Matthew shrugs out of his backpack as he gets a feel for the knife in his hand. The blade is a lot longer than the knives he is used to using, which he figures will come in handy right about now.

The Beet slowly approaches Matthew with its clawed appendages reaching for him. By now, the drool that once gently dripped down the creature's tentacles is now pouring profusely.

Suddenly, the Beetle spits a spray of its drool at Matthew, which he dodges at the last possible moment. He looks at the wall where the spit had landed as he remembers what James had said about the Beet's venom.

Knowing that he got lucky with his last dodge, Matthew charges the Beetle and takes a hold of one of its clawed arms. The creature doesn't have time to react before Matthew slashes at the nearest join on its arm with his knife. The clawed appendage writhes as Matthew tosses the now-loose limb away from his prey.

Retreating a few paces, the Beetle looks down to its missing arm which now has a geyser of its light blue blood shooting out. It doesn't have time to look back up before

Matthew takes another run at the beast and sinks his knife into its neck.

The Beet throws Matthew back against the wall of the cavern once more and Matthew splashes to the muddy ground. He anxiously searches for his knife in the mud near where he had landed to no avail. Looking up, Matthew realizes that his blade is still buried in his adversary's neck.

Out of sheer desperation, Matthew charges once more. The Beet is ready for him this time, and it takes a hold of his chest with its clawed arm. It starts to squeeze, and Matthew feels its claws digging into his flesh. The pain caused by the Beet's pinching causes lights to flash on the edges of Matthew's vision. Suddenly, he snaps into all-out survival mode, and the amount of adrenaline coursing through his veins seemingly doubles.

Matthew flails about as the Beet lifts him from the ground. As he swings his arms and legs, praying that he can make contact with something that will save him. After several seconds he remembers his blade.

Matthew is now face-to-face with the Beet, and he can't help but notice the increased flow of drool as it drips down the monster's tendrils. Matthew continues swinging his arms about in order to keep the Beet preoccupied as he carefully kicks at his knife. After several attempts, he makes contact with the knife's handle.

The blade digs deeper into the Beet's neck while also getting tweaked just so. With that, the Beetle suddenly goes limp and it drops Matthew to the ground. The Beet collapses without so much as a whisper, and it lands with a mighty splash beside Matthew.

Matthew lets out a long unsteady breath as he closes his eyes. After a few moments, he opens them and turns to see the Beet's venom-drenched tentacles which had landed far too close to Matthew's head for his liking.

Matthew moans as he stares up to the sky above as he wishes he was home. Not only home, but home with Dixie. He longed to eat some of her lukewarm, watery stew which she would spend the entire day making. Matthew closes his eyes as he imagines what his homecoming will be like.

"Congratulations, Matthew," Rav'ian sounds from above.

"Thanks for the help," Matthew mutters sarcastically as he struggles out from under the Beet whose heavy neck had landed on top of him.

Matthew slips in the mud as he slowly struggles to his feet. Once he is standing, he takes a step forward, only to stumble and fall back to the ground. He grunts as his head slams into something hard, which he quickly realizes is his wayward rifle.

"I lied to you earlier," Rav'ian admits as Matthew rises to his feet once more.

"What about?" Matthew inquires, hoping that the Toaz wasn't about to hop down and try to finish him off.

"The invades are no less menacing when they awaken," Rav'ian replies, "And yet you still defeated the beast."

"No thanks to you," Matthew whispers to himself as he pulls his knife out of the Beet's neck.

Matthew kneels beside the Beet's head as he slowly decapitates his defeated foe. Once he finishes, he lobs off its venom-soaked tentacles and tosses it up to where Rav'ian is.

"You may want to claim additional trophies from this kill," Rav'ian advises, "I have yet to see one defeat such a mighty foe on their own."

"Then why did you leave me to do it alone?" Matthew demands, his irritation getting the best of him.

Matthew stoops beside the dead creature's body as he carves away a large chunk of the Beet's shell. He isn't sure if he wanted to make a breastplate out of the piece, or a shield, but he feels inspired to fashion some sort of armor out of the creature.

"Because I have yet to see any less than five soldiers defeat one of the invaders," Rav'ian reports after a long pause.

"So, does that mean I'm going to be some kind of legend then?" Matthew asks with a chuckle as he frees part of the shell from his kill. He winces as the shell breaks free when the skin on his chest starts burning. He looks down and sees that he isn't bleeding a whole lot, instead his skin is blistering where the Beet had grabbed him. He shakes his head and resolves to ignore the pain as he does his best to hide his wound.

"Indeed," Rav'ian affirms, still staring down at Matthew.

"So how do I get out of here?" Matthew asks after looking around the hole he is stuck in. As far as he can see, there is only one way in or out, and that is the hole that is above his head.

"I have a rope," Rav'ian sounds as she lowers a line down to Matthew.

"Thanks," Matthew nods as he sheathes his knife. He fetches his backpack and then he lashes both his rifle and the Beet's shell to it to make transporting it a bit easier. Content, Matthew grabs the rope and then climbs up.

"How did you know to kick the blade?" Rav'ian asks once Matthew is topside once again.

"I didn't," Matthew cedes as he looks down to his chest which is bleeding through his uniform. From what he can tell, the Beet must have just barely nicked him when it grabbed him, however, there still was the issue with the blistering.

"Interesting," Rav'ian mutters as she scans Matthew's face for several moments. Eventually, she must see what she had been looking for because she breaks eye contact and hands Matthew the Beet's head, "This belongs to you."

"So, am I going to make a helmet out of this like the others have?" Matthew inquires.

"Yes," Rav'ian replies as she looks to the horizon.

Feeling like something isn't adding up, Matthew presses, "So, all of this was just for a helmet?"

"Yes," Rav'ian answers as she turns

around and starts off back toward the trenches. After several steps, she continues, "It is also a rite of passage that newcomers must complete in order to be truly accepted."

"I take it most people get the Beets when they are still asleep?" Matthew asks as he follows after Rav'ian.

"Yes," she replies simply.

Chapter Three

The Bulwark, Allegra

"I guess this means we can officially welcome you to The Bulwark," James announces as he looks at the head Matthew had tossed at his feet.

"Quite the baptism by fire," Matthew grunts as he stares at James with more than a hint of malice. Rav'ian's words had resonated with Matthew, and now he can't help but distrust James.

"Oi, Robinhood," a man calls from inside the bunker James is still standing at the door of, "This the Mud Pup you told us about?"

"It is," James affirms as several people come into view behind James.

"Welcome aboard," the man nods approvingly to Matthew after looking at the Beet's head. He stoops down and picks up the head nodding as he inspects it.

"Let me show you to your bed," James eventually requests as he steps aside to let Matthew through the narrow door.

"I think I'd rather stick it out on my own," Matthew refuses James's request, "I like sleeping under the stars anyways."

"But kid, we got bets to win!" James pleads, likely realizing that he is about to lose Matthew.

"Thanks for the pointers," Matthew nods as he collects his prize from the reluctant arms of the man who had been examining it.

"Are you sure you aren't interested in my hospitality?" James asks with a threatening tone.

"I've heard a lot about you and the others," Matthew replies, "I am very sure."

"Have it your way," James seethes as he spits to the side and subsequently slams the door to his hideout shut.

"Your actions confound even me," a voice Matthew recognizes to be Rooch's sounds from nearby.

"I think I'll be better off without them," Matthew shrugs at the large Arrandorran.

"I informed him of what the Thief and his companions do," Rav'ian sounds from several meters away. For one reason or another, she had kept her distance the entire time Matthew had spoken to James.

"Intriguing," Rooch nods as his head sways to-and-fro.

"So, I guess that means I'm on my own

then," Matthew frowns as he looks up and down the trench he is in.

"I can speak with my people," Rav'ian sounds after a few moments, "The tale of your valor is sure to win their respect."

"That would be great," Matthew smiles to his Toaz companion.

As much as Matthew hated giving up his chance to be surrounded by some of the few humans on the front, he couldn't see himself lodging with people like James. Especially after learning of everything they did.

"I trust it was my stories that eventually convinced you?" Rav'ian prods as she stares at Matthew.

"Yeah... I don't think I could ever bring myself to eat the Beets," Matthew shudders at the thought, "Do they really do that?"

"Yes," Rav'ian nods as she bows slightly to Rooch. She turns and starts off down the trench as she continues, "However, I find their cowardice to be their greatest flaw."

"Well, my people don't take to the warrior lifestyle that your people do," Matthew shrugs, "A lot of us seek a life of peace."

"There are times for peace and times for war," Rav'ian counters, "My people can thrive in peacetimes, but we refuse to shy away from war. I have observed that you, Matthew, are much more like us than you may realize."

"I don't know if I could sleep in the mud like you do though," Matthew chuckles after a beat.

"That would be unnecessary," Rav'ian sounds before she too laughs.

"Will your people really accept me, even after I killed one of them?"

"Of course. You defeated Riaan in fair combat."

"But I… I killed him."

"Many hostilities among our people result in death. Many believe there is more honor in death than there is in defeat."

"If you say so," Matthew frowns.

Matthew and Rav'ian plod through the maze of trenches for some time before Rav'ian finally tells Matthew to wait outside of what appears to be another large bunker. She makes Matthew stand a few paces away as she knocks. Without another word to Matthew, Rav'ian is welcomed into the bunker, leaving him completely alone in the dingy trench.

Matthew waits patiently for at least a half-hour before his exhaustion gets the best of him. Realizing he may be waiting for a long while, Matthew drops his pack and takes a seat. He props his head on his good arm, which he is resting on his knee and he starts examining his various wounds. Oddly enough, much of his right side is blistering in the same way his chest had been. This worries Matthew and he considers tracking down Rav'ian for some help before nodding off.

•••••••••••••••

"He is not much to look at, is he?" a feminine voice sounds, gently rousing Matthew from his sleep.

"He is the best warrior I have seen come from your people in a long time," Rav'ian's voice counters.

"That isn't too difficult," the voice says with a chuckle.

"You have not seen him fight," Rav'ian maintains. After a few moments, she asks, "Do you think you can help him, healer?"

"I've done all I can do for him, now all we can do is wait," the one Rav'ian referred to as the healer replies.

"I trust in your abilities," Rav'ian assures the healer.

"I heard the others say he was a sailor," the healer sounds, she continues in a mutter,

"Very interesting indeed."

By now, Matthew is fully awake, but he is doing his best to look like he is still fast asleep. He is laying down somewhere a lot warmer than where he had fallen asleep, which he finds both soothing, and alarming. Part of him worries about his gear, but he is sure that Rav'ian kept track of it for him.

"What are sailors?" Rav'ian inquires after a long beat.

Matthew feels something being pressed against his chest which immediately makes him feel woozy from the immense pain that starts screaming inside his brain. He struggles to remain conscious to no avail.

•••••••••••••

"Hey, wake up," the feminine voice that had awakened Matthew earlier sounds. Matthew quickly remembers that Rav'ian had called her the healer.

"Where am I?" Matthew moans without opening his eyes.

"You're in my medical ward," the healer replies, "Rav'ian brought you here, do you remember that?"

"The last thing I remember is Rav'ian

taking me to the Toaz bunker," Matthew mutters as he opens his eyes and slowly sits up. He takes a small bowl of soup from the healer and he nods his thanks to her.

"Interesting indeed," the healer sounds.

Matthew looks at the healer who he quickly sees is a human. Not only that, but she is also quite beautiful. Matthew is about to say something else when the door leading into the underground medical ward eases open.

"Has he awakened?" Rav'ian inquires as she peeks her head through the door. Matthew looks past her and sees that it is still dark out, which he finds relieving.

"Yes," the healer replies from beside Matthew. She steps aside so Rav'ian can see him.

"Are you aware that you were poisoned?" Rav'ian asks Matthew as she enters the subterranean barracks and approaches him.

"Was it that Beet I fought?" Matthew inquires as he looks down to where his uniform should have been.

Rather than seeing the light brown material, he sees his tanned chest which is boasting a large angry-looking wound. He raises the arm Riaan had bitten to touch his chest in order to poke at his injury when he sees several matching spots dotting the better portion of his arm.

"It would seem so," the healer nods as she looks Matthew over.

"It doesn't feel too bad," Matthew shrugs after a beat.

"That is because I spent the entire day tending to you," the healer laughs.

"The entire day?" Matthew asks dumbly. Part of him doubts that he could have slept through an entire day on Allegra. His stomach growls, reminding him of his need to eat, and he quickly gulps down some of the soup that the healer had given him.

"Yes," the healer nods as she watches Matthew eat.

"Will I be alright?" Matthew inquires as he looks down from his bowl to the purplish swelling on his chest. He nervously looks between Rav'ian and the healer when they don't immediately reply.

"We—well, Marie, is uncertain," Rav'ian replies as they both continue staring at Matthew with sad looks.

"I've never actually treated anyone for this kind of venom," the healer Rav'ian referred to as Marie reports with a nod, "No one has survived an up-close encounter like the one Rav'ian says you had."

"She is attempting an experiment to save you," Rav'ian adds after a few moments.

"Well, do I have to stay here?" Matthew asks with a frown.

"No," Marie replies, looking rather offended.

"Marie utilized the Latcher I recovered in addition to the head you recovered in order to create an antivenom of sorts," Rav'ian informs Matthew as he slowly swings out of bed.

"Well, thank you," Matthew nods to Marie who appears to enjoy receiving credit for her work.

"You are very welcome," Marie smiles before she quickly looks away and retreats to a nearby cot that has a Toaz in it.

"Would you like to accompany me on tonight's hunt?" Rav'ian inquires as she helps Matthew to his feet.

"Last night's hunt didn't go too well for me," Matthew chuckles as he stares at his wounds.

"The others are expecting you," Rav'ian insists, "Tales of your hunt have spread like wildfire."

"I wonder who told everyone about it,"

Matthew mutters as he levels an accusing stare at his Toaz companion.

"Everyone helped spread the word," Marie tells Matthew as she draws near. She wraps a large bandage around Matthew's chest as she continues, "They needed the morale boost. I can only do so much here to keep our people fighting."

"So, where does that leave me?" Matthew asks as he looks at the duo.

"It leaves you with a tough act to follow," Marie responds as she tosses Matthew a new brown shirt.

"Wait, so you're telling me that you go on hunts every night?" Matthew asks Rav'ian in surprise.

"We venture beyond the trenches no less than twice every night," Rav'ian affirms, "For the nights are long, and our enemy are many."

"What do you do during the day?" Matthew inquires as he slowly pulls his new shirt over his head.

"We defend The Bulwark and struggle to stay alive," Rav'ian replies as she grabs Matthew's backpack from a line of gear.

"Nights here are usually twenty-two hours long while the days are thirty-five hours,"

Marie adds, "So we rest up as often as we can."

"Why are the days so long?" Matthew inquires as he straightens out his shirt.

Matthew admires his new uniform, which is both thicker, and fancier than his original one. This shirt makes him look far more like a soldier in uniform than his plain shirt which is now out of the picture.

"Allegra rotates slowly, and it rotates at a slight axis," Marie promptly replies. She grabs a bag which she then tosses to Matthew before returning to her work.

"Matthew, it is time for us to leave," Rav'ian sounds as she hands Matthew his backpack, "We cannot miss the hunting party."

"Thanks again, Marie," Matthew nods to the healer before he follows Rav'ian out the door.

"Interesting indeed," he hears Marie whisper as the door shuts behind him.

"Marie has been with my people for some time now," Rav'ian informs Matthew as they make their way through the trenches toward the frontmost line.

Matthew remains silent, pushing down his desire to know more about the beautiful healer who had attended to him for countless hours. Matthew is afraid that if he learned more about her, he may fall for her. He couldn't risk falling for another girl while Dixie was at home.

Rav'ian seemingly understands that Matthew doesn't want to talk about Marie, so she too falls silent. They continue through the mess of man-made ravines until they finally find themselves at the fringes of a large group of Toaz.

A Toaz speaker Matthew thinks he recognizes as Trellik is addressing the group, but Matthew can't understand what he is saying. Trellik continues speaking for quite some time in what Matthew reasons is the Toa language. Judging by the faces of the Toaz around Matthew, the speech is a good one. Every so often, Matthew thinks he hears some familiar names, but he can't be certain.

"For Riaan," seemingly the entire group sounds once Trellik finishes his speech. They suddenly raise their various weapons into the air with a shout, which catches Matthew off-guard.

"Trellik has commissioned us to a hunt which we shall honor Riaan with," Rav'ian informs Matthew once the cheering has stopped.

"What do I need to do?" Matthew

inquires as he watches the crowd of Toaz disperse. Most of them disappear over the top of the trench, but a handful crowd around Matthew.

"You are to claim the greatest sum of prizes in Riaan's name, or we shall kill you," Rav'ian replies.

"Kill me?" Matthew whispers nervously as he looks around the circle of Toaz who had formed around him.

"No, that was a jest," Rav'ian assures Matthew with her oddly humanlike laugh. Looking deeply into his eyes, she continues, "However it would bring great honor to both you, and Riaan's household if you brought in the greatest sum of prizes."

"What do we do with the prizes?" Matthew inquires, still unsure as to what had been done with his own trophies. Part of him fears that someone stole the head he had in addition to the shell.

"They shall be burned in a funeral pyre," Rav'ian replies, "And a memento of sorts will be made for the hunter who brings in the greatest catch."

"Well, let's get this over with," Matthew nods as he looks to the nearest ladder. To his dismay, every way out for him has been blocked off by the crowd of Toaz who had gathered around him. Matthew eventually looks to Rav'ian and whispers, "What do they want?"

"They wish to be present as you receive your first accolade," Rav'ian replies with her toothy smile.

"My first—" Matthew starts before Trellik suddenly emerges from the crowd and silences him with his booming voice.

"Matthew Campbell, valiant hunter," Trellik greets him. He crosses his arms over his chest as if he is hugging himself before he continues, "We welcome you as one of our own."

"Tha—" Matthew starts before he is elbowed in the side.

"Quiet," Marie whispers to him from his side. She must have snuck up behind him without so much as a sound. She quickly follows up her order with a softer voice, "This is an important ritual for them."

"Tonight, we welcome you, even as one of our own depart from us," Trellik continues before he slips back into what Matthew is sure is the Toa language. Trellik continues for some time before the crowd behind him parts.

The crowd allows a short female Toaz to waddle through. Her scales are nearly black, which Matthew finds intriguing. Up until now, every Toaz he had seen had lighter-colored scales. Following her are several other Toaz, all of whom have similarly dark scales.

"Our armorer has toiled tirelessly that we might bestow upon you a gift worthy of a great hunter," Trellik eventually continues as he motions toward the black female Toaz which had led the small procession. The rest of the newcomers assemble in a tight circle around Matthew and Trellik, which Matthew assumes must be part of the ceremony.

One of the Toaz who had accompanied the armorer steps forward. They present a black helmet; which Matthew can see was made out of the head that he had lobbed off of the Beetle the night before. As the Toaz bows, he announces, "A helm formed from the head of your first hunt,"

Matthew is about to speak again, but he decides to look over to Marie out of the corner of his eye. Marie notices Matthew's inquisitive look, and she shakes her head slightly. Matthew takes this as her way of telling him to keep silent.

By the time Matthew looks ahead again, the helmet is gone. He considers asking where it went but is cut short when it is plopped on top of his head. Matthew does his best to not flinch as a set of arms reaches around him to secure a chinstrap into place

"This shall protect you in your next battle," the armorer informs Matthew.

"Crafted from the shell of your first trophy," another one of the dark-scaled Toaz sounds as he lifts a large piece of armor above his head for all to see. Matthew examines it closely, and he quickly sees that the piece is meant to protect his torso. Much of the Beet's shell went into creating the breastplate of the armor, but smaller fragments had also been utilized to protect his back and sides as well. After a long pause, the Toaz passes the armor to one of his companions, and they approach Matthew.

The Toaz who now has the armor stands before Matthew and quickly says a few things in his native tongue. Unsure of what was said, Matthew glances over to Marie once more.

"Stretch your arms out," Marie instructs with a hurried whisper.

Matthew immediately complies, feeling more than a little foolish. Once his arms are outstretched, the Toaz around him quickly open the piece of armor up and then wrap it around him. With the armor in place, the Toaz proceed to tie a few knots on Matthew's side to fix the armor in place.

"This armor shall counter many of the invader's attacks," the armorer explains as she nods approvingly at how well the piece fits Matthew.

Matthew looks over to Marie yet again to see if he is allowed to thank everyone for the armor, and she finally nods. Smiling, Matthew looks to the assembly before him and says, "Thank you for everything. I hope to make all of you proud."

Matthew's words are met with a sudden and loud cheer, which makes him jump slightly. Without waiting another moment, the assembly disperses, disappearing over the top of the trench as they head out for the night's hunt.

The Hunt

The Battle for Allegra

Episode Three

Chapter One

The Bulwark, Allegra

"Are you not coming with us?" Matthew asks as he looks down to Marie who is still in the trench that he and Rav'ian had just come out of.

Marie looks up to Matthew and gives him a wry smile. She shakes her head and starts leaving before she calls back, "You've got your job, I've got mine."

"We require her services here in order to aid our wounded," Rav'ian explains, "The Coalition did not provide us with medical staffing, and thus Marie filled the role."

Matthew nods in understanding. *Although I definitely would have liked Marie's company up here,* Matthew thinks. As much as

126

he loved Dixie, he had to admit that he had developed a slight crush on Marie in the very short time since he had met her. The girl is both beautiful and smart, much like Dix. Come to think of it, Matthew's crush may just be caused by his missing Dixie.

Matthew pauses a moment to look around and he notices something—or more accurately, the absence of something. Looking over to Rav'ian, he points out, "I can't help but notice I'm the only human up here."

"Our orders currently require that we simply maintain our position. My people cannot remain idle while there is a fight to be fought, and so we fight."

"Wait, you're telling me that we don't have to be out here?"

"That is correct, but we expect this will change in short order. No war is won on the defensive."

"Do you at least get something out of this?"

"We gain stories and honor."

"I mean do you get extra rations or something like that?"

"Unless we are granted some from those we rescue, no."

Matthew frowns, unsure of what to ask

next. The entrepreneurial side of him can't help but wonder why someone would risk their lives for just about no gain. The rest of him wonders why anyone would even come out here even if there was something to be gained.

"We received reports that approximately ten invaders were assembled nearby!" a nearby Toaz calls from a small ridge ahead of Matthew and Rav'ian.

A nearby assembly of Toaz make their way toward the Toaz who had made the announcement, and Matthew begins to follow them before Rav'ian takes a hold of his arm. She pulls him back to herself and holds him there for a few moments longer than Matthew would have liked. He is about to say something when Rav'ian finally speaks.

"There are many among my people who believe we should not treat you as we do," Rav'ian starts as she stares toward the group of Toaz who are being briefed on the Beets. After another longer than necessary pause, she continues, "The one way that you might be accepted is if you bring in the most trophies this night."

Matthew gives her a quizzical look before he sighs and tells her, "I know, you've already told me as much! I've got to bring back the most heads to honor Riaan and his household."

"This would also serve you," Rav'ian reminds Matthew as she finally releases his arm.

"Well, now we missed out on joining that hunting party," Matthew mutters as the group of Toaz disappear over the small hill that the announcement had been made on top of. He looks back to Rav'ian who is silently scanning the horizon. Matthew waits a few more moments before asking, "What are you looking for?"

"Signs of a… I believe your people call it a hive."

"A hive? So, we're looking for a bunch of Beets?"

"That is correct. Such a target would yield the greatest quarry."

"Won't it be crawling with the Beetles?"

"They will be hibernating for the night,"

"But won't there be a *lot* of them?"

"The estimates I have heard report nearly twenty of your '*Beetles'* for every hive."

"What if they wake up though?"

"Then we die with honor," Rav'ian replies with her perfect laugh. She reaches behind her into a backpack that Matthew hadn't

129

noticed until now and she produces a small helmet of her own. She quickly straps it, and a pair of gauntlets, on as she starts walking away from Matthew.

Matthew chases after her, stumbling several times in the mud. Once he catches up to his Toaz companion, he asks, "Why don't you have more armor?"

"Armor like your own does not suit me," Rav'ian replies simply.

"What do you mean?"

"As your people say, it does not suit my style."

Matthew cocks his head slightly, as he decides if Rav'ian is trying to explain fashion to him. After a beat, he admits, "I'm still not following…"

"Perhaps this will aid your understanding." Rav'ian sounds as she swings a fist at Matthew.

Matthew is taken off-guard, and Rav'ian's scaled fist smashes into his jaw. Worse yet, her momentum puts him off-balance, sending him sprawling into the mud.

Matthew spits out a mouthful of mud as he picks himself out of the mire. Now that he has tasted the mud, Matthew is confident that the stories of the dirt being made wet with blood were false. This muck was definitely more akin to the sludge found in his fishing ship's bilge.

Rav'ian takes advantage of Matthew's lapse in attention, and she quickly wraps her arms around Matthew's throat in a chokehold. Matthew looks down and sees a line of spikes on Rav'ian's gauntlets. He remembers a similar line of spikes on the legs of the Beet he killed the night before.

With the spikes pressing against his throat and jugular, Matthew feels his pulse quicken. He is about to throw Rav'ian off, or just roll on top of her until she yields when he realizes that she isn't actually applying pressure around his throat. Evidently, she isn't trying to kill him.

Trusting his previous impressions of Rav'ian, and hoping he read his situation right, Matthew announces, "Ok, I get it," he slowly rises to his feet, Rav'ian still on his back. Thanks to his strength, he hardly notices her weight.

"Good," Rav'ian sounds from her perch before she lets go of him and drops back to the ground. Matthew turns around and sees her grinning widely. After a few triumphal beats, she continues, "I cannot risk any weighty armor like your own, as such would impede my fighting abilities."

"You could have just explained it like that," Matthew points out as he rubs his jaw where Rav'ian had hit him. Despite her sleek frame, Rav'ian really could pack a punch.

Rav'ian lets out something that sounds like a giggle as she turns. She starts heading the direction she had been going a few moments before without so much as a word. Matthew starts following her once more, and this time he is sure to give her a little more space—just in case.

•••••••••••••

"The hive is near," Rav'ian whispers as she slows to a stop.

Matthew lets out a long breath as he too stops. He and Rav'ian had been forging their way through the boggy landscape for quite some time now. If Matthew had to guess, he would say that they had been going hard for about two hours now.

"How near?" Matthew asks warily as his eyes drop to the ground. He starts scanning his surroundings for any signs of the Latchers that Rav'ian had found the night before.

Rav'ian stoops down to the ground and she drives her knife into a pile of mud that Matthew had failed to notice. The Latcher inside squeals and writhes a moment before it dies. Rav'ian collects her prize as she answers, "I am unsure."

Unsatisfied with her answer, Matthew presses, "But since the Latcher is here, they've got to be close by, right?"

"This is my understanding, yes," Rav'ian agrees as she drops her trophy into her bag. She stands and scans their surroundings, likely hoping to find some dead giveaway.

"Could the hive be in one of the hills?" Matthew asks as he looks at the nearest hill. He stares closely at it for a few moments before he notices a small hole in its side, which he assumes might be the entrance into the hive. Pointing, he tells Rav'ian, "I think that one might actually be it."

"It appears like you are correct." Rav'ian agrees as she stands beside Matthew.

Frowning, Matthew recalls the events from the night before. As epic as that fight was, he preferred the idea of killing the Beets in their sleep this time. Looking to his companion, he inquires, "So, do we go in without any lights then?"

"Such is the way we avoid death, yes." Rav'ian replies with a purposeful nod as she marches toward the apparent hive.

"But how will we be able to see in there?" Matthew presses as he follows her, "It will be too dark for us to be able to make anything out."

"What do you suggest?"

"I don't know… I just don't like the idea of getting stuck in there if one of them wakes up."

"Then we must be swift, they rise at first light."

"But what if we wake one up?"

"Such an occurrence is most uncommon."

"Such an occurrence is uncommon?" Matthew demands dumbfounded, "It happened to me last night!"

"Light awakens them, as does heat," Rav'ian explains as she stops at the hole at the base of the hill Matthew had pointed out.

Matthew takes in the entrance, and he frowns once more as he realizes that the hole is easily large enough to accommodate three of the Beetles. Not only that, but the mouth of the hive appears to be quite a bit taller than the Beet Matthew had killed the night before.

Peering into the vast tunnel, Matthew searches for any signs of movement. He whispers a quick prayer for everything to remain still, and sure enough, nothing moves. After several moments, Matthew looks back to Rav'ian who is also standing idly at the entrance.

"Do you have any of your rope?" Matthew inquires.

Rav'ian produces a large coil of rope from her backpack. Handing it to Matthew, she asks, "What have you devised?"

"In case we get turned around in there, we'll have this to guide us out," Matthew explains as he ties one end of the rope around a nearby rock. He gives it a few tugs to seat the knot before he continues, "I did something like this back at home when my friends and I explored the caves around Crail."

"I would very much enjoy learning more about your home some time," Rav'ian informs Matthew as she takes a knife in each of her hands.

"And I yours," Matthew nods in response and he fumbles around with his belongings a few moments before finding his own knife. He considers grabbing his rifle for a moment before he remembers how ineffective it had been the night before.

Resigning himself to his fate, Matthew takes his first step into the hive. Matthew slowly unravels the rope behind him as he and Rav'ian descend into the dark depths of the tunnel.

The air is both cool and damp against Matthew's skin, and he shivers slightly. He tries to assure himself that his shuddering is only from the cold, but he inwardly knows his own fear is also to blame. He continues slogging through the thick mud which clings to just about everything it touches.

"So, has anyone else been stupid enough to go into one of these hives?" Matthew asks as he and Rav'ian continue slogging down the dark cave.

"I have yet to hear such stories," Rav'ian replies quietly.

Matthew chuckles, largely for his own sake. Turning back to Rav'ian, he inquires with a sly grin, "Does that mean we're doing something new, or does it mean that everyone else died?"

"I am unsure," Rav'ian promptly replies. Her footsteps stop and are quickly replaced by a loud splash.

Worried, Matthew stops and whispers,

"Are you alright?"

"Yes, all is well." Rav'ian's voice sounds. Matthew hears the sound of her blade sawing through something before she explains what happened, "I stumbled upon one of the invaders."

"I take it you already killed it?" Matthew inquires as he sheaths his knife. He stoops down and follows his rope back toward Rav'ian in order to investigate.

"Correct," Rav'ian replies proudly as she pushes something at Matthew. She catches Matthew off-guard, and he stumbles backward.

Matthew trips over himself as he slips, and he then slams into the wall of the tunnel he and Rav'ian are in. His hands sink into the mud as he tries to pick himself up. He freezes when his right hand touches something hard. Matthew's blood runs cold and he whispers just loud enough to be heard, "Rav'ian, am I near the Beet you killed?"

"No," Rav'ian replies simply. Her backpack rustles slightly as she stows away her first trophy of the night.

"Then that means…" Matthew mutters to himself as he slowly reaches into his belt with his left hand and produces his knife. As he brings his knife to bear, Matthew grips the spiny leg of a Beetle with his right hand.

The leg suddenly twitches, its spines ripping through the tough skin on Matthew's palm. Unwilling to allow the Beet to fully awaken, Matthew starts stabbing wildly into the mud where the Beet is hibernating.

After several stabs, Matthew finally hits what he recognizes as part of a Beetle's shell, and he quickens his pace. Stabbing time and time again, Matthew eventually finds a soft spot in the creature's impenetrable shell. Capitalizing on his discovery, Matthew drives his blade as deep as it will go into the soft spot.

By now, the Beet has awakened, but Matthew's assault has handicapped it somewhat. The beast tries rising from the mire it is in, but it fails miserably. Matthew continues his assault all the while, and eventually works his way up to the Beet's neck.

All too aware of the damage that the creature's venom can do, Matthew summons all of his strength to keep the beast's head beneath the mud. The Beet writhes beneath him as it tries to buck him off, but Matthew's previous attacks have already weakened it too much.

Before long, Matthew finds a gap in the creature's naturally armored neck. Smiling victoriously—albeit with his jaw clenched due to the adrenaline coursing through his veins—Matthew drives his knife into the Beet's neck. The beast starts jerking around erratically as it panics, but Matthew's grip is too much for it. Matthew jerks his blade about inside of the Beet's neck and it quickly succumbs to its wounds.

"Alright, that's one for me!" Matthew announces proudly as he works up the rest of the way to the Beet's head. He starts carving away at its neck as he continues, "I guess we're tied now."

"Unfortunately for you, this is not the case," Rav'ian announces from deeper within the tunnel. She continues with a triumphal voice, "I slew another one of the invaders as you struggled with your first."

"How…" Matthew whispers to himself in awe. Once again, Rav'ian had proved that grace may in fact beat brawn.

Unwilling to fall behind this early in the hunt, Matthew quickly bags his first head. Standing, he starts trudging through the mud once again, this time feeling around for any signs of a Beet. After several steps, Matthew's foot brushes past another Beet leg, and he quickly kills it.

Having removed the Beet's head, Matthew looks over to Rav'ian and happily announces, "I think I'm getting the hang of this!"

"This is good," Rav'ian's voice sounds in response further down the tunnel.

"Don't get too far ahead," Matthew warns as he picks up the rope he is using as their impromptu bread trail.

"This would not be an issue if you were swifter." Rav'ian points out in a teasing tone.

"Hey, I just thought of something," Matthew declares as he bags a third Beet head, "How are we going to transport all these heads?"

•••••••••••••

Matthew and Rav'ian toss yet another Beet head on top of the pile of thirty or so others. The head lands with a dull crash and it quickly rolls to the base of the mountain of death. Matthew lets out a long, content sigh as he takes in the evidence of his and Rav'ian's hard work.

Clearly content with their haul, Rav'ian takes a seat in the marsh, and she quickly sinks in several centimeters. Rav'ian and

Matthew both stare at the pile of heads for several minutes in absolute silence. After nearly five hours of trekking through the tunnels in the Beet hive, both of them are spent. Between the physical exertion of slogging through the mud, and the emotional draw from the constant fear of the Beetles awakening, Matthew knows that he is ready for a long night's—or more accurately day's—rest.

Rav'ian shifts and slowly rises to her feet. After a moment, she looks over to Matthew and informs him, "It appears as if our only option will be to take several trips."

"We could string a few heads together and make a chain of sorts," Matthew points out as he rakes his mind for any possible ways to get out of taking several trips. Matthew knows that he won't be able to weather a few trips between here and the trenches.

"I do not understand," Rav'ian admits as she looks between Matthew and the pile of heads.

"Well…" Matthew starts before trailing off. Realizing that his idea would be better explained via example, he grabs Rav'ian's rope and then takes a hold of two Beet heads.

Matthew finds a nearby rock and he takes a seat on it as he carves two of the

Beet's eyes out and then he hollows out a small channel between the two chasms. He then fishes the rope through the small tunnel and shows Rav'ian his creation. Nodding, he continues, "It's like putting beads on a string."

"This appears to be very tedious work," Rav'ian frowns as she watches Matthew, who is butchering his second head.

Shrugging, Matthew replies, "It sounds a lot easier than taking a few trips between here and the Bulwark."

Matthew's final comment seems to sway Rav'ian over to his side, and she quickly joins him. In short order, she is prepping the heads for Matthew to string. They make quick work of their string of gore, sliding the final head on in time to hear gun reports not too far off.

"We should assist them," Rav'ian announces dutifully as she looks off toward where the gunfire had come from.

"Didn't you say that the Beets are just about impossible to kill once they are awake?" Matthew asks pointedly as he suppresses the urge to shudder in fear. In reality, he is more interested in avoiding another close encounter with one of the Beetles.

"Be that as it may, we are obliged to assist one another out here." Rav'ian replies in

142

a tone that tells Matthew that there is no talking her out of her latest mission. After a short beat, several additional shots sound off, proving someone is still fighting for their life.

Sighing, Matthew resigns himself to his fate. It seems like he is destined to follow Rav'ian to the end. Shrugging, he cedes, "Well, let's bring these along so we don't have to double back."

Several more gunshots sound in the distance, seemingly working to force Rav'ian's hand into complying to Matthew's request. A few faint voices are carried over to the by a slight breeze that has picked up. The light wind also brings with it the smell of sulfur and smoke.

"Very well," Rav'ian says, agreeing to Matthew's terms. She picks up one end of the rope of heads and starts off toward the battle in progress.

"Any idea why the Beets might have awakened?" Matthew inquires as he takes up his own end of their gore-chain, which is dripping with the Beetles' light blue blood.

"Perhaps a newcomer used their light, as you did." Rav'ian offers as she increases her pace slightly.

Nodding, Matthew slowly agrees,

"Perhaps,"

Matthew and Rav'ian make their way through the muddy warzone and then up a nearby rise. As they crest one of the highest hills in the valley, they see the cause of all the commotion.

In the distance, Matthew can see at least fifty bodies of people who are dressed in dark blue Coalition uniforms. Said bodies are scattered around what remains of what appears to be a Coalition shuttle.

The shuttle has been reduced to a smoking shell of the ship it once was. Flames are still rising high from the cockpit and the engines. What appears to be burning bodies are scattered in its immediate vicinity, every soldier lying where they fell.

"We are too late," Rav'ian mutters softly as she stares at several of the nearest bodies that are strewn about on one of the hills between them and the battlefield. Many of the corpses are congregated outside of what appears to be another Beet hive, much like the one Matthew and Rav'ian had just been inside of.

Matthew stares at the remains of the battlefield in awe. What is even more concerning than the field of dead before him is the eerie lack of any Beetles. Frowning, he eventually asks, "Where are all the Beets?"

"This worries me as well," Rav'ian sounds, "But I assume the invaders returned to their hive upon neutralizing our soldiers."

"All except those," Matthew says as he points to a handful of Beets that appear to be chasing down a squad of soldiers in the distance who were unfortunate enough to have engaged them. They are fighting for their lives on the other side of the small valley from Matthew and Rav'ian.

"We must assist them," Rav'ian announces dutifully.

Matthew frowns as he looks over the field of bodies between him and the soldiers Rav'ian wanted to help. He shakes his head, fearing that only the worst could happen if they went through there.

Before Matthew has the time to explain how bad of an idea it is to charge through the killing field, Rav'ian is already running. He dumbly looks to her end of their rope of trophies and sees that she has abandoned it in order to try to save those on the other side of the valley.

"We can't just go through there!" Matthew calls out as he drops his end of the trophy rope and chases after her.

Rav'ian doesn't so much as turn as she replies, "It is the shortest route."

Matthew lets out a long, unsteady breath as he resigns himself—yet again—to his fate. If he made it through the killing field ahead then he was a lot luckier than he ever thought he was. He slowly blinks before he fixes his eyes on the horizon in order to maintain his bearing and he continues chasing after Rav'ian.

Matthew doesn't make it far when he trips over the body of one of the fallen soldiers. Thanks to his fixation on the horizon, he had ignored the obstacles underfoot. He lands face-first into the tattered remains of another slaughtered soldier.

"Rav'ian!" Matthew calls out once he picks himself up from the bloody mess he landed in. Looking up, he sees that she has stopped and is looking back to him. He spits some of the dead soldier's blood out of his mouth before asking, "What do the Beets eat?"

"I doubt you will relish the answer." Rav'ian's voice sounds in reply after several moments.

Matthew lets out a long, loud groan of agony before the entirety of his stomach's contents make a move for the outside world. He is throwing up for nearly a minute before Rav'ian comes up behind him. She stops just beyond the blood bog that was a Beet feeding ground not too long ago.

"Are we just going to leave them out here like this?" Matthew demands once his stomach settles slightly.

"There are more pressing matters for us to attend to." Rav'ian sounds after several beats.

"But if we don't do something, the Beets will just keep eating them." Matthew points out as he looks to the carnage around him where soldiers had been ripped apart for food.

"To wait here is to join them," Rav'ian shakes her head as she points at the dead all around Matthew. Looking to the hills where the soldiers are still fighting for their lives, she continues, "We must press ahead and aid the others."

Matthew takes one last look at the dismembered bodies around him as he idly wipes his hands off on his pants. Sighing, he eventually cedes, "Fine, let's go."

Rav'ian starts off without a word, and Matthew follows in suit. They jog as quickly as they dare past the wreckage of the shuttle, doing their best to avoid all the bodies on the ground.

"Do you hear that?" Matthew questions as he suddenly stops. Listening intently, he hears a faint clanking from the inside of the burning gunship.

"It is likely nothing," Rav'ian assures Matthew as she looks longingly toward the hills where there is still some gunfire.

Matthew nods absently as he resumes his trek toward the hills. After a few beats, he asks, "Can we check it out after we save everyone?"

"Yes," Rav'ian promises, "Perhaps we might return with additional aid as well."

"That'd be helpful," Matthew nods to himself as he casts a backward glance to the ruined ship.

•••••••••••••

Matthew and Rav'ian survey the surrounding hillsides for any signs of the Beets. The gun reports have died down considerably, which worries Matthew. *Either we just won, or everyone's dead.* Matthew reasons to himself as he lays on his stomach beside Rav'ian.

"I see eight Beets near the ridge,"

Matthew mutters under his breath just loud enough for Rav'ian to hear. He slowly points toward the Beets that are idly milling about on a nearby hill.

Matthew turns and sees that Rav'ian is still scouring their surroundings. After a few moments, she faces Matthew and asks, "Do you see any of our allies?"

"I don't see any signs of them," Matthew reports feeling more than a little relieved. As he saw it, if there weren't any signs of anyone getting killed here, perhaps they all got away.

Rav'ian nods slowly before she grabs her rifle and flips the cover off of her scope. Without any warning, she takes a shot and one of the Beetles falls to the ground.

Knowing that the Beets would likely charge them, Matthew quickly follows Rav'ian's lead, letting off several rounds toward the Beets. After a few brief moments, three Beetles are all lying on the ground, their blue blood seeping into the miry earth.

By now, the Beetles have started rushing around, trying to find Matthew and Rav'ian. As far as Matthew can tell, the echoing gun reports are discombobulating the Beets, hamstringing their efforts of finding him and Rav'ian.

Before too long, the remaining five Beetles are all lying dead alongside their companions.

"I do not see any additional invaders," Rav'ian reports once she has scanned their still surroundings.

Matthew glances around the hills, inwardly wishing that it was lighter out so he could make out more details. Sure, the moons above did grant a good amount of light, but there was nothing like real sunlight.

"That was a little too easy," Matthew breathes as he continues staring at the fallen Beets in his scope. For how ferocious the Beetles were in close combat, they weren't very threating from afar.

"This is why we are told to neutralize them from a distance," Rav'ian replies as she slowly starts rising to her feet.

A few bullets whizz through the air, far too close for comfort. Matthew instinctively reaches up and yanks Rav'ian to the ground beside him and away from danger. With Rav'ian out of the line of fire, Matthew does his best to wriggle further behind the muddy ridgeline he is on, away from the sortie of bullets.

"The Beets don't have guns like that,

right?" Matthew inquires, doing his best to be heard above the sound of the gunfire and splashing of bullets in the muck.

"They do not," Rav'ian affirms.

Frowning, Matthew concludes, "So, we're getting shot at by our own people then."

"Yes, but I would assume they are not from the Bulwark." Rav'ian agrees as she removes her backpack.

Matthew watches as Rav'ian rifles through her bag for a few moments before he finally asks, "What are you looking for?"

"A signal flare," Rav'ian readily answers as she continues her search to no avail.

"I'm sure they'll realize we're not Beetles sooner or later." Matthew offers with a passive shrug. As he finishes speaking, the gunfire dies down. Curious, Matthew removes his Beetle head helmet and peeks over the ridge before he continues, "I guess they're done now."

"See? I told you they were friendlies!" someone shouts accusingly from the bottom of the hill Matthew is looking over.

"How were we supposed to know that?" a soldier demands in response.

Matthew watches intently as a handful of soldiers in dark blue Coalition uniforms start emerging from all around. From this distance,

Matthew can't quite make out their faces, but judging by their voices, they are quite scared.

"I'm sorry about that," the man who had been shouting a moment ago apologizes as he waves for Matthew to come down and join him and his people.

"They want us to join them," Matthew tells Rav'ian, who evidentially gave up her search for the flare.

"They just fired upon us," Rav'ian reminds Matthew with a chiding tone.

"They said sorry," Matthew points out as he rises to his feet.

"Your kind never ceases to confound me." Rav'ian shakes her head as she stands beside Matthew.

"Thank you for the save," the shouting man sounds once he sees Matthew and Rav'ian standing. Matthew reasons the man must be the one in charge of the unit of soldiers below since he is doing all the talking for the group.

"Is this everyone?" Matthew asks as he looks at the sorry group of twenty or so soldiers. He starts down the hill, Rav'ian in tow.

"Yeah, we lost five guys when those... *things*... came out of their holes." The man in charge reports. He looks back to some of his

152

men before he continues, "Our gunship dropped me and my team of marines here about forty minutes ago. We're supposed to join up with the other teams—"

"You won't be joining up with them," Matthew interrupts, "They're all gone."

"What do you mean?" the man asks, clearly taken off-guard by the report.

Matthew frowns as he continues down the hill, trying to formulate his response. He briefly glances over to Rav'ian who doesn't look like she is about to speak up. Sighing, he informs the soldier, "Their ship crashed next to a Beet hive. We think you're the only survivors."

"But there was a whole company of marines on that shuttle…" The man trails off as he looks past Matthew to Rav'ian. The confusion evident on his face, the man looks back to Matthew and slowly inquires, "What are you doing with a Toaz?"

"Killing Beets, same as you," Matthew replies dismissively.

"Wait, are you a Mudder?" the man presses.

"Yep, I got on Nelson's bad side." Matthew shrugs, "So here we are, just in time to save you and your team."

"Ah, Nelson's not the best guy to get mad." The man chuckles. He extends a hand to Matthew and smiles, "I'm Second Lieutenant Seville Wyndover."

"Matthew Campbell," Matthew smiles back as he takes the man's hand and gives it a firm shake. Pointing to his Toaz companion, he continues, "And this is Rav'ian Chekkier."

"A pleasure," Wyndover nods as he stretches a hand out to Rav'ian, "I have heard of your clan's accolades."

Rav'ian takes his hand and gives it a quick shake before retreating behind Matthew. Despite his curiosity as to why Rav'ian's demeanor had changed, Matthew decides to leave her be. She could explain herself later.

"What are you and your team doing out here?" Matthew asks with a small amount of hope welling up inside his chest. Perhaps Wyndover was just the first of a new Coalition offensive to end the war.

"It was supposed to just be a glorified scouting mission," Wyndover replies passively before he looks back to his team of marines. Frowning, he turns back to Matthew, "Can you take us to the crash site to look for survivors?"

Nodding, Matthew answers, "Yes, in fact, Rav'ian and I were planning on doing just that."

"Let's get moving then, I don't want to waste any more time here. Lead the way." Wyndover announces as he makes a hand motion to his team. His soldiers quickly form up behind him, and he nods to Matthew.

"You got it," Matthew nods to Wyndover. Turning, Matthew starts climbing the hill he had just descended. To his surprise, Rav'ian is already at the top of the hill, scanning their surroundings.

"What's wrong with your friend?" Wyndover asks in a whisper as he follows Matthew up the small hill.

"I don't know," Matthew admits with a slight grimace. If there was anything he hated in life, it was not knowing what was wrong with his friends.

Wyndover and Matthew both watch Rav'ian as they continue up the hill. After several beats, Wyndover acknowledges, "She doesn't seem too fond of marines."

"Oh," Matthew sounds as a look of realization shines in his eyes. Looking to Wyndover, he whispers his revelation, "It's probably because of how the Coalition attacked her homeworld. They must have sent in marines, so your presence brings back bad memories."

"That'd make sense," Wyndover mutters as he glances back to his team.

"It would appear like we are alone," Rav'ian announces from her perch once Matthew and the others are a few paces away.

Matthew nods to Rav'ian and then he looks to the group of marines. There are twenty-three soldiers in total, and they all appear to be accustomed to war. Matthew reasons that most of them must be career soldiers, judging by their age and scars. Wyndover who appears to be in his early thirties is likely the oldest of the group.

"Let's get moving, we don't want to be out here when the sun rises!" Matthew announces to the squadron.

"You heard him, marines! Double time!" Wyndover calls to his soldiers who surge ahead at a brisk march.

Matthew looks ahead and sees that the valley with the crashed shuttle is glowing red. He isn't sure why he hadn't noticed the glow before, but now it is unmistakable.

"Matthew," Rav'ian beckons from the rear of the column of soldiers.

"What is it?" Matthew asks as he draws near to his Toaz companion.

"I would appreciate it if we did not dwell long with these soldiers." She replies as she eyes the marines ahead of them. Frowning as best as her reptilian face allowed, she continues, "I do not like being in close proximity with them."

"Is it because of what they did to your homeworld?" Matthew inquires, curious if his initial assumption was correct.

"Yes," Rav'ian murmurs. Her gaze snaps up from the platoon and she focuses on the fiery horizon, "But they have done much more to wrong my people since then. I do not trust them."

Matthew follows Rav'ian's stare and he can't help but think that the fires have seemingly died down some. Nodding, he eventually says, "I'll be sure that we can send them on their way as soon as possible."

"Thank you," Rav'ian breathes.

Chapter Two

Somewhere on the Front, Allegra

"Can I get a hand over here?" one of the marines shouts from a large piece of wreckage.

"Go, I'll finish up here," Wyndover tells Matthew and a handful of other marines who are all gathered around a soldier whom they had found just barely clinging to life.

Matthew jogs over to the marine who had called out and he takes a hold of the massive piece of scorched metal. The steel is warm to the touch, and Matthew can just make out the Coalition 'X' insignia through the soot.

"On three, I need all of you to lift." The marine who called everyone over sounds, "There's someone under here."

"You two get ready for anything! We don't know if our friend here is alone." Matthew orders two nearby soldiers.

The soldiers train their rifles on the hunk of the transport's hull as the man who called everyone over counts to three. Matthew grits his teeth as he exerts all of his strength. Everyone's combined efforts quickly free the

158

soldier who was completely covered by the piece of wreckage.

"What happened here, marine?" Wyndover's second in command demands of the burned and bruised soldier. Wyndover had introduced the man as Platoon Sergeant Killian.

"Something shot us down…" The soldier replies after a cough. She reaches up to her face in a sad attempt to brush away a stray lock of her black hair, but she flinches when her fingers make contact with the severe burns that cover her forehead.

"What do you mean you got shot down?" Killian presses as he glances around the valley, likely searching for anything to verify the woman's story.

"I—I don't know, sir," she babbles, "We were flying over this valley when there was an explosion… Our ship cracked in half—have you found my commanding officer? Second Lieutenant Jenkins, he—"

"We're still pulling bodies," Killian interrupts, "Did you see where you were shot from?"

"No, I was in the aft cargo bay with the mechs. I was running some last-minute checks, one of the mechs were missing…"

"What do you mean missing, soldier?"

"We had five in my cargo bay... or at least we were supposed to. I went down to prep the mechs for drop, and one wasn't there."

"Are you saying someone hijacked it?"

"I d—don't know... I... I—it..." The woman slumps in Killian's arms, and he quickly checks her pulse.

"She's alright, just passed out." Killian sounds as he continues holding her. He looks around for a moment before he nods toward a nearby sheet of metal, "Bring that to me, I want this girl carried out of here when we're ready to go."

"Yes, sir," two marines sound as they race over and retrieve the piece of wreckage. They bring it back and get the woman situated atop of it.

"What are mechs?" Matthew inquires as he stoops down beside the unconscious woman.

"Mechanized warriors," Killian replies as he dresses the woman's burns.

"I'm not following," Matthew frowns.

"O'Brian, can you tell our Mudder friend here all about mechs?" Killian orders a nearby soldier who is fiddling with a severely damaged piece of tech.

"Yes, sir," O'Brian affirms as he ushers Matthew away from Killian. He leads Matthew beside a heap of metal before he announces, "This is a mech."

"What, this?" Matthew wonders aloud as he takes in the wreckage of what once was a mech.

The mech appears to have two thick legs which lead up to a thick body that resembles a spaceship's cockpit more than a torso. Attached to the body of the mech are two arms and two very large shoulder-mounted artillery pieces.

"Yes," O'Brian replies as he climbs on top of the ruined piece of machinery. He hops into a small recessed area in the mech's body before he continues, "The pilot and gunner ride in here. From this little cockpit, they wield enough firepower to destroy a small city."

"…or a transport…" Matthew mutters as he puts together a plausible scenario for what took out the shuttle. He looks up to O'Brian, his fear evident, "What if someone on board this ship stole that missing mech and brought the ship down?"

"Now why would anyone do that?" O'Brian challenges Matthew's storyline,

"They'd get stuck out here just like the rest of the crew."

Unfazed Matthew continues, "But there are terrorists who I'm sure would be willing to sacrifice themselves to take out a bunch of Coalition soldiers."

"Terrorists? I don't think so."

"There's a group of Fulcrum people back at the Bulwark," Matthew presses, knowing that he was giving up James's secret.

"Fulcrum fighters, eh?" O'Brian muses, "Keep that quiet for now, we don't want our guys getting any more nervous. I'll pass the message along for you."

"Matthew!" Rav'ian calls from the outskirts of the crash site. She had insisted on remaining at a distance, thanks to her distrust of the Coalition marines. In order to remain useful, she volunteered to patrol the surroundings for any signs of Beets or survivors.

"What is it?" Matthew asks as he leaves O'Brian and the mech to join her.

"Tracks. I believe they belong to one of the marine's mechanized warriors." Rav'ian answers as she points at a line of tracks that leads away from the crash site. Matthew's eyes follow the tracks over the nearest hill, which coincidentally is also on the way back to the trenches.

"You don't think James and his friends had anything to do with this, do you?" Matthew hears himself asking before he can suppress the idea.

"I do believe that the Thief and his allies would leap at the opportunity to steal a mechanized warrior for themselves," Rav'ian affirms as she looks to the hill that the mech had gone over.

"But do you think that they'd kill a hundred people to do that?" Matthew presses, his voice quivering ever so slightly at the thought.

"I am unsure," Rav'ian admits as she pauses to examine Matthew's face. After a few moments, she asks, "Do you believe that the Thief and his allies did this?"

"I don't know," Matthew frowns as he glances back to the wreck. He removes his helmet and runs his hand through his greasy hair as he thinks about the possible implications if James was in fact involved in this bloodbath. Sighing, he plops his Beet head helmet back on top of his head and says, "Let's tell Wyndover about the tracks."

Rav'ian nods in response and she

follows closely behind Matthew as he makes his way through the battlefield to where Wyndover is. Wyndover is busy directing the collection of the dead as they are put into body bags which had been found in the wreckage. When he sees Matthew approaching, Wyndover takes his leave and meets him halfway.

"I know how rough it is for you guys on the front, so I'm going to leave some supplies behind." Wyndover starts as he motions toward a large pile of armaments, food, and medical supplies. Nodding, he continues, "It's the least we can do after you saved our skin."

"What are you going to do with the bodies?" Matthew inquires as he looks over to the nearby Beet hive. He shudders slightly as images of what the Beets must have done flash through his mind's eye.

Frowning, Wyndover looks back to the growing assembly of body bags, "I called for a pickup, they should be here in a matter of a few hours."

"Will they be here before daybreak?" Matthew demands.

"They should be," Wyndover nods once again as he glances at the nearby hive which has remained unnervingly quiet.

"Good," Matthew sounds, relief flooding through his body. He couldn't bear to see another ripped apart soldier that the Beetles had fed on. After a silent moment, Matthew glances over to Rav'ian who appears very out of her element amidst all the marines. Sighing, he proceeds to tell Wyndover, "There were some mech tracks leading back to the trenches. I don't know this for sure, but Rav'ian and I may know the responsible party."

"The higher-ups have already signed off on all the mechs. They think everything is a total loss, hence how we'll be able to leave so much stuff behind for you." Wyndover informs Matthew as he looks to the mech tracks. Shaking his head, he continues, "You're free to try and recover it yourself, but no one will come looking for it. Killian already told me about your friends, so I'll be sure to keep an eye out for any more unsavory types in the future."

Matthew's blood runs cold at Wyndover's report. Eventually, he stammers, "W—wait, they're just going to let them get away with it?"

"If I had it my way, I would hunt them down and string them up for what they did." Wyndover announces in a loud voice. He takes a step closer to Matthew before he continues with a softer tone, "But the higher-ups are more worried about other things, so they don't care about a few dead marines—much less any terrorists. They see our deaths as the cost of doing business."

"But—"

"I lost a good friend on that ship. Now he's going to go home in a bag. If there was anything I could do to avenge him, I would, but my hands are tied."

"I'm sorry,"

"It would mean the world to me if you could find the people who did this and kill them." Wyndover whispers, "That way I could tell his family that their husband was avenged the next time I go home to Secora. Can you do that for me?"

"I—I" Matthew stammers, his fear getting the best of him. He doesn't know if he could actually kill anyone that was supposed to be a friendly—much less someone he knew like James.

"Thank you," Wyndover nods as he claps Matthew on the back and leaves him alone with Rav'ian.

"I didn't say I would do it..." Matthew mutters mostly to himself.

"And yet you neglected to say you would

not." Rav'ian points out as she leaves Matthew to resume her perimeter sweep.

"What have I gotten myself into?" Matthew wonders aloud once he is alone. He lets his shoulders slouch before letting out a long loud sigh.

"Hey, would you give me a hand with this?" someone calls out to Matthew from a nearby piece of banged up machinery.

•••••••••••••••

"Thanks for everything," Wyndover shouts to Matthew barely loud enough to be heard over the roar of the dropship's engines that had come. Wyndover nods to Matthew as they shake hands one last time, "We wouldn't have made it without you!"

"And thank you for the gear!" Matthew calls back as he thinks about the massive plunder Wyndover ensured went 'missing' for Matthew's sake.

"It was the least we could do," Wyndover replies as he takes a step away from Matthew and Rav'ian. Nodding once more, he continues, "Remember everything I told you!"

"I—" Matthew starts to protest.

"We shall." Rav'ian interrupts.

Wyndover seems to be pleased with Rav'ian's response, and he turns to join his comrades aboard the massive dropship. He turns once he steps into the dropship's side doors and he waves to Matthew and Rav'ian. The transport's large metal blast doors slowly slide shut in front of Wyndover as Matthew waves back.

The dropship's engines roar even louder as it slowly rises into the air. Once the ship is airborne, its engines quiet down slightly and the ship begins turning to return back to base.

"I hope all of this doesn't wake up the Beets..." Matthew sounds as he glances over to still silent hive.

Before Matthew has a moment to continue, the dropship's various weapon systems spring to life. In a moment, the ship's heavy machineguns and its larger cannons release a hail of munitions upon the hive.

The hive is consumed in a fiery blast that is too bright to look at. Matthew looks away momentarily to save his eyes. When he turns back to where the hive had been, all that remains is a smoking crater.

Small pieces of debris are falling all around, and Matthew feels his hair stand up on end when he realizes that some of the fragments belong to slain Beets. Slain Beets that had feasted on humans not too long ago.

"If we return for our trophies, we may not make it to the Bulwark before daybreak." Rav'ian informs Matthew as the dropship speeds away.

"What do you think we should do?" Matthew asks as he watches the dropship slip out of sight over some nearby hills.

"I desire to retrieve the trophies; however, I do not require you to assist me."

"If you're going, then I'm going." Matthew announces resolutely.

"Very well," Rav'ian nods as she smiles slightly.

"I'll bring the mule along so we won't have to carry everything," Matthew reports as he turns and starts climbing up the hill that Wyndover had his people stash everything behind.

"This sounds like a good plan." Rav'ian nods as she takes out her rifle and carefully scans their surroundings.

When Matthew was told that he was being given a mule to move the supplies, he couldn't help but imagine an actual animal. He was relieved when he learned that a 'mule' was actually just a six-legged piece of machinery that served as an all-terrain packhorse for the marines. The mule is controlled by its clucky onboard computer that allows it to follow orders and do a very limited number of other tasks.

"Rav'ian, I'm sorry that took so long," Matthew apologizes, "I'm sure you wanted to get more Beets tonight."

"Second Lieutenant Wyndover's gifts will more than make up for any lack we have." Rav'ian's voice sounds in reply.

"Mule, follow me," Matthew orders the odd machine once he can see it. A handful of lights flash to life and the mule turns and starts ascending the hill to meet Matthew. Matthew turns to Rav'ian who is still on the lookout for Beetles. He waits for her to look up to him before he asks, "Why did you volunteer us to hunt down the mech?"

"They must be brought to justice for what they did," Rav'ian replies simply as Matthew makes his way down the hill toward her.

"But what if we have to hunt down James?"

"Then we will do so diligently. Those responsible for slaughtering these soldiers must be held accountable and answer for their actions."

"I don't know if I could kill any of them though…" Matthew groans. *Killing Beets is one thing, especially when they fight back. But I couldn't kill another human or a Toaz—could I?* Matthew thinks to himself with a sense of foreboding.

"When the time arrives, I do not doubt that you will make the correct decision." Rav'ian maintains steadfastly.

Not convinced, Matthew shrugs and decides to drop the matter. Fortunately, Rav'ian doesn't seem to be a fan of small talk, so they proceed in silence toward the string of heads they abandoned all those hours ago. The thick mud makes retracing their steps easy and they find the trophies without too much difficulty.

"You know, I was a little worried these wouldn't be here when we came looking for them." Matthew admits with a chuckle as he helps Rav'ian secure the trophy string to their heavily ladened mule.

Rav'ian peers around a large sack that is atop the mule and gives Matthew a curious look. After a moment, she inquires, "What was the cause of this worry?"

Shrugging, Matthew replies, "Things get

taken when they're left unattended."

Taken by whom?" Rav'ian asks with a laugh as she motions around them, "We are entirely alone out here."

"I guess that's true," Matthew sounds as he nods absently. Looking around, he eventually inquires, "So are we still not going to make it back to the trenches before daybreak?"

"I do not believe so." Rav'ian shakes her head as she gazes toward the western horizon.

Worried, Matthew asks, "How bad is it out here in the morning?"

"Some mornings are calmer than others," Rav'ian replies simply.

"So, we shouldn't worry?" Matthew continues badgering Rav'ian.

"Worry will not aid our return."

Why can't she just give me a straight answer? Matthew wonders as he shakes his head and starts slogging through the mud on his way back to the Bulwark. The mule immediately starts following him its electric motors humming cheerfully as it clumsily chases after Matthew.

"Matthew," Rav'ian beckons after he has taken a few steps.

"Yes?" Matthew chimes back without turning.

"Would you like some new boots?" Rav'ian asks. Matthew looks back to her in time to see Rav'ian toss a pair of boots to him.

"Thanks," Matthew says as he catches the boots and then proceeds to stare at them for several moments. For a split second, he wonders where they might have come from, and then he recalls all of the dead they had just helped to clean up. He grimaces and nearly drops the boots in disgust when Rav'ian sees his expression and interrupts his thoughts.

Rav'ian quickly tries to reassure Matthew, "The previous owner no longer needs them, whereas you do. Second Lieutenant Wyndover noted that you lacked boots and found these for you."

"Alright," Matthew cedes as he looks down to his mud clad shoes that have been thoroughly soaked through. He is about to stoop down to shed his shoes when Rav'ian laughs.

"Sit on the mule to dry your feet." Rav'ian instructs, "Your people's feet are far too susceptible to foot issues as it is. You need to wash them properly when we return to the Bulwark."

"Alright," Matthew nods as he climbs on top of one of the sacks that are fixed on the mule's back.

Rav'ian quickly takes the lead and the mule starts following her. The mule rocks to-and-fro as it plods through the mire. Matthew turns his focus to his feet. With his change in focus, he immediately takes note of how badly his feet hurt. He flinches as he tries to free his foot from his mud sodden shoes, which really sends the point home that his feet are in dire straits.

Matthew closes his eyes and clenches his jaw, doing his best to ignore the pain as he rips one shoe off. Much to Matthew's surprise, his skin is still attached to his foot, which puts his greatest fears to rest. That being said, they are very sensitive and have been rubbed raw in some spots.

The cool night air on his exposed foot sends shivers up Mathew's back, and he quickly grabs some bandages from his pack to wrap up his foot. With his foot now covered, Matthew proceeds to slip on the first boot. He then repeats the same process with his second.

Matthew immediately rips his foot out of the second boot when he feels it touch something out of place. He immediately dumps out the boot's content and is met with a few odd pieces of paper. Momentarily putting his curiosity aside, Matthew drives his foot home in his scavenged boot.

Matthew hops off of the mule, and he can't help but sigh when his feet remain perfectly dry despite the muck he is standing in. He then grabs the paper that he found in the boot and picks up the first scrap.

Matthew is greeted with a small photo whose colors have grown faint over the years. In the picture, there is a man and a woman who are about his parents' ages. The couple is smiling happily as they hold their hands out in order to show off their wedding bands.

Matthew's prying eyes fall onto the next photo which is of the couple and their kids. Matthew's heart grows heavy when he realizes that these kids just lost their father and the woman lost her husband. A lump rises in his throat and he shoves the stack of family photos into his pocket.

What would my family do if I don't make it home? What will they tell Dix? Will anyone even be told what happened to me? Matthew finds himself wondering as his own mortality becoming glaringly obvious. He continues sloshing through the mud beside the mule as he thinks, *I wonder if any of my friends are going to not make it home. Will I have to break the news to their families like Wyndover?*

"Matthew, stop!" Rav'ian shouts, snapping Matthew out of his thoughts. He slides to a halt and looks over to her with a look of surprise. Before he has a chance to ask what was wrong, she looks at him and inquires, "Are you even looking where you're going?"

Matthew looks down to his feet and sees a strange heap of metal. While he is examining it, Rav'ian tosses something at it and it snaps shut. Matthew jumps backward in shock when he realizes the contraption is a very large trap.

"Woah!" Matthew exclaims, his eyes wide. He waits for his heart rate to decrease before he thanks Rav'ian for the save.

"You must remain vigilant out here," Rav'ian advises as she approaches the trap and goes about resetting it. With the trap set once more, she explains, "Some of the other humans in the Bulwark built these ingenious contraptions. There are traps similar to these throughout the battlefield. They work remarkably well—I never cease to be amazed by what your people can create when they apply themselves."

Caleb Fast

Chapter Three

Somewhere on the Front, Allegra

"First light!" Matthew announces as he looks to the western horizon and yawns.

He had noticed the light gently growing to the west for several minutes now, but he failed to mention it since he was so used to it rising in the east. Prior to making his announcement, Matthew even checked his compass several times in doubt, certain that the sun always rose in the east.

"Indeed," Rav'ian nods as she looks to the west as well.

"The sun rises in the west here?" Matthew asks with a curious grin. He had heard that some planets spin like this, but he had never actually seen one.

"Yes," Rav'ian answers.

"So, does that mean that the Beetles will be coming out soon?" Matthew asks groggily.

Rav'ian answers as she looks down to the trenches where they are still heading, "I expect many have already awakened."

Yawning once again, Matthew looks down from the horizon line to the trenches that he and Rav'ian are still a ways away from. Inside he knew that he should be more worried, but after being awake for perhaps twenty hours now, he is thoroughly spent. Matthew stretches and takes a long, deep breath as he assures himself that he will be sleeping soon.

Shrugging, Matthew fiddles with his rifle and announces, "Well, I hope they don't bother us."

Rav'ian remains silent as she slowly surveys their surroundings for the billionth time. Matthew chuckles softly as he thinks about how hard of a time anything would have trying to sneak up on her. Between Rav'ian's roving stare and amazing spatial awareness, she is a survival machine.

The pair proceed in silence as they stumble along, both in dire need of rest. Before too long, Matthew can hear a few voices emanating from the trenches ahead of him. He sighs, happy to be reunited with his allies at long last.

"Matthew, we cannot proceed further." Rav'ian suddenly announces. Before Matthew has time to respond, she tells the mule to stop, and she drags him down to the ground behind it.

"What's wrong?" Matthew moans as he picks himself out of the mud and tries to get as much of it as he can off his pants before it soaks through. He is careful to stay behind the mule through this whole process, knowing Rav'ian must have some reason, but he can't help but feel annoyed once she doesn't immediately reply. Frowning, he repeats his question, "Rav'ian? What's going on?"

"I noted movement in the distance." Rav'ian eventually reports as she looks longingly toward the trenches that are just out of reach.

"Think it might have been the Beetle snipers?" Matthew inquires.

"Yes,"

"So, we're stuck here until night."

"That is correct,"

"And if any other Beets come a little too close, we're just about done for."

"It is not likely that we would survive such an encounter, I fear you may be correct."

"Then we have to figure out a way to keep moving." Matthew declares as he takes a mental inventory of everything he knew they had on hand. He isn't sure what all they had in on the mule, but he did know that there were some smoke canisters, which he figures are their best bet.

Rav'ian is watching Matthew, and when she sees realization dawn on his face, she inquires, "What are you considering?"

"We'll make a smokescreen," Matthew informs her as he slowly reaches up to the mule and starts opening one of the bags on top of it.

Rav'ian nods slowly before quickly peeking around the mule to the hills. She immediately pulls back behind their cover and is followed by several bright beams of light that crack like lightning. Rav'ian looks over to Matthew and frowns before she says, "The invaders are aware of our presence."

"We'll be out of here soon enough," Matthew assures her as his fingertips come into contact with something that reminds him of the smoke grenades. He rises slightly to reach further into the bag and is immediately hit in the head with something very hard. Matthew drops to the ground, his ears ringing, and his heart thudding violently. Everything is in a slight fog, and he is consumed with one thought: *Get back to cover.*

Matthew rolls back behind the mule where he remains perfectly still for several minutes before his brain catches back up to what is happening. His head is throbbing, and he slowly reaches up to his helmet. His fingers quickly find a hot spot on the helm's surface, and, out of pure curiosity, he pulls his helmet off. Matthew looks to the spot his fingers had found and sees that there is a sizeable divot where something had hit him. He frowns as he watches a small coil of smoke rise from the hole.

"...are you well?" Matthew eventually hears Rav'ian's voice demand over the sound of the thudding and ringing in his ears.

"I think so," Matthew manages as he reaches up to his head and finds a large goose egg. He slowly traces around the elevated sore on his head with his fingers before resolutely plopping his helmet back into place.

Matthew looks over to Rav'ian who promptly admits, "I was worried for you."

"Don't worry, I'm alright. It'll take a lot more than that to kill me." Matthew assures her with a laugh.

"I have never seen someone survive a hit from one of the invader's snipers." Rav'ian muses as she looks up to Matthew's helmet.

"As I said, I'm hard to kill!" Matthew laughs once more.

By now, Matthew's heart rate has

slowed considerably, and he is able to think straight again. He looks up to the bag on top of the mule and he takes a firm hold of it before tugging it down on top of himself.

Now fully obscured by the mule, Matthew proceeds to rifle through the sack in relative safety. He picks one smoke grenade out after another and soon has a pile of six canisters. Content, Matthew looks over to Rav'ian and nods.

"Are you certain this plan will indeed work?" Rav'ian queries.

"We're dead if it doesn't," Matthew shrugs before trying to offer her a reassuring smile. He then pulls the pin on the first canister and is rewarded with a faceful of white smoke.

Matthew quickly tosses the canister to his right a short way before he lightly coughs against the smoke that had hit him. Chuckling, he shakes his head before repeating the process a few times and tossing the grenades all around him and Rav'ian.

The smoke quickly envelops the mule, and the duo hiding behind it, and Matthew tentatively removes his helmet and sticks it on his rifle's barrel. He raises it above the mule and he waits a moment to allow for it to get shot. The shot never comes, and Matthew

183

nods to Rav'ian.

"What of the supplies?" Rav'ian asks as she looks up to the mule she and Matthew are leaning against and then to the sack Matthew had pulled down.

"We'll bring it with us, we've got plenty of cover." Summoning all of his strength, Matthew forces the heavy bag from atop of himself and he works it back onto the mule. He then drops back down beside Rav'ian to tell her it was time to go when a few beams of light start shooting wildly around them, followed by their customary thunderous claps.

Rav'ian flinches as one of the shots hit the ground far too close for comfort. Looking to Matthew, she points out, "It seems as if the snipers have realized what you were intent on doing."

"But they can't actually see us," Matthew assures her, "They're shooting wildly, trying to keep us pinned down."

"We cannot risk taking a direct hit ourselves," Rav'ian reminds him as she points at his helmet.

"We can't risk staying here either." Matthew asserts, "Just keep your head down, and stay in front of the mule."

"I am unsure—"

"Go!" Matthew calls as he tells the mule to proceed at full speed toward the trench line.

Matthew then pushes Rav'ian ahead of the mule, and he does his best to keep up with the two of them as the sniper fire continues cutting through the thick cloud of smoke.

Relegated

The Battle for Allegra

Episode Four

Chapter One

The Bulwark, Allegra

"Just run!" Matthew commands when he notices Rav'ian slowing down slightly, "Don't worry, I'm right behind you!"

Rav'ian heeds Matthew's words and she quickens her pace. Matthew hopes against all hope that he and Rav'ian are still heading in the right direction. Unfortunately, he can't be sure thanks to the thick cloud of smoke that he had deployed.

The sniper fire has intensified since Matthew first tossed the smoke grenades. He isn't certain, but part of him wonders if the Beetle snipers knew that he and Rav'ian had just slaughtered so many of their friends.

One of the sniper beams hits the ground nearly a meter away from Matthew's feet, snapping him back to the task at hand of running for his life. The ray cracks loudly, and the mud sizzles where it had been hit. Not in the mood to get shot again, Matthew ducks down slightly and surges ahead.

Another sniper bolt strikes the mule and burns a hole into its side. The mule continues lumbering ahead seemingly unfazed through the storm of sniper fire.

"You're almost there, come on!" Matthew hears someone beckon from ahead of him.

"Ack!" Rav'ian screams as a sniper bolt cuts into her thigh. She quickly stumbles and falls to the ground where she clenches her leg and squirms around.

"I've got you," Matthew calls out as he races over to Rav'ian's side.

Matthew slides to a stop beside her and he stares as the scorched hole in her leg for a few moments. Another loud crack from a sniper makes Matthew flinch and he immediately scoops up Rav'ian. Scared for his, and Rav'ian's lives, Matthew carries her in his arms the rest of the way to the trenches.

Before Matthew realizes it, he is at the

edge of the frontmost trench. He then carefully hops down, doing his best to not jostle Rav'ian, who had fallen silent. Now protected by the trench's high walls, Matthew relaxes slightly and lets out a content sigh.

"Well, that's a new one." A nearby human remarks as they examine Matthew.

"Can one of you get Marie?" Matthew huffs, his arms still clenched around Rav'ian who is beginning to stir.

"Who's Marie?" one of the Mudders inquires as they cock their head.

Sighing once more, Matthew levels a stare at the small gathering of human Mudders and asks, "Just track down a Toaz, they'll know who she is. Tell them Rav'ian got shot."

A few people scurry away in order to fulfill Matthew's request, leaving just a handful of curious faces who continue ogling him. They remain silent, save the occasional whisper.

After a minute or two, one of the onlookers asks, "So, what's a Toaz?"

"She's a Toaz," Matthew answers simply as he jerks his chin toward Rav'ian. Frowning, he prods, "Are you guys new?"

"Yeah, just shipped in from Galatia," one of the men promptly replies. Smiling, he nods, "We were told that we'd be able to fight for our freedom."

"Your freedom?" Matthew asks curiously as Rav'ian mumbles something.

"Galatia's a prison world, mate," another soldier with a strange accent informs Matthew as he kicks some mud off his boot. Likely seeing that Matthew isn't following, he continues, "We gots ourselves in a mite of trouble few years 'ack. Me frien's and I are fixin' to go straight af'er we done 'ere."

"So, they just left you guys here on the front?" Matthew asks, trying to conceal his worry.

As much as he liked the idea of having even more humans fighting by his side, Matthew is beginning to wonder if there were any other good humans out there in the galaxy. Between this lot of convicted criminals and all the Fulcrum guys with James, Matthew can't help but feel out of place.

"Aye," the man answers as he takes a few steps closer to Matthew. The man is stout, and he has a wild black goatee to match his equally wild eyebrows and hair. Nodding, he eventually introduces himself, "Name's Reginald Greenfield, me frien's call me Reggie."

"Well, Reggie, I'm Matthew," Matthew

nods in return before he looks down to Rav'ian who appears to be on the verge of saying something.

"Good t' meet ya," Reggie smiles, revealing a mouthful of metallic teeth. He then motions to two other humans and continues, "This 'ere be me crew... rather what's 'eft of 'em at least."

The first person Reggie motioned toward steps forward. She is short and her auburn hair is braided and secured to the back of her head with a length of wire. She examines Matthew a moment before she introduces herself with a smile, "I'm Louise, Louise Glendoveer."

"And I'm Alois, Louise's big brother." A young man sounds as he steps forward. Alois is much taller than Louise and he looks far more rugged as well. To seal his menacing look, much of the right side of Alois's face is scarred from severe burns.

"Are not," Louise counters as she narrows her eyes and scowls at Alois. She quickly looks back over to Matthew to explain, "We're twins—"

"—And I am five minutes older," Alois finishes with a mocking laugh as he elbows his sister in the side.

Matthew chuckles at the twin's teasing of one another, but his amusement is cut short as Rav'ian moans in pain. Worried for her sake, he says, "It's great to meet you all, but I—"

"Move!" Rav'ian sounds, cutting Matthew off.

Rav'ian's eyes are fixed on something above them, and Matthew's blood runs cold when he realizes that it must be the mule. He quickly tosses Rav'ian's form easily a meter from where he is sitting before rolling after her. As he rolls, he sees the various onlookers also diving for cover.

Not fast enough to avoid the danger, Matthew is suddenly buried beneath the mechanized mule, and all the equipment it was ferrying. Matthew grunts as he tries to free himself from beneath the mule to no avail. He tries to take a deep breath when he suddenly realizes that he is sinking into the mud at an alarming rate.

"Get me out of here!" Matthew calls out as panic starts to set in.

His fear driving him, Matthew starts thrashing about until he throws one of the bags of supplies off of himself. He then starts clawing his way out of the mire and away from the mule. He sputters, coughing up a mouthful of mud before he looks over to see Rav'ian, who is on her side, watching him.

"I apologize for not providing you with a greater warning," Rav'ian sounds with her strange frown.

"It's fine," Matthew assures her after a cough. He takes a drag from his canteen and swishes the water about for a few seconds before spitting it out, along with all the remaining filth in his mouth. Rising to his feet, Matthew turns and asks, "Reggie, are you and the other alright?"

"Aye," Reggie replies from his hiding spot. The others slowly peek out from where they had been hiding as well.

"What is that thing?" one of the ex-prisoners asks as they gawk at the mule.

"It's a mechanized transport for supplies," Matthew replies as he lightly kicks at the mule that had yet to move.

"Is it dead?" the man presses as he rises from where he had taken cover.

"I sure hope not," Matthew frowns as he stoops next to the mule. Realizing that he had more pressing things to attend to, he turns and helps Rav'ian to her feet.

"What's in the bags?" Reggie queries as

he approaches the mule.

"A lot of gear from a gunship wreck," Matthew replies as he helps Rav'ian limp toward the heap of metal. He sets her on top of the mule's body as he continues to Reggie, "There's a lot more out there still, you and your people might want to get what you can tonight."

"Is it safe to go out there at night?" Alois asks as he looks down at Rav'ian. Frowning, he gives Matthew a worried look.

Nodding, Matthew assures him, "It's a lot safer than it is during the day."

Matthew reaches into his backpack and pulls out some gauze. He then rifles around in his med pack for a few moments before he finds some burn cream. He pulls it out to apply to Rav'ian's leg, but she quickly pushes his hand away and shakes her head.

"This does not work on my people," Rav'ian explains with a wince.

"Then what can I use?" Matthew asks.

"The healer will possess what is required," Rav'ian sighs as her eyes squeeze shut.

"Is there any way I can help?" Matthew questions, hating how useless he felt.

"You cannot," Rav'ian replies as she lets her head rest on the mule.

"Whereabouts is this shipwreck?" Reggie asks once he sees that Matthew had finished with Rav'ian.

"I don't know for sure," Matthew admits with a shrug, "But you should be able to follow our tracks back to it without too much difficulty."

Approaching Matthew, Louise asks, "Why aren't you going to return to it? If there's so much stuff to be had, I would think you would be interested in it."

"Rav'ian and I have something else to take care of first," Matthew tells her as he looks to Rav'ian. Part of him wants her to nod in agreement at least before he commits both of them to Wyndover's mission. When Rav'ian doesn't show any sign of response Matthew sighs in defeat.

"And what might that be?" Louise presses as she stands a couple paces away from Matthew and the mule. Oddly enough, she and her brother hadn't gone running for cover as the others had. Instead, they seem to have only retreated several meters away.

"I can't say at the moment," Matthew responds, knowing the importance of keeping the mission under wraps.

"And why's that?" Alois butts in as he

joins his sister.

"Because I—" Matthew starts before cutting himself off. He pauses a moment to consider how to phrase his response before he just goes for it and says, "Because I don't trust you guys yet."

"Listen here, just because we—" Someone starts before Louise cuts them off.

"He has no reason to trust any of us, he has only just met us." Louise sounds in defense of Matthew. She nods at Matthew for a moment before leveling an accusing glare at Reggie, "A lot of us would be better off if we didn't trust people too fast."

"Oi, you can't go blamin' me fo' tha'!" Reggie exclaims.

Louise snorts before she mutters, "No, I'm pretty sure we can."

"He did get us out of there," Alois points out in a whisper.

Shaking her head, Louise counters, "No, you got us out. And you've got the scars to prove it."

"But he waited for us," Alois maintains.

"And then he got us arrested, what's your point?" Louise demands.

"Now you can't be bringin' tha' up now," Reggie cuts in.

"Enough!" Matthew interrupts their argument, "Rav'ian needs silence so she can rest. You can fight elsewhere."

"Where are they?" Matthew hears Marie's voice sound from nearby.

"Over here, Marie," Matthew calls out as he raises his hand as high as he dared. By now, the dense cloud of smoke has cleared, so the Beet snipers would have a clear shot to blow his hand off if he raised it too high.

Marie materializes from the group of ex-inmates and she stops dead in her tracks when she sees the mule and all the supplies it had been carrying. She cocks her head to the side and looks between Matthew and the bags of supplies for a few moments. After several awkward moments, she finally asks, "Where did you get all of this?"

"A Coalition troop transport got shot down, just about everyone was killed," Matthew reports, "One of the survivors—a Second Lieutenant—made sure Rav'ian and I got everything we needed. They said they knew how bad it was for us on the front."

Marie smiles excitedly and approaches Matthew with a bounce in her step. Once she is alongside the mule, she asks, "Is there any medical supplies? We've been out of so many

196

things for so long."

"Check out this bag," Matthew instructs as he pats one of the larger bags. He smiles knowingly as Marie tears into the sack and starts pulling out various odds-and-ends.

"This is amazing…" Marie starts as she slowly peels out a large piece of medical equipment. Once she has it out of the bag, she gently kisses it before going on to explain herself, "I'll finally be able to do bloodwork for everyone now."

Matthew nods slowing, wanting to celebrate with Marie, but also worrying about Rav'ian. When he sees Marie go back to exploring the bag's content, he interrupts, "That's great, but Rav'ian's in bad shape."

"Right, I'm sorry," Marie sounds as she pulls herself away from her early Christmas gift. Looking to Rav'ian, she starts talking, seemingly to herself, "Severe burn… Looks like it's just a flesh wound…"

"Can you help her?" Matthew interrupts Marie once again.

"Yes, yes," Marie nods absently as she reaches into a small satchel that she is wearing. She pulls out a strange orange ointment that smells like rotten seaweed and starts putting it on Rav'ian's leg where the sniper bolt had burned her.

Rav'ian moans as Marie applies the ointment, but she doesn't sound like she is in too much pain. Before long, Rav'ian opens her eyes and looks up to Matthew who is cradling her head. She smiles at him briefly before turning her attention to Marie's work.

"How long until she'll be back on her feet?" Matthew asks as he gently wipes some dried mud from Rav'ian's face.

"She should be quite capable once she has rested," Marie replies as she finishes applying a copious amount of the ointment to Rav'ian's leg. Marie goes on to wipe her hands off on a towel before she grabs the gauze Matthew had pulls out earlier. She then wraps Rav'ian's leg up tightly, which arouses a pained grunt from Rav'ian. Once Marie ties off the bandage, she looks up to Rav'ian and asks, "Is that better?"

"Yes," Rav'ian replies as she slowly exhales, "Thank you, healer."

"Well, if I understand it right, it's Matthew you should be thanking," Marie announces as she smiles to Matthew. Nodding to Matthew, she continues, "His efforts brought you both back to me—I mean us."

"Thank you, Matthew," Rav'ian smiles

as she closes her eyes and exhales once more.

"I am needed back at the medical bunker," Marie announces suddenly. Standing, she nods curtly to Matthew and Rav'ian before spinning on her heels and leaving the way she had come.

"What about the medical supplies?" Matthew calls after her as he looks at the pile of gear she had been fixating on moments before.

"Bring them to me later!" Marie's voice sounds in response.

"She finds you attractive," Rav'ian mutters in a bemused tone. Grunting, she tries to climb off of the mule.

Matthew waits for Rav'ian to stop before he sounds, "I don't think you're ready for that."

"But I must accompany you in the search for the stolen machinery." Rav'ian protests weakly.

"I don't know how helpful you will be like this," Matthew reasons as he points toward Rav'ian's leg. After a moment of thought, he offers, "How about I just scout things out and then come back for you later? That way you can rest up."

"I believe you are in need of rest as well,

Matthew," Rav'ian reminds him with a knowing look.

"Ugh, you're right," Matthew moans as his head suddenly starts pounding. He massages his temples for a few beats before yawning deeply. Rubbing his eyes, Matthew continues, "I need some sleep."

"You're free to stay in our camp," Alois offers with a welcoming smile.

Matthew smiles back and nods his thanks. Without turning to his companion, he asks, "What do you say Rav'ian?"

When Rav'ian doesn't reply, Matthew spins around and sees her chest slowly rising and falling as she breathes. Her eyes are closed, and he quickly realizes that she had fallen asleep.

"Louise should be able to get you're A-TUT back up and running if you would allow it," Alois volunteers his twin.

"My what?" Matthew asks in confusion.

Pointing at the mule, Alois clarifies himself, "That's an all-terrain utility transport—A-TUT for short. A lot of marines call them mules."

"Ah, right," Matthew nods enthusiastically, now understanding. He quickly regrets his nodding as it causes his head to throb once more. He moans before continuing, "Go ahead, please."

"Louise, if you would," Alois invites his sister.

"I don't have any of my tools," Louise protests as she raises her hands to show that she doesn't have anything.

"Matthew, are there any tools we can use on that A-TUT?"

"I think so, have at it," Matthew replies as he rubs his face tiredly. Knowing that he is on the verge of passing out, Matthew decides to busy himself with putting away the gear Marie had taken out of the bag.

"Ah, just what I needed," Louise sounds from another bag as she produces a toolbelt. She quickly drops to the ground and gets to work behind the mule.

"Oi, what're you doin' down there?" Reggie demands as he emerges from the group of ex-inmates that had gathered once again.

"Mister Campbell here needs our help," a slurred reply comes from Louise. She pops back up into Matthew's view with a wrench in her mouth. Pulling it out, she continues, "I just need a couple more seconds and I think I can get it running again."

"That was fast," Matthew muses as he finishes stowing away the last of the loose cargo.

"It was an easy fix," Louise explains, clearly savvy enough to skip the long explanation.

"Then get on it," Reggie orders.

Matthew watches as Louise silently slips back under the mule. A moment later, it whirrs back to life and its motors' contently hum at the ready. Nodding approvingly, Matthew smiles and thanks Louise for her work.

Smiling sheepishly, Louise shrugs, "It was nothing, really."

"Regardless, I owe you one," Matthew insists before yawning once more. He examines Louise for a few moments as she avoids eye contact with him before he finally says, "And you can keep the tool belt as my thanks."

"Are you sure?" Louise asks excitedly. She finally looks up in order to search Matthew's eyes.

Smiling, Matthew assures her, "You have more use for it than I ever will."

"Thank you," Louise smiles broadly as she takes another look at her new tools.

Matthew sees Louise look covetingly at

the sack that she had pulled the belt from and he quickly asks, "Is there anything else that you'd like out of there?"

"Well, there's—" Louise starts before she clamps her mouth shut. Shaking her head, she declines, "No, this is more than enough, thank you."

"Well then, I guess we had best be getting to your camp then," Matthew sounds resolutely, "Rav'ian and I need to rest up before we head out on our special assignment."

"They're stayin' in our camp?" Reggie demands of Louise and Alois.

"Aye, sir," Alois readily replies, "If you haven't noticed, there aren't a lot of humans around here that we can trust."

"There are alien races you can trust here," Matthew interjects, "Just look at Rav'ian."

"I ain't seen her do nothin' yet," Reggie declares, clearly not convinced.

Louise quickly adds, "Alois and I will share our own supplies with them, you don't need to worry about them taking anything of yours."

"I ain't rightly sure this is smart, we don't know 'im!" Reggie protests as he points a shaking finger at Matthew.

"Alois and I will keep an eye on them," Louise offers as she looks over to Matthew. She continues as she shrugs and points at Rav'ian's leg, "There's not much else we can do today anyways. You can see what'd happen to us if we went over the top."

The moment Louise stops talking, Alois starts in, "I promised him that he would be able to stay in our camp, if only for the day."

"I don't think—" Reggie starts.

"Frankly I don't care what you think anymore," Louise interrupts, "Alois and I are taking Matthew and his friend in regardless of what you think."

Taken aback, Reggie tries once more, "How dare you, I'm your leader! I—"

Shaking her head, Louise scowls and interrupts Reggie once more, "Your leadership stuck us in a Galatian prison."

Undoubtedly feeling insulted, Reggie tries once more to defend himself, "I—"

"We're leaving," Louise announces as she scowls at Reggie. Turning, she starts marching away and calls back, "Now."

"Isn't he in charge of you two?" Matthew asks as he starts after Louise who appears to not care if anyone is following her. After a few steps, he looks back to see that both Alois and the mule are following him.

"He used to be," Alois replies, "But there isn't much of a command structure in prison."

"About that, what did you do to get stuck there?" Matthew inquires, his curiosity getting the best of his manners.

"We were accused of illegal salvaging," Alois replies with a nod as he pulls up alongside Matthew. Smirking, he continues with a chuckle, "Problem is, we were supposedly on a government contract at the time."

Perplexed, Matthew presses the matter further, "So, they just locked you up?"

"No, they turned our ship into space junk first," Alois frowns, "Just the three of us survived. There was a crew of thirty-eight onboard, plus an additional twenty people we were transporting."

"They killed that many people?"

"From what I've heard, they do stuff like that all the time."

"So how did the three of you make it out?"

"We all got on an escape shuttle and then the Coalition fleet picked us up once they blew up the *Cherry Picker*."

"*Cherry Picker*?"

"That was the name of our ship."

"Interesting name," Matthew nods before he looks back to ensure that Rav'ian is still on the mule. Seeing that she hadn't moved from her perch, he asks Alois, "If Reggie isn't in charge of you two anymore, why are you still with him?"

"He waited for us to get to the escape shuttle. If he left without us, we would be dead right now. His waiting saved our lives."

"I thought Louise said you saved her life."

"I did, then Reggie saved the two of us."

"How long were you guys in prison?"

"Believe it or not, we were out of there within a week."

Once Alois stops talking, Louise halts and turns to add, "Yeah, I think the Coalition started arresting random people in order to have them join this little war."

"Why would they do that?" Matthew asks, admittedly worried. The more he heard from the twins, the more he feared that everything he heard about the Coalition was true. Perhaps the Coalition was, in fact, the cruel overlords that James had tried to convince him they were.

"My guess is they don't have enough soldiers quite yet," Alois replies, "Louise has been telling me about what she thinks is going on for a while now."

"Either they don't have enough soldiers, or they want more humans on the front." Louise informs Matthew, "Most everyone who was killed on our salvager were all alien races, just like it is up here."

Confused Matthew asks, "Now why would they want more humans up here in the line of fire?"

"I don't know," Louise admits, "All I know is there was no other reason for us to get sent to Galatia only to be immediately offered freedom if we fought for Allegra."

"And you agreed?" Matthew asks dumbly.

Frowning, Louise cocks her head and slowly answers, "Yes, because the alternative was a lifetime in the mines of Paradise. We figured a few months of being enslaved as soldiers beat a lifetime of it."

"Sorry, this is all just a bit much for me," Matthew cedes with a shrug and an awkward chuckle, "We don't get much news of the outside world where I'm from."

"And where is that?" Louise inquires,

"You know a lot about us now, and we don't know much of anything about you."

"I'm from a nearby world called Sinclair where I used to be a fisherman," Matthew replies simply. Chuckling, he adds, "I always wanted a way out so I could see the galaxy, and now here I am."

"Not everything you expected, huh?" Louise laughs. Before Matthew has the time to reply, she asks, "Matthew, where is the medical bunker that Marie lady said she wanted you to drop your stuff off at?"

"Just follow the signs that say field hospital," Matthew instructs as he points to a dingy sign that is mounted on a nearby trench wall.

Chapter Two

The Bulwark, Allegra

"My head..." Matthew moans as he reaches up to press his palms against his eyelids.

Opening his eyes, Matthew is greeted with a view of the interior of the tent he had fallen asleep in hours before. He remains still for a few beats as his mind slowly replays the events from before his nap.

He and the twins had dropped off the medical supplies at Marie's bunker after an unsuccessful search for her. Once they did that, the twins led Matthew to their camp as he told them about himself. They had taken an avid interest in him, which Matthew found rather entertaining.

"Welcome back to the land of the living, Matthew," Louise's voice cheerfully chirps from somewhere outside of the tent.

"How long was I out?" Matthew groans as he slowly sits up, his abs aching at the effort.

"My count is twelve hours," Alois answers from nearby. He chuckles as he continues, assumedly to Louise, "Which means I won our little bet."

"Fine, fine," Louise snaps. There is some shuffling outside before Louise finally sounds, "Matthew, your friend Rav'ian has yet to wake up. I doubt she'll be up any time soon though."

"Why's that?" Matthew inquires as he emerges from his tent. He looks up to the sky and is greeted with an impossibly bright sun. Squinting, Matthew reckons that either Allegra's sun is a lot larger than Sinclair's, or Allegra is a lot closer to its sun.

Matthew takes in the surrounding trench that he is in which is one of countless similar trenches that make up the Bulwark. This particular trench is a lot drier than the rest, save a few mud puddles and a small trickle of water on its far end. The tents are all situated around the recessed cul-de-sac of sorts.

Louise stands, startling Matthew who quickly looks over to her. Seeing that she has Matthew's attention, Louise replies, "Her wounds are still healing, I'd say that she has least a few more hours before she'll be ready to head out."

"That Marie lady sure knows her stuff," Alois muses.

"Yeah," Matthew agrees with a laugh, "I don't know where she learned it all, though."

Louise walks over to a pile of gear next to the tent Rav'ian is staying in and she stoops down to pick up her own equipment. Standing once more, she shoulders her bag and assures Matthew, "We'll figure that out eventually, I'm sure."

"The machine…" Rav'ian mutters from within her tent.

"Matthew, Rav'ian is talking about a machine, does this mean anything to you?" Louise asks with a perplexed look.

Matthew finishes slipping on his other boot before standing upright and nodding wordlessly. Part of him had wished that Rav'ian would be ready to accompany him on their hunt when he woke up. Frowning, he now realizes that he is on his own.

"What kind of machine are we talking about?" Alois queries as he grabs his own gear.

"Where are you two going?" Matthew asks, trying to avoid Alois's question.

"With you," Louise replies readily as she puts out the small fire she and Alois had been cooking over. Smirking, she continues, "You've got us for the long haul."

Unwilling to put the twins in the line of fire, and wary of letting them know too much, Matthew starts, "I can't ask you to—"

"Reggie is dead, Matthew," Alois interrupts.

"I had Alois check it out, he says it looks like he was killed by a human," Louise finishes as she bites her lower lip in an attempt to hold back tears.

Matthew looks between Louise and Alois for a few moments before he finally asks, "Any idea on who it was?"

Alois scans Matthew for a few seconds before he finally admits, "I tried tracking them down, but I lost their trail after a while."

Once Alois finishes talking, Louise pipes up, "My bet is that whoever killed Reggie is also the person that you are after."

"I want to accompany you to see if I can find the tracks of the person who killed Reggie," Alois adds once his twin had finished.

"And what about you?" Matthew asks Louise.

Frowning, Louise announces, "Odds are that whoever killed Reggie is waiting for us to split up so they can take us all out one at a time."

"Is there something you're not telling

me?" Matthew asks, feeling like something isn't adding up.

"The Marie lady is still unaccounted for," Alois reports, "As are several people who met you when you returned to the trenches."

"It sounds like a lot more than a coincidence to me," Louise asserts.

"So, you want us to all stick together just in case," Matthew nods in understanding. Frowning, he looks over to Rav'ian, who is still asleep and asks, "But what about her?"

Louise, who apparently already worked everything out, quickly responds, "You said those of her kind can be trusted. We can leave her with them while we do your thing."

"Makes sense," Matthew sounds as he gathers his gear. Looking to the mule, he continues, "I think I'd like to leave all the gear with them too, just in case. But I will be bringing the mule along with us in case we need it."

"Could we leave our stuff with them as well?" Louise asks.

"Yeah," Matthew affirms, "That's probably your best bet."

"Alois, can you load all our stuff up?" Louise asks of her twin. She frowns as she slowly nods and continues, "And bring

Reggie's stuff too, he won't be needing it."

"On it," Alois sounds as he quickly starts collecting items from three of the tents that are scattered around the campsite.

Louise grabs her rifle and starts walking around the camp, peeking inside of each tent as she goes. Every so often she stops to poke around in someone's belongings before she moves on the next. After searching a few tents, Louise waves Matthew over.

Cocking his head, Matthew asks, "Aren't we going to help pack?"

"No, that's Alois's thing," Louise replies, "He likes doing the physical side of things while I take care of the planning."

"Yeah, I noticed you do a lot of planning," Matthew chuckles as he recalls how often Louise's ideas are brought up in conversation.

"He says I was born with both our brains," Louise chuckles as she looks over to her twin. Still staring, she continues, "It's been a bit of a catchphrase of sorts for him as long as I can remember."

"Well, it sounds like he's a great tracker," Matthew offers as he stops beside Louise.

Nodding, Louise agrees, "Yeah, we both

have our own sets of skills."

"So, what did you want me over here for?" Matthew asks.

"Check out the guy in the tent," Louise instructs.

Matthew stoops down and peeks through the tent's flap. He is immediately greeted with the face of a dead man. The man's face is locked in an eternal scream that sends shivers down Matthew's spine. Matthew jumps away from the dead man's tent and crashes into the neighboring one. As he fumbles around trying to free himself from the mess, he is greeted by another dead body.

"They were all here when we got here," Louise informs Matthew as she helps to free him from the tent he had entrapped himself in. Once Matthew is to his feet, Louise continues, "When we left this morning and found you and your friend all the tents were empty. By the time we got back after dropping off all the medical supplies, half of the tents were full of dead guys."

"Think it was the same people who killed Reggie?" Matthew asks with a dry mouth. He can't help but worry that Louise may be lying to him about how long the bodies had been here.

Nodding, Louise points at some

footprints and replies, "Alois says some of the tracks match, so yeah."

"And you said it was a human that did it?"

"Alois says the prints were definitely human."

"Well, there aren't a lot of humans up here. The ones I do know are terrorists. Suffice to say, I think they probably are involved."

"Think we should take the dead guys' gear? They won't be needing it any more than Reggie does."

"As much as I hate the idea, you do have a point."

"Hey, you're a salver now. It's what we do!"

"A what?"

"Salver. It's short for salvager—you're one of us now, boss."

"Boss?"

"Alois and I took a vote while you were asleep, you're our new boss."

"I don't think—"

"The voting session is over, congrats skipper. ...You know, Alois even came up with a clever name for you already too!"

"Do I even want to hear it?"

"Oh yes, it's a gem."

"Alright, go for it."

"So, you know how we are called Mudders?"

"Yeah?"

"And you're a sailor…"

"And?"

"And since you're in charge that makes you a skipper. So, Alois told me that we should call you 'Mudskipper' for now on."

"Mudskipper?"

"Aye, Mudskipper Matthew. You're our captain now!" Louise declares happily. Alois overhears her and starts laughing as he gives Matthew an exaggerated salute.

"Oh joy," Matthew mutters, mostly to himself.

••••••••••••••

With Rav'ian, the trophies from last night's hunt, and all the gear stowed away with the Toaz, Matthew can't help but feel free. As he sees it, he suddenly doesn't have as many burdens. Sure, this feeling may just be temporary, but Matthew intends to make the most of it.

"So, we're looking for some really big tracks," Alois sounds, pulling Matthew out of his state of bliss.

Nodding, Matthew replies, "Yeah, big prints from a large machine."

"We're not hunting down a mecha, are we?" Louise whispers.

"That's exactly what we're after," Matthew responds, no longer willing to hide the truth from his new crew. So far he had only heard of the mech being called a mech or a mechanized soldier of some sort, but he had to admit he liked the sound of mecha too.

"You truly intend to track down a mechanized marine?" Louise asks with wide eyes.

Shrugging, Matthew offers, "For what it's worth, it was stolen."

"Stolen, how?" Alois quickly demands.

"I don't know how," Matthew admits with a frown, "All I know is that there are nearly a hundred dead marines out there and the mech is the only thing that walked away from the crash site."

"And there's just three of us going after whoever did this?" Louise asks, her worry evident.

Frowning, Matthew replies, "I don't know who else we can trust right now—beside the Toaz. And right now, I think the Toaz will be better off if we left them out of this. That way they can keep track of things around here. Just in case something bad happens."

"I don't think this is the best idea," Louise maintains as she quickly glances over her shoulder.

"Bad idea or not, it has to be done," Matthew shrugs, "You said so yourself, these are probably the same people who killed Reggie."

"Stop," Alois sounds as he slides to a halt in front of Louise and Matthew. He crouches and Louise follows in suit.

"What is it?" Matthew whispers as he stoops down and presses himself against the trench wall.

As Matthew's body presses into the porous wall, he feels the warm mud seeping through his clothing. Oddly enough, he doesn't find the mud nearly as distasteful during the day thanks to its warm embrace. He reaches down and takes a handful of the mud and squeezes it, watching carefully as it oozes between his fingers.

"Back up," Alois orders as he starts retreating. Louise and Matthew are quick to comply, and they make their way back from where they came.

"It looks like we're being hunted," Louise whispers to Matthew, "Alois found a crude trap in our path."

"Are you sure it was meant for us?" Matthew breathes as he looks back to Alois.

"It's new, way too new to be for anyone other than us," Alois reports, "And I think it was set by the same person who killed Reggie. They left the same tracks."

Nodding, Matthew surmises, "So either we're next, or they know we are on to them."

"I'm sure—" Louise starts before getting cut short by a gunshot and a splash in the mud near her head.

"Hit the deck!" Matthew calls out as he drops to the ground and looks to where he had heard the gunshot.

About fifteen meters ahead Matthew sees the intersection he and the others had passed through just a few minutes before. From one of the intersecting trenches, Matthew can see the barrel of a rifle sticking out from the shooter's hiding spot. Pointing, he reveals the attacker's location to Louise.

"Think it's just him?" Louise demands as she pushes a crate in position so she can hide behind it.

"I sure hope so," Matthew calls as the

shooter blindly opens fire around the corner they are hiding behind.

"Alois, where are you?" Louise shouts as she looks behind her and Matthew. Matthew follows her gaze and sees that Alois is no longer behind them.

"He must have gone over the top!" Matthew announces before he starts digging into the earthen wall he is pressed against. At first, he uses his fingers before he quickly changes gears and uses the small shovel he has strapped to his backpack.

"Alois, look out for the snipers!" Matthew warns as he cranes his neck out from the foxhole he is digging. He then quickly ducks back behind his cover as another volley of weapons fire sounds off.

"Now we know there are at least two of them," Louise acknowledges as bullets smack all around them with renewed fervor.

"I hope there aren't a lot more than that," Matthew grunts as part of his mud wall explodes as it is hit in the latest volley. Wiping some grime from his face, he takes hold of his rifle and looks over to Louise.

Louise gives him an expectant stare for a moment before asking, "What are you thinking?"

"Alois is probably sneaking over there to take them out, right?" Matthew asks as he presses himself even further into the soft earth.

"I would assume so, yes," Louise nods.

Nodding back, Matthew instructs, "Then we need to occupy those guys long enough to let him sneak up on them without being noticed."

Louise quickly sticks her own rifle out from behind her cover and opens fire in the general direction of their assailants. Matthew glances around the corner of his small crevasse once more and sees that Louise's assault sent the attackers back behind into hiding. Using this to his advantage, Matthew motions for Louise to cover him as he prepares to charge down the trench.

"Look out!" Matthew hears someone shout in the attacker's direction. This call is immediately followed by a loud grunt, and Matthew reasons that Alois must have gotten to them.

Hoping to get to the assailants in time to help Alois, Matthew charges down the trench. After a few short steps, Matthew sees one of the shooters racing toward him, Alois hot on his heels.

The man is wearing a mask, which

makes Matthew nervous. The nervousness must be mutual because the man slows slightly when he sees Matthew charging him, but that isn't enough to stop him completely.

Locking his jaw, Matthew lunges toward the man, his arm already swinging toward his target's face. Seeing this, the man stops altogether and he raises his arms to try and protect himself.

Matthew's fist crashes into the man's arms with a loud crack which is immediately followed by a scream of pain. The man crumbles to the ground in front of Matthew, cradling his right arm protectively.

"Who are you?" Matthew demands as he rips the man's mask off. He then takes a handful of the man's hair and pulls at it until he can see the man's face.

"No one," the man seethes through clenched teeth.

"You know, that's weird because you look a lot like someone I saw with James earlier."

"You should have accepted his invitation when you had the chance," the man fumes. He tries to spit on Matthew, but fails miserably, managing only to cover his own face in spittle.

"This is the guy who killed Reggie," Alois

informs Matthew once he catches his breath.

The man tries to jerk away from Matthew before responding to Alois, "You can't prove anything."

"Alois?" Louise prods as she looks expectantly to her brother.

"The footprints match," Alois declares, "It's him alright."

"What do you two want to do with him?" Matthew asks of the twins.

"Let me gut him like I gutted his friend," Alois demands as he takes a step forward, a bloody knife in hand. The man whimpers in fear and he tries to break away from Matthew's steely grip.

"Not yet," Louise shakes her head.

"Please, no…" The man whimpers as he squirms slightly.

"Would he actually do that?" Matthew whispers to Louise.

"If you can answer some of our questions, we might just spare you," Louise informs the captive.

Just who are these people? Matthew thinks to himself as he glances between Alois and Louise. Looking down at the man beneath him, Matthew gets a sour taste in his mouth. Releasing his grip, Matthew lets the man drop to the ground. Shaking his head, Matthew protests, "We're not torturing—*I'm* not torturing him."

"Please, I'm just following orders," the man blubbers further.

"If you don't tell us everything right now, then we won't have any choice other than—"

"I... can't be a part of this..." Matthew announces as he raises his arms in surrender, "Do what you think you have to do."

"You can't let them do this to me!" the man whines as he looks to Matthew in fear, "Help me!"

"Did you kill their friends?" Matthew asks the man.

The man responds after several moments, tears streaming down his face, "Yes, but I—"

Shaking his head, Matthew starts walking away. The man whimpers behind him before Matthew announces, "Then I can't help you, you're a murderer."

Matthew quickens his pace slightly and is around the corner when the man finally calls out, "If you leave me now, then you no better than I am!"

Shaking his head, Matthew slips behind the corner he and the twins had been attacked from. He is immediately greeted with the sight of a man whose guts had quite literally spilled from his abdomen.

Swallowing, Matthew resists the urge to vomit as images of the Beet feeding ground from the night before flash before his mind's eye. Grimacing, Matthew dry heaves a few more times. Frowning, Matthew inwardly congratulates himself for not actually puking.

Turning, Matthew finds someone's backpack and he stoops down beside it. Opening it, he rifles through its contents and quickly finds a blanket. Pulling it out, he unfolds it with a shake and covers the unsightly mess Alois had caused.

In the distance, Matthew can hear cries of pain sounding as the twins retrieve the information they desired from the assailant. Doing his best to ignore the suffering he had allowed; Matthew covers his ears and stoops down in the mud. Shuddering, he closes his eyes and lets out a guttural shout to try and overpower the man's cries.

●●●●●●●●●●●●●●

Matthew wakes up with a start as he hears the sound of boots sloshing in the mud nearby. Gripping his rifle, he looks up and sees Louise and Alois approaching him.

Frowning, he looks back down to the ground. *I just let them torture a man*, Matthew thinks in disgust, *I just… let it happen*.

"Matthew, we're done," Louise sounds as she places a hand on Matthew's shoulder.

"Did you kill him?" Matthew asks without looking up.

Louise laughs and then continues after a few moments, "No… we took him to the Toaz once we were finished with him."

"We didn't torture him, don't worry," Alois quickly adds, "He told us everything before we got the chance."

"Who are you guys, really?" Matthew demands as he looks up to the twins.

"We were with the Resistance years ago," Louise responds, suddenly very forthcoming, "Alois and I were… shock troopers of sorts. We were shipped all across Coalition and neutral space to fight and to train troops."

Confused, Matthew cocks his head and continues his questioning of the odd duo, "I'm sorry, how old are you two? And I thought you said you were arrested without any reason?"

"We're twenty-three," Alois answers,

"And we weren't doing anything illegal."

"At the time!" Matthew exclaims, "But you guys had a history that would be more than enough to get you sent to prison."

"We didn't leave any trace of our presence anywhere we went," Louise argues as she and Alois pull Matthew to his feet, "And we had a cover story for where we were and what we were doing for all the years we were with the Resistance."

Pulling away from the twins' reach, Matthew demands, "And why should I trust you now, since you've kept this much from me?"

Chuckling, Louise gazes into Matthew's eyes. Smirking, she looks him up and down and admits, "You shouldn't, but I think you can see that you don't have any other options at this point."

"Are you threatening me?" Matthew inquires as his hand instinctively reaches for the knife in his belt.

"Alois, no," Louise warns as she stretches her arm out to her brother. Matthew then sees that Alois has his own knife in hand and he looks far too ready to use it again. Alois relaxes slightly and Louise proceeds to assure Matthew, "I have no reason to threaten you, I'm just pointing out that you probably won't make it on your own now. Besides, you need our help to get your mecha."

"So, I don't have a choice. I have to either trust the two of you or die?" Matthew asks as he eyes the twins. *How did I end up here, where all the humans have such violent histories?* Matthew wonders as he rubs his face.

"We can't guarantee your safety if you go out on your own," Louise offers with a shrug.

Matthew gives Louise a curious look as he asks, "And why are you two so committed to protecting me?"

"We heard about your fighting ability when we landed here," Louise starts, "Suffice to say we were curious. When we saw that chain of Beetle heads on your A-TUT, we knew you lived up to the stories."

"Up until last night, all I've done was protect myself," Matthew tells the twins as he shrugs.

"And you learned how to do all of that on a fishing ship?" Louise asks curiously.

Nodding, Matthew replies, "Yeah, a few of the guys on the crew were veterans. Some used to be in special ops units."

"And they trained you?" Louise asks,

clearly surprised. Chuckling, she levels an accusing stare at Matthew and continues, "That's highly illegal. I'd say you are in no position to judge us—"

"They didn't train me, I just watched them fight and copied it. I used their moves against them when we'd fight." Matthew answers, trying to gloss over the fact that it took several years before he was even faintly proficient.

Repositioning her gear, Louise starts marching down the trench they had been ambushed in. She tosses a rock and there is a loud crash, which Matthew reasons must be the trap going off. She slips out of sight, leaving Matthew and Alois.

"If you ever try pulling a knife on her again, you're going to end up like him," Alois warns Matthew as he uses his knife to point at the man he had gutted earlier.

Louise sticks her head around the corner she had disappeared behind and announces, "Well, we're going to need those fighting skills if we're going to find your stolen mecha."

"Wait, so you're still going to help me?" Matthew asks, surprised.

"As I said, you need us, and we

probably need you." Louise's voice sounds in reply as she starts off down the trench once more, this time with Matthew and Alois in tow.

Chapter Three

The Bulwark, Allegra

"Well, it looks like we've found the tracks," Matthew notes as he pokes at one of the large prints in the ground with his foot.

"Are they as recent as I think they are?" Louise inquires of Alois.

"They aren't too recent," Alois shakes his head, "The mecha likely passed through here several hours ago."

"Well, if the mech was taken by James's people, then it shouldn't be too far away, right?" Matthew asks.

"I believe that's going to be the case," Louise agrees.

The trio follow the tracks of the missing marine mech as they lead away from the trenches and further behind friendly lines. The mountains loom ahead of them, as do the limited artillery pieces that line the various ridges.

To believe James and I just passed through here two nights ago... Matthew muses to himself with a chuckle. He looks to the mountain pass he and James had passed over in order to reach the front and sighs. *A lot has changed in the course of just a couple of days.* Chuckling, Matthew mentally corrects himself, *A couple of Allegrian days at least. What is that? Three or four normal days?*

"These are the same tracks as the two men who attacked us," Alois reports as he points to two sets of footprints that cut across the trail the mech had left. Several other sets of footprints also crisscross the mech's trail, possibly in an attempt to throw off those who may attempt to follow it.

"Should we follow these back to where they came from?" Matthew asks as he veers away from the mech's tracks and pursues the much smaller footprints.

"No, these tracks will take us on the most direct route," Louise counters.

"Why?" Matthew asks as he stops, "If I were on foot, I would have taken the shortest way back to the trenches."

Motioning for Matthew to return to her, Louise sounds, "They probably took the shortest route on their way there in order to hide their mecha as quickly as possible; they didn't want anyone to see it in daylight. Their people, on the other hand, needed to cover their tracks and ensure that they didn't come from the same direction of their hideout."

"Think of those footprints as a decoy of sorts," Alois offers as Matthew rejoins them.

"So, what all did the guy you questioned say?" Matthew asks as he plods alongside Louise.

Looking over to Matthew, Louise replies, "He said that they've got a lot of people with the mecha. If we're going to do this, we can't risk getting spotted."

"So keep your eyes open, we can't let anyone sound the alarm," Alois warns as he scans the surrounding landscape.

•••••••••••••

Dropping to the ground, Matthew slowly looks over to where Louise is laying. She glances over to him and gives him a reassuring nod before turning her attention back toward the small dugout Alois had pointed out ahead of them. Matthew peeks over the small crater he and the twins are hiding in to follow Louise's gaze.

Ahead, Matthew can just make out the form of a few helmets sticking out from some trenches. A couple helmets bob up and down as the wearer walks from one end of the trench to another.

"What's the plan?" Matthew whispers just loud enough to be heard by the twins.

Rolling closer to Matthew, Alois answers, "We go around on the south side."

"South..." Matthew mutters, mostly to himself as he looks distastefully at what appears to be a bombed out building.

The trench leads all the way to the derelict building which appears to be heavily defended. Matthew slowly swallows a lump in this throat as he continues scanning the hostile stronghold. Much of the building looks like it is on the verge of collapse, and the remaining portion looks very much haunted.

"I'm seeing some movement in the building," Louise points out.

Frowning, Matthew adds, "I'm willing to bet that the mech is going to be in there."

"It'd be a great hiding spot," Alois agrees.

Matthew, Alois, and Louise all watch the building in complete silence for several moments. Sure enough, there is a good amount of movement within the structure. Matthew counts at least eight people milling about around the ruin in addition to the six or so in the trenches around it.

Worried, Matthew looks over to the twins and asks, "How are we going to—"

"Don't move!" someone calls out menacingly from behind Matthew.

"I guess we found our way in…" Louise breathes.

"What do you mean?" Matthew asks. A moment later, he hears the man who told them not to move start approaching them.

"Shut up!" the man warns as he clicks his safety off.

"Who's this, Dominic?" another voice sounds from behind Matthew and the twins.

"These three are spying on us," the first man, Dominic, replies.

"Think we can take two guys?" Louise whispers barely loud enough for Matthew to hear.

Alois whispers something in reply, but Matthew can't make it out. Judging by the soft grunt Louise makes, Matthew assumes Alois's response wasn't satisfactory.

"You, stand up," Dominic orders as he kicks Matthew's foot.

Matthew rises to his feet slowly and he watches the twins closely, praying that they make a move. Once Matthew is all the way to his feet, the man behind him turns him around roughly. Matthew is now looking at the two men who snuck up on them face to face.

"He's the one James brought in," the other man sounds after he scans Matthew's face for a moment.

"The fighter?" Dominic asks, his face betraying both his curiosity and nervousness.

Nodding, the second man starts, "Yeah, you'd better be careful."

"Maybe I should just shoot him," Dominic mutters as he scans Matthew's face, likely searching for any signs of a fight.

Shaking his head, the second man shoots down the idea, "No, James will—"

In an instant, Matthew takes a hold of Dominic's rifle. Breaking it away from Dominic's grip, Matthew smashes the weapon against Dominic's chin and then unleashes a volley of bullets that tear into the second man.

Knowing that all the noise he made would draw a lot of attention, Matthew immediately drops back to the ground. Closing his eyes, he takes a long, unsteady breath.

Shooting a Beet is one thing, this… this is completely another… Matthew thinks as he feels some tears welling up in his eyes. His lips tremble slightly as he thinks about how he just killed two people. Two living and breathing human beings.

"Matthew, are you going to be alright?" Louise whispers slowly. She touches Matthew's shoulder which makes him flinch and pull away.

"He'll be alright," Alois sounds.

"I just killed them," Matthew whimpers.

"Weapons fire!" someone shouts from the direction of the delipidated building.

"Check it out!" another voice orders.

"It sounds like our cover's blown," Louise points out before she peeks over their meager cover at the hostiles beyond.

Chuckling, Alois proceeds to remind Matthew, "They were talking about killing you, you shouldn't feel bad about what you did."

"You may have just saved our lives," Louise quickly adds in an effort to ease Matthew's conscience.

"Sal, Hunter, check it out!" one of the hostiles calls out.

Matthew is about to say something when the thunderous reports of an explosion sound in the valley. Soon thereafter, the earth beneath Matthew and the others starts shuddering. The blasts continue going off continuously, each blast reverberating through Matthew's bones.

"Who's shooting?" Matthew calls out, trying to be heard over the blasts. As soon as he finishes, another explosion sounds nearby, showering Matthew and the twins in dirt.

"What?" Louise shouts back, barely loud enough to be heard over the countless detonations.

"Looks like artillery!" Alois calls out, "We need to find cover!"

"Artillery?" Matthew asks, mostly for his own sake.

Turning over onto his back, Matthew looks to the trenches in the valley below and is greeted with a sight that sends shivers down his spine. All across the Bulwark, explosions are going off and there are people running to-and-fro. A light blue fog has descended across the trenches, reminding Matthew of James's words.

That must be the gas James told me about… Matthew thinks as his eyes grow wide. Memories of James's warnings flash through his head and he gets a sinking feeling in his gut. James had warned that the gas would drive people to turn on their fellow soldier. He also warned that not every artillery blast resulted in an explosion. That some shells waited for people to draw closer before they were activated to infect the unfortunate soul who stumbled across it.

Terrified, Matthew glances over toward where the nearest artillery round had crashed moments before. Matthew cranes his neck to get a better look at the nearby crater where it had landed. Sighing, Matthew notes that the round had evidentially detonated and not released any of the toxic gas.

"Looks like we got lucky," Alois sounds before falling into a brief coughing fit.

After several still moments, Louise points out, "The artillery seems to have stopped."

Frowning, Matthew announces, "But now we're in for some real trouble."

"What do you mean?" Louise asks.

"James told me that the Beet's artillery opens up a whole new can of worms," Matthew replies with a slight grimace, "Some of the shells release a toxic gas that drives people crazy. Those caught in it start killing everything in sight."

Cocking her head, Louise inquires, "Are you sure you can trust him on that?"

"He thought I was going to join him when I first came, he didn't think he needed to lie just then," Matthew answers, "So, yeah, I think I can trust what he told me early on."

Alois lets out a long, low whistle before saying, "If that's the case, then I think our friends over there are in big trouble."

"Why do you say—" Matthew starts to ask before he risks a glance at the trench and derelict building. He is greeted with the sight of a blue fog over the trenches and even parts of the structure.

"Charlie, what are you doing?" someone cries out from the ruin. They start to say something else but are silenced by a spurt of gunfire.

"I guess we can assume that not everyone is infected quite yet," Matthew frowns.

"Then we use this to our advantage," Louise announces as she quickly checks her gear, "Let's get in and out while they are killing each other."

"We have to avoid the gas," Matthew warns, "Otherwise we'll end up at each other's throats as well."

"Alois, did you bring any of Reggie's supplies with you?" Louise inquires as she slowly rises to a crouch.

"I brought some," Alois responds as he kneels next to his twin. He shrugs off his pack and opens it before continuing, "What do you need?"

"Do you have his gas mask?" Louise queries.

Chuckling, Alois declares, "Believe it or not, I do!"

"Alright then, masks on," Louise instructs.

"Hang on, how do we know that we can only be infected by breathing it in?" Matthew challenges.

"You've got me there," Louise admits, "What do you think we should do?"

Matthew scans the building for several moments. Nodding slowly, he takes in every detail that he can. As far as he can tell, only the part nearest the trench line appears to be affected by the gas that is now dissipating. There are several doors leading into the building, only one of which currently appears to be outside of the cloud.

"It looks like the south door will be our only way in," Matthew reports as he motions toward the furthest door.

"South door it is," Louise nods as she pulls off her pack. Setting her bag down in the mud, she proceeds to pull out a gas mask. Once she has her mask strapped into place,

Louise finally offers, "I think we should have these on, just in case."

"Can't hurt," Alois quickly agrees as he fishes two masks out of his bag. He hands one off to Matthew before fixing his own into place.

"Murry, stop!" another voice calls from the damaged structure. This call is immediately followed by several sets of gunshots and nearly as many screams.

"We're going to have plenty of resistance in there," Alois points out as he slowly nods. He then trains his rifle on the trenches and slowly swivels from one side to the next.

Nodding, Louise suggests, "So we make sure no one is left standing to resist us."

Startled at Louise's words, Matthew quickly protests, "Now hang on here, I'm not shooting any—"

"And we're moving," Louise interrupts as she rises to her feet and starts off toward the door Matthew had pointed out.

Matthew is about to argue when the twins both race out from their cover and make a break for the building. Shaking his head, Matthew gives chase. *Whatever these two are up to, I hope I don't get shot for it,* Matthew thinks to himself as he pursues the cryptic duo.

"Hold," Alois sounds as he slides to a stop beside the door. His back is up against the wall nearest the door and his hand is on the handle.

"Matthew, stay behind us," Louise instructs, "We'll clear the way for you."

"But we still don't know if they're actually bad guys," Matthew weakly argues, still feeling squeamish after killing the two men who had found him moments before.

"They're hostile alright," Louise announces steadfastly.

Frowning, Matthew gives in, "I just hope you're right, I have a bad feeling about all of this."

Retrieval

The Battle for Allegra

Episode Five

Chapter One

The Bulwark, Allegra

"Watch your right!" Louise calls out her warning as she points at a small group of soldiers that are dug into the nearby mountainside. The soldiers appear to be preoccupied as they fight amongst themselves, which Matthew finds oddly reassuring.

"They look like they're busy," Matthew reports as he turns away from the small squad Louise had pointed out and looks back to Alois.

Matthew and the twins had stopped at the southmost door and remained completely silent for several moments now. Louise explained that she and Alois wanted to listen for any signs of hostiles inside. After hearing quite a bit of activity, Louise reasoned that they should continue waiting until things cleared up slightly.

"Incoming," Alois reports as he motions with his weapon behind Matthew.

Matthew spins around and sees that there are a handful of soldiers shambling toward him and the twins. The soldiers' skin is discolored, and their eyes are very much blank. Frowning, Matthew thinks, *I guess James was telling the truth about what gassed soldiers look like.*

"They've been gassed!" Matthew declares as he raises his weapon and prepares to fire.

"That one's already been shot..." Alois breathes as he cocks his head slightly.

"I don't like the sounds of that—" Matthew mention but he is cut off when one of the gassed Mudders lunge forward. Instinctively, he pulls the trigger on his rifle and releases a stream of bullets that rip into the nearest soldier.

Matthew calms down slightly when the soldier he shot doubles over and stops moving. To his concern, however, the remaining gassed soldiers continue approaching them.

"Should we shoot?" Alois asks as he

glances over to Matthew.

Louise spins around and points out a group of gassed Mudders that are approaching from their rear. She fires a few rounds before shouting, "That's a yes!"

Matthew glances over his shoulder to the hostiles Louise had pointed out. He looks just in time to see Louise unload the rest of her magazine on them. Seeing that the job is done on that end, Matthew turns back to the afflicted soldiers in front of Alois.

"That's all I needed to hear," Alois declares happily before unloading on the hostiles before him.

Matthew quickly sees that Alois's firepower isn't enough to take care of the growing group of gassed Mudders and he tenses up once more.

Gritting his teeth, Matthew tightens the grip on his rifle, and he decides to join in. Opening fire, Matthew helps Alois mow down the remaining gassed soldiers.

"That wasn't so bad..." Matthew muses with a nod. He smiles, realizing how he and the twins made such quick work of the hostiles.

"So, what should we call those guys?" Alois asks after a few moments.

"What do you mean by that?" Matthew

inquires.

"The crazy guys?" Louise asks, surprised.

Nodding, Alois affirms, "Yeah, I was thinking something along the lines of "gassers" since they were gassed."

"Sounds good to me," Louise responds as she nods approvingly at Alois's name proposal. She glances up from the sights of her rifle that she still has trained on their surroundings.

"What is it with you two and naming things?" Matthew asks incredulously.

Chuckling, Alois confidently replies, "If I can put a name on it, I can shoot it."

"Wait, you gave me a name—" Matthew starts but is cut short when he is hit by a large drop of something. At first, he thinks that it may be raining, but then he remembers that it hadn't rained on Allegra yet.

Looking up, Matthew is greeted with a sight that makes his heart stop momentarily. His voice is caught in his throat, which causes him an odd pain that makes him wince slightly.

His eyes still wide open, Matthew eventually coughs and lets out a concerned shout. Above him are a large group of gassers that are reaching down toward him and the twins from the second story of the building.

"What is—" Louise starts before she sees what Matthew had taken issue with. Raising her weapon, she calls, "Alois, up top!"

Before either of the twins have a chance to fire, the gassers start pouring over the ledge, falling toward them.

Instinctively, Matthew opens fire once more. He tenses up again and prays that he can kill all the gassers before they can kill either him or the twins.

Several gassers land dead on the ground, remaining where they land. By now, the twins have their weapons free and they are letting loose on the gassers that are still coming over the top.

Matthew flinches as a gasser gets shot far too close for comfort. To his horror, the gasser's blood splatters all over his mask. In his brief lapse of attention, three gassers hit the ground, untouched by the twins' gunfire.

The trio of gassers quickly work their way to their feet. Matthew watches with a mix of disgust and intrigue as the gassers work their ridged bodies and begin approaching him.

Realizing that the twins hadn't noticed the gassers, Matthew trains his weapon on them. He pulls his trigger a few times to no avail. Turning his weapon onto its side, Matthew checks his mag and sees that he is out of ammo.

Before he has a chance to grab a new magazine one of the gassers takes a hold of his shoulders. Matthew looks up in time to see another gasser reaching for Louise and he acts.

Releasing his rifle, Matthew takes a hold of the nearest gasser's face and he drills his fingers into its eyes. Simultaneously, he grabs his sidearm and opens fire wildly at the gasser that has yet to reach Louise.

Thanks to the suddenness of Matthew's attack, Louise looks over to him and sees his dire straits. She spins around and shoots the gasser nearest her that Matthew had unsuccessfully shot at before turning her weapon on the remaining two.

"Thanks," Matthew breathes as the gasser in front of him crumbles to the ground. He holds his hand up in the air where he had been holding the gasser and he gawks at the blood that it is running from his fingers all the way down to his elbow.

"And thank you," Louise nods before looking back up to the ledge the gassers had come over.

"Looks like that was all of them," Alois reports after a few moments.

Sickened, Matthew decides to offer an idea, "You know, maybe we could just hold off on this attack—"

"Fall back!" someone cries out from the other side of the door, interrupting Matthew.

"Get out of here!" another voice orders from much closer.

"Back up, they're coming!" Louise warns as she steps away from the door.

Taking a few steps away from the doorway, Matthew points to a nearby empty trench and proposes, "We could hide in there."

"Go," Louise nods as she starts for the trench.

"We'll wait this out at the pass!" the second voice advises from inside. A moment later, the door bursts open. Several people race out of the door but stop as soon as they see Matthew and the twins. The man at the front of the line levels his weapon at Matthew as he demands, "Who are you?"

Raising his hands in surrender, Matthew glances over to the twins. Frowning, he sees that they also have their firearms raised. Matthew looks back to the men who had just left the building and he can't help but fear for him. The twins had proven that they are very capable when their lives are on the line. Hoping to save the newcomers' lives, Matthew pleads with Louise, "Don't kill them."

Louise chuckles and looks over to Matthew. She cocks her head for a moment before politely requesting the group of men from the building, "Please, drop your weapons."

"No way, you first," the man at the front of the group laughs. He looks to his six companions briefly before he continues, "We've got you outnumbered."

"That's not going to help you," Alois warns the group. He turns on the laser sight on his rifle and a red dot appears over the heart of the man at the front of the group.

"And why do you say that?" the man asks pointedly after briefly examining the laser sight on his chest. His voice quivers slightly as he continues, "If you don't let us go, then we're dead anyways."

"Then get out of here," Louise responds as she motions with her weapon for the group to leave.

When the group of men doesn't immediately move, Matthew offers, "If you lower your weapons then we can keep talking."

"And if not?" one of the men asks skeptically.

Shrugging, Matthew replies, "Then my friends will do what they think they need to."

The man who seems to be in charge cuts in, "We have to get away from here, you don't know what's happening in—"

"We know what's going on, we just have one question," Louise interrupts the man, "Is there any large military equipment in there?"

"What kind of equipment are you referring to?" the man asks hesitantly.

"Big mobile gun platform," Alois responds as he spread his arms apart to signify just how large the marine mech is. He waits a moment before letting his arms drop to his sides. Sighing, he tries to further explain, "You couldn't have missed it, it just came in a few hours ago."

"I'm not supposed to say," the man answers in a weak attempt to deflect Alois's questioning.

"I doubt you're supposed to abandon your post either," Louise points out, her weapon still trained on one of the men before her.

"He didn't say that he didn't see it," Matthew reminds Louise, "So I'm willing to bet that our mech is in there."

"Makes sense to me," Alois agrees with Matthew as he lowers his weapon slightly.

"Get out of here," Louise orders the group once more as she motions again for them to move out. Before giving the men a chance to react, Louise demands with a lot more fervor, "Move it!"

At this, the men make a run for the nearby mountains that lead away from the gas-filled valley. They whisper to one another as they make their retreat, but Matthew can't make out anything specific. After several silent moments, the group disappears into a nearby trench that leads part way up the mountainside.

"It sounds like it's clear inside now," Matthew reports after pressing his ear against the door which is now closed. He looks around a moment and sees that the gas is now dissipating. Pausing for a few beats Matthew also notes that the bombardment had abated as well.

"I know what you're thinking," Louise starts, cutting off Matthew's thought process. Matthew looks over to Louise and sees her looking at him through her mask with a raised eyebrow. Shaking her head once, she continues, "We're leaving the masks on, just to be safe. We don't know how long the gas stays in the air after the bombing ends."

"We still don't know if the gas is only dangerous if we inhale it," Matthew points out, "What if the cloud can kill us just by touching our skin?"

"We're just going to have to try our luck," Louise offers with a shrug.

Frowning, Matthew nods slowly and eventually agrees, "Let's get that mech."

"Stay behind me, Matthew," Alois instructs with a nod as he returns to the door. He swings it wide open and steps through his weapon at the ready.

"This isn't our first raid, don't worry," Louise assures Matthew as she follows Alois through the doorway.

Sighing, Matthew follows the twins. As much as he trusted the two of them, he can't help but feel nervous. He knew he could trust Rav'ian, or at least he thought he could after his very short time here. On the other hand, he had only known the twins for a matter of a few hours. *Maybe I'm just being too hard on them,* Matthew reasons to himself, trying to convince himself that he can trust them after such a short while. Stepping through the doorway, the realization hits him, *I really don't have much of a choice at this point.*

Inside the old structure, Matthew is greeted with a surprisingly well-kept interior. A lot of work seems to have been done recently to extend the life of the building. Despite the rough exterior, and the fact that the sky is visible throughout most of the room, Matthew can't help but feel slightly at home here.

Along several walls, new temporary roofs have been installed to keep various areas dry and out of the sunlight. New shiny steel flooring has also been installed in several portions of the complex to keep people off of the original earthen floor. A mix of scaffolding and new construction cover the bulk of the walls, especially near the renovated areas. All in all, Matthew can't help but admire the efforts that had gone into making the place livable.

"Looks like they've put a lot of time into this place," Alois muses as he nods approvingly at their surroundings.

"Indeed," Matthew agrees with a half-chuckle. It was nice to know that at least one of the twins thought like him.

"I don't see any signs of a fight," Louise announces as she scans their surroundings for hostiles, "All the action must be deeper inside."

"Not all of it," Matthew mutters loud enough for the twins to hear. Frowning, he points toward a pair of boots that are peeking around a nearby corner. Blood is spattered all around the inanimate boots.

"That makes one dead," Louise sounds as she looks over to the corner Matthew had pointed out.

"I'm sure there's plenty more where that came from," Alois adds as he approaches the corpse that the boots belonged to. He steps around the corner and slips out of sight.

"Where did they got all of this?" Louise wonders aloud as she approaches a nearby piece of equipment. She fiddles with it for a moment before it hums to life. Nodding approvingly, she announces, "This is a top of the line generator."

"I'd bet they took it from the wreck," Matthew ventures a guess.

Nodding in agreement, Louise declares, "Well, if they got this from that wreck, then I definitely want to check it out too. I'm sure there's some stuff left that I could use."

"There's nothing left over here," Alois reports as he returns from his short adventure.

"How many dead?" Louise asks.

"Fifteen," Alois replies curtly as he looks

over his shoulder.

Worried, Matthew inquires, "No survivors?"

"Not one," Alois shakes his head, "The gas is thick on that end of the building."

"And how do you feel?" Matthew asks as he eyes Alois.

Looking down to his feet briefly, Alois reports, "I feel fine, I guess the gas is only dangerous if you breathe it in."

"Good to know," Matthew acknowledges.

"Jonas, get out of here!" a voice echoes down a nearby hallway. A spurt of gunfire roars shortly thereafter making Matthew jump slightly.

"We've got incoming," Louise calls as she takes several steps away from the hallway the voice had come from. She crouches behind a nearby stack of crates and readies her weapon.

"What if we just let them go like the others?" Matthew begs, hating the idea of killing more people. Not only that, but the idea of shooting at people as they retreated made him sick.

"We can hide in the hallway Alois just came back from," Louise offers without turning away from the hallway.

"Let's do that then," Matthew agrees as he rises to his feet and races away.

After reaching the hiding spot, Matthew stops and waits for the twins to join him. Once they have done so, he takes a hold of his weapon and readies himself to shoot any threats. *Shooting anyone who has been gassed is a lot easier than shooting a normal person,* Matthew thinks to himself as he slowly inhales.

"What about the prisoners?" a feminine voice asks from the down hallway.

"They're all gone, Joleen," another person replies.

"All of them?" the woman, Joleen, asks. Her awe and fear are evident in her voice.

"They're coming, run!" a new voice shouts. A moment later, a resounding stampede begins, its echoes thundering down the hall.

"What are you doing?" Louise asks as she crouches beside Matthew who is still peeking out from their hiding spot.

Weapons fire sounds from down the hall, grabbing Matthew's attention. After several short spurts, a voice calls out, "Jonas, I said get out of here!"

"I'll be right behind you, don't worry," another person replies dutifully.

"Might as well cover those guys as they retreat," Matthew shrugs as he clicks his safety off.

Louise tugs on Matthew's pant leg to get his attention and he looks down to her. Seeing that she had his attention, Louise reminds him, "We still may have to shoot them. But you don't have to do anything like that. Alois and I can take care of them."

Nodding slowly, Matthew is about to thank Louise when a handful of Mudders pour out of the hall. Louise and Matthew both tense up, startled by the sudden intrusion.

"Door's open, let's go!" one of the Mudders exclaims as they make a break for the door.

Matthew and Louise retreat further behind their corner in hope to stay out of sight. There was no need for them to be seen if it wasn't entirely necessary.

"Jonas, they're hot on your heels!" the woman, Joleen, warns as she stops at the mouth of the hallway. She raises her weapon and opens fire down the corridor at an unseen enemy.

One of the Mudders peeks back through

the exit and calls back to Joleen, "Come on, let's go!"

"Kennedy, I can't go without Jonas!" Joleen argues as she reloads her weapon. She resumes firing the moment she finishes and calls out, "You're almost there, Jonas!"

"We'll cover you!" Matthew calls out from his hiding spot as he emerges slightly.

"Who are you?" Joleen demands as she briefly looks over her shoulder.

"We're the ones who are going to let you get out alive," Louise cuts in before Matthew has a chance to respond.

"That's good enough for me, come one!" the woman at the door, Kennedy, announces.

"Let's go, they're right behind me!" Jonas shouts as he races past Joleen. He stops entirely in order to grab the woman and push her ahead. Once Joleen starts moving, Jonas instructs, "Don't stop until you're at the pass."

"What about you?" Joleen asks as she slowly shuffles toward Kennedy. She continues looking to Jonas as she walks backward toward the doors. When he fails to reply in a timely matter, she presses, "Jonas?"

Handling his weapon, Jonas answers, "I have something I need to do first, I'll catch up with you later."

"And what might that be?" Louise demands as she emerges from the corner.

"Who are you?" Jonas demands as he trains his weapon on Louise.

"Look out, they're here!" Joleen shouts as she raises her weapon and opens fire. Her bullets tear through a handful of gassed soldiers—or gassers, thanks to Alois's name proposal. She stops them before they can reach Jonas and the others. Joleen stops shooting a moment to tell Jonas, "If you stay then—"

"Go!" Jonas shouts to her with what appears to be all the conviction he can muster.

Joleen and Kennedy slowly exit the building and then disappear altogether. Matthew and the twins train the weapons on both the man named Jonas and the hallway the murder-crazed gassers had come through. After several still moments, Jonas finally glances at Matthew and the twins and he gives them a curious look.

"What are you supposed to be heading back for?" Matthew asks, already convinced that he knew the answer. The marine mech was probably the most valuable piece of equipment on the grounds.

"Nothing," Jonas replies slowly as he glances between Matthew and his companions.

"Then you're useless to us," Louise announces as she points her weapon at Jonas's head.

"Woah, hang on," Matthew cuts in with a whisper just loud enough to be heard by Louise.

"I think I hear more gassers coming," Alois reports after several hollow-sounding screeches resonate from down the hallway the others had come down.

"Think you can take all of them on by yourself?" Louise asks Jonas who appears to be thoroughly terrified.

Alois elbows Matthew and winks before offering, "We could leave Jonas with them."

Matthew quickly realizes that the twins are putting on a show which calms him slightly. Fortunately, Jonas doesn't catch on and his eyes grow wide at the twins' words. He trembles slightly as he looks around for some sign of deliverance.

"So, are you going to help us, or not?" Louise presses after several tense moments.

"There's a mechanized marine," Jonas admits, "I am supposed to move it if we ever evacuate this location."

"And now you're going to take us to it," Louise instructs, "No funny business or we leave you for the gassers."

"What am I going to tell the others?" Jonas whimpers.

Chuckling, Alois offers, "Tell them that you got mugged."

"That's not going to help me," Jonas shoots as he gives Alois an irritated look. He shifts his weight from one foot to the other before ceding, "But I guess I don't have much of a choice."

"You've got that right," Louise affirms.

Matthew considers saying something, but he can't help the feeling that any actions on his part would only foul up Louise's plans. As he is thinking, Louise shoots him a look that tells him to keep quiet.

"Now drop your weapon," Alois instructs as he approaches Jonas.

"Wait, you can't expect me to go back in there without a gun!" Jonas exclaims far too loudly. In response to his outburst, several gasser screeches resound from down the hallway.

"Great, you blew our cover," Alois moans. He closes the remaining distance between him and Jonas as he shakes his head. Once in front of Jonas, Alois rips the man's weapon out of his hands and prods him forward with his rifle. Once Jonas is moving toward the hallway, Alois finally continues, "And yes, I do expect you to go in without a gun. In fact, I expect you to lead the way."

"If I die then you'll be stuck in here," Jonas warns through clenched teeth. Alois meets Jonas's veiled threat with a rough shove forcing the man further forward.

Unamused, Alois seethes, "If you want to live then you'll get us out of here sooner rather than later."

Matthew and Louise start following Alois and Jonas from a distance. They slip into the hallway and are greeted with a sight that initially soothes Matthew. After a few steps, however, Matthew's brain starts screaming various warnings at him. *Where are all the gassers?* Matthew wonders, his blood growing cold.

The long corridor is full of various odds-and-ends, bodies included. Scattered between the various doors that line the hallway there are more bodies than Matthew cared to count. Many of them appear to have belonged to gassers, judging by their discolored skin. That

265

being said, more than a few corpses are severely disfigured, likely due to the gassers' attacks.

Jonas steps over the body of one of the gassers and lets out a brief scream of terror when it takes a hold of his ankle. Before Alois has time to react, Louise is already firing. The gasser immediately goes limp, releasing Jonas's ankle.

"Are there any other routes we can take?" Matthew asks, trying his best to sound unafraid. However, despite his best efforts, Matthew's voice comes out rather strained.

"If we can get to the second level, we might be able to avoid a lot of fighting," Jonas replies. Matthew can't help but sigh softly when Jonas doesn't seem to notice his nervousness.

"And how would we do that?" Matthew prods as he glances back to the room they had left just a few moments earlier. Part of Matthew doubts Jonas's words. Not only had Jonas not proven his trustworthiness but there was also the matter of the gassers that had rained down on Matthew and the twins from the second level when they first arrived here. Matthew shakes his head slightly trying to get those images out of his head. Frowning Mathew thinks, *Killing Beets is one thing, I don't know if*

I can keep doing this though.

"There's a stairwell up ahead a few doors," Jonas answers as he points to a nearby doorway.

Louise swings her weapon behind her as she scans their rear. After a few silent moments, she turns back around and nods, seemingly to herself. Louise takes a few steps before she warns Jonas, "If this is going to be some kind of a trap, remember you're the one who will get shot first."

"Or killed by a gasser," Alois adds with an optimistic tone.

"Do you want me to die?" Jonas demands as he stops altogether. When Alois doesn't immediately respond, Jonas continues, "If that's the case, then you might as well kill me right now."

"Keep moving," Alois instructs as he pushes Jonas forward once more.

"We aren't going to kill him, are we?" Matthew whispers to Louise once they start moving again.

"Probably not," Louise replies in a silent voice as she steps over the corpse of a soldier whose body is on top of a fallen gasser.

"Probably?" Matthew presses.

"If he does what we ask him to then we'll

let him go," Louise assures Matthew.

Admittedly still worried, Matthew asks, "But what will he tell his superiors? I doubt that they'll let him off the hook after losing their only mech."

"What are you proposing?" Louise asks as Alois and Jonas reach the door that the staircase is supposed to be behind.

Shrugging, Matthew offers, "If this all works out, maybe we could bring him back to the trenches with us."

"Aren't James and the rest of the Fulcrum people there too?"

"They are, but what else can we do for him?"

"We could let him go."

"Let him go?"

"If we send him packing once we're done here, he might be able to get away from anyone who might want to track him down."

"And what if he can't get away?" Matthew asks as they step through the doorway and start up the single flight of stairs.

"Then, depending on who catches him, he'll probably be killed."

"Killed?"

"Both the Fulcrum and the Coalition don't take kindly to deserters. But I'd think this is the best chance he's got."

"That doesn't sound like too much of a chance to me," Matthew mutters mostly to himself.

"He's the one who joined up with the Fulcrum," Louise replies with a shrug. Her response seems very dismissive, which makes Matthew think that she may want to just kill Jonas once he led them to the mech.

Chapter Two

The Bulwark, Allegra

Matthew steps through the door at the top of the stairwell and is met with the barren second story of the building. Looking around, Matthew can see that this level had a long way to go before it was anything close to being as livable as the downstairs had been. There are very few walls up here, and the handful that are present aren't in great shape.

A gentle breeze wafts through the open exterior walls and sends a few loose pieces of paper flying. Shouting can be heard from the warzone outside where countless Mudders are fighting for their lives.

Matthew looks up to the ceiling and is greeted with a beautiful sky. The deep blue canvass above him is dotted with a few wayward clouds. Hiding amongst the clouds is a pale disk that peacefully watches over on the warzone. Sighing, Matthew wishes he was on that moon right now, far away from the fight.

Matthew halts after taking a few steps into the room and looks around. The vast space is hauntingly empty, a fact that normally

270

would concern him, but now he found it calming. After a moment, Matthew thinks, *I wonder if the Beets are using this to their advantage… With all the gassers keeping everyone busy, this would be a great opportunity for them to try and take over the Bulwark. And if the Bulwark falls, that'll give the Beetles a sure way out to the rest of the planet.*

"Looks like we're alone," Matthew announces as he turns to face the twins once more.

"Seems like all the gassers must have jumped when we first got here," Alois reasons, trying to make heads or tails of the absence of life.

"Jumped?" Jonas asks.

Chuckling, Alois replies, "When we first got here, they all jumped down to try and kill us."

"I'd say there were at least thirty of them," Louise adds. Looking over to Matthew, she nods and continues to him, "Thanks again for the save."

"I'm pretty sure you're the one who saved me," Matthew chuckles as he blushes. He is thankful that his mask is obscuring his face because he doesn't like the idea of the twins seeing just how hard he was blushing. A moment later his mask fogs up and he realizes his blushing had caused a whole new problem for him.

"Where to Jonas?" Alois prompts after a few still moments.

"West end," Jonas replies as he points to a large set of double doors on one of the few walls. Nodding, he quickly adds, "That'll lead out to the second level of the garage on that end of the complex. That's where we keep the mechs."

"*Mechs?*" Matthew asks in surprise. He glances between the twins for a moment, hoping that they heard what he did. After seeing no obvious reactions from them, he presses, "Mechs, like multiple mechs?"

"Yes?" Jonas replies, saying it as more of a question than anything.

"How many do you have in there?" Matthew demands as his heart skips a beat. His eyes go wide as he considers the ramifications of the presence of multiple mechs. Amazed, Matthew thinks, *If we can get our hands on several different units then we can really stand a chance against the Beets. Not to mention the Toaz will be a lot better equipped for their nightly hunts.*

"Seven..." Jonas replies worriedly.

Nodding dumbly, Matthew eventually murmurs, "I guess we'll be taking a few trips then."

"You can't take them all," Jonas quickly argues.

"We can do whatever we want to," Alois reminds Jonas as he makes a big show of having a weapon.

"No, I'm not saying that," Jonas shakes his head. He glances over to the double doors before explaining himself, "Six of them are smaller units that run off of liquid fuel. Those six ran out of juice a while ago and we haven't been able to get enough to run them. We have some fuel, but we use it in our other vehicles. The newest mech is nuclear powered. We were hoping it would last us until the end of the war."

"How small are the other six?" Louise demands as she approaches Jonas.

Jonas takes a half-step back, his fear evident on his face. He raises his hands slightly in surrender before answering, "They're single-man units—"

"How big are they and how much do they weigh?" Louise interrupts as she motions for Jonas to hurry up and explain himself.

"The little ones are just shy of four

meters tall and they're about three meters wide. They weight a little more than four metric tons apiece."

"That's pretty big," Matthew declares with a low whistle.

"How big is the nuclear unit?" Louise queries.

Now knowing the drill, Jonas quickly reports, "It's about three times as big and four or five times as heavy."

"Why does it matter?" Matthew asks Louise after she had been nodding thoughtfully for several moments.

Louise looks over to Matthew and he can see the twinkle in her eye through her mask's visor. A smile in her voice, Louise giddily replies, "I'm thinking we should be able to carry the smaller mechas with the one big one. It may take a few trips though."

"But they don't have any fuel," Matthew reminds her.

Nodding absently once again, Louise assures Matthew, "If these units are anything like the others I've seen, they're very forgiving with the types of fuel they take."

"That they are," Jonas affirms, "They can run off of diesel, hydrogen, alcohol, or other flammable fuels like those."

"Or a cocktail of all three," Louise amends.

"You gotta love those engineers," Alois chuckles, "They really thought of everything with those mechas."

"First off, we still don't have any fuel," Matthew reminds the group. Worried, Matthew can't help but feel like he is the only sane person here. The twins look over to him and Louise is about to respond before Matthew continues, "And second off, how can they run off of several different types of fuel? Everything I've ever seen only works with one."

"I can make some alcohol without too much effort," Louise responds confidently, "And as for the engineering side, that's a bit more complex."

"I'd say a lot more complex," Alois adds with a laugh, "I've seen the engine compartment on those mechas, it's crazy."

Louise nods in agreement before she goes on to explain, "Well, quite simply, the engines on these mechas are fed by a few different intake systems. Depending on the fuel type you put in they use a different system to fuel the engine."

"That doesn't seem too complex," Matthew shrugs.

Louise laughs before countering, "No, it's pretty complicated in there, I just explained it as simply as I could."

"Alright," Matthew gives in, not wanting to get into a technical argument. He had worked on a few different engines in the past, so he knew a thing or two, but he was all too aware that he wasn't an expert.

"Well, let's get going then," Alois sounds, likely pickup up on the tension in the air. Matthew nods appreciatively to him for breaking the silence that had fallen.

At Alois's prompting, the group makes for the double doors. They cross the vast empty room and are careful to avoid any spots where the floor had given way. This was easier said than done and there were several times where Matthew thought someone was going to fall through. In some spots, the floor creaked so loudly that quite a few gassers down below stirred to life and let out their belch-like screams.

Matthew continues alongside the others, doing his best to not fall through the creaky old floor. Matthew looks down to his feet to further ensure that his footing is true when one foot shatters the floorboard beneath it. Matthew catches himself before he can fall all the way through, and he helplessly looks up to the twins. Knee-down, Matthew's leg is stuck in the floor and he can feel cool air wafting up his pant leg from the ground level beneath him. Several gasser shrieks sound below and Matthew prays that his leg is out of their reach.

Alois leaves Jonas's side and walks over to Matthew. Once next to him, Alois takes hold of Matthew's backpack and pulls him out of the hole and up to his feet. Setting him down, Alois laughs and announces, "I've never seen that before."

"Me either," Matthew nods as he looks through the hole he had fallen through. He stares at the floor beneath him feeling more than a little lucky. Several gassers rush aimlessly below and one of them stares through the hole back up to Matthew. Matthew quickly looks away before announcing, "Well, this route doesn't seem too much safer than the downstairs one was."

"At least there are less gassers," Alois offers with a shrug. Nodding to Jonas he instructs, "Let's go."

Nodding, Jonas starts leading the way once more, now without the urging of the barrel of Alois's rifle. He looks over his shoulder as he informs Matthew and the twins, "Once we're in the garage I'll have to access the main computer to open the bay doors. It's password-protected—"

Before Jonas has the time to finish his statement, he falls through the ground to the floor beneath. Several dozen gassers start shrieking fanatically before Jonas lets loose a cry of terror. Matthew takes a step toward the hole that Jonas made when he fell through the floor when the ground suddenly shudders.

"Jonas!" Louise calls as she also approaches the hole.

The floor beneath Matthew and Louise buckles and starts to give way. For the briefest moment, Matthew's mind flashes back to his father's fishing ship as the floor starts shuddering.

Images of a massive lightning storm make Matthew freeze as he recalls the night that he and the rest of the ship's crew nearly died. An errant bolt of lightning had struck both the ship's mast and the bridge. By all accounts, the ship was at the mercy of the sea. At one point during the effort to save the ship, a sneaker wave washed over the deck. The first mate saw it coming and threw Matthew out of its path. When Matthew picked himself off the ground he discovered that the man gave his life to save him.

"Run!" Matthew orders as he takes hold of Louise. The ground beneath Louise starts to give way as Matthew throws her toward a sturdier section of the floor. Matthew tries to follow her but is too late.

As the ground beneath him starts to disintegrate, Matthew dives forward in an effort to spread out his weight. As he does so, Matthew pulls out his knife and drives it into a floor joist that appears like it will be able to hold him.

Despite his best efforts, the ground beneath Matthew falls to the level below with a loud crash. The frenzied gassers beneath him all fall silent as they are crushed beneath the tons of debris.

Matthew coughs as a huge cloud of dust is kicked up by the collapse. At first, he thinks nothing of it but then he quickly realizes that his mask had fallen off at some point. Terrified, Matthew continues clinging to the handle of his knife that had held firm. His feet are dangling over the chasm below which is fortunately void of any gassers for the moment.

"Matthew!" Louise calls out worriedly from somewhere beyond the haze.

Coughing again, Matthew reasons that

the air must not be dangerous to breathe anymore since he is still alive. Not even the dust cloud seemed to be too hazardous, which, again, Matthew reckons to be the case since he isn't dead yet.

Well, I guess Jonas was breathing the air without a mask, Matthew thinks as he hangs on for dear life. After a few moments, Matthew works his way on top of the beam that had saved his life. Straddling the joist, Matthew coughs a few more times as he tries to blink away all the junk that had gotten into his eyes.

"Matthew!" Louise calls out once more.

"I'm here," Matthew manages before he falls into another brief coughing fit.

"Are you alright?" Louise asks, her voice much nearer now.

"I don't think I broke anything, if that's what you're asking," Matthew sputters. He wrenches his knife out of the wooden beam he had lodge it into and then sinks it back into its sheath. Coughing once more, Matthew quickly works up the will to shimmy his way along the beam to safety.

"Where are you?" Louise calls into the cloud.

Still sliding up the beam, Matthew assures her, "I'm coming, don't worry."

As soon as he finished talking, Matthew emerges from the densest part of the cloud of dust. After a few more scooches Matthew can just make out Louise's silhouette as she impatiently paces to-and-fro. He continues working his way closer to her until she stops and he is at her feet.

"You saved my life," Louise whispers to Matthew as she helps him up. She spoke with a notable amount of awe in her voice, which Matthew finds odd.

Smiling, Matthew chuckles and returns, "Of course I did."

"Thank you," Louise nods. She cocks her head for a moment as she examines Matthew. After a few moments, she peels off her mask and smiles.

"I was thinking," Alois announces, abruptly ending the moment Matthew and Louise were sharing. He takes a few steps toward them as he continues, "With all that new medical equipment, do you think that Marie lady and her people might be able to do something to save the gassers?"

"When we find her, you can ask her yourself," Matthew assures Alois. He can't help but worry about Marie's wellbeing.

Groaning, Matthew rubs his eyes in an

effort to get the grit out of them. When that doesn't work, Matthew reaches behind him and fumbles around with his backpack until he gets a hold of his canteen. After blindly unscrewing the lid, Matthew proceeds to empty its contents into his eyes and all over his face.

"Feel better?" Alois asks as he gives Matthew a surprised half-grin.

Groaning, Matthew replies, "I'm not sure if better is the word."

Louise looks around for a few moments before she announces, "Well, it looks like our only way out now is through the garage bay."

"She's right," Alois confirms, "The ground between here and the stairwell we used is gone."

"And we don't want to drop back downstairs," Matthew adds as several new gassers let out their blood-curdling cries. Frowning, Matthew looks to the garage's double doors and reminds the twins, "Jonas said we can't get out of the garage without his passcodes."

Louise starts toward the door before she announces, "My bet is we don't actually need those codes. We're stealing a massive piece of military equipment here."

Chuckling, Alois starts after his sister

and reiterates her point to Matthew, "Translation: We'll be able to shoot our way out."

Matthew follows the twins to the doors and they all pause at the entrance long enough to check their weapons. Once they are sure that everyone is set, all burst through the double doors in unison, weapons raised.

The garage is slightly more updated than the first room Matthew and the twins had been in. Much of this portion of the complex appears to have been finished not too long ago. Unlike the first room, the garage has one solid roof that is lined with a mismatched assortment of lights.

The garage has one large shop floor where the bulk of its equipment is situated. Above the floor are several catwalks and raised platforms where people can work on larger equipment like the mechs from above.

Quite a few hoists, cables, and air hoses hang down from the ceiling giving the impression of vines hanging from trees in a jungle. Near the center of the garage is one massive mech surrounded by several smaller units. In many ways, the group of mechs reminds Matthew of a hen and her chicks.

Under normal circumstances, Mathew

would be awestruck by the sight of so much equipment in one room. This garage had at least ten times more tools than Crail's workshop ever did. The main issue, however, was the fact that the garage is just as filled with gassers that hadn't yet taken notice of Matthew and the twins.

"Gassers!" Alois alerts the others as he opens fire. The moment Alois fires, all the gassers in the garage spin around and start charging them.

Matthew freezes for a moment as he tries to take a quick count of all the gassers. As far as he can tell, there are at least thirty gassers on the various catwalks and platforms that crisscross the second story of the large garage. Matthew peers over the ledge of the platform he is on and sees an untold number of hostiles racing about in an unnerving sea of humanity.

"We don't have enough ammo to take them all on," Louise warns after she neutralizes a handful of gassers in their immediate vicinity.

"Then what do we do?" Matthew demands as he unloads on a stream of hostiles that are coming up one of the few stairwells that reach the shop floor.

"We have to cut them off!" Louise shouts

as she kicks a gasser that had gotten far too close.

Looking around once more, Matthew sees eight different stairwells scattered around the massive garage. Frowning, he announces, "I don't know how we're supposed to do that. A lot of the stairs are too far away to get to."

"Then we'll just have to blow the catwalks then," Alois offers as he mows down a group of gassers that are approaching on a nearby footbridge. He expends the last of his mag on another group of gassers before quickly reloading. After finishing off that group, Alois informs the others, "I only have one more mag after this."

"I've got two," Louise reports.

Matthew takes a quick inventory of his munitions before sheepishly admitting, "I've got five."

"Well, ammo isn't quite a concern right now then," Alois announces with a laugh.

"I see a computer console," Louise says as she takes a step toward the unit. Looking back to Matthew and Alois she requests, "I need you two to cover me as I try to open the doors."

"You've got it," Alois affirms with a nod.

Matthew looks over to Louise for a

moment as she turns on the computer terminal. Part of him wanted to watch her do her magic, but a gasser's squawking pulls him back to his task at hand.

Spinning around, Matthew mows down a handful of his adversaries. With them attended to, Matthew opts for a new tactic and he fishes one of his few grenades from his pack. *Three grenades*, Matthew tells himself as he handles the first explosive.

Summoning his throwing skills from his years of retrieving fishing traps, Matthew throws his first grenade for all he was worth. Much to his satisfaction, he hits his mark and it comes to a rest at the top on the nearest staircase.

The gassers that are nearest where the grenade landed pause a moment to congregate around the grenade, seemingly curious as to what it was. Matthew cocks his head as he watches them. As near as he can tell, they appear to be conversing with one another.

"What's happening?" Alois demands from behind Matthew as he stops shooting. After a brief pause, he reports, "They all stopped running."

At a loss for words, Matthew stammers,

"I—I think they're communicating—"

Matthew is about to continue when his grenade explodes, sending every gasser in its immediate vicinity flying. The staircase buckles now that the upper portion had been so battered. A moment after the blast, the stairwell groans and collapses to the floor below.

Suddenly, all the gassers shriek in unison. Their cry is so loud that Matthew and the twins have to cover their ears. Then, as suddenly as their cry began, the gassers fall silent and resume their charge with a new fervor.

"Well, now they're mad," Alois declares as he prepares himself for the gassers' next run at them.

Matthew throws his last two grenades at two of the remaining nearby stairwells. Matthew whistles to get Alois's attention and then tosses two mags to him before he turns to Louise and demands, "Any idea how much longer you'll be?"

Louise glances over her shoulder and calls back to Matthew loud enough to be heard over his gunfire, "I can't get to the doors, but I think I can do something else to help us out."

"Sooner rather than later please!" Alois chimes in.

Alois mutters something under his breath before turning his attention away from the gassers. Matthew and Louise glance over to him in time to see him open fire on the cables that are holding up one of the walkways he had been working to keep clear.

Alois lets off a handful of well-aimed rounds and a large portion of the catwalk breaks free. With a loud groan, the footbridge twists and buckles. It continues doing so for several seconds, sending the few gassers on it flying. Just before the last gasser falls off, the bridge breaks itself apart and showers down on top of the gasser below.

"That'll work," Matthew mutters barely loud enough for Alois to hear over the din. Matthew then nods appreciatively to Alois before turning back to the task before him.

"Just make sure you don't knock out the one between us and the mecha!" Louise warns as she returns to her work.

Matthew and Alois continue knocking out catwalks for all they're worth while simultaneously working to keep the gassers away. Once again, Matthew is thankful for his shooting skills that he got from his days on the fishing ship. *Who would have thought a fisherman would be ready for war?* Matthew thinks to himself as he chuckles.

"You're a lot better of a shot than I am," Alois congratulates Matthew after they had been shooting for a while.

"You can thank my father for that," Matthew replies as he shoots one final cable on the last unneeded footbridge.

"I'll be sure to do that," Alois nods as he and Matthew both turn to cover the final remaining catwalk.

"How much longer for you?" Matthew asks Louise once again as he turns to her.

Louise is mouthing out words as she reads to herself and continues typing away. Matthew is about to repeat himself when she responds, "Just a minute…"

A crash sounds behind Matthew and he spins around in time to see that the last catwalk he had fired on had only fallen on one end. Much to his alarm, the end that had fallen and turned the small footbridge into a ramp. Even more alarming than that is the fact that the gassers have also taken note of their new route up.

"Guys, we're in trouble!" Matthew calls as he opens fire.

"What do you me—" Alois starts before he turns and sees Matthew's predicament. He and Matthew exchange startled looks before Alois shouts to his twin, "We need to go, and we need to go now."

"Almost got it..." Louise mutters, mostly to herself.

"Do you have any more grenades?" Alois asks Matthew as he joins him at the top of the accidental ramp.

"No," Matthew replies, his voice sounding hollow.

Matthew quickly glances behind himself for a moment to ensure that the catwalk leading to the large mech is clear. As he turns back to the ramp Matthew notices a large barrel of fuel. He pauses as his brain races and gives him a clever—albeit dangerous—plan.

"I need help over here," Alois reminds Matthew who is still staring at the fuel cask.

Matthew turns around long enough to empty the rest of his mag into the oncoming gassers. With that done, Matthew drops his weapon and races over to the fuel drum. He unscrews a small cap on its top and peeks in. Smiling, Matthew takes a whiff of the fuel inside and notes that it is diesel.

Replacing the cap, Matthew topples the large cask and sends it rolling toward the ramp with one hard kick. Once the barrel is moving,

Matthew calls out to Alois, "Move!"

Alois glances behind himself and quickly sidesteps away from the barrel's path, kicking Matthew's weapon out of the way as he does so. A moment later, the barrel rolls onto the ramp, mowing down every gasser in its way.

Matthew races over to the top of the ramp and rips Alois's weapon from his hands. A moment later he opens fire on the diesel barrel and pops it full of holes. After firing several rounds there is finally a spark and the surrounding area is consumed in a roaring flame.

"Done!" Louise announces joyously as she spins around to face Matthew and Alois. She waits long enough for both the men to face her before continuing, "We have to get to the mecha—like right now."

Matthew is about to argue when a gasser that is on fire starts climbing up the ramp. His eyes wide, Matthew promptly agrees, "Yep, time to go!"

"And here I didn't think those guys could get any scarier…" Alois mutters, sounding completely dumbfounded. He takes back his weapon and lets off a few rounds into the nearest burning gasser. Shaking his head, Alois turns and follows Louise.

Matthew pulls up the rear as he drives his last remaining mag home. Shaking his head Matthew thinks, *If we get out of here, I owe Louise big time.*

"I've only got about ten rounds left," Alois reports after checking his magazine.

"Here, take one of mine," Louise volunteers as she hands him a mag.

Frowning, Matthew admits, "I just loaded my last one as well."

"You need it more than I do since you're pulling up the rear," Alois says as he passes Louise's mag back to Matthew.

"So, what's the rush?" Matthew calls up the line to Louise who seems to be in quite a hurry.

Glancing over her shoulder, Louise replies, "I set things up so the welding and cutting equipment will explode. If we're lucky, the fuel tanks will also catch fire and blow."

"If we're *lucky?*" Matthew inquires, missing how being caught in an explosion made them lucky.

Nodding, Louise continues onward and informs Matthew of her desired end goal, "The explosion and ensuing fires should kill a lot of the gassers."

"And what about us?" Matthew asks,

knowing that he must be missing something.

"We'll hide in the mech," Alois answers on Louise's behalf, "It's made for war, so a little fiery explosion shouldn't hurt us if we're inside."

"And if we don't make it there in time?" Matthew prods as they all stop long enough to mow down a small group of gassers that are standing between them and their mech.

"Then we're dead anyways," Alois argues. He fixes his rifle to his pack before declaring, "I'm flat out of ammo."

"I'm on my last mag now," Louise adds as she reloads her weapon.

"I can't spare anything!" Matthew shouts as he spins around and opens fire on the horde of gassers behind them.

By now, the diesel fire Matthew had started has died down to the point that gassers can pass through and not be consumed by fire. The gassers seem to be making the most of this opportunity and they are charging with all they have.

"Cut them off!" Louise calls as she races on ahead. Matthew glances over his shoulder and he sees that Louise had stopped beside the largest mech. As soon as she stops, she starts shooting the cables on the catwalk ahead of her.

Matthew takes in the mech now that he is a lot closer, and he can't help but admire it. Between the unit's massive scale—standing nearly 12 meters high—and the apparent attention to detail, the mech looks like a work of art.

However, said work of art is clearly meant for destruction. While the mech has two arms and walks on two legs like a human, that is about where the similarities stop.

The unit doesn't have a head, instead, it has a large torso that appears to have a cockpit built into it. The mech's arms have two very large cannons where its hands ought to have been which really makes it look like a war machine.

At the mech's shoulders there appear to be two mortar-looking attachments. Matthew also notes that there are two smaller machineguns near the mortars that appear to be able to swivel. Unfortunately, the mech's roof appears to be flat and void of any weapons which piques Matthew's interest. Matthew lets out an impressed whistle as he imagines the machine storming into battle.

"Not bad…" Matthew whispers to himself.

Matthew looks at a large insect that is

emblazoned on the side of the mech's hull. The bug's rear end is glowing on odd burnt orange, which Matthew finds odd. Beneath the critter, there's a word that reads *Firefly*. The orange color from the bug's butt is accentuated by some tasteful coloring that decorates the mech's exterior.

"She's a beauty!" Alois declares happily.

Nodding in agreement, Matthew tears his eyes away from the mech and agrees, "Yeah,"

"We have to cut them off!" Louise impatiently repeats herself.

"You heard her, Mudskipper," Alois nods to Matthew reassuringly, pulling him back to the here and now. Matthew watches as Alois races over to his Louise and the mech.

Not wanting to waste any time, Matthew starts running down the catwalk after Alois. As he runs, Matthew shoots each cable as he passes it. After blasting holes through several cables, the lines fray and the footbridge begins to rumble and warp. Satisfied, Matthew stops shooting and he joins the twins at the mech.

"So, what are we waiting for? Why don't we hop in?" Matthew queries as he looks down at the gassers below that now appear almost ravenous. A bile-like taste rises in the back of

Matthew's throat as he looks on to the gassers with a sense of disdain and fear.

Opening up a small panel beside the entrance hatch to the mech's cockpit, Louise explains, "We're locked out for the time being. It's a safety protocol to make sure the mech isn't stolen or broken into."

"Well, we know it's possible since someone else did it before they brought down that troop transport," Matthew affirms as he scans their surroundings. After a short while, his eyes fall on a collection of canisters near the mech. Hoping he is mistaking, Matthew asks Alois, "Is that what I think it is?"

Alois follows his gaze and frowns in concern as his eyes lock onto the assortment of welding gear. After a short pause, Alois affirms, "It sure is."

Turning around, Matthew stoops down next to Louise and in a low whisper, he asks, "Exactly how much time did you give us, Louise?"

"Enough," Louise replies simply before she reaches over and clamps Matthew's lips shut with her fingers.

"Hm," Matthew lets out a thoughtful, albeit surprised, hum as he looks down to Louise's fingers. Pulling away from her grasp,

Matthew stands and then states, "I get it. Shut up."

"Mhmm," Louise grunts in reply as she returns to her work.

"She didn't happen to tell you how long she gave us, did she?" Matthew asks Alois.

"Shh!" Louise demands impatiently.

A little touchy, isn't she? Matthew thinks to himself with a chuckle. He stares ahead blankly as he allows his mind to wander for the first time since he arrived on Allegra.

Louise sure reminds me of Dix. She's just as strong-headed… volatile too. Matthew muses as a slight smile stretches across his face. He looks upwards as he follows the train of thought, *I wonder how Dix is doing right about now. Forget that, I wonder how everyone is doing back home. Between all of us who were taken, that's a good amount of jobs being left undone.*

"That's it," Louise announces proudly as she steps back from her work. A hum sounds from within the mech and the entrance hatch slowly eases open. Louise nods to Mathew and Alois before stepping through the hatch and into the mech. After a very brief moment, she sticks her head back out and advises, "You two better come in here."

"Is something wrong?" Matthew asks as he ducks through the small hatch.

When Matthew climbs into the mech's cockpit, he is pleasantly surprised. The interior of the unit is a lot larger than he expected. Chuckling, he finds it rather spacious and slightly luxurious as well. A few large structural supports jut out from the mech's exterior hull into the cockpit area, taking away from the otherwise open layout in the cockpit.

The cockpit's four seats are all matching black leather with tasteful orange stitching. The same burnt orange color is carried over on various decals throughout the interior and Matthew can't help but admire the design.

The seats in the cockpit are situated in pairs with three stairs leading down to the lowest two that appear to be reserved to the pilot and copilot at the nose of the mech. The upper two seats have a little more wiggle room around them and they are surrounded by various gauges and consoles. Shrugging, Matthew figures these seats must be for the gunners.

"I gotta ask," Matthew sounds in an effort to get the twins' attention. They both look over and Matthew queries, "What's up with the roof? Why's it flat?"

"It's flat so shuttles can land on it," Louise replies dismissively before she takes a seat in one of the chairs at the front of the cockpit.

"Really?" Matthew asks as he gives Louise a curious look. He is unsure how a ship could land on top of a comparatively small machine like the mech without crushing it.

"Sure," Alois affirms before he sits in one of the chairs at the back of the cockpit. He swivels his chair around and starts rattling away on one of the consoles.

Before Matthew has the time to say anything else, the twins both start laughing. Matthew looks over to Louise now feeling thoroughly confused and left out.

"I'm kidding, Mudskipper," Louise admits after composing herself. Louise sees that Matthew can't make heads or tails of what's going on so she goes on to explain, "The top is flat because this mecha must not be meant for the real fighting. Generally, the frontline units have some sort of huge armament up there. Odds are this one's roof is supposed to be used to transport stuff or something like that."

"Now that makes a lot more sense," Matthew laughs now understanding what the joke had been.

"If you look over there you can see all that empty area in the wall," Alois adds as he points to a spot beside the other gunner station, "That's where all the guts and tech for the bigger gun usually goes.

"Thank you," Matthew nods appreciatively, happy that the twins are filling him in on even more stuff that he previously had no idea about. Despite their help, Matthew has a feeling that the twins would continue making his learning process rather difficult for as long as they could.

"Alright, come on up here and take a seat, Mudskipper," Louise invites Matthew as she points to the chair on her right.

"You don't expect me to drive this thing, do you?" Matthew inquires as he takes his seat.

"Of course not," Louise replies cheerfully, "You're of more use to me if you're shooting bad guys. Anyone who can shoot so well that Alois compliments them belongs in the gunner's seat."

Cocking his head, Matthew looks over to Louise and inquires, "Then why am I sitting up here?"

"For the light show," Louise smiles before pointing out the cockpit window.

"I am not going to miss any of those gassers," Alois announces confidently as he takes a seat on the stairs between Matthew and Louise.

Louise looks out to the garage just beyond the cockpit window and stares blankly for a moment. Smiling slightly, she then counts down on her fingers as she says "Three... two... one..."

A moment after Louise hits one, the world beyond the mech seemingly catches fire. It all starts with a handful of small explosions scattered throughout the garage, but the flames quickly spread. Countless vehicles burst into flames as their fuel tanks rupture and shoot out geysers of fire. Shortly after that, several large storage vats also catch fire and Matthew has to briefly look away as the flames grow surprisingly bright.

"Well, I think that'll take care of all the gassers," Louise eventually acknowledges, her surprise evident in her voice.

"That was a lot more fire than I expected," Matthew declares as the fires die down to the point that he can look outside once more.

The flames beyond the mech's cockpit window are still towering high. If Matthew didn't know any better, he would think that the garage was only one story tall, since he can't even see the actual ground floor through the towering flames.

The ceiling above the mech has given way allowing the think smoke from the fires to escape. Every so often, Matthew thinks he can just make out a glimpse of the blue sky above through the dense smoke, but he can't tell for sure.

Louise flicks a few switches as she looks outside before she mutters something to herself. After several attempts, she announces in a flat voice, "Well, I think we're stuck here for the time being. I can't get this thing moving."

"Let's rest up then," Alois recommends, "No need to waste any energy if we can't do anything."

"Agreed," Louise nods before she flips a switch that causes several electric motors to start humming. A moment later, several thick steel shades emerge from the hull around the cockpit window and they slowly close, blocking out the light from the outside world. Once the large plates finish moving, Louise informs Matthew and Alois, "I'm shutting off battery power now. I'll turn it back on when we wake up."

"Will we be safe in here?" Matthew asks as he looks around the dark compartment around him. He can't see anything; much less be able to defend himself if there was anything dangerous in here.

"Perfectly safe," Alois assures Matthew, "Nothing in here can get through the armor on this mecha."

"When I wake up, I'll check to see if it's safe for us to leave the mecha," Louise volunteers, "If the fires have died down, and if there aren't any gassers out and about, then I'll get the reactors fired up too."

"Then we're home free," Alois finishes, a smile in his voice. He takes a sharp breath and there is some shuffling before he grunts from somewhere behind Matthew. Alois sighs before whispering, "I'm beat."

"Sleep tight," Louise sounds from her seat. A few moments later, her breathing slows down considerably and it falls into a peaceful rhythm. Behind her and Matthew, Alois is now snoring softly as he sleeps as well.

Well, I doubt I'll ever be able to fall asleep that quick, Matthew thinks to himself with a chuckle. Shaking his head Matthew finds a more comfortable position in the large seat he is in and tries to clear his mind so he can sleep.

Chapter Three

The Bulwark, Allegra

"Up and at 'em boys!" Louise calls cheerfully.

Matthew sits bolt upright, which isn't saying much since the chair he is slept in didn't allow him to recline. Regardless, Matthew is awake now, and he squints as he tries to see anything in the dark cockpit.

As Matthew looks around, Louise flips a switch and the steel shades over the cockpit window recede, bathing Matthew in the bright Allegrian afternoon sun. Matthew winces at the harsh and sudden light before he raises a hand to try and keep the sun out of his eyes.

"How long were we out?" Matthew groans as he stands from his seat. Stretching, Matthew realizes how stiff his back is, and he swears to himself that he will never sleep in that same position ever again.

"Five hours," Alois reports from behind Matthew.

Matthew turns and sees that Alois had sprawled out in the open area between the two gunner seats. Chuckling, Matthew can't help but feel jealous of the man's sleeping arrangement. Matthew turns and sees that Louise is already partially covered in grease and she gives him a curious look after he had been staring for a few too many seconds.

"I got the reactor fired back up while you two slept," Louise announces as she turns away from Matthew and takes her seat. Facing the cockpit window, she flips a few more switches and the mech shifts slightly. Nodding approvingly, Louise adds, "Everything seems to be in order."

"So, we're all set?" Matthew asks as he takes a hold of his chair to stabilize himself as the mech moves once more.

"The mecha is ready to walk," Louise replies with a nod. Glancing back to Alois, Louise asks, "Are we ready to shoot?"

"I'm reading full ammo on all weapons," Alois reports from his seat, "I guess whoever stole this baby must have not needed to shoot anything."

"That's a yes," Louise chuckles before she looks over to Matthew. She nods toward his chair and he quickly takes a seat.

Matthew looks out to the charred world beyond and he shudders slightly as he remembers how many gassers had been out there just a few hours ago. Now all that remained of them was blackened concrete and ash. Looking to the walls of the garage, Matthew asks what he thinks is the obvious question, "So, how are we going to get out of here? The walls are all still up."

"Let's see," Louise replies as she looks back to her brother. Chuckling, she passes along Matthew's inquiry, "Alois, should we walk through them, or blow them up?"

"As much as I'd like to shoot our way out of this one, let's save our ammo," Alois responds, sounding slightly distraught with his answer.

"Alright, strap in, this'll be a rough ride!" Louise warns before she takes a hold of the controls before her and drives the mech forward at full speed.

Matthew takes a hold of the various straps that make up his harness and he hurriedly straps them into place. Without a moment to spare, the mech smashes through one of the garage's walls and emerges on the other side seemingly unphased. Rubble and dust rain down on the mech as Louise eases off the controls and they slow to a stop.

Matthew looks down to his harness that he is gripping so tight that his knuckles have turned white. He slowly releases the harness before he asks, "What about the other mechs in there?"

"I doubt they'll be going anywhere any time soon," Louise replies sadly, "I checked them out before you two woke up. The fire seems to have permanently taken them out of commission."

"I take it they weren't run dry after all?" Alois inquires.

"I guess not," Louise affirms, "They had enough fuel left in them that they caught fire. A few of them seem to have exploded as well."

Sighing, Alois offers, "Well, at least we got one."

"But we still don't know who brought the shuttle down," Matthew points out as he frowns. He had promised, or more accurately be coerced into pledging that he would hunt down the guilty party. Now he had the stolen mech but not Wyndover's revenge.

"And the Toaz's healer Marie is still unaccounted for," Alois adds from his seat.

"Well, I got good news for the two of you," Louise announces as she drives the mech forward at a leisurely pace. After the mech had taken a few steps, Louise continues, "First off, the computer I accessed said that

Marie was being held in the Fulcrum bunker. They had a couple of injuries last night when they stole this thing and they needed her to take care of their people."

"That'll make things difficult," Matthew mutters to himself as he wonders just how many people would have to be killed in order to free Marie. After a few moments of thought, Matthew realizes that he isn't even sure if he can make it through the front door of the bunker Marie is supposed to be in.

"As for the ones who took the troop transport down," Louise starts as she reaches over to a nearby keyboard and types away. She is surprisingly good at typing as the mech jostles everyone with each step. After a few moments, a small screen flashes to life, drawing everyone's attention. Louise taps a few more keys before an image with five people fills the screen. Nodding slowly, Louise announces, "Those are you killers."

"Five of them?" Matthew asks as his voice squeaks. Hunting down one person was one thing, a whole group of people was entirely another. Swallowing a lump in his throat, Matthew can't help but feel like he had bitten off more than he could chew.

"Three actually," Alois amends as he

joins Matthew and Louise at the front of the cockpit. Pointing as best he can at two people on the screen, Alois explains, "I know for sure that those two were gassers we killed."

"So, there's a chance we already got all of them?" Matthew inquires as he examines the faces of the remaining three strangers.

"No, I saw those two walking around before we left the Bulwark," Louise shakes her head as she points at two of the on-screen figures.

Matthew scans the outside world as the idea of hunting down three more people starts to set in. Not only would these people likely be living, breathing, fully human targets, but they would likely know that Matthew and the twins are onto them.

That meant they would be doing their best to survive.

They'd try to cling to life no matter what.

And then Matthew would come in just to kill them.

"Well, I'm starving," Alois declares as the mech continues waddling toward the Bulwark. He slips behind Matthew once more and reemerges with three packets of food. He drops a packet in Louise's and Matthew's laps before tearing open his own.

Matthew looks down at his ration and grimaces. Thanks to the idea of hunting down several people, Matthew had no desire to eat. A bitter taste rises in the back of his throat as he imagines throwing up if he tried to force the food down.

Knowing that the twins would try to make him eat if he made a fuss, Matthew quietly tucks his packet between his seat and the control panel. He has no intention of feasting while the idea of killing humans filled his mind.

Matthew looks out ahead of the mech to the Bulwark trying to get his mind off of the notion of hunting humans. The sight before him only serves to further churn his stomach.

Columns of smoke are rising all across the Bulwark. Matthew can just make out the forms of several dozen bodies all around the nearest trenches.

Fires are glowing red as far as Matthew can see going up and down the trench lines. In the distance, Matthew can see explosions going off, far from the Bulwark as the handful of friendly artillery positions finally return fire on the Beets.

The Beetles had evidentially not made a move beyond the gasser artillery strikes several hours ago. That being said, from Matthew's vantage point, the Beets seem to have dealt a huge blow to the Mudders today.

"I hope Rav'ian and Marie are alright," Matthew whispers to himself before uttering a quick prayer on their behaves.

Sanctuary

The Battle for Allegra

Episode Six

Chapter One

The Bulwark, Allegra

To say that the Bulwark had seen better days was an understatement. Seemingly everything that could burn had either already been scorched and reduced to ash, or it is still on fire. Fortunately, Matthew can't feel any of the heat from the firestorm outside, thanks to the mech's thick armor that he and the twins are inside of. That which couldn't burn hadn't escaped the damage dealt by the Beets' attack. Large chunks of metal from various constructs are splintered so badly Matthew can't even recognize what they once were.

Matthew rises to his feet from the copilot chair he is in and cranes his neck to look along

313

the trench line. Sure enough, the desolation appears to be just as severe everywhere he could see.

Matthew can't help but sulk when the vainness of his worry for Rav'ian and Marie finally strikes him. If the destruction all around him and the twins was any indicator, there shouldn't be anyone left alive.

"I'm sure they're both fine," Louise assures Matthew when she sees how worried he looks. Nodding resolutely, Louise continues, "Marie and Rav'ian both seemed very capable at defending themselves."

Frowning, Matthew continues scanning the Bulwark hoping to see any signs of life. Discouraged by the lack of movement, Matthew bites the inside of his cheek out of concern before muttering, "So did a lot of people."

"From what I heard, there were a lot of bunkers all over," Alois adds optimistically, "I'm sure plenty of people were able to find cover in time."

"I sure hope so," Matthew says with a frown as he drops back into his seat.

"Well, we'll have better luck finding people on foot than up here," Louise reports after everyone had been staring outside for several still moments.

Knowing Louise was right, Matthew starts to get up when he realizes that the Fulcrum may try to reclaim their prize. Worried, Matthew points out, "But we can't just leave the mech sitting out here though. Anyone could come along and steal it again."

"I'm sure your Toaz friends would be willing to watch it for us," Louise shrugs. Without waiting for a response, Louise rises out of her seat and walks to the back of the mech. Louise taps a few buttons and checks a few systems before she finally offers, "You and Alois can start your search. I'll drop *Firefly* off with the Toaz and then find you."

"What if the Fulcrum people try to hunt you down before you get back to us?" Matthew asks as he recalls the ambush that they had been caught in that morning. If it weren't for them all fighting together, Matthew was sure he would be dead right now. Or, at the very least, be a prisoner to the Fulcrum.

Louise and Alois exchange a look that makes Matthew feel very uneasy. He is about to say something when Louise finally starts, "Matthew, you know that guy Alois and I were questioning?"

"Yeah, the guy you said told you

everything," Matthew nods as images of the man flash before his mind's eye.

"We lied to you about him," Alois admits, "He's dead."

"Oh," Matthew breathes as his heart skips a beat. Part of Matthew had questioned the twins' original story about how the man told them everything and how they had let him go, but he still hoped it was true.

After seeing the twins fight and kill so many gassers and seeing how passive they were when Jonas died, Matthew knew they were stone-cold killers—or at least a lot colder than he was. But, even with all the pain Alois and Louise could inflict, Matthew can't help but feel a little safer with them around.

Provided they don't ever turn on him.

But, even if the twins didn't turn on him, Matthew isn't sure how he felt about them lying to him. Sure, their initial lie allowed him to think nothing bad had happened. However, now that he knew what they did, Matthew isn't sure how to feel.

Seeing that Matthew is conflicted about their actions, Alois goes on to explain, "We left his body outside of the Fulcrum bunker with a note. It was a warning to leave us be."

"Seems rather excessive to me,"

Matthew grumbles, "Besides, how do we know that they won't come out after us out of revenge?"

"We've dealt with people like them before. We'll be fine." Louise tries to reassure Matthew.

Not convinced, Matthew presses, "And if we aren't?"

Alois steps between Matthew and Louise's seats and confidently declares, "If they try anything, we'll just have to send a stronger message."

"And the last message was a very strong one," Louise tells Matthew with a grimace. Shuddering, she quickly adds, "I hope we don't have to do anything like that again."

To appease any remaining doubts in Matthew's mind, Alois quickly adds, "But as I said, we've dealt with people like them before. One body on their doorstep and they should avoid us from now on."

"I just hope you're right," Matthew sighs. Looking between the twins, Matthew notes that they both are wearing looks of distaste. Nodding to himself, Matthew thinks, *Maybe they aren't all that bad.*

Louise turns away from the cockpit window and reminds Alois and Matthew,

"We've only got two hours until nightfall so we should get moving."

Worried for Louise's safety, Matthew prompts, "And you're sure we should split up?"

Nodding slowly, Louise offers, "We can stick together if you want to, but that might delay our rescue of your girlfriend."

"I—uh. She's not—uh,"

"Don't worry, I know she's not your girlfriend," Louise assures Matthew with a laugh. Smiling mischievously, she quickly adds, "I'm just teasing you, no need to fuss."

Admittedly still at a loss for words, Matthew stammers, "I—I wasn't fussing, you just caught me by surprise."

"Yeah, yeah," Louise makes a show of her rolling her eyes. She and Alois exchange a look and begin chuckling at Matthew's expense.

Several excruciatingly long moments pass as the twins poke fun at Matthew and Marie. As much as he hated being the subject of their jokes, he had to admit that they were on to something. He did have a bit of a thing for Marie as much as he hated to admit it.

Sure, Marie was absolutely amazing, but Matthew was spoken for. He had a girl waiting for him back home. Matthew lets out a long breath as he closes his eyes and he draws up an image of Dixie. She personified everything he ever wanted in a woman. Or at least he thought she did. Now that he was so far away from home and seeing so many new things for the first time, Matthew can't help but wonder if his love for Dix was premature. Similar to one's first crush, Matthew feared, his love for Dix could be jaded by an absolute lack of knowledge on how the galaxy spun. He didn't know anything before he left Sinclair and now, he had seen and heard about things that no one even dreamed about back home.

What if Dix doesn't like who I become after all this? Matthew thinks to himself in worry. He hated the thought, but he knew that men seldom returned from war the same. Factor in everything Matthew had learned about the Coalition in his first few days here, and even more fear seeped into his bones. The fear left Matthew feeling as bone-cold as he did on the nights that he slept outside exposed to the frigid nighttime breezes over the ocean back home. A cold so absolute that the idea of warming up beside the fire sounded more painful than pleasant due to the starkness between the cold and the heat. Matthew feels a tear well up in one of his eyes as the realization hits him; he wasn't going to return home anything like how he had left. Doing his best to hold back tears, Matthew thinks, *I'm going to end up just like the grumpy old veterans from my father's crew... Dix won't stick around me after all of this, she can do so much better for herself than what I will become.*

Louise suddenly snaps out of the teasing mood that she had been in and she announces in a very businesslike tone, "I think it would be best if I dropped the two of you off here, otherwise the Fulcrum people will see and hear us coming."

"Yeah, these things definitely weren't made for stealth," Alois agrees with a chuckle as the *Firefly* lets out a long loud whine before it lowers itself closer to the ground so Matthew and Alois can disembark.

The *Firefly* stops after a few seconds and Louise looks to her controls before she tells the others, "This is as low as we get, get out of here and get moving. I'll catch up to you as soon as I can."

"Before we go, I have something I have to ask," Matthew addresses the twins before Alois has the chance to open the rear hatch of the *Firefly*.

"Which is?" Louise prods after a

moment.

"How can we be sure that the Fulcrum won't target you once they realize that we are coming after them?" Matthew asks, hoping that the twins could see his thinking. It was one thing to scare them off and then leave them alone, it was entirely another to proceed to hunt them down.

"They should be able to see that we are just reclaiming what's ours," Louise shrugs, "If not, I can handle myself."

Alois stands at the rear hatch for a moment and he frowns as he thinks about Matthew's words. He opens his mouth to say something before he clamps it shut again and he turns and swings the door wide open. Stepping out, Alois assures Matthew, "As we said before, we've dealt with people like them in the past, they won't be ones to initiate anything after what we did."

Nodding, Louise affirms, "Yeah, they're scared of us and it will take a lot of convincing from the Fulcrum leadership to convince their goons to come after us any time soon. Besides, they're probably going to be busy dealing with the gassers just like everyone else."

Matthew considers arguing but he knew

that it was futile. He hadn't ever been in a situation like this before and, as the twins have stated several times now, they are the experts here.

Shoving down the mess of emotions that are raking through his chest, Matthew rises to his feet shakily. Resigning himself to the task of rescuing Marie no matter the cost, Matthew makes for the rear of the *Firefly* in order to catch up to Alois who had already left the mech and slipped out of view.

"You forgot your stuff, hotshot," Louise reminds Matthew after he had taken a few steps.

"Oh, thanks," Matthew winces as he realizes that he was not putting on as brave of a face as he thought he was.

"Just keep your cool, Mudskipper," Louise directs Matthew as he returns to his seat and gathers his gear. She continues as he straps everything into place with quivering hands, "Alois will keep you safe and I'll be back before you can miss me."

Matthew nods wordlessly to Louise before he turns and finally leaves the cockpit. He was as ready as he was ever going to be and there was no point in tarrying inside where nothing would get done.

"Godspeed!" Louise calls out to Matthew once he reaches the hatch.

"Thanks," Matthew says as he steps out. The moment he is through the door Matthew coughs. The air outside of *Firefly* sears his lungs as Matthew's entire body tries to tell him that there isn't enough oxygen for him to survive out here. Squinting against the acrid air Matthew's eyes begin watering in an effort to clear away all the filth that is suspended in the air all around him. Still coughing, Matthew staggers out the door without wishing Louise Godspeed in return.

Much to Matthew's concern, Alois is currently engaging with a handful of gassers that are emerging from somewhere beyond his limited field of vision. Curious, Matthew peeks around the expanse of hull that is obstructing his view and he sees that the gassers are slowly filing out of what appears to be a bunker.

"Oh no…" Matthew whispers to himself as he takes in a surprised gasp. He had hoped against all hope that the countless bunkers would keep more people safe from the gas, but he now saw that that might not be the case. Matthew's lungs burn at the air he had just taken in and he immediately wishes that he still had his mask. However, it seemed luck was not on Matthew's side since he had lost it several hours ago. Matthew quickly pokes his head back into the *Firefly* and he takes a quick breath of fresh air before pulling himself back out. He would have to make do with the cool, clean air that was escaping the *Firefly's* interior for the time being.

"Get back in your lousy holes!" Alois's voice demands as he takes a brief break from shooting. He drops the magazine out of his weapon and quickly replaces it. Alois then charges forward, shooting the whole way.

Matthew briefly wonders where Alois might have gotten his new munitions when his eyes fall onto a small open hatch beside the entryway of the *Firefly*. Peering in, Matthew is greeted by a plethora of filled magazines, quite a few grenades, and a lot of other odds and ends. He pokes around for a moment as Alois continues shooting and he lets out a discontent groan when he fails to find a replacement mask. He would have to find a mask soon if he was going to make it very long in this foul air.

"You going to help Alois, or should I?" Louise's voice questions from within the *Firefly* as Matthew stocks up on ammo and grabs himself some new grenades.

Matthew peeks around the corner once more at Alois, who is currently standing his ground several paces away from the afflicted bunker. The initial trickle of gassers has grown to a steady stream that Alois clearly cannot handle for much longer.

Taking hold of the ladder that extends to the roof of the *Firefly* for support, Matthew leans out and he carefully lines up a shot with his free hand. After emptying the remainder of his clip at the emerging hostiles, Matthew pulls himself back to a standing position and he reloads. Frowning, Matthew decides that it was in everyone's best interest if he admitted defeat and let Louise deal with the threat.

"Go for it!" Matthew prompts Louise as he braces for the *Firefly* to stand up and swing around to bring its weapons to bear.

"Alois, fall back!" Louise's voice rings over some loudspeakers that must be affixed to the exterior of the *Firefly*.

"Got it!" Alois's voice comes back in reply and Matthew watches as Alois makes a run for it.

A moment later the sound of quite a few electric motors whine and Matthew sees that Louise is using one of the larger shoulder-mounted cannons to render her aid to Alois's war effort. Realizing that Louise was about to fire such a large caliber weapon, Matthew quickly moves to cover his ears.

"Goodbye gassers!" Louise shouts in a voice loud enough that Matthew can hear her through his hands that are covering his ears.

Matthew presses his hands even tighter against his head and he then feels the *Firefly* shudder as a massive gun report races through his bones while momentarily deafening him as well. He had expected a big blast, but this was a lot more than he could have imagined. Not even a second later—and long before Matthew could have recuperated—the sound of an explosion echoes from the direction of the bunker that the gassers had been coming out of. Matthew continues covering his ears for a few seconds as the lights from the initial explosion and the subsequent fires illuminate his surroundings.

Slowly removing his hands, Matthew chuckles and admits, "That was a lot bigger than I expected."

"What?" Louise shouts back to him.

"That was really big!" Matthew calls in to Louise who appears to be just as deafened as Matthew was right now.

"Yeah!" Louise nods, "Next time we will

need to close that hatch though!"

"Oops, sorry!" Matthew apologizes in a loud voice as he realizes that his actions inflicted the pain on Louise.

"Well that's a new one," Alois shouts loud enough to be heard from below.

"Yeah," Matthew agrees as he coughs once again at the air that feels almost as thick as water. Without saying anything more to Louise, Matthew slams the hatch shut behind himself and he decides that his best bet would be to get to the ground. *I just need to get beneath the smoke. Since smoke rises, the ground should be a safer bet,* Matthew reasons to himself, *Then I will be able to breathe.*

"Alright, what's the plan, Mudskipper?" Alois prompts as the hatch behind Matthew seals itself shut with a high-pitched whine that Matthew can just hear over the ringing in his ears.

"I—" Matthew wheezes, still unable to speak. Coughing, he focuses on moving and he forces himself down a few steps that take him from the small recess where the hatch is on the *Firefly* down to the ground below. Once he is on the ground, Matthew tries again, "We—"

"Put on your mask," Alois instructs as he

points to his own respirator.

"Don't... have... one..." Matthew sputters pathetically.

Pointing over Matthew's shoulder Alois says, "You've got one on your pack right there."

Confused, Matthew reaches over his shoulder where Alois is pointing, and he feels around for the mask. Sure enough, Alois was right, and Matthew quickly pulls the piece of equipment to his face. Pressing the godsend of a mask tightly against his face, Matthew coughs as he takes a few breaths of the mix of bad air that had been caught in the mask when he put it on, and the fresh air that the unit is gracing him with.

A few moments pass and Matthew finally has enough oxygen in his lungs to be able to speak again. Taking one more deep breath Matthew finally responds, "I don't have a plan."

"It's up to you to think of one on the way then," Alois shrugs as he starts toward the nearest trench.

Matthew follows after Alois, deeply thankful for the mask that he is now wearing. He wonders for a moment where it might have come from when he realizes that Louise had likely given him hers. He smiles, happy that she would look out for him like that. *It's good to know that they really do care about me.* Matthew thinks with a smile as he looks back to the *Firefly* which rises back to its full height with another loud whine.

"Louise must have stuck her mask on your pack before you left," Alois says as the *Firefly* starts toward the trenches on its own heading.

Nodding, Matthew agrees, "That's what I was thinking."

"She probably has a backup. Either that, or she has a plan to pick up a new one."

"I hope she'll be fine without one…"

Alois lets out a loud laugh that knocks his mask loose. He quickly reaches up to fix it back into place before he assures Matthew, "Trust me, she's heartier than you would think."

"I can assure you that I have put that together already," Matthew laughs as he recalls the day's previous excitement. In just a few short hours, the twins had taken him from a Beet killer to a hunter of men. Or, more accurately, men and mechs.

Matthew watches as Alois drops down into the nearest trench and he can't help but hold his breath as he listens for any signs of danger. Hearing none, Matthew closes the remaining distance between him and the hole and he jumps down beside Alois who is carefully scanning the trenches that their current dugout leads into.

"Where are all the bodies?" Matthew asks when he sees that there isn't any sign of a fight around him and Alois. With all the damage that the bombardment had caused earlier, Matthew had expected to see a lot more evidence of the hurt it had brought.

"Everyone must have left when everything started," Alois reasons as he slowly starts down the nearest trench that would take them toward the Fulcrum bunker.

"Think they all made it to safety?"

"Couldn't tell you."

"I wonder how many people we lost..."

"Don't worry about that. Worrying won't change anything about the past, it will just get you killed now."

"Well there isn't a lot for us to be worried about right now," Matthew points out as he motions at their eerily still surroundings. The only signs of life that Matthew can see are a bunch of sodden footprints in the mud that he and Alois are presently trudging through.

"That doesn't mean that we shouldn't

focus," Alois reminds Matthew as he leads the way around another bend.

Matthew silently follows Alois around a few more twists and turns when the telltale sound of gunfire finally cracks over the roar of the fires that are blazing all over the trenches. Worried, Matthew scans Alois for a reason to be scared. Seeing none, Matthew sighs and tells himself that he is just overreacting. Shaking his head, Matthew thinks, *I'm on the frontlines of a planetwide war. Of course there will be gunfire.*

"Got a plan yet?" Alois asks as he stops just shy of an intersection in the trenches. He peeks around the corner as he had done several times now and then he settles against the wall he is leaning up against.

"I didn't know that you were serious about having me make the plan," Matthew admits with a frown.

"Well, I was serious."

"I don't have a plan though,"

"If you don't come up with one then we are going to be walking right into the Fulcrum bunker."

"Are you serious?"

"I don't kid around about these kinds of things."

"Well, I'm sure that they are expecting us, so there's something that I have to factor in..."

"Why would they be expecting us? They're going to be busy fighting off the gassers like we were."

"I'm sure they will be, but odds are that someone found out about our little raid on their complex. There's no way that no one mentioned to them that we were stealing their mech. If that's the case, then someone in the Fulcrum will likely figure out that we might be coming for them next."

"And then you have the Toaz who might be interested in recovering their nurse too," Alois adds after a few moments.

"Exactly," Matthew nods, "So we won't want to come from either the north or the southwest, since that's where they would expect either us or the Toaz to come from."

"So, we approach from the east?"

"I think we should approach from the southeast. We don't know what's going on on the easternmost lines, since that's the front. The southeast should be our best bet."

"See there? You're already the Mudskipper that Louise and I knew you could be."

"I'm not sure if my plan means anything," Matthew argues. He isn't even trying to be modest by saying it, he truly doubted that a plan to circle around merited any recognition. There was nothing special about it.

"It does when you see what I see," Alois fires back as he motions with his head around the corner that he had stopped at.

"Well, what do you see?" Matthew asks as he cranes his neck slightly to try to see around Alois.

"Don't look now," Alois says as he pushes Matthew back against the wall. Motioning for Matthew to turn back the way he had come from, Alois proceeds to fill Matthew in on what he saw, "I saw some Fulcrum guys waiting for us down that way. Several of them were hiding."

"So, I was right then?"

"They're either waiting around for some of the gassers or they are waiting around for us."

"And I take it you have a good feeling that they are waiting for us?"

"There's no reason to be hiding from gassers. Gassers don't shoot at you."

"Not yet at least," Matthew laughs as he retraces his and Alois's steps.

"You know, that is odd…" Alois mutters to himself.

"What's odd?"

"The gassers aren't shooting at us."

"So?"

"Well, I've been thinking about them. If they can walk and make sounds, then why can't they do other stuff too?"

"Are you saying that you *want* them to shoot at us?"

"No, but I am saying that I wouldn't be surprised if they started doing just that."

"I don't know, walking is one thing. Shooting at something—shooting accurately especially—is entirely another."

"I'm not quite convinced," Alois maintains, "There are some weird things out there."

Matthew nods, realizing that Alois is right, but he doesn't immediately say anything. He isn't sure what to think. Taking a few more steps, Matthew finally veers off from their original path in order to circle around both the Fulcrum roadblock and their bunker. Sure, circling around to approach from the southeast would add a lot of time, but it was a safer bet. Matthew also hoped that approaching from the rear would prevent any excessive bloodshed.

Lord willing, he and Alois would be able to get in and out undetected.

Chuckling, Matthew shakes his head and pledges, "If the gassers start shooting then I am blaming you."

"That's fair," Alois shrugs and laughs. Shaking his head, he is quick to point out, "But *you* are the one who said that the gassers aren't shooting yet."

"Yeah, yeah," Matthew grumbles, knowing that Alois was right.

"Speaking about gassers, you hear that?" Alois inquires as he raises his weapon and trains it on the lip of the trench that they are in.

Matthew pauses dead in his tracks and he warily raises his eyes above him. He listens intently for several moments to the gentle crackle of a nearby fire and the popping of gunfire that is close enough to make him nervous but far enough away that it didn't pose an immediate threat. Matthew tries to listen for anything else, but he fails to hear anything. After a few long moments, Matthew finally asks, "What is it?"

"Nothing," Alois chuckles, "I just thought it would be convenient if some gassers showed up right then."

"Wow, thanks so much," Matthew grumbles sarcastically. Shaking his head, Matthew starts down the trench ahead of him once more and calls back to Alois, "Come on, we've got a bunker to crack."

"You mean a damsel in distress to rescue," Alois amends.

Chapter Two

The Bulwark, Allegra

"What's our headcount up to now?" Alois asks from behind Matthew.

Matthew glances back to Alois for a moment to see what the man might be talking about before he suddenly slips. Catching himself before he falls all the way into the filthy mire beneath him, Matthew then returns his focus to the task at hand. He had to cross this section of trenches to save Marie.

Matthew grimaces as he looks down at the newly formed stains on his uniform. This 'water,' if he could even call it that, was some of the most putrid liquid he had ever seen. And now here he was, wading through a muddy trench of it alongside Alois. Up until today, he would have never entered such a filthy mess, but preferences like that change quickly when someone's life was on the line.

The boggy mixture of ash, water, dirt, and who knows what else reaches all the way to Matthew's waist and he can't help but feel thankful for the mask that he is still wearing. If it weren't for the mask's filters, Matthew was sure that he would be throwing up from the smell right now. Even with the filters, he can still make out the scent of rot that the bilge carries.

"What do you mean by our headcount?" Matthew asks after he yanks his foot out of a patch of mud that he can't even see through the swampish muck. The mud feels as if it is tugging at him, beckoning for Matthew to join it at the bottom.

"How many gassers have we killed since we left Louise?" Alois clarifies.

"I don't know," Matthew answers honestly. He had little interest in keeping track of his kill count on a good day, a bad day like this further removed his urge to keep track of such things.

Alois grunts behind Matthew as he rips his own foot out of the quicksand-like mud that had caught Matthew a few moments before. Matthew glances behind him and sees Alois stumble out of the hole before he recovers and eventually asks, "Think it's over twenty yet?"

"I really don't know. I don't care either."

"Well, we need to keep track because Louise is going to be counting hers."

"Let her, I really don't care," Matthew maintains as he hopes that Alois would just drop the matter. He really didn't want to dwell on the idea of ending the life of another person—even if they were a gasser.

"I'd say we've killed at least twenty gassers for sure," Alois rambles on as he and Matthew begin rising out of the deepest part of the flooded trench.

Matthew sighs, knowing full well that Alois wasn't about to move on. Closing his eyes, Matthew thinks, *When things calm down around here, I'm taking a week off. Well, maybe not a whole week, I don't know if I would be allowed to do that... maybe just a day?*

Matthew continues thinking as he works his way out of the cesspool of a trench and he doesn't realize that he had tuned Alois out until his thoughts pause long enough for Alois's voice to be heard again, "...with all those gassers we ran into when you took that wrong turn I'm sure we're well past twenty though. I think we could tell Louise that we made it to sixty or more, what do you say?"

"Alois, please, I *really* don't care!" Matthew begs, "I don't like keeping track of gasser kills, it makes me sick."

"You'll get used to it sooner or later," Alois assures Matthew, "Or at least sort of used to it... what I'm trying to say is that you will learn to deal with it a little better. Some people get to the point where it doesn't faze them at all."

"So, where are you on that journey?"

"Far enough along that it scares Louise sometimes."

"Does it scare you?"

"Used to."

"Used to?"

"Well, you can get over that too. You get to the place where you realize that hating yourself doesn't do anything to alleviate guilt. When you realize that you start to feel less guilt. Once that happens, you're home free."

"Home free?" Matthew parrots Alois's closing statement to himself. He hated the idea that anyone could get to the point where killing something that looked like them didn't bother them. How could anyone get to that point?

Sure, the gassers were actively trying to kill him, but did that make them any less human? Even the gassers that he had killed today that were once Arrandorrans and Toaz made Matthew want to cry as he pulled the trigger. Maybe there was still enough of the person that used to be inside of the gasser still. Maybe that little remainder was fighting against what the gas did to them to try to regain control. What would that make Matthew if he killed them? He would be condemning them then and there!

Matthew's chest aches like he had just inhaled a bunch of boiling hot smoke. His heart hurts in a way that made him wonder if someone had ripped his chest open long enough to beat his heart like a punching bag. Nothing about the last few days felt right to him. Now that he thought about it, even the thought of killing another Beet made him sick.

"You know that you will have to learn how to deal with killing things sooner or later, right?" Alois asks Matthew as the two of them take the final few steps out of the waterlogged ditch.

"No, I don't!" Matthew finally snaps, "I can struggle with it every time and I will! I'm killing people that I spoke to just a few hours ago! That is *supposed* to bother you! That's what makes us human, we don't just kill people!"

Alois looks at Matthew for a moment before he says, "If they try to kill you then they lose their right to be called a person."

"No, it doesn't!" Matthew cries out, wondering what could possibly be wrong with

Alois. There is no way that anyone could look at things with such a dispassionate view of what made a person a person.

"Then why wasn't this an issue for you earlier?" Alois asks.

"Why wasn't what an issue?"

"Killing stuff."

"I've never killed a person before today!"

"You killed the Beets, aren't they people? Or did they lose that title when they attacked you? Were they suddenly less alive when you realized they were your enemy?"

"I—I… Well—"

"Or those flying lizards that you told Louise and me about, were they any less alive just because they were snatching the fish that you killed in order to feed their offspring? You killed them too."

"Well, that's different—"

"There's nothing different about it. Don't hurl stones at me if you aren't ready to get them thrown back. The galaxy is a lot more black and white than you think. Things can lose their right to live if they threaten your own livelihood."

"Is that why you tried pulling your knife on me?" Matthew asks as he remembers how willing Alois had seemed to be to kill him when

Matthew had challenged them.

Alois walks past Matthew and he takes a seat on a rickety bench that is sitting beside the wall of the trench that he and Matthew are in. Removing his boot, Alois lets the water drain out and he watches as it drips to the sodden ground below. Looking back up to Matthew, Alois finally replies, "You went for your own knife first, as soon as you did that, you crossed a line."

"And I suddenly wasn't worth anything to you," Matthew states, hoping against all reason that he was misunderstanding Alois.

"It was your choice, not mine. Anyone who threatens those I protect forfeits their right to life. So long as you don't threaten me or Louise again, you are on the list of those I protect."

Completely dumbfounded, Matthew simply stares at Alois in silence. There was no way that the man could see things the way he said he did. As Matthew stares, Alois turns his attention back to his feet and he empties his other boot of the water inside of it before he busies himself by wringing out his socks.

Seemingly content with his work, Alois then puts his socks and boots back on. Standing, he looks around for a couple of moments and then his eyes settle on Matthew, "If you are just going to stand there then I will find my own way to the bunker. If we don't get there soon then Louise won't stand a chance."

Matthew watches, still completely lost, as Alois then marches off. Something about the hollowness in Alois's eyes. In many ways, Alois suddenly reminded Matthew of the feral dogs from back home. The dogs, like Alois, weren't outwardly aggressive, so long as you didn't interfere with their pack. The moment you did, then you were forever a threat to them. Sure, you might be able to win their trust by leaving out scraps of food and showing them various bits of kindness, but at the end of the day, they were animals. Animals that were, for the most part, in it for only themselves. The was no trusting them in your darkest hour.

"Wait up," Matthew hears himself saying before he had the unction to stop the words from pouring out of his mouth. Almost unwittingly, Matthew begins following Alois as well.

I don't want to do this. I don't want to storm the Fulcrum bunker. I don't want to follow Alois. I don't want any of this. Matthew thinks his brain rapid-firing everything that was wrong with what he was doing. Taking an unsteady breath Matthew then tells himself, *But I have to do this. For Marie, for Rav'ian, for everyone. Just like back at home, sometimes you have to work with people you don't like for the good of everyone.*

At that last thought, Matthew's mind wanders back to his years as a fisherman. Sure, this had only been a few days ago, but it suddenly felt like a lifetime had passed.

Matthew's memories quickly settle on a week where his father's fishing ship had been out of commission due to a storm that nearly sank it. Rather than sit things out and wait for the repairs to be completed, Matthew's father had decided to send out his crew to work on some of Crail's other fishing vessels. He had explained that there was no time to sit around because they had to meet the Coalition quota. No number of excuses could stave off the Coalition's rage when a quota wasn't met, so Matthew's dad did everything he could to make up for his inability to fish.

In order to truly make a statement and lead by example, Matthew's father, Heron, was the first to volunteer to work aboard another ship. This ship, everyone knew, was captained by Heron's most bitter rival, McCluskie—a man who truly was in it for himself. Whenever things went bad for McCluskie he weaseled his way out of the repercussions. Time and time again, that left Matthew's dad to pick up the tab.

Then, despite Matthew's begging, Heron signed up Matthew to work alongside him on McCluskie's glorified piece of driftwood. Heron explained that Matthew had to be willing to take on the worst task before he asked anyone else to do anything like it. In this case, that meant that Matthew and his dad would fish with a man everyone knew hated them. With the example set, they could ask the rest of their crew to work on the friendlier boats.

Matthew chuckles as he recalls the happier times from those long nights on McCluskie's boat. Sure, there weren't a whole lot of good times as McCluskie took advantage of Heron and Matthew's efforts, but Matthew's dad had a way of making even the worst things more bearable. All the long nights and even longer days were accompanied by grand stories from Heron, stories that Matthew knew he would never have the pleasure of hearing again. During that dreadful week, Matthew learned that his father was much more of a man than Matthew thought he could ever become. He did things that no one else could dream of doing, and he then made sure that no

346

one glorified him for it.

Heron had shared stories about his time as a soldier. About how he had fought off terrible foes and taken on impossible odds. He shared about how he had done all of this to earn the right to his land on Sinclair. He recounted tales of his darkest days which seemingly all crescendoed into impossible victories. It was on that dreadful boat of McCluskie's that Matthew learned about what it meant and what it took to be a man.

Alois suddenly speaks up, pulling Matthew away from his memories, "I know you don't understand where I'm coming from, and I am okay with that, but I need to know that I can trust you to have my back."

"I'm with you," Matthew assures Alois as a hint of pride wells up in his chest. As far as Matthew is concerned, he was going to be a hero and he was going to make his father proud. What he was about to do was just going to be the first grand story that he would have to his name. This one daring rescue was going to set off a chain reaction of triumphs. This chain reaction would then undoubtedly change the tide of the war. Or at least that's how Matthew was painting the picture for his own conscience.

"Good," Alois's always simple reply reaches Matthew.

Alois slows to a stop and Matthew keeps his distance. Listening carefully for several moments, Matthew tries to hear what might have caused Alois to stop. Hearing a few hushed tones, Matthew realizes that he and Alois are not alone. Curious, Matthew eventually asks in a whisper, "Any idea who they are?"

"Shhh," Alois urges as he cranes his neck in an effort to better make out the voices.

Matthew makes a face, admittedly off-put by Alois's shushing. He is about to say something when he opts to bite his tongue. Knowing that Alois had a reason to be listening so intently, Matthew knew it had to be something important. Matthew quickly resolves to try to listen in on what was being said as well.

"...now what, Jane?" Matthew can just make out the first voice.

A woman coughs before answering, "Well, we cleared out all the gassed guys, why don't we get back to the others?"

"Are you sure they want us to go back early?" the first voice asks.

Jane chuckles before she replies,

"There's clearly no one else back here, Tony. I'm sure we'll be fine."

"Think we should torch the bunker just to be safe?" the first voice that belonged to Tony asks.

"It can't hurt," a third person offers, "Make sure we really got everything."

"But we know we got all of them," Jane points out, "There's no use in spending any more time in there."

There is a brief shuffling as someone seemingly searches through a bag for something. The noise stops and Tony argues, "No, I'm with Juan. Let's light it up and call it good."

Jane lets out a discontent grunt before she says, "Well, you two can waste your own supplies lighting it up, I'll wait over there."

"Incoming!" Alois whispers urgently as he presses against the wall he and Matthew are leaning against.

"We'll be back out here in a minute," Tony reports.

"Keep an eye out for any more of the gassed people," Juan requests.

"You got it," Jane pledges, her voice much closer now than it had been a few seconds before. The squeal of a rusted and warped door opening cries out from where Juan and Tony were and there is a brief commotion as they slip in. A beat passes and Jane begins muttering under her breath, "Those idiots are going to get themselves killed. And what did they think I was going to do out here anyway? Of course I'm going to stand watch!"

"No, she's not," Alois whispers just loud enough for Matthew to hear. Before Matthew has the chance to beg for the woman's life, Alois is already whipping around the corner.

"Wait!" Matthew urges as he darts after Alois hoping that he might be able to call him off of Jane before he kills her.

By the time Matthew is around the corner, Alois is already dragging Jane's squirming form through the mud back to him. Matthew lets out a brief sigh of relief when he sees Jane's terrified eyes look to him beggingly as Alois maintains his firm grip around her neck and over her mouth. *At least she's still alive,* Matthew thinks as he loosens up and lets out a brief sigh. Following Alois back behind their corner, Matthew reasons to himself, *Sure, things could be better for her right now, but this beat being dead.*

Alois pulls Jane a short way away

before he stops and tells her, "I need you to answer some questions for me, can you do that?"

Jane nods once and she loosens up noticeably. As she loosens up, the look of terror also leaves her eyes. As far as Matthew can tell, she is very ready to cooperate.

"If you so much as talk too loud I will kill you," Alois threatens Jane as he prepares to release his grip over her mouth.

At this, Jane stiffens once more, and she looks between Alois—who she can just see at the corner of her vision—and Matthew. Matthew can see that the terror had returned to her eyes and his heart seemingly leaps inside of him as it tries to elicit an outward response from him.

Swallowing a lump in his throat, Matthew finally speaks up, "So long as you cooperate, we won't do anything to hurt you."

Alois makes a face at this, and Matthew can see that Alois likely had different plans. Odds were that he had been intent on killing Jane once she told him what he needed to know, just like he had with the last man he interrogated. Matthew assumed that this was one of the many ways that Alois kept his people safe—he tied up every loose end.

Matthew watches as Jane slowly nods and he then nods to Alois as he requests, "Alright, she's ready. Can you let her go now?"

"Don't you try anything," Alois warns as he slowly removes his hand from the scared girl's mouth. When Jane doesn't cry out for help, Alois then removes his other arm from around her neck.

Jane looks between Alois and Matthew as she slowly rubs her throat. Matthew can tell that she is gauging her chances if she either made a run for it or tried calling for help, which initially makes him nervous. The thoughts appear to quickly subside, and Jane resigns herself to her fate. Taking a deep breath, Jane finally asks, "What do you want to know?"

"How many people are guarding the Fulcrum bunker?" Matthew asks.

Jane chuckles, "We're getting straight to it then? There are a lot of guys, I don't know how many for sure though. There are definitely too many for just you and your... friend here to take on though."

"He asked for a number, not an opinion," Alois says menacingly as he takes a hold of Jane's arm.

Jane lets out a quiet yelp and she quickly gives Matthew an apologetic yet pleading look. Seeing that she wasn't going to be punished for her yelp, Jane reports, "I don't know for sure how many people there are. I would say at least forty though—probably more!"

"Is that where you're keeping Marie?" Matthew presses as he peeks around the corner that Jane and the others had been behind not too long ago.

"We need her—" Jane starts before Alois tightens his grip on her arm. Getting the message, Jane quickly changes gears and, dropping her head, she answers, "Yes."

"How well defended is she?"

"Pretty well, as I was saying, we need her. If her guards don't raise the alarm, then the people she is helping will."

"Would my friend and I be able to get in and out without too much trouble if we were quiet?"

"I told you, there are too many people. There's no way that you could get her out!"

"That's not what I wanted to hear," Matthew mutters, mostly to himself, as he lets out a long sigh. So much for the easy heroics that he had hoped for.

"Odds are that our people will let the healer go once she finishes helping us with our wounded. She refused to come to our bunker willingly, so we had to take matters into our own hands!"

"And how long would that be?" Matthew asks hopefully. From what he knew of James, the man didn't seem like he would kill Marie when he was done with her. She was too valuable. It also wasn't likely that he would keep her since they would eventually run out of wounded soldiers. They rarely did any fighting as it was, so they had no reason to hold her after that.

"I don't think your friends would part with such a valuable asset so easily," Alois argues, making a point that Matthew had overlooked in his optimistic worldview.

"Well there's no way that you could ever get her out otherwise," Jane shoots back defiantly, "Now let me go!"

"I'm the one calling the shots here," Alois warns as he narrows his eyes at Jane. He tightens his hold of Jane's arm, even more, to send the point further home.

"It doesn't sound like it," Jane points out defiantly. Turning to Matthew, who she can see is in charge, she begs, "Please, I don't want the others to know that I ratted our people out! I won't tell anyone about the two of you, I swear!"

"Oh, I know you won't," Alois chuckles, "Because they would kill you if you did."

Nodding feverously, Jane agrees, "Exactly, so please let me go!"

"Not going to happen," Alois shakes his head, "You are still of too much use to us."

"What do you mean?" Jane asks, frightened.

Cocking his head, Matthew can't help but wonder what is going through Alois's head. Worried, he seconds Jane's question, "Yeah, what are you thinking?"

"She's our ticket in," Alois announces, "All we need now are two Fulcrum uniforms— and I know just the place where we can get them."

"Wait, please don't hurt them!" Jane begs, "They're just—"

Jane is cut short when Alois shoves a wad of cloth into her mouth. Jane tries to spit it out, but Alois was ready for that and he already has a full band of cloth wrapped around Jane's head to hold the gag in place.

"Please don't hurt her," Matthew requests as he mentally kicks himself for not speaking up sooner. With how rough Alois is currently being, every dream of the grandeur of wartime heroics was fading. As far as Matthew was concerned, there was nothing honorable about manhandling a woman, like Alois currently was.

"She'll be fine, I just don't want her squealing on us," Alois assures Matthew. He then ties up Jane's arms and legs in a few smooth movements as he continues, "And I don't want her running off on us either."

Jane lets out quite a few grunts and squeals in protest as Alois finishes tying her up and Matthew can't help but feel bad for her. *But, our hands are just as tied as hers are,* Matthew reasons, *If we let her go, then we're just as good as dead. Marie would probably suffer a similar fate as well.*

"Let's go get our outfits," Alois announces once he is sure that Jane won't be going anywhere.

Matthew winces as Jane's look of panic intensifies at Alois's words. He momentarily considers keeping quiet, but his heart ends up winning the internal argument yet again, "If it's at all possible, can we avoid killing them?"

"Can't make any promises," Alois shrugs as he hoists Jane's tied up form over his shoulder. He starts toward the battered bunker door that Tony and Juan had disappeared into a few minutes prior with Matthew in tow.

Jane begins making muffled sounds again as she tries to appeal to Alois and Matthew through her gag. It is obvious that she doubted Alois's intentions and that she thought he would kill her friends. Matthew looks away from Jane and Alois as he slowly follows them, no part of him enjoyed watching Jane's garbled pleas.

Grasping for an excuse to spare the lives of the two men inside the decrepit bunker, Matthew asks, "Do we really need the uniforms? What if we found another way to sneak in?"

Shaking his head, Alois stops just outside of the rickety old door. He sets down Jane with a lot more care than he had picked her up with before he tells Matthew, "Even if we didn't need the uniforms, we still need to make sure that these two don't sound the alarm when they don't find our new friend, Jane."

"Well, let's do this then," Matthew concedes after Jane stops gurgling with her own wordless protests.

"I'm going to open this door, now," Alois informs Jane, "If you so much as scream, I kill you. And just know, if you alert your friends and they try to fight us, they *will* die."

Jane nods in understanding and Matthew can see her swallow. Her eyes are wide with well-founded fear. After a few brief seconds of staring at Alois, her gaze shifts to Matthew. Matthew's heart sinks even further when he sees the pleading look in Jane's eyes. His heart didn't sink because he felt any worse for all of this—he already felt absolutely horrible—but what caused his heart to sink now was the thought that everything was out of his control. It wasn't up to him if Jane's friends opened fire or not. It wasn't up to him if Alois shot them dead in return. Matthew's lip quivers and he is thankful for his mask. This way no one can see how bothered he is by all of this.

"Remember, they started this fight when they took Marie," Alois stresses the reasoning for all of this to Matthew. As soon as he finished speaking, Alois swings the door to the bunker wide open and he readies his weapon.

Matthew stares into the darkened room beyond the door and he wonders why there wasn't any lighting. Shrugging, Matthew decides this was rather unimportant and he prepares himself to delve into the shadows. Before he has the chance to take a step, two beams of light from within the bunker shine toward the ajar door, and Matthew instinctively shies away from the opening. Once he is away from the doorframe, Matthew looks over to Alois and sees that he had slipped away from the door as well.

"Jane, weren't you supposed to stand watch?" Tony's voice sounds from within the bunker as the echo from the door's squeal continues resounding through the subterranean room.

There is a brief shuffle inside before Juan queries, "Jane? Is that you?"

"I'm going to check on her," Tony volunteers as the soft plod of footsteps on packed earth nears Matthew and Alois.

Alois motions for Matthew to hide and Matthew presses himself further against the wall that he had retreated to when the duo inside the bunker flashed their lights at him. He draws in a sharp breath before he holds up a finger in front of his mouth—or more accurately his respirator—urging Jane to remain quiet. So long as she didn't blow their cover, Alois would be able to take out Tony without much of a fight. All things considered; this was one of their best bets to get the uniforms without any bloodshed. Sure, the Fulcrum uniforms weren't too different from the standard Mudder outfits, but the slight changes would, Lord willing, grant Matthew and Alois the cover they needed to get in, grab Marie, and get out without raising an alarm.

"Jane, if this is one of your pranks, it isn't funny," Tony warns as his footsteps near the doorway.

A laugh sounds from within the bunker before Juan points out, "She does have a knack for scaring us."

"And this is one of the creepiest ones to date," Tony confirms, "The dead people all around here don't help either."

"Nope," Juan agrees, "Hopefully we can get this fire started already."

"Jane, this isn't funny—" Tony peeks his head out of the doorway and Alois immediately grabs it.

Ripping the man out of the bunker, Alois envelopes him in a far-too-tight bear hug as he strangles the breath out of him. Tony squirms around but he can't move too much, thanks to Alois's firm grip. Realizing all was lost, Tony changes gears and he tries calling out a warning to his companion, but his cries are negated thanks to Alois's hold over his mouth. As the seconds slowly tick by, Tony's movements grow slower and slower and his eyes rove his surroundings with less and less urgency.

Nearly a minute passes and Jane finally lets out a fearful whimper when Tony finally falls completely still. Alois holds the man for a few more seconds, despite Jane's muffled pleas, before he finally drops Tony's still form.

Tony crumbles to the ground and Matthew catches his breath. *Did Alois really just kill him?* Matthew wonders to himself in awe, *And did I really just stand here and watch!?* Matthew's thoughts are cut short when he sees Tony's abdomen rise with a shallow breath. Sighing, the fear that had been gripping Matthew's chest leaves him and he thinks, *Alright, he's alive. One down, one to go. I can do this.*

"Tony?" Juan's voice sounds after a few eternal, still seconds. Matthew lets out a breath that he had been holding when he realizes that Juan had somehow missed Alois's takedown of Tony.

"See?" Alois asks Jane who is still looking at Tony since he hit the ground. Jane slowly lifts her eyes to Alois who casually offers, "That was painless enough."

"Tony, I know you're out there, you're not going to scare me," Juan says with a laugh.

He hammers away on something metallic inside of the bunker for a few more seconds before he calls out, "Guys, come on, I need some help with this thing."

"Think you can knock him out if he doesn't come out?" Matthew asks Alois when Juan doesn't make any immediate moves for the door.

"It'll be a lot harder," Alois admits, "I don't know."

"That's what I was afraid of," Matthew frowns as he looks down at Tony's unconscious form.

"Tony, come on already!" Juan demands.

"I've got an idea," Matthew announces as he turns Tony over and quickly strips the man of his jacket.

"Better do it quick," Alois advises as he stares into the darkened bunker.

Dropping his pack, Matthew then begins pulling on the muddied jacket. Knowing that looks wouldn't be enough, Matthew tries his hand at imitating Tony's voice, and, using his impersonation, he asks Alois, "Think this voice will fool Juan?"

"You could have had me fooled," Alois confesses. Nodding once, Alois adds, "Just don't do too much talking. It may sound good enough to me, but Juan knows this Tony guy better than I do. He'd be able to pick up any differences."

"Got it," Matthew affirms in his Tony impression. Taking a deep breath, Matthew prepares himself for what he was about to do. If all went according to plan, he would have Juan's uniform and the guy wouldn't know what hit him.

"You had better hope he doesn't actually look at you," Alois points out, "And you should lose the mask since our friend here didn't have one."

Matthew nods to Alois as he hastily buttons up Tony's jacket. The jacket is adorned with Fulcrum insignias and several odd badges that attest to the man's various feats, but their meanings are lost to Matthew. Taking a deep breath, Matthew prays that the jacket would be enough of a ruse since Tony's pants matched his own. Removing his mask, Matthew cautiously inhales the air around him which is a lot less smokey now. Content, Matthew surveys his disguise and nods approvingly at it.

"Try the hat too," Alois recommends as he stoops down to pick up Tony's hat that had fallen into the mud during the scuffle.

"Good idea," Matthew thanks Alois in his impersonation of Tony's voice as he jams the hat on. Hoping to further conceal his identity, Matthew then pulls the cap's rim low over his face, just to be safe.

"Perfect," Alois nods. Looking down at Jane, Alois asks, "What do you think?"

At first, Jane looks shocked at Alois's asking for her input, but she quickly recovers. Scanning Matthew, Jane bobs her head side to side in a way that told them that the look could be improved.

"Tony, come on! I need your help already!" Juan's voice calls out from the bunker with a lot more irritation than it had held earlier.

Matthew winces at Juan's demand before he asks Jane, "What else do you think I should do then?"

Jane's eyes squint as she thinks, and she then motions with her head at the muddy ground.

Nodding in understanding, Matthew scoops up some mud and he dirties his face. Having applied a good amount of the filth, Matthew smiles to Jane and says, "Thanks,"

"Bring Jane with you," Juan requests, "We're going to need her help."

"Jane's busy," Matthew lies in his best

Tony impression to date.

Juan grumbles under his breath for a moment before he calls out, "Tell her to get un-busy! And what took you so damned long?"

"I had to pee," Matthew lies.

"You took your time peeing,"

"Well, I had to get some privacy," Matthew offers, wondering if that was at all in character with what the real Tony would do.

"I'm sure you did, now get in here and bring Jane!"

"What should we do?" Matthew whispers to Alois.

"I don't know," Alois shrugs, "Think of something."

"Um—why don't we see if just you and I can do it?" Matthew requests, his mind racing. Taking a step into the bunker, he adds a lie that he hopes would sell the idea, "Jane's in one of her moods again."

"You always got to try doing things yourself," Juan grumbles. Throwing a tool across the bunker, Juan angrily shouts, "Fine! We'll do it your way, as always."

Matthew quickly closes the distance between him and Juan and he does his best to step around the handful of dead gassers. In retrospect, it would have been wise to pull the flashlight off of Tony. Juan is hunched over what appears to be an old generator that came from who knows where. His flashlight is trained on the opening that his head is in which, Matthew hoped, would make it so Juan would have to really look at him to see through his ruse. So long as he didn't give Juan a reason to look up, everything would be fine.

"What do you need lifted?" Matthew asks, still hoping that his Tony impression was good enough.

"Are you really that stupid?" Juan demands as he pulls himself away from the old piece of machinery. He turns to Matthew and he says, "As I said before, we just have to turn the crank to see if the engine is seized. We aren't lifting anything."

Matthew lets out a brief sigh when he realizes that Juan hadn't made him yet. Odds were that Juan couldn't see a whole lot because the rest of the bunker was so dark. The flashlight had partially blinded him, much to Matthew's benefit. Taking the last few steps, Matthew stands beside Juan and he makes like he is about to try to turn the crankshaft with a large breaker bar. The bar is currently stuck on the crankshaft's pully bolt on the front of the large engine, assumedly right where Tony had left it.

"Alright, this really is a three-man job, but let's see if we can do it with two…" Juan starts as he focuses on poking around inside the open hatch that his flashlight is trained on.

Matthew waits a beat as Juan's head dips back into the open hatch. Making the most of his time, Matthew takes several deep breaths to steady his nerves. *Hopefully, Juan goes down as easily as Moon and Walskie did on my first day*, Matthew thinks as he examines the man. *If I can't knock him out, then I'm in trouble. Things could get ugly really quick… I need the perfect opening.*

Matthew is soon rewarded with the opportunity he had been waiting for, and Juan turns around and begins fiddling with some wiring. In one swift movement, Matthew rips the breaker bar off of the bolt and he brings it crashing down on the base of Juan's skull.

"Ow, Tony, what are you doing!" Juan shouts as he rears his head upward as he spins around. Reaching up with one hand he feels the spot that Matthew had hit. Scowling, he demands, "What the Hell is wrong with—"

Before he can think, Matthew swings the bar at Juan's head once more, cutting the man off midsentence. Matthew misses his mark slightly, and he ends up hitting Juan's wrist instead. Much to Matthew's benefit, the sound of breaking bone accompanies the crash of the steel on flesh.

"Ah!" Juan cries out as he rips his now-broken wrist away from his head where he had been cradling his wound. With his good arm, Juan then rips the breaker bar out of Matthew's hands, and he seethes, "How about I beat you over the head with this now?"

Knowing that he was now at a disadvantage, Matthew charges straight for Juan before the man can react. Matthew leaps into the man's chest and he wraps one arm upwards behind Juan's head as his other arm works to immobilized Juan's good arm.

"Wait a minute, who *are* you?" Juan asks as he struggles to free himself from Matthew's grip. Evidently, his eyes had finally adjusted to the darkness. Either that, or he finally realized that his friend wouldn't be attacking him so aggressively.

"Matthew!" Alois calls from the entrance to the bunker. A moment later, Matthew hears the safety on Alois's weapon click off.

"Hold on!" Matthew tells Alois as he puts all his effort into reaching the wound he had made on Juan's head.

"Matthew?" Juan parrots Alois as the gears in his head finally start working.

Juan loses his focus long enough from saying Matthew's name that Matthew is able to press his fingers into a bloodied, wet patch on the back of Juan's head. Juan cries in pain as Matthew presses as hard as he can, and Juan drops to the ground. Matthew falls with Juan and they struggle for the upper hand on the earthen floor of the bunker.

Juan quickly rips his good arm out of Matthew's grip, and he swats Matthew's hand away from his head wound. A moment later, Juan kicks Matthew square in the chest, sending Matthew careening through the air.

Matthew crashes to the ground about a meter away from Juan and he looks over to Alois. Alois has his weapon trained on Juan who is rising to his feet as best he can with just one arm. Holding a hand up to Alois, Matthew shouts, "Don't shoot!"

"Then hurry up!" Alois demands. Glancing somewhere outside, Alois says something else that Matthew can't make out. Frowning, he looks back into the bunker to report, "We've got gassers incoming!"

Matthew rises to his feet as fast as he can, and he makes another run at Juan as

Alois steps out of the bunker and begins firing at the gassers outside. Juan is all too ready for Matthew this time, even though he still is on the ground. Kicking wildly, Juan makes contact with Matthew more than a few times.

"Get away from me!" Juan cries out as he fends for his life.

"Just—give—up—then!" Matthew tells Juan between his various attempts at getting to the man. The moment Matthew finishes his demand, Juan delivers a perfect kick to Matthew's mouth and Matthew's lip splits open. At this, Juan relents momentarily and Matthew breaks through his leg-defense. Knowing that he didn't have much time, Matthew straddles Juan's gut and he wraps his hands around the man's throat.

Juan struggles for breath and he tries to kick at Matthew from behind. As he kicks, Juan also swings both his good and bad arm at Matthew's face in hopes that that would make Matthew loosen his grip. Matthew squints his eyes to try to keep them from being clawed out and he does his best to ignore the pain of being kneed in the back as Juan struggles to free himself.

As Juan's attempts to break away from Matthew drag on, Matthew's grip grows tighter and tighter. *I must be doing this wrong if he isn't unconscious already!* Matthew thinks as his fingers sink firmly into the flesh of Juan's throat.

Juan continues gasping for breath to no avail and Matthew closes his eyes in order to avoid staring into the man's bulging eyes. A few more seconds pass and Juan's movements grow slower and weaker, but Matthew's grip remains firm. As Matthew saw it, there was no way in telling if Juan was just putting on a ruse. The weak gasps from Juan degrade to a gargle and then Juan falls completely still.

"We're out of time, just kill him!" Alois shouts from outside of the bunker.

Matthew slowly opens his eyes and he is greeted with a sight that he is sure he would never forget. Beneath him, Juan's eyes are still open, but they are glazed over and slightly bloodshot. Shocked, Matthew immediately tears his hands away from Juan's throat and he leaps to his feet. Juan's head lolls to the side and a thin trail of blood seeps to the ground from between his lips.

"But I was just choking him…" Matthew whispers to himself in terror as he looks down to his hands. Hands that had now killed another human being. Matthew's heart feels like it stops altogether as he thinks, *I'm a killer now. Even if the Beets and gassers didn't count, this did. What have I done?*

"Good, you finally knocked him out," Alois acknowledges from the door, "Now pull him out here and don't forget his jacket!"

"He's dead," Matthew mutters as Alois turns and quickly fires a few rounds at an unseen target.

Alois looks back to Matthew and he urges, "Come on! We're cutting it close here! I already cut Jane's legs loose so she can walk. I'll be carrying Tony; you carry your guy!"

Matthew tears his eyes away from Juan's corpse and he watches as Alois stoops down and picks up Tony's still form.

Matthew lets out a shaky breath and he drops to the ground beside Juan. He begins reaching for the first button on the man's jacket when he suddenly vomits up the small amount of food and water that he had taken in over the last few hours.

Outside, several gassers shriek, and Matthew can even hear what he thinks is Jane's own muffled cry of terror. Recovering as best he can, Matthew quickly pulls off Juan's jacket and he is careful to keep both Juan's body, and the clothes he killed the man for, out of the puddle of vomit that he had just made.

Wiping his mouth and eyes with his sleeve, Matthew takes one last look at Juan before he spins around and runs for the exit. The moment he is at the door, Matthew dives for his pack and he rips out an incendiary grenade that he had taken from the *Firefly's* supply cache.

As he pulls the grenade's pin, Matthew looks into the bunker long enough to see Juan's body which is being illuminated by the flashlight he had been using. Something about the spotlight on the body made Matthew even sicker to his stomach, but he doesn't have anything left in him to vomit up. Matthew throws the grenade at the far side of the bunker and it lands a lot closer to Juan's body than he could have hoped for. Clenching his eyes shut, Matthew then slams the door to the bunker. He was never going to be the same after this.

"Come on!" Alois urges without looking at Matthew.

Alois and Jane are both standing a few paces in front of Matthew, but they have their backs turned to him. Tony's unconscious form is draped over Alois's shoulder as Alois continues doing his best to keep the horde of gassers at bay as they race toward them.

Matthew reaches over to his rifle that he had left outside, and he opens fire past Alois. Without taking his finger off the trigger, Matthew empties a mag at the nearest gasser with a guttural cry that leaves his throat feeling raw.

Chapter Three

The Bulwark, Allegra

"Don't stop moving!" Alois urges as he continues fighting.

"My foot," Matthew complains weakly as he looks down to his gnarled appendage.

He had managed to get his foot caught in some barbed wire which was buried in the mud nearly an hour ago and it hadn't stopped oozing blood since then. Provided, it was rather hard to tell what was blood, and what was just mud right now though. Thanks to the drenched state of the trenches that Matthew and the others had been slogging through almost nonstop, everyone's feet were caked with mud.

"You just need to hang on for a little while longer," Jane tells Matthew as she frantically looks around. Frowning, she adds, "We just need to find a good spot where we can get you taken care of."

"You know, I like her a lot more without a gag," Alois chuckles, "Sorry about that."

"As I said before, we're on the same side right now," Jane replies as she lays

Matthew's arm over her shoulder so she can help him walk.

"For now, at least," Alois fires back, "There's no way we can trust you once the gassers are taken care of."

"That would happen a lot faster if you just gave me a gun!" Jane fires back, repeating her plea for a weapon. She had been asking for one since Matthew had convinced Alois that they could remove her gag. Matthew had started pressing Alois to remove Jane's gag not too long after they made a run for it from the bunker that Matthew had torched.

"That's never going to happen, love," Alois shakes his head.

"Please stop calling me that," Jane requests yet again as Matthew stumbles alongside her.

Alois grunts in response to Jane's request and he focuses on shooting a few more gassers instead.

The gassers, much to Matthew's dismay, had begun climbing up and out of the trenches in order to travel unimpeded by the narrow channels. Up until then, the trenches had served as the perfect kill boxes for the survivors to defend themselves from the masses of gassers. Now the gassers were literally everywhere, and the trenches were even more dangerous since the gassers could now come down from above.

Matthew had initially made a case for traveling up top, like the gassers, in order to make better time and have the high ground. Unfortunately, that plan backfired epically. The harebrained idea was what got Matthew's foot destroyed by the barbed wire and it crescendoed with every gasser taking note of Matthew and his team. Since then, the constant flow of more gassers had kept Matthew and Alois's guns very busy.

"Any idea how far away the nearest bunker is?" Matthew asks weakly as his injured foot drags in the mud. He didn't have the energy to keep his foot lifted anymore, so it served as more of a dragnet for more sharp objects hidden in the mud than anything else right now.

"The closest one is the Fulcrum bunker to the west," Jane answers as she points to their left, "And yes, I am well-aware that you two don't want to go there, Alois."

"She learns quick," Alois muses as he slowly peeks around another corner. Tony is still draped over Alois's shoulder which only slowed the group down further. Alois had tried letting Tony walk when he finally woke up the first time, but the man ended up making a run for it. Alois quickly caught him and put him in another sleeper hold. Since then, Alois had not put the man down, which really impressed Matthew who was dog-tired from just carrying his pack as he stumbled along.

"Is he always that way?" Jane whispers to Matthew.

"So far, yes," Matthew affirms. He is thankful that Jane had seemingly forgiven him for killing Juan. Rather than hate him for killing the man, Jane seemed to be perfectly neutral about the whole thing. If Matthew wasn't mistaking, he is sure that Jane only really cared about Tony. It was almost like Juan had just been a third wheel that slowed her down. Matthew lets out a pained chuckle before he cedes, "But I've only known him for a few hours."

Staring ahead, Jane's face contorts into the briefest of grimaces. She quickly puts her neutral face back on before she flatly says, "Lovely,"

"Yeah," Matthew agrees with another chuckle.

Matthew and the others continue through the trenches in silence for several minutes as the sound of gasser shrieks rise from seemingly all sides. Spurts of gunfire are sounding from just about everywhere and Matthew reasons that the sounds of battle are drawing the gassers away from him and the others. As far as he was concerned, everyone that was shooting right now was saving his life.

"Is it just me, or did I just hear Louise's voice?" Matthew asks when he hears the faintest hint of a semi-familiar feminine voice in the distance.

"You're hearing things," Alois states as he slows down considerably. He slowly puts Tony down and he begins poking at the trench's wall on his left.

The wall isn't too special, as far as Matthew can tell, minus the fact that it is bristling with splintered shards of wood and metal. Generally, the trenches were lined with planks of wood and sheet metal that were more or less smooth. These retaining walls served to hold the earth back. So long as the walls stood, no one would be buried alive. Matthew had seen quite a few sections of trenches that had either filled in when the retaining walls failed and he had seen even more that had been reduced to splinters in artillery strikes, like the one Alois is fixated on.

Matthew frowns as images of the other destroyed sections of trench flash through his head as he and Jane watch Alois.

"Am I missing something?" Jane asks.

Matthew gently shakes his head as he answers, "I don't think so."

"This looks like it's part of an old structure," Alois finally lets the two of them in on his thoughts, "I think there might be a bunker in here."

"I hate to be the bearer of bad news," Jane starts as she takes in the scene before her and Matthew, "But I don't think there's anything left in there. It clearly took a pretty big hit a long time ago."

"Oh, it looks fine," Alois argues, "The blast looks like it just collapsed the entrance."

Matthew examines the remnants of a large crater that appeared to be rather old. Matthew hadn't been on Allegra long enough to gauge just how old the crater was for sure, but he is confident that it was at least a few weeks old. Several rotting corpses lie all around Matthew and the others as another telltale sign that the bunker Alois is trying to unearth had been abandoned for quite some time.

Matthew exchanges a look with Jane that tells him that she thinks the same thing he is. Clearing his throat, Matthew offers, "I think we'd have better luck if we kept moving. Maybe we can find somewhere that's… somewhere that's still standing. We can rest up there and then head out later tonight or even tomorrow morning."

"That's right…" Jane mutters as she looks up to the twilight skies, "I forgot the nights were so long."

"Yeah," Matthew nods, "It's hard to get used to."

"You're telling me," Jane laughs, "I've been here for a week and a half already and I'm still not used to it. You've only been here… what? Two days?"

"I've technically been here for three days now," Matthew clarifies.

"Three days, not bad," Jane nods approvingly as she and Matthew watch Alois drop his pack and whip out a folded-up entrenchment shovel.

"Well, I was unconscious for one of those," Matthew sheepishly admits before he laughs. It was strange to think that he had slept through a full 35-hours of daylight. Worse still, he had done that on just his second day on Allegra. Shrugging, Matthew adds, "Feels a lot longer than the three days though—and I'm not just saying that because the days are longer here."

"Wow, you're still such a Mud Pup," Jane chuckles, "I'm surprised you managed to sleep through a full day uninterrupted though."

"I was in the infirmary," Matthew explains, "Got hit with some Beet venom."

This really gets Jane's attention and she eyes Matthew sideways for a moment in a mixture of surprise and skepticism. Nodding slowly, Jane observes, "And you survived? Interesting..."

"Yeah—" Matthew starts before Alois interrupts him.

"Just help me dig," Alois urges, "I think we've finally caught our break."

"Not much of a break," Jane whispers to Matthew as she helps him hobble over beside Alois.

Balancing on one foot, Matthew leans against a nearby section of wall that is still standing for support. As much as he wanted to be a better help, he couldn't. Being crippled, even if that only extended to his foot, was quite the hindrance.

Matthew, Jane, and Alois quickly find their digging rhythm where Alois and Jane dig while Matthew busies himself with pulling out any debris that impeded their work. Several comparatively still minutes pass and Matthew begins to let his mind wander as he continues clearing the way for Alois and Jane to dig. As his mind wanders, Matthew listens to the noise of the battle against the gassers all around him.

To the west, where Matthew knew the Fulcrum bunker is, the fighting seems to be the most severe. If Matthew isn't mistaking, it sounds like the entirety of the Fulcrum gang is fighting over there. North of Matthew and the others, the fighting also sounds rather intense, but it seems to be a lot more spread out than that of the fight to the west. It almost sounds like they are running cleanup operations to route out the last of the gassers. To the south and west things seem a lot calmer, but there is the occasional spurt of gunfire and the rare explosion as well. And then Matthew hears the same voice that he had heard earlier.

"They disappeared around here," Louise's voice faintly sounds as it is carried along by the wind.

"But the sighting is nearly a half-hour old," a Toaz voice sounds in reply.

"But we've got tracks," Louise fires back. Matthew chuckles as he hears the fiery spirit in

Louise's response, even at this great distance.

"Is that blood?" the Toaz asks.

"Yes, one of them must be hurt," Louise replies, "We need to…"

Matthew frowns when the wind shifts, and he can't make out the voices in the distance anymore. He tries moving his head about in an effort to make out anything, but he fails to hear much beyond the fighting that is now upwind.

Clung!

Matthew jerks his head back to the task at hand at the sound of metal hitting metal. Looking at the pile of debris, Matthew sees that Alois and Jane have both frozen. Matthew sees Alois's shovel which is still buried in the mud and his eyes follow it up Alois's arms to his surprised face. Alois then begins looking between Jane and Matthew excitedly as if to ask, *'Did you hear that too?!'*

Without saying a word, the trio begin tearing into the dirt with a vengeance. Any doubts that they had are now dashed as they are all consumed with one thought, *There's something down here.*

"I see steel!" Alois exclaims as loudly as he dared.

"I've got a handle!" Jane declares as

she shovels away a large hunk of dirt.

Matthew rips a final large beam away from the work area and he is awarded with a sight of a steel door. The door isn't massive, it's barely large enough for two people to squeeze through simultaneously, but it's a door. It's an escape out of the current nightmare that they are living in.

"Finally!" Alois whoops as he and Jane quickly clear away the area around the door. The moment the doorway is clear, Alois takes a hold of the handle and gives it a tug.

Matthew darts out of the way as the door falls forward toward him and the others. Initially landing on his bad foot, Matthew's leg gives way because of the pain and he lands face first in the mud. As Matthew slowly picks himself up, he finds himself staring directly into the face of one of the corpses that litter the ground outside of the old bunker. Matthew lets out a short, startled scream as he pushes himself away and he rises the rest of the way to his feet as a shiver runs down his back. Matthew fidgets for a few seconds afterward as the shivers continue, and he begins to wonder if any worms or corpse maggots might have gotten in his shirt when he was on the ground. He is about to reach into his shirt to check when he hears Alois whoop for joy once again.

"There it is!" Alois declares happily, drawing Matthew's attention.

"We don't know how deep it goes," Jane points out as everyone focuses on a small tunnel that is just large enough for someone to crawl through on all fours.

"And I doubt it would be easy to crawl back out," Matthew adds as he sizes up the meager hole. Crawling in was always the easy part, backing up was difficult when one got stuck.

"Well, I'm not going in," Jane opts out immediately.

"I don't think you'd be too good at guarding both Tony and Jane," Alois remarks to Matthew.

"Great," Matthew says with a frown. Sighing, Matthew thinks to himself, *Well, I've been volunteered. Or, more accurately, voluntold.*

"We only need somewhere to hide out because of *you* anyways," Alois adds unhelpfully.

"I'm not sure how true *that* is," Jane whispers as she helps Matthew remove his pack.

"Doesn't matter," Matthew shakes his

head, "I'll fit in there a lot easier than Alois anyways."

Once Matthew's gear is on the ground, Jane eyes his gun and asks, "Can I have a gun to help stand guard now?"

"Nope," Alois dismisses Jane's request once again as he swipes Matthew's gun away from her.

"Seriously?" Jane asks incredulously, "If I was going to shoot you guys, I would have done it by now. I've had every opportunity!"

Taking a seat on Matthew's pack, Alois argues, "We don't arm our prisoners of war."

"Come on!" Jane exclaims. She looks down at Matthew who is sizing up the hole once more and she begs, "Please? You know as well as I do that Alois won't be able to hold off a horde of gassers."

Matthew chuckles, knowing full well that he didn't want to partake in this argument. As it turned out, perhaps he wasn't getting the short straw after all. He would much rather venture into the hole than out here and bicker with Jane. Before Jane can press him for his response, Matthew climbs into the narrow tunnel with a flashlight in one hand and a knife in the other; there was no knowing what else might be down here.

"So, is that a no?" Alois inquires sarcastically as Matthew crawls through the darkness.

Once again, Matthew opts to ignore the argument, and instead, he proceeds onward. After crawling two meters or so, the tunnel is far too dark to see in. Frowning, Matthew reluctantly flicks on his flashlight. He knew that he was using up his priceless batteries, but if he didn't, he might not be alive to use them much longer.

The flashlight illuminates the tunnel ahead of Matthew and he immediately sees that it takes a sharp turn upwards several meters ahead of him. He also sees that it gets a lot tighter.

Resigning himself to his fate and praying the whole way, Matthew presses on. He is quickly forced from crawling on his hands and knees to his elbows and knees. After forcing his way a little further, he is forced to lie almost flat as he worms himself on ahead.

With a dreadful sense of claustrophobia setting in, Matthew's heart begins racing. He had never been scared of tight spaces, but something about the uneven and questionably secure earthen walls stressed him out to the point that his heart is beating in his ears. Not only that, but he feels like his chest is being pressed so tight that he can't even take in a whole breath.

As he thought all of this, an explosion somewhere on the surface shakes the tunnel that Matthew is in, and he is showered in dirt clots. *Please don't let me die like this!* Matthew thinks desperately as his heartrate rises even higher. Another explosion sounds and even more dirt falls, and Matthew offers up a brief, whispered prayer, "God, if I'm going to survive this war, then help me survive this night. If not, take me now."

The moment Matthew's prayer is over, the explosions stop. Not entirely convinced that he was still alive, Matthew tentatively opens his eyes. *I'm still here… for now, at least*, Matthew thinks as he nervously begins nibbling at his lip, *Maybe I should have specified what* 'now' *meant though. Now could mean a few seconds from now, if you think about it…*

"You still with us?" Alois asks, his voice echoing ever so slightly off of the soft dirt walls.

Matthew takes a deep breath and he takes a quick mental inventory of his appendages. He wiggles his fingers before him and then his toes that are somewhere behind him. Besides the pain that the wiggling caused

Matthew's injured foot, everything seemed fine. Content that those smallest appendages still worked, Matthew shakes the rest of his body around a bit and he nods, mostly to assure himself that he was still alive. Satisfied with his test, Matthew replies, "Yeah, almost there."

"Well, we've got a surprise for you when you get there," Alois reports.

"Can't you just tell me what it is?" Matthew asks as he forges ahead.

There is a brief commotion of hushed voices well behind Matthew before Louise's voice sounds, "Told ya I'd find you!"

"I told the others that I heard your voice!" Matthew declares happily, "They said I was crazy."

"Did not!" Alois upholds.

Chuckling, Matthew counters, "You said I was hearing things. Last I heard, that was the same as calling someone crazy."

"He could have been calling you a prophet," Jane offers.

"A prophet?" Matthew laughs, "I like that, but I don't think so."

"I like Mudskipper more than prophet anyways," Louise adds.

Before Matthew can sound his agreement to Louise's claim, he finds himself at the end of his small tunnel. He has to worm his way onto his back, rather than his front in order to get over the lip that he had seen earlier. Pulling himself out of the tunnel completely, Matthew looks around the bunker that he is now in as he illuminates it with his flashlight.

Empty, Matthew notes to himself. At first, he is discouraged, but he isn't sure what the reason was. He had thought that there would be corpses of people that had died down here when the exit had been sealed off, but there aren't any. Instead, the bunker appears to be fully stocked with supplies, bunks, and even a generator, among quite a few other things. Realizing that he had no issue with the lack of rotting corpses, Matthew's concern quickly turns into glee.

Sticking his head back into the tunnel that he had come from, Matthew calls out to his companions, "Come on in, this place is perfect!"

"Ladies first," Alois's voice offers.

"You just don't want the tunnel to cave in on you," Jane fires back before Matthew can hear her grunt and he sees her start down the tunnel toward him.

"You'll want to go through the last bit on

your back," Matthew advises, "It'll be easier to get out that way."

Content that he had completed his job, Matthew turns back around, and he continues examining the bunker that he is in. Everything seemed so perfect. *It seems almost too perfect,* Matthew considers, *Especially when you look at the dire straits that the entryway is in.*

This bunker appeared untouched by the mud and mire of the outside world. It truly appeared to be untouched. At a complete loss, Matthew begins shuffling toward the nearest cabinet, but he stops himself when he remembers his foot. Looking down, he realizes that he is dirtying the pristine concrete floor below him.

Raising his injured leg, Matthew hops back to the pile of dirt that is obstructing the entry tunnel. Halfway there, he laughs to himself as he recalls a similar scenario where his mother had scolded him for tracking in bloody fish guts into their house.

Smiling at the memory, Matthew lowers himself to the ground and he gets comfortable as he leans his back against the soft dirt. Closing his eyes, Matthew lets the memory run its course in front of his mind's eye.

The day had been a lot sunnier and warmer than most winter days back home. Not only that, but the fish had been a lot easier to catch, which was a very rare occurrence on sunny days. Excited to have nearly half a day of sunlight left, Matthew had quickly finished his fishing duties and helped pack away the day's catch.

Once the various chores were done, Matthew raced home. He was set on cleaning up nicely and surprising Dix. The only thing that stood in his way, he would later discover, was a hunk of dead fish that had somehow lodged itself in the arch of his boot.

Matthew's mom had been in the kitchen when he made it to the door, and he had excitedly greeted her. Once she got over her initial surprise, she looks down at Matthew's feet and saw the bloodied prints that he had left behind on the whitened wood floors. Without even telling him what was the matter, Matthew's mom had chased him out of the house with her broom. With him out of the house, she then proceeded to chase him out of the front gate as well.

Laughing to himself, Matthew remembers how the smell of fish and the dark bloodstains on the wood had never fully washed out after that day.

Sighing, Matthew's heart sinks as he realizes just how much he missed home.

"What's so funny?" Jane inquires as she wriggles out of the tight tunnel and gives Matthew a strange look.

"Just remembering home," Matthew replies simply.

Nodding knowingly, Jane asks, "Feeling homesick?"

"A bit," Matthew nods back. He is about to say more when Jane stops him.

"Woah!" Jane exclaims, "This place *is* perfect!"

Looking around at the room once more with Jane, Matthew agrees, "Yeah—"

"Except for that," Jane mentions as she points toward some of the footprints Matthew had left, "I take it those were from you and not some freaky monster?"

"Yeah," Matthew nods embarrassedly. He feels almost like he had committed some form of heresy by being the first one to muck up the otherwise pristine underground chapel.

"I'm just glad it wasn't me," Jane laughs as she removes her filthy boots and walks around the large room.

"Yeah, lucky you," Matthew chuckles at

the girl's honesty.

Louise and Alois follow shortly thereafter and Matthew exchanges similar conversations with them. Sure enough, everyone seems very happy with the bunker.

"So, is this our new home?" Alois asks the question that had to of been on everyone's heads. He finishes tying Tony's unconscious form to one of the bunk beds before he turns around and explains, "Because it's not like anyone is going to miss this place."

"I know I won't be parting with it any time soon," Jane steadfastly declares as she reclines on the bunk that she had claimed.

"Maybe not, but you will be parting with that bunk," Alois says as he picks Jane up with one arm and carries her to another berth. Once he sets her down, he enlightens the group, "I always get the bunk nearest the door."

"But there isn't a door," Jane laughs.

Raising an eyebrow, Louise points out, "She's not wrong, you know."

"Eh, semantics," Alois waves them off.

"There's a big word for you," Louise teases as she kneels in front of Matthew. She sets out several items that she had picked up from all around the bunker between her and Matthew. Surveying the items quickly, Louise nods confidently and she then carefully removes Matthew's tattered boot.

"I picked it up back on the *Cherry Picker*," Alois admits, "I like the sound of it."

"The *Cherry Picker*?" Jane queries.

"That was their ship," Matthew explains as he does his best to not cry out in pain as Louise pulls his boot the rest of the way off.

"Hmm," Jane mumbles, "Strange name."

"It was a salvage rig," Alois defends the name of his old home.

"Well, I guess that makes more sense," Jane offers a slow nod of partial approval. Turning to Matthew, she inquires, "Why didn't you just say that up front?"

Matthew doesn't reply as he clenches his jaw shut and closes his eyes as hard as he can to keep from letting out either a cry or a moan of pain. A moment later, Louise begins pouring water over his abused foot and Matthew loses control. Jerking his foot away from Louise, Matthew lets out a yelp and he holds his foot as close as he can, which—thanks to the stiffness that holding the leg up for so long had caused—wasn't too close.

"Oh, man up," Louise scolds, "If we don't get your foot cleaned up then you'll lose it."

"That doesn't mean that didn't hurt!"

Matthew defends his actions as Louise pulls his foot back over the bowl that she had set out.

"So, Alois," Jane turns her attention to the man that had taken her bed, "Can I have the top bunk? I'm a fan of being close to the exit too."

Alois eyes Jane for a moment before he relents, "Fine"

"Great," Jane smiles as she skips over to her new spot and she happily crests the ladder to her perch.

"One more thing," Alois says once Jane is topside.

Jane cocks her head and prompts, "What?"

"Well, you're going to need one of these if you're going to keep anyone from kicking you out of your new home," Alois tells her as he finally gives the girl a rifle. Or, more accurately, he returns the rifle that he had taken from her when he and Matthew captured her.

"Is that a good idea?" Louise whispers to Matthew as she finally lowers his foot into the bowl before him. She watches Jane out of the corner of her eye as she gently pours some more water on top of Matthew's foot.

Matthew takes a very deep breath to

keep from squirming too much and Louise quickly finishes pouring the water on his foot. A second or two pass and the stinging subsides enough that Matthew can reply, "We're about to find out."

"Alright, but what about Tony?" Jane asks after quite a few very stressful moments.

"Well, I'm not about to give him a gun," Alois shrugs, "He hasn't earned my trust yet."

"Huh," Jane mumbles. Frowning, she looks down at the gun in her hands once more before she hands it back to Alois. Seeing his surprised expression, she explains, loud enough for everyone to hear, "I don't have anyone I need to defend myself from down here."

"Ha, cute," Louise says just loud enough for Matthew to hear.

"I take it you're sleeping with your weapon tonight?" Matthew asks quietly.

Shrugging, Louise casually answers, "I do anyways."

"Of course," Matthew nods.

"What does that mean?" Louise asks pointedly as she stops fishing through the bottles of medical stuff that she had taken from a nearby crate.

Feeling like he had just really fouled

things up, Matthew stammers, "N-nothing… you just—I—well…"

"Slow down, you're going to hurt yourself," Louise teases as she flashes a brief smile at Matthew. Content that Matthew hadn't meant anything outwardly offensive, Louise returns to the task at hand, and she adds a few things to the basin that Matthew's foot is in.

"Thank you," Matthew eventually gushes.

"Well, I couldn't just let your foot bleed out all over our pretty floor," Louise shrugs.

"No, I mean thank you for everything. You and Alois have done so much for me and I don't even know you guys."

"Well, we aren't just doing this out of the goodness of our hearts. Sure, that's a part of it, but it isn't the main reason."

"Well, what's the main reason?"

"Well… Alois and I—we… the two of us haven't had the easiest go. We've learned how to find people we can trust. People that will look out for us just as much as we will look out for them. Oftentimes those people are the ones that need a little more help from us, but, so long as we know we're safe, we're willing to do that."

"Oh, well… thank you for picking me. I

don't know how I would have done anything that we did today without you two."

"You're resourceful, you would have figured it out," Louise nods approvingly at Matthew. Smiling, she adds, "That's just one of the added bonuses of our choosing you. Besides, your way with the ladies just won us a new ally."

Matthew follows Louise's gaze, and he sees that Jane and Alois are currently chatting like longtime friends. If Matthew was reading the duo's body language right, he would say they were engaged. The two of them seem so entirely transfixed in the other's words.

"You sure it's my way with the ladies?" Matthew finally asks once Alois gets Jane laughing so hard that she starts snorting.

Chuckling, Louise admits, "I guess my big brother is a smoother talker than I ever gave him credit for."

"Seems so," Matthew agrees as his eyes shift to his submerged foot.

"I stuck in everything I knew would help pull out the junk in your cuts," Louis explains when she sees that Matthew's attention had moved to his foot. Nodding at her assortment of medical supplies, she says, "I threw in a bunch of Epsom salts and some antibiotic ointment. I put in some lavender oil to soothe the pain too. But don't come after me for malpractice later, I'm no doctor."

Chuckling Matthew reasons that Louise's approach probably wouldn't do him too much harm. Shrugging, Matthew opts to thank her instead, "It looks great, thanks. I don't think I would have been able to actually take care of my foot anyways."

"I'm glad to help," Louise smiles as she moves to sit beside Matthew. A beat passes and she tells him, "Once we've soaked your foot for a while, I'll dry it off and bandage it. We'll need to find you some new boots too."

"Ain't that the truth," Matthew agrees as he looks at his discarded boot. The thing still did resemble a boot, more or less, but Matthew knew that it wouldn't do him too much good in its current state.

Several hours pass and Matthew and Louise sit in peaceful silence despite their both being wide awake. Alois and Jane have long since fallen asleep in their respective bunks, leaving Louise and Matthew alone. Matthew isn't sure if he isn't talking because of his exhaustion or if he felt like he shouldn't disturb the stillness and apparent holiness of their new sanctuary.

"Now that we've got a place to call home, I feel a lot safer," Louise breaks the silence.

"Same here, this beats a tent."

"It beats a lot of things. I don't know if I've ever lived somewhere so nice."

"Me either,"

"What do you think we should call this place?" Louise asks after a beat.

"You want to name it already?" Matthew laughs.

"That's what Alois and I do," Louise shrugs, "We name things."

"I don't know,"

"I was thinking we should name it Sanctuary."

"Sanctuary?" Matthew cocks his head. He isn't sure why, but he really liked the name already.

"Yeah, like a church."

"That's funny," Matthew sounds as he lets out a soft chuckle, "I've been thinking this place felt awful church-like."

"It's so peaceful and pure," Louise agrees.

"Sanctuary it is then," Matthew declares with a nod. Looking around the room, thoughts of stained glass and tapestries play in his imagination as he considers going all out and making their new home a chapel for the frontlines.

Several minutes pass and Louise eventually breaks the silence, "Sorry we couldn't save your friend Marie today."

"We did our best, I'm sure she'll be fine for another day."

"I'm sure she will be too. The Toaz told me all about her. She sounds smart and resourceful."

"From the little bit that I know about her; I'd have to agree."

"It's funny because the Toaz are convinced that the two of you are going to get married."

"Huh," Matthew grunts, "Weird."

"Oh, don't deny it," Louise teases as she gives Matthew a playful shove that causes him to wince when his foot shifts in the bowl. Seeing that she had hurt him, Louise promptly apologizes.

"It's fine," Matthew assures her. Pursing his lips, he asks her something that had been troubling him, "What happened to the Toaz you were looking for us with? I heard them with you earlier."

"Oh, they went back to their bunker

when we found you. There was a whole team of Toaz that escorted me here. They were worried about you, so they pulled their people away from gasser hunting. You really made a good impression on them."

"Sounds like I do that with a lot of people," Matthew says as he makes a face. He isn't sure how he liked being so popular with everyone. After growing up with such a small group of people in Crail, the idea of hundreds of people knowing him left Matthew feeling... strange. He didn't have a grid for understanding what to do with so many people. Part of him felt like what he thought the early colonists would have felt like when their planet was years away from their nearest neighbor. He had grown up so alone and now the whole galaxy was open to him.

Nuzzling closer to Matthew, Louise leans her head on his shoulder, and, with a yawn, she requests, "Well, don't stop being you, it might just save our lives one day."

Secured

The Battle for Allegra

Episode Seven

Chapter One

The Bulwark, Allegra

Matthew's eyes gently flutter open and he finds himself in the exact same position that he had nodded off in. He closes his eyes a moment to take a deep yawning breath before he looks around the bunker. The room is dark, and Matthew can just make out the forms of his various companions.

Oddly enough, he was finally the first one awake for a change. Yawning once more, Matthew slides away from Louise. Not wanting to wake her up, he gently lays her down.

Just a few Allegrian days ago he had been back home. He had been safe, warm, and fed. Thanks to his baptism by fire on this

405

war-torn world, it felt like an entire month had passed, at the very least.

Looking around the bunker once more, Matthew can't help but realize just how badly he had to go pee, and he allows himself to hope that there might be a bathroom in the bunker somewhere. He doubted that there would be since so many of the bunkers in the Bulwark didn't have restrooms, but he still hoped.

"Let's see here..." Matthew whispers to himself as he shuffles his way past the various bunk beds in the subterranean barracks. As he walks, Matthew hobbles slightly thanks to his injured and bare foot. Sighing, he tells himself, *I got to find a new pair of boots, maybe there's a pair for me down here somewhere.* At this, Matthew begins scouring the lockers beside each bunk and he takes a mental inventory of everything he sees as he searches.

Matthew lets out a defeated sigh when he fails to find any boots, but he can't help but feel excited with the other odds and ends that he had found. Not only were there plenty of interesting items including spare munitions, weapons, and clothes, but there were plenty of bunks for more soldiers to join Matthew and his growing band. All in all, Matthew counted a total of seventeen bunks or thirty-four individual berths.

Upon nearing the western end of the bunker, Matthew finds a small doorway that extends northward and he allows himself to get his hopes up. Perhaps there was a lot more to this bunker than he originally had suspected.

Taking a step around the bunk nearest the door, Matthew takes a hold of the handle and he lets out a slow breath. With all the gassers out and about, there could be some gassers just on the other side of the door. If there were, then he might just be condemning his team to their deaths.

As Matthew considers his options, his urge to pee reaches a crescendo and he begins shifting from one side to the other in a potty dance of sorts. Grimacing slightly, Matthew realizes that he was at the point of no return. If he turned back now, he would wet himself.

Matthew presses his ear against the door, and he listens intently for a few seconds for any indications of trouble. Besides the sound of his moving around, however, he can't hear anything. Taking another deep breath, Matthew turns the handle and he tugs gently on the door.

Much to Matthew's surprise, the door seems all too happy to open and is swings wide, bathing Matthew in cool air. Stepping through the yawning gateway, Matthew prepares himself to meet his fate. Matthew takes a few steps before he realizes that he had best shut the door behind him, and he quickly does so. With the door now shut, he realizes just how dark it is down here and he fumbles around until he fishes out the small flashlight that is in his pocket. No, this wasn't truly a life or death emergency, and as such wouldn't warrant the flashlight's use, but Matthew didn't care. All that mattered to him, at this moment, was finding somewhere to relieve himself.

Shining the flashlight down the hallway, Matthew's jaw drops. Rather than abruptly ending after a meter or so, as he had expected, the hallway continues on for at least fifteen meters. The hallway's walls are comprised of smooth concrete walls which appear to be rather new. The concrete itself isn't entirely smooth, which attests to the idea that this bunker may have been hastily erected near the start of this war. Overhead, light fixtures hang as a constant reminder that Matthew still needed to get the generators fired up so he wouldn't waste his flashlight's batteries needlessly.

This place is massive! Matthew thinks as the sense of awe wears off enough that he remembers why he had come this far.

Letting out a relieved moan, Matthew sees the bathroom sign above his head. Relieved, he races through the door and down a short hallway to the men's restroom. After a good minute or so, Matthew finishes up and he tentatively approaches the sink. Eying the faucet skeptically, he eases the handle upwards and sighs when nothing comes out. Frowning, he pushes the small handle back down in defeat.

To Matthew's surprise, that effort yields him a splash of water and Matthew cocks his head to the side. *That was weird… What if I try it again?* Matthew thinks as he pumps the handle a few more times and is rewarded with even more water. He then pumps with one hand as he washes the other before he swaps hands and returns to the hallway that he had been in earlier.

"Man, I had to pee," Matthew says to himself as he lets out a chuckle. He can't help but smile stupidly as he relishes the euphoria of peeing after holding it for far too long.

Matthew's thoughts are cut short when an explosion somewhere overhead reverberates through the soil and shakes the bunker that he is in. *Almost like the war thought that it needed to remind me that it was still going on,* Matthew thinks as he warily eyes the ceiling overhead. Despite the safety that he had thought the concrete bunker's roof would provide, Matthew can't help but notice the dust falling as each blast shakes another cloud loose. His lip quivers slightly as he thinks, *Perhaps the ceiling isn't as solid as I thought it was...*

Ahead of Matthew, an odd scurrying sound whispers from the end of the main hall that branched off from the barracks room. His brows furrow from a mixture of curiosity and fear and his heart leaps in surprise at the thought that there was something else down here with him. Despite this, Matthew decides to check things out.

Flashlight in hand, Matthew approaches the large steel door where the noise had come from. Knowing that opening any more doors could prove fatal, Matthew looses his knife from its sheath and he holds it in his free hand.

Passing an ajar door, Matthew quickly glances in. Looking around he sees even more

410

crates of supplies, including an open box of flashlights and batteries. Smiling contently, Matthew picks up a new flashlight and jams it, and three small battery packs, into his back pocket. Looking around further, Mathew is greeted with even more supplies, gear, and food.

At the far end of the supplies room, Matthew is greeted by another door. Excited, he races over to it and tests its handle. To his disappointment, it is locked. Frowning, Matthew lets out a saddened sigh as the joyous curiosity that he had just felt is hemmed back by an unfortunate reality. Looking the door up and down, he notes that it is made of steel and he sighs. Still eyeing the door, Matthew finds himself thinking, *I wonder what might be behind this thing... It's gotta be important for the door to be locked like this. Maybe the twins might be able to get through.*

Matthew's eyes drop in defeat at the thought of his first dead end and, as they drop, he sees a label on a box that piques his interest. *Boots!* Matthew thinks with a broad smile as he rips the lid off the crate. Peering into the bulky wooden crate, Matthew can see dozens of boots which all have their sizes printed on a tag that is holding each pair together. Searching frantically, Matthew doesn't see his size on his first pass, but he catches it on his second.

Matthew's heart skips a beat as he realizes his good fortune. *I'm not going to have to go barefoot!* Matthew hears himself celebrating inside of his head. The excitement causes Matthew's hands to shake and he momentarily can't retrieve the boots. Closing his eyes, Matthew offers up a quick prayer of thanks as he thinks back to the last time that he had been this excited.

It had been nearly a year ago and Matthew still can't help at the memory whose details had fogged slightly thanks to the passage of time. He can't recall just what time of day it was, only that it was under the heat of an unforgiving sun that left him with a massive sunburn that ended up blistering the next day.

Under normal circumstances, Matthew would have gone below decks to get away from the sun. There wasn't much use in getting burned topside when fishing was so much of a waiting game during the daylight hours.

However, that day there weren't any ordinary circumstances; Matthew and the rest of his dad's crew had a score to settle.

The day before, some sort of massive

fish had ripped through their ship's nets and cost them most of the day's catch. Not only did Matthew and the others have to face the shame of a return voyage home with empty holds, but they also knew that their future catches would never be as large—not with their biggest and best net gone.

So, Matthew and his father's crew did what any man who had been ashamed would do.

They decided that they would hunt down the object of their pain and destroy it.

The day wore on at such a dreadful pace that Matthew remembered how he had started listening in on and internalizing the same defeatist thoughts of his father's crew. Not only were they sitting out in what turned out to be the hottest day in the planet's recorded history, but they were seeing almost no bites on their lines as well. Despite being in the same location as they had been in the day before, their fish had seemingly moved on.

Matthew chuckles softly as he recalls the next part of the story. Shaking his head as the stupid grin remains, Matthew sits down and begins strapping on his brand-new boots.

Matthew remembered how he had considered leaving his fishing line unattended so he could go talk to his father and see what he thought about their misfortune. He had figured that there had to be a reason which a seasoned sailor like his father would be able to come up with. Fish didn't just disappear without a trace for no reason.

That was when Matthew felt just the slightest movement on his line. An inexperienced fisherman could have mistaken the faint tug as just that of the ocean's tide, but Matthew knew the difference. He knew that a fish had just bumped into his bait as it examined it.

Before Matthew could call out to the others that he had a bite, the fish latched on and immediately tried taking off with Matthew's lure. Matthew had immediately worked his way over to the nearest fighting chair and prepared for a long struggle. He knew that he had a big one on the end of his line and he was certain that it was the previous day's perpetrator.

Over an hour passed and Matthew had waved off several people who had offered to take over for him. He knew he could have used the help, but this fight was personal. This fish had threatened his livelihood and he was making sure that he set an example to the other fish to never do it again.

By the time the massive fish was close enough to see through the aqua-colored waters, Matthew knew the day had been won. He also knew that he had truly captured the fish that broke their nets, thanks to the fact that the netting was still caught in some of the massive fish's fins.

When word got to Matthew's dad that the fish was within view, had their net still, and was absolutely massive, he did what few others would intentionally do. Matthew's dad drove their ship into a nearby sandbar in the open sea. Thanks to his father's quick thinking, Matthew was able to wrestle the fish into calmer and shallower waters where the rest of the crew was able to swim out and kill the fish.

Even cut into pieces, that one fish filled their ship's hold and they had to summon another nearby fishing vessel to take the rest of the catch and pull their ship off the sandbar.

Thanks to that day's hard work, Matthew had recovered his father's nets—saving the family business, and he also set the record for the planet's biggest fish ever caught. The celebrations that ensued also elevated Matthew within spitting distance of his father's legendary status in their village.

Behind Matthew, the faint scratching

sound that drew his attention earlier sounds ripping him away from his fond memories. Reluctant, Matthew decides that he had to leave his newfound motherlode to investigate. Pursing his lips, Matthew allows himself one last look around the riches of the room that he had found, and he leaves it without so much as a word.

Passing another door on his right, this one closed, Matthew finally reaches the door that the noise had been coming from. He tentatively touches the handle—half expecting to be shocked the moment that he touched it. When nothing bad immediately happens, Matthew grips the handle a little more firmly with three of his fingers as his remaining two continue holding his knife. Taking a deep breath, Matthew resolves to finish his exploration before waking up the others to share in the riches that he planned on discovering behind this door.

Matthew turns the handle and he eases the door open as slowly as possible as he clicks his flashlight off. If there was something dangerous in here, Matthew didn't want it leaping at him like the Beet had when he shined his flashlight at in on his first hunt.

Stopping dead in his tracks, Matthew's

breath catches in his throat. An ever so faint light is glowing from somewhere beyond the door and outside of his field of view. That same light just betrayed the movement of some creature's shadow.

"This was a bad idea," Matthew whispers to himself as he realizes that his appendages had grown cold from the fear that his discovery had caused. *I'm not alone down here...* he notes with a shudder. Pursing his lips, the train of thought drags on ahead, *Well, what should I have expected? I heard something moving.* Taking one last breath to steady himself, Matthew breathes, "No going back now. I'm doing this."

Matthew waits just long enough for his eyes to adjust to the faint lighting before he eases the door the rest of the way open.

This room, like most of the compartments in this bunker, is filled with crates. To Matthew's dismay, however, crates stood as both a bane and a benefit. On the one hand, they would be filled with wonderful life-giving supplies. On the other hand, they provided cover for whatever creature might be down here.

The key difference that stands out to Matthew is its sheer size. The ceiling stands much higher than that of the main bunk room and the auxiliary rooms and it seems to extend farther as well.

Matthew slips through the door at long last and he ensures that it shuts behind him. If worse came to worse, he wanted to be sure that his careless exploration didn't get the rest of his team killed.

Looking around once again, Matthew estimates that the room is nearly thirty or forty meters long and about thirty meters wide. The structure is reinforced with several pillars, several immense concrete rafters, and countless steel beams the latter two of which both track with the ceiling's gentle curve.

Peering toward where the glow is originating, Matthew notes that there are several crates in the way. *Crates and hiding spots*, Matthew corrects himself. Knowing that he had to check it out, Matthew quietly descends the stairs that the door deposited him at the top of. Cautiously shuffling along, he makes every effort to not make a sound. If there was a gasser or a Beet in here, Matthew wanted to be the one doing the surprising this time.

Matthew presses his back against a massive crate which he reasons must be large enough to fit a good-sized car and he takes several breaths to steady himself. Just around the corner of this box lay the object that is faintly lighting the room.

Taking a final steadying breath, Matthew finally peeks around the corner of his hiding spot.

Or at least he tried to.

Instead, Matthew slips on a slick puddle at his feet that he hadn't noticed and he hits the ground hard in the aisleway. His knife clatters to the ground and comes to a rest about two or three meters away and his flashlight bounces somewhere behind him—fortunately still turned off.

His back to the object that is now shining like a spotlight on Matthew, he freezes in sheer terror. There was no knowing what might lay behind him.

Hardly a second passes before Matthew considers turning around to take a look at the object. This thought is immediately followed by one that is telling him to flee while he could.

Before Matthew can come to a decision, a warning growl sounds from behind him.

Wondering what might be the best course of action, Matthew briefly considers remaining absolutely still. The Beets and gassers didn't seem too terribly bright to him, so—Matthew hoped—that he might be overlooked if he played dead.

And then the sound of clawed feet begins approaching Matthew from where the growl originated. If Matthew isn't mistaking, he can just make out the sound of two sets of feet.

There's two of them?! Matthew thinks as he fails to suppress a slight shudder.

His movement seems to be noted, and the creatures behind Matthew stop once more. As they stop, there comes another low growl.

"This is how I go," Matthew breathes as he clenches his eyes shut. After his previous prayer to either make it through the war or die that night, Matthew had hoped that he was square with God.

Now he wasn't so sure.

The growling dies down once more and the creatures begin approaching Matthew. Oddly enough, the duo seem to be in some sort of strange lockstep—the moment that one of them picks up their clawed talons the other's foot touches the ground.

What if I just snuck a look? Matthew wonders, *Maybe I'll see a weak spot? One I might be able to capitalize on like with the Beets?* Resolving to go down fighting, Matthew slowly reaches toward the knife that he lost. Knowing that he couldn't reach it, he simply hoped that he might test just how much he could move before the two creatures reacted.

By now, Matthew can hear the Beets' breath. Oddly enough, the two of them seem to be breathing as one, as he can only hear one inhale and exhale.

Maybe they're breathing at the exact same time? Matthew estimates as he makes a confused face, *No, that doesn't add up… How could that work?*

Before he can make his move, a damp appendage from one of the creatures prods at his butt ever so gently. As it prods, Matthew stiffens and that sends the creature skittering away before it begins growling once again.

Deciding that enough was enough, Matthew lunges for his knife, grabs it, and then spins around with the knife sticking out toward the creatures.

But, to his surprise, there is just one four-legged creature.

A creature, Matthew notes, that looks nothing like any Beet he had seen thus far.

As Matthew eyes the furry critter before him, he notes that its coat is comprised of three colors, brown, black, and white.

421

The creature's white-tipped tail raises, and it begins slowly swaying from side to side as the creature cocks its head at Matthew and its floppy ears perk up slightly. By now, it is no longer growling and there seems to be some sort of spark of recognition in the animal's eyes.

"What are you?" Matthew asks the creature before him as he cocks his head right back at it. A sly grin tugs at the sides of his mouth as he can't help but notice the friendly demeanor of the animal. Perhaps this small beast was a lot friendlier than a Beet.

The animal keeps its ears perked up and its head cocked slightly as it gingerly makes its way toward Matthew.

For one reason or another, Matthew doesn't feel threatened this time. As he scans the animal, he tries to place where he had seen such a beast before. Squinting, he scours his memories of the textbooks that he had brushed through in school, and—after a few long beats—he comes up with his answer.

"You're a wolf!" Matthew exclaims to the creature. Happy that the animal is something that came from earth—a nice change for someone on the front that was on alien overload—Matthew rises to a crouch. Smiling,

Matthew thinks, *Maybe this wolf can be our new house pet.*

The 'wolf' stops, and it cocks its head at Matthew once more. As far as Matthew can tell, it didn't like the sudden outburst.

When the 'wolf' sees that Matthew is done yelling, it resumes its approach. As it draws near, Matthew can't help but notice how the 'wolf's' coloring is off. It is unlike any of the wolves in the book he had seen. Not only is its coat different than Matthew recalled, but its ears were weird too; rather than the wolves' pointed ears, this one had floppy ones.

As he watches the animal, Matthew recalls how he had read that it was omnivorous, and he remembers how he had seen some packs of meat in the storage room that he had surveyed before entering this room.

"Hey, buddy, do you want something to eat?" Matthew asks as he reaches his hand out to the 'wolf'.

The 'wolf' leaps out of Matthew's reach and away from his outstretched hand, but it doesn't run away.

After quite a few of the 'wolf's' approaches, it finally comes close enough for Matthew to take a hold of the band of fabric around its neck and he does so slow enough to keep from scaring the animal off. Despite the textbook's saying that wolves were fearsome hunters, this one seemed very timid.

"You know, I could use another hunting partner out there," Matthew announces as he looks his new companion up and down. As he examines the creature it presses itself tightly against his legs, so much to the point that Matthew topples over.

To Matthew's initial concern, the 'wolf' lunges at him the moment that he lands on his rump and it begins licking at Matthew's face. Laughing in a mixture of confusion and happiness, Matthew pushes the animal off himself and he asks, "What was that?!"

The 'wolf' cocks its head at Matthew before it lowers its front paws and shakes its raised rump and tail about. Panting with its tongue sticking out, the 'wolf' then lets out a short, but loud, bark.

Flinching slightly, Matthew asks the 'wolf,' "And what was that? Aren't you supposed to howl? Or… was that a howl?"

When Matthew doesn't do anything else, the 'wolf' comes back to him and it sits beside Matthew. All of three seconds pass before it starts leaning against Matthew again, but he was ready for its weight this time.

Once again, Matthew's attention turns to the band around the animal's neck and he takes a hold of it. Rotating it around the 'wolf's' neck, Matthew sees a string of numbers which he assumes must be the animal's identification.

"Huh, they didn't even give you a name..." Matthew mutters as he looks his newfound companion up and down. He's about to say more when he remembers the matter of food and he hesitantly asks the animal, "So... are you hungry?"

At first, the animal didn't really react to Matthew's talking—at least not until he said the word 'hungry.' The moment that word left his mouth, the 'wolf' goes absolutely berserk and it started bouncing around in tight circles.

"I take that as a resounding 'yes.'" Matthew notes with a laugh. Waving for the 'wolf' to follow, Matthew requests, "Come on, let's go get some of the meat I found in the other room."

Matthew begins to retrace his steps and he steps over the puddle that he had slipped in. As he does so, he laughs as he realizes that the puddle was in fact the 'wolf's' urine. A moment passes before that laugh becomes a grimace when Matthew notes that the urine had soaked through one of his pant legs and is now touching his bare skin. Matthew is about to react further when he reasons that he had touched a lot worse things on the front and he opts to just shrug it off for now.

Leading the way to the storage room, Matthew ushers the 'wolf' on ahead of him through the door leading into the massive room and then into the storage room. Ripping open a package of what simply claimed to be '*meat*,' Matthew passes it along to his companion who greedily chows it down.

Laughing, Matthew opens another package and passes it to the animal as he observes, "You must have been starving in there."

When the 'wolf' downs the second ration of '*meat*' Matthew stops himself from opening up a third. Despite the wolf's' appetite, it didn't look like it had been starving. If anything, it seemed to be a little overweight, if nothing else.

The 'wolf' looks up to Matthew expectantly and he shakes his head at it. The animal's weight attested to the contrary of a starving creature that had been sealed underground for too long.

Turning around, Matthew motions for his

new pet to leave the storage room as he says, "How about I show you to the others before we think about giving you anything else to eat?"

The 'wolf' lets out a whine before it does as Matthew requested. As it exits the storage room, Matthew can't help but wonder how much the animal actually understood. It seemed like it only really picked up on certain keywords if nothing else.

"Nope, this way," Matthew beckons when he sees the 'wolf' start toward the large room that he had found it in. Motioning toward the room to the barracks, Matthew doesn't wait to see if the 'wolf' was following because he is sure that it is.

Grabbing the door handle to the barracks, Matthew briefly considers checking if his newfound friend was nearby when its now-familiar form presses against his leg once again. Chuckling, he opens the final door and ushers the 'wolf' on ahead to meet the others.

Chapter Two

The Bulwark, Allegra

"Matthew!" Louise shouts the moment that the door opens, "We were getting ready to mount a search for you!"

"Woah," Matthew breathes as he freezes. Louise's shouting had startled both him and his 'wolf' who is now looking up to him expectantly.

"What were you doing?" Louise demands.

"Looking around," Matthew shrugs, "I found the bathrooms and some other things."

"Dibs on the shower!" Jane calls as she hops up from the bench that she had been tying up her boots at.

"I didn't even notice that there was a door back there," Alois admits, "Sorry everyone."

Nodding, Louise consoles her brother, "Don't worry, I don't think any of us did since it was tucked away behind those lockers."

"I know I didn't," Matthew agrees.

Sighing, Louise says, "We should have looked around before we passed out last night, it was a bad call on all of our parts."

Matthew nods for a few somber moments before he excitedly announces, "Oh! And I found a wolf! He's super friendly."

"A wolf?" Louise asks as she stiffens.

"Yeah," Matthew nods as he motions for the animal to approach his friends. The 'wolf' quickly complies, and it trots toward the others. Nodding Matthew reports, "He doesn't have a name, so I figured you and Alois might want to name him too."

Laughing, Louise announces, "Matthew, that's no wolf."

"What do you mean?" Matthew asks as he cocks his head. He pauses a moment as he wonders if he had always cocked his head this much, or if it was the 'dog's' quirk that he had so readily picked up.

"Wolves are a kind of dog... or are dogs a kind of wolf...?" Louise trails off as she considers her words and she eventually shakes her head. She smiles at the dog before she finishes, "Either way, they're in the same family, but they aren't the same thing. Wolves are dangerous, dogs aren't."

"Usually, at least," Alois amends.

"Right, usually," Louise agrees as she stoops down and slowly extends a hand toward the dog.

"It's not just any dog," Jane announces happily, "It's a beagle! One of my favorite breeds."

"It sure is a cute one," Louise smiles, "I doubt he'd be too terribly useful on the front though."

"Yeah, their bite isn't too scary," Jane approves with a laugh, "But their noses are great. I'm sure this one could really help us track some stuff down if we needed. I think we'll be able to make good use of him."

"I bet he could warn us of gassers too," Alois thoughtfully adds after a few moments.

"Sounds like we've got ourselves a new teammate," Louise smiles as she nods to the beagle that she is still stroking.

"So, what about a name for him?" Matthew prompts as Jane and Louise continue playing with the latest addition to the team.

"Well, he was stuck down here in Sanctuary..." Louise points out. Nodding slowly, she offers, "What about 'Monk?'"

Matthew laughs before he agrees, "Monk is good, I like it."

"I hope you guys know I'll be calling him Monkey if that's what you go for," Jane warns.

"That's even cuter!" Louise squeals.

"Yeah… I'm just gonna stick with Monk," Matthew announces.

"Monk it is," Louise nods. Looking down at the dog, she playfully asks, "How do you like that name, Monk? Huh? Is it good?"

Monk simply wags his tail and then offers a short and playful bark in response. Monk's bark makes Matthew laugh and he briefly wonders if the dog knew what was even going on right now.

Still playing with the beagle, Louise asks Matthew, "So, did you really think Monk was a wolf, Matthew?"

Shrugging, Matthew answers, "Yeah, it fit the bill, more or less."

"You've never seen a dog before?" Louise asks.

"Nope, never."

"You poor thing, dogs are the best."

"They appear to be plenty of fun."

"They are, I love them. Alois doesn't care for them too much though, he's allergic."

"It's just a minor allergy," Alois interjects, "Besides that, I like them a lot. They're great companions and they make my job easier."

"Should we take Monk out of here?" Matthew asks, worrying for Alois's health.

Shaking his head once, Alois answers,

"Nah, I should be good, so long as Monk doesn't climb into my cot or make too much of a mess. As I said, my allergy is minor."

Once Alois finishes, Jane pipes up, "My mom was super allergic to dogs, so we never got to have one. Not growing up, at least. I got a pair of dogs when I decided to leave home. Trike and Spike. They were Pitts."

"Pitts?" Matthew inquires. By now he is standing beside the two women as they continue playing with their newfound pet.

"Pitbulls," Jane clarifies.

Cocking his head, Alois asks, "Where'd you come up with the names?

Nodding, Jane explains, "Trike had three legs, she was born like that. Spike had a wacky wart or something on his head, so it was either Unicorn or Spike for him."

"Spike was definitely the better call," Louise giggles.

"What happened to them?" Matthew asks, "Did you bring them with you?"

"The Coalition put them down when they conscripted me," Jane frowns, "It was hard at first, but a lot has happened since then, so it feels... distant now. Almost like it was part of another life..."

"That why you joined the Fulcrum

group?" Matthew asks, wondering just how a nice girl like Jane might have ended up with a crew of such monsters.

Shrugging, Jane hesitantly answers, "Well, that was a part of it. They promised that we'd be able to bring about the end of the Coalition."

"Why else did you join then?" Louise presses.

Jane looks around the room for a few beats as if she is looking for the others' encouragement to continue. When no one moves to interrupt her, she finally explains, "There aren't a lot of places for humans to be accepted here on the front. Matthew here is an exception to that rule, of course, but the rest of us weren't so lucky. The Coalition made a lot of enemies among the aliens—and those aliens blame humans as a whole for their terrible lots in life because of that."

"I've heard that's an issue on some planets," Louise nods, "Lots of people—aliens included—have grudges and bad blood."

Jane nods in agreement before she continues her monologue, "The guys who recruited me for the Fulcrum made sure that the only aliens we fought beside were... friendly toward humans. That and they also tried to get all the humans they could to join us just so we could have some people we could trust."

"I was told that the Fulcrum didn't do much of any fighting," Matthew points out.

"There weren't a lot of friendly aliens to work with," Jane shrugs, "But your Toaz friends aren't the best sources of information on fighting spirits. They're born and bred for war and they're doing more fighting than just about everyone on the front. Because they're doing so much, they think that no one else is doing much of anything."

"I don't know," Matthew shrugs, "All I've seen the Fulcrum do is try to kill me and the twins while we're behind friendly lines."

Cleary offended at that statement, Jane fires back, "And all I've seen is you killing us—erm—I mean them... I guess I'm one of you guys now, after all..."

"Yeah, you're one of us," Alois assures Jane.

Chuckling softly, Louise warns, "You've got that right. So, don't be surprised when your old friends try shooting at you the next time you see them."

"Oh," Jane squeaks as the reality that Louise just warned of begins to set in.

Without skipping a beat, Louise changes gears and asks, "So, Matthew, what else did you find in your exploring?"

"Loads of supplies and a huge room… Come to think of it, it could be a hangar of sorts."

"A hangar, out here?" Alois demands, his skepticism nearly dripping through his voice.

Shrugging, Matthew replies, "I know, it's weird, but it was just such a big room. It reminded me of the place where we got our mech."

"You guys really got a mech?" Jane asks in surprise, "I heard whispers that you did, but I didn't see how you could have…"

"Don't worry, we didn't go in and kill all of your friends who stole the thing," Louise assures Jane, "They were just about all gassers when we got there."

"Just about?" Jane whispers under her breath.

Louise doesn't seem to hear Jane and she continues, "We left it with the Toaz for safekeeping but, if we actually have a garage for it, I guess we'll be able to keep a closer eye on it."

"Did you see anything else?" Alois asks

Matthew, "Any other ways in and out that we might need to worry about?"

"There were some rooms I didn't venture into, but nothing that I saw seemed too entrance-like..." Matthew starts, "But I didn't do too much snooping around either."

"I guess we had best scout out our base then," Louise announces, "What say you, Mudskipper?"

"That sounds like our best bet," Matthew agrees, "Maybe we'll find something of value that we might be able to buy Marie back with."

"Umm..." Louise says before falling silent. She rises from Monk's side and then pulls Matthew a few paces away before she whispers, "I don't think we should be doing any negotiating with them. Since we're still hunting down the other three people that brought down that transport, we probably shouldn't be painting ourselves to look like friendlies so soon. We'd undo whatever good graces we fell into when we take those three out."

"I guess I did promise Wyndover that I'd avenge his team..." Matthew mutters as he considers Louise's words.

Louise doesn't wait for Matthew to say anything else before she continues, "I think it might be best if we left Jane behind too, just in case she freezes up. She probably knew a lot of the people that we might be killing today."

"But she's part of our team now," Matthew reminds her.

"And so is the Toaz, Rav'ian," Louise points out, "But she's not here either."

"So, what are you saying?" Matthew asks.

"I'm saying we should leave Jane here to guard Sanctuary," Louise says flatly, "If she's still here when we're back, then we know that she can be trusted. If not, then this is her out and she can leave as soon as we're gone. She might slip out and warn her friends that we're coming. She might not. Either way, this could be a great test of her loyalties."

"But what if she sees through that plan?" Matthew asks worriedly.

"That would just make things better, she'd know to be on her best behavior if she wants to stick around," Louise assures him, "Besides, we really do need someone to hold down the fort while we're away. The three of us—you, me, and Alois—we're a great team together. We don't know about Jane, not yet at least."

"Fine," Matthew cedes, "We can leave Jane behind *this* time. That's it though!"

"That's all I'm asking for."

"I hope she doesn't feel like we're intentionally leaving her out…"

"Well, we are. This is the way we need to do this."

"But I don't want to do anything more to hurt her… I already killed one of her friends…"

"And we're about to kill even more of them. This is going to be the easiest thing for her."

Matthew scans Louise's eyes for a few moments as he searches for some sign of foul play. Seeing nothing in her eyes other than her earnestness, he sighs and says, "Alright, we'll leave her to guard Sanctuary."

"Even if she begs to come along?"

"Even then."

"Good," Louise nods as she pulls away from Matthew. Once she turns back to the group, Louise announces, "Let's check things out down here, we've got places to go and medics to rescue."

"Why don't you guys get going and I'll take an inventory of everything?" Jane volunteers.

"Wait, what?" Louise asks, clearly surprised by Jane's offer,

Speaking carefully, Jane answers, "I

know that you won't want me coming along as you break into the Fulcrum bunker to save your friend. I don't want to be there either. I'll stay behind and check out what all we have."

"Well, that settles it then," Louise shrugs. Turning to Alois, she asks, "That sound good to you?"

Nodding, Alois responds, "Yeah, but what should we do with our prisoner here?"

"We'll take him with us and see if he can get us in without a fight," Matthew cuts in before Louise can give her response, "If everything goes smoothly, then we can leave him with his people."

"And if not, then he'll be the first to die," Louise announces.

"We're not shooting an unarmed man," Matthew snaps at Louise, "And if the Fulcrum people start shooting, then we'll shoot back at them, but we aren't going to shoot Tony."

Tony, who had been listening from his bunk, lets out a loud breath of relief at Matthew's closing statement.

Seeing that Tony was finally awake, Matthew asks him, "Will you cooperate with us so we can get our friend back?"

Tony nods feverously in reply.

"See, he's on the level," Matthew tells

the others.

"And what if his friends shoot him instead?" Alois inquires.

"Then we'll have to find ourselves a shooting solution," Louise answers readily.

Chapter Three

The Bulwark, Allegra

"The Fulcrum bunker is just over there," Louise informs Matthew and Alois.

"We know," Alois grunts as he pauses long enough to cut a strand of barbed wire that had caught his pant leg.

"I feel like it would have been easier to just take the trenches," Matthew groans as his hands sink deep into the mud and he feels something jerk away from him when he touches it. Trying his best to ignore the thoughts of unseen monsters traversing the mud beneath him, Matthew continues crawling ahead on his stomach with a newfound burst of energy. He wasn't about to die up here and let whatever it was below him to eat his corpse.

"As I said before, they'd expect us to come from there," Louise reminds Matthew.

Tony mutters something through his gag which everyone agreed to leave on.

"No one asked you, Tony," Louise snaps as she continues worming her way through the mud.

"It's surprisingly quiet up here now,"

Matthew points out as he allows himself a brief glance up and down the Bulwark. The gassers had fallen silent since he and the others had fallen asleep in their bunker. The fires that had been blazing when Matthew and the twins returned earlier that night had also largely died out.

"Sounds to me like we finally beat back the gassers," Alois agrees, "Took long enough."

"Odds are that most everyone was just trying to wait the gassers out while just a few people cleared the trenches," Louise surmises.

Tony mutters something through his gag once more but Matthew can't make out any of the words.

"No one's talking to you, Tony," Louise angrily reminds the man who, despite being gagged, seemed very talkative.

Louise's words silence everyone, and they continue crawling. In some areas, they even have to wade across deep craters that had filled with brackish water and quicksand-like mud. In addition to the difficulties in crossing the hostile terrain, Matthew and the others are constantly reminded to keep their heads down and stay low as gunshots and shouts sound from all around.

There is a splash behind Matthew, and he glances behind him at Tony who had been pulling up the rear.

"Keep moving," Matthew urges Tony who had stopped in one of the deeper craters.

Tony grunts and mutters in response and his head and shoulders wriggle from side to side as he seemingly walks in place. Matthew can't help but notice that Tony is dripping with the filthy water and he even has some mud sticking to his face in places that Matthew hadn't seen before.

"What's the holdup?" Louise asks.

Without initially answering, Matthew slowly turns around and begins sliding back into the crater that he had just emerged from. Before he's too far in, Matthew shrugs off his pack and he then glides down its slick slope. He claws at the mud to stop himself from getting too far in when his descent becomes uncontrollable. When he finally remains his footing, Matthew answers Louise, "I think Tony's stuck."

Frowning, Louise watches Matthew and says, "Then let him be stuck, we all got through easily enough."

"I don't think so," Matthew shakes his head before he rises from a crouch all the way to his feet to keep his head above the water in the crater. Approaching Tony, Matthew continues, "We've made it this far."

Tony mumbles something else as Matthew draws near.

"What?" Matthew asks as the hairs on the back of his neck stand on end. He can't tell if Tony's muffled words are a warning, but he can tell that something is amiss.

Tony continues his wordless mumbling and his wiggling seems to grow more frantic.

"I told you, I'm coming..." Matthew reminds the man as he wades closer to him.

By now, the mud beneath the water is so thick that Matthew has to work to take each step. The effort to simply free his foot reminds him of how hard it was to pull up an anchor on his father's fishing ship without the aid of pulleys or anyone else.

Matthew stops about a meter shy of Tony and he weighs his options. As was the case when rescuing a drowning person at sea, Matthew is sure to keep Tony at a distance or risk getting pushed under as the man tried to save himself. Biting his lip in thought, Matthew weighs his options.

Nodding resolutely, Matthew decides on his course of action, "Alright, I'm going to reach out to you and then pull you—"

Tony lunges toward Matthew and Matthew shoves him away instinctively. He knew that he couldn't risk getting pulled under as he tried to help Tony or else they both might die.

Tony grabs once more and Matthew takes a clumsy step back as he pushes Tony away again. As he does so, he sees a look in Tony's eyes that looks more bloodthirsty than frightened.

"What are you doing?" Matthew demands, "Calm down!"

Tony swipes at Matthew without answering him and he finally gets a hold of Matthew's arm. A sharp biting feeling follows Tony's steely grip. Not wanting to go down with Tony, Matthew quickly shakes himself free of Tony's hold.

Taking one more step backward, Matthew finally trips and he slips and then falls. Matthew hits the water with a splash and he doesn't have enough time to take much of a breath before he sinks.

The mud seemingly pulls at Matthew like it has the desire to devour him like an unseen sea monster. The further Matthew sinks into the mud, the more it pulls.

Sitting up as best he can, Matthew blindly begins yanking on one of his legs in an attempt to free it from the mire that is pulling him further down. Things would be a lot easier if he could see, but he knew that there was no hope for that in this thick of mud, so he keeps his eyes clenched shut.

As Matthew struggles, he hears Tony continue splashing. He does his best to ignore Tony's struggling and he finally frees one of his legs.

I'm so glad I learned how to hold my breath... Matthew thinks as he tries scooping some of the mud that had gathered in his lap away. The swampish muck is working at burying him alive and he knew that he had to keep as much of it off himself as possible if he was going to make it out of this. Gauging the burning in his lungs, Matthew tells himself, *I've got another thirty seconds maybe...*

Before he has the chance to free his other leg, Matthew feels a sharp kick to his stomach which knocks the wind right out of his screaming lungs.

Tony! What have you done! Matthew hears himself shout within his head as he keeps himself from gasping like his body had tried to do already.

446

There's a hollow feeling in Matthew's throat somewhere beneath his Adam's apple as he forces himself to leave his lungs empty.

To try and now would be to drown.

Now frantic, Matthew feels around for his other leg and thinks, *Got to get my leg free. Soon as I do that—*

What Matthew can only guess is a gunshot sounds from somewhere above him. The sound seems to be very far away, but Matthew is certain that it was very close. He knew that sounds traveled strangely from the surface world to the waters below. Following the single shot, the whipping currents from Tony's frantic movements immediately halt. A moment later, Matthew hears a splash and the sound of rising bubbles of air as something sinks in the water nearby.

Why'd… they… shoot him? Matthew lazily thinks, the thought was surprisingly hard to come up with. Knowing that this was a sign of his brain saving what little oxygen he had left, Matthew feels a distant, yet also distinct, panic set in. He didn't have much time left like this.

By now, Matthew can feel some tears squeezing out from his tightly clenched eyes. His whole body screams at him in an effort to

447

compel him toward the surface.

If only he could obey.

A lone bubble rises from one of his nostrils where it had been keeping itself from soothing Matthew. The bubble, unlike Matthew, is unimpeded by the mud.

His resolve giving way to his body's instincts, Matthew helplessly thinks, *That's… it, that's…. all… I've… got…*

Before his lungs can answer their call to be filled, Matthew hears a louder splash sound from the water's surface.

They're coming, he thinks excitedly but also seemingly from a distance.

With one sudden tug, Matthew feels a thick forearm rip him upward. The abrupt force of the pull makes Matthew unintentionally take in a lungful of the thick water.

Coughing the water that felt like spoiled milk up, Matthew feels himself emerge from the water's cool embrace. He was finally free from the involuntary baptismal tank. Seemingly as soon as he is out of the murky liquid, his savior throws him toward the waterline.

Matthew feels like he's floating as he gasps at the air that is now around him. Oddly enough, the air feels remarkably cold in comparison to the mud's hold.

Crashing to the solid earth once more, Matthew lets out a deep cough, expelling most of what remained of the crater's depths. His lungs then continue their greedy effort to be filled and, this time, Matthew allows them that pleasure.

"Matthew!" Louise calls but her voice sounds distant.

Matthew's gasps die down to a pant as he realizes that he really is still alive. Alois had dived down and fished him out of the watery grave that he was about to call home.

"Matthew! Come on!" Louise continues babbling from her spot a million miles away.

Matthew is about to respond, but he feels something cover his mouth and nose tightly, stopping the words right in his throat. A moment later, a flood of water crashes into his face and all over his head. The torrent continues far too long, and the hand pulls away the moment that it finally stops.

Gasping once again for air, Matthew sits bolt upright, and he tries raising his arms to fend off whoever it was that just tried to kill him.

Or at least that was the intention.

Instead of battling off a horde of psychopaths that thought that drowning was something to be trifled with, Matthew's arms and face crash against something much softer. Softer and warmer.

Matthew's eyes snap open and he sees Louise's surprised gaze meeting his own.

A brief moment passes before Matthew realizes that his lips are clumsily pressed against Louise's and his arms are more or less holding her close.

"Ah!" Matthew sounds as he pushes himself away and he shuffles backward a few scoots. His eyes wide, Matthew blabbers, "Sorry, I—well I uh…"

"That's one way to say thanks," Louise giggles as she reaches up to her face to wipe away some of the mud that her and Matthew's encounter had left.

"Glad it was you and not me," Alois chuckles at his sister who is still crouching right beside him, "That was a close one."

Still shocked, Matthew continues his apology, "Sorry, I wasn't trying to—uh… kiss you…"

"Only thing you have to be sorry about is how sloppy it was," Louise continues teasing as she clears away some more of the mud that Matthew had shared with her.

"Sorry for covering your mouth, there were some freaky maggots that were all over your face and we needed to wash them off," Alois explains before Matthew can have the chance to respond to Louise.

"Maggots?" Matthew asks dumbly as he shudders. There were few things in life that he found as disgusting as those bulbous larvae. The ones that jumped and could bite were the worst.

Grimacing Alois nods, "…Yeah… you'll probably want to check yourself for any more of them. These things were something else, nothing like anything I've seen before."

Not waiting for Alois to say anything more, Matthew races over to his pack. He immediately rips out his water bottle and showers himself with its contents. Shuddering and feeling like his whole body might be covered with the grotesque creatures, Matthew starts smacking his pant legs in an effort to kill anything that might have gotten inside them. As he beats at his clothes wildly, Louise comes up behind Matthew and starts toweling him off as best she can with a shirt.

"Looks like we got most of them," Louise finally declares.

"I… never want to do that again," Matthew shudders.

"I'd say you still made out, though," Alois

tells Matthew.

"Yeah, since you saved me," Matthew nods as he takes the towel-shirt from Louise and starts wiping his arms clean. Looking over to Alois, he says, "Thanks for that."

"Of course," Alois nods, "But that wasn't what I was talking about."

"What were you talking about then?" Matthew asks as his eyes turn to the waters that he had nearly drowned in. Thanks to the low lighting, he can't see a whole lot, but what he can see is that the water is a lot darker now than it had been on their first crossing. He shudders and grimaces as he reasons that the discoloration could a mix of the maggots, mud, and Tony's blood.

"Your friend there had a knife," Alois reports, "He was trying to slash at you."

"I shot him as soon as I realized that he had the blade," Louise admits, "Sorry, I know how you wanted to keep him alive."

"But I was trying to save his life..." Matthew mutters as he looks out to the place where Tony had been standing not too long before.

As he stares, Matthew crushes the towel-shirt over the arm Tony had been grabbing and he lets out a surprised squeal.

Looking down, he sees that his arm is bleeding.

"Looks like you didn't get so lucky," Alois notes as he pulls Louise's water bottle from her pack. Approaching Matthew, he warns, "I'm gonna try to wash it out some."

"Go for it," Matthew grunts as he looks away from his damaged arm.

Without another word, Matthew feels the stabbing sensation of water being dropped on his open wound from a good height. The cold water mixes strangely with the warm blood and mud within Matthew's wound. Despite his best efforts, the odd feeling causes Matthew to focus on his injury and he groans as he also picks up on the searing pain. The pain is comparable to someone sticking their hand up beneath his ribs and then yanking out on them like they were trying to rip them out altogether. The main difference being that this is in his arm and not his abdomen.

After nearly a minute that feels more akin to thirty, the cascade stops.

"I think that's it," Alois announces.

"Are there any maggots in there?" Matthew asks hesitantly, unwilling to look for himself.

Matthew feels as someone pulls the

flesh on his arm apart and he groans in pain as his arm bucks slightly. After a few seconds, the person removes their hand and Matthew can feel as his wound closes itself back up as best it can on its own. Oddly enough, the pain seems to be a lot more bearable when the flesh is closed back up.

"Nope, you're clean," Louise reports, "I'd say you're clean enough to wrap it up too."

"Let's do that then," Matthew nods as he finally turns to see his arm.

Looking at his injured arm, Matthew can still see that the flesh isn't completely closed up and a good amount of blood is seeping out of the semi-open gash. Hoping that wrapping the wound tight and closing it back up would reduce the pain further, Matthew tears into his pack with his free hand and he pulls out some gauze and a long strip of bandaging cloth.

"Let me do it," Louise request with an outstretched hand.

"Please hurry," Matthew begs as he hands off his means of salvation.

Louise nods as she quickly gets to work on Matthew's arm. As she wraps it, Alois frees something from his own medkit. For one reason or another, he turns around so Matthew can't see him working on whatever it is.

454

"How come you're always the one getting hurt?" Louise laughs as she begins wrapping Matthew's arm up, "First your foot, now this? Then there was that stunt back where we got the mecha too."

"I don't know," Matthew responds as he shrugs with the shoulder of his uninjured arm to keep from jostling Louise's work.

"I think you just like seeing me fix you up," Louise winks, "You got a thing for girls wrapping bandages?"

His eyes growing wide, Matthew sputters, "What? No—"

"First Marie, now me..." Louise interrupts, "I'm seeing a pattern."

"I'm sorry, I didn't mean to kiss you, it was an—"

"I'm just teasing you, Mudskipper," Louise laughs. Looking up to Alois, she asks, "You set?"

"Yep," Alois nods.

"All set for what? Are—" Matthew's voice catches as Alois spins around and drives a needle deep into the flesh of his bicep on his injured arm. His eyes wide, Matthew is at a complete loss for words.

"There's a cocktail of painkillers and some stuff to make sure you don't keel over on us from anything that might have gotten into your blood," Alois explains simply as he pulls out the now empty syringe.

"Ow?" Matthew moans, saying it as a half-question. Rubbing the spot that the needle had entered, he sighs, "Thank you guys for everything."

"We're just doing what we can to keep our little crew alive," Louise smiles warmly. Matthew can see a new twinkle in her eye that seemed to be new, but he does his best to overlook it.

Several moments pass as everyone checks their gear and Matthew finally asks, "So, now what?"

"I'd say we should stick to the original plan," Alois answers.

Looking at Matthew's arm, Louise says, "We'll have to give you some sort of waterproof layer for that bandage if we're going to keep crawling though."

"I can use my jacket," Matthew nods as he turns to his pack which he still hadn't put on.

"Before you do that," Alois starts, interrupting Matthew's action, "I think I see something we should check out."

"What is it?" Louise asks as she and Matthew look up to Alois who is the only one of them standing.

"Follow me," Alois replies simply as he drops to a crouch and shoulders his pack onto his back. Still crouching, he stealthily works his way southwest.

"Must be something important," Louise shrugs as she helps Matthew to put on his own pack.

"Thanks," Matthew nods, "Let's get going then."

Matthew lets Louise take the lead and he follows the twins as best he can as they make their way to some point to the southeast that Alois had found so intriguing. For Matthew, he can't help but be thankful that he and the others are not crawling on their bellies anymore. Not only did that promise to keep his arm clean, but it also meant that he wouldn't have to feel any more strange creatures sliding through the mud.

"There we are!" Alois whisper excitedly, "I knew I saw a light!"

"Why are we whispering?" Matthew inquires as he joins the twins beside a chunk of stone that had been kicked up by one of the Beet's artillery strikes.

"I see our way into the Fulcrum bunker," Alois answers as he points into the crater that the stone they are behind most likely came out of.

Following Alois's arm, Matthew sees a small light on the far side of the crater. The light is dim and it is shining through a small slit in some subterranean structure. If Matthew isn't mistaking, the slit is about half a meter wide and no more than four centimeters high.

"I hate to be a downer, but I don't think we can get in through there," Matthew points out.

"It looks like the wall is made of corrugated steel," Alois says in response, "We can force our way through if it is."

"But what if the bunker is full of gassers?" Matthew asks, "If this crater was caused by one of the gas shells, then the bunker would have been caught in the cloud."

"Judging by the blast radius, I doubt this was anything but a high explosive," Louise shakes her head, "We'll be fine."

Still not too fond of the plan, Matthew presses, "Alright, so, say we got in, then what?"

"Then we try our best to not get seen or heard," Louise shrugs, "Get in and out before anyone knows what happened."

"And if we get seen?"

"Then we'll just have to shoot all the same people that we would have if we took the front door approach. Probably less people, actually."

"You're saying this is the best option for not killing people?"

"I sure think it is, sneaking around usually leads to a lot less shooting that frontal approaches, last I checked."

"What do you think, Alois?" Matthew asks as he turns to his silent companion.

"I think we should check it out," Alois answers.

"Well, let's go then," Matthew says with a sigh. As much as he liked the plan, he can't help but worry that everything might go belly up on him again. Despite his concerns, Matthew knows that the twins' plan was their best—and safest—plan. Not only did it promise them a quick and potentially bloodless entry, but it was also covert enough that they might be able to not sound the alarm. *Things are going to work out. I know it. We're going to get in, get Marie, and get out. No one needs to and no one will die.* Matthew thinks to himself with every vestige of confidence that he can muster.

"Stay low," Alois instructs as he closes the remaining distance to the opening into the bunker ahead of them.

"Stay quiet and tread lightly," Louise warns as they make their way through the crater.

The earth within the crater is a lot dryer than the slush that Matthew and the twins had made their way through to get this far. Looking around, Matthew reasons that this was because the explosion had dug beneath the sodden earth while simultaneously baking it in a short-lived kiln of sorts. Matthew didn't really care how the earth remained dry, so he quickly cuts that train of thought. All that mattered to him now was reaching the light ahead of him. The sooner he was there, the sooner this would all be over.

"Any idea how long until daybreak?" Matthew asks nervously as he and the others slow a few meters away from the light.

"I think we have no more than an hour before first light," Louise reports, "So we'll have to make the most of our time in there. I don't want to have the Beet snipers shooting at us."

"Me either," Alois agrees, "I had never seen sniper fire that intense before we saw you dive into the trenches. How did you make it through all that anyway, Matthew?"

Matthew shrugs before he answers, "To

be honest, I don't really know. The mule took a lot of hits for Rav'ian and me, so I have that thing to thank. The smoke grenades were a huge help for sure, but there were just so many shots… There's no way that we should have survived that."

"It does seem like you are very hard to kill," Louise points out with a laugh.

"Which is interesting for how many times you get hurt," Alois adds in a whisper as he stops altogether right beside the hole that the light is peeking through.

"Now what?" Matthew inquires of the twins as he peeks into the hole at the bunker beyond. Sure enough, Matthew can see several Fulcrum insignias on several folded uniforms and even a banner that he can see hanging.

Carving away a small seat into the freshly disturbed dirt, Louise takes a seat. Wrapping her arms around herself, she lets out a relaxed sigh and answers, "Now we sit tight."

"Wait?" Matthew asks, taken aback, "Wait for what?"

"We can't just go charging in there without some intel," Alois explains, "We're going to listen to what's going on in there and then pick our opening."

"But we don't have a lot of time left to do that," Matthew points out, "The Fulcrum people will probably start waking up with first light, right alongside the Beets. We'll be caught between the two of them when we try to escape!"

"What are you proposing?" Louise asks skeptically.

Frowning, Alois quickly argues, "We can't just charge in there without some idea of what we're getting in to!"

"That's what we were going to do in the first place," Matthew points out.

Staring intently at the hole that he and the twins are congregated around, Matthew sighs. He drops to his hands and knees and sticks his face right up against the hole. Looking around, Matthew can't help but notice how the room appears to be completely void of human life at the moment.

As he stares, Matthew hears the faint sound of voices that seem to be somewhat muted. Curious, Matthew repositions his head and he realizes that the room before him is very small. Not only is the room small, but it is also separated from wherever the voices are talking by a door that appears to be very solid.

"What do you see?" Louise asks after

several minutes.

"I think we should be able to get in without anyone noticing us," Matthew answers as he retreats from the hole far enough to begin clawing at the dirt around it.

As Matthew and the twins dig, he can't help but marvel once more at how dry the soil is in comparison to the mud that is everywhere else. His digging efforts quickly diminish as he begins toying with the dirt in his hands and pushing around the firm clots. No, the dirt wasn't dry by any definition of the word, but it was a lot closer to it than anything that Matthew had seen since arriving at the Bulwark.

"What is it?" Louise asks worriedly as she and Alois stop digging as well and they both look to Matthew.

"It's just so... dry," Matthew answers, immediately feeling dumb for how interested he is in the dirt.

"Yeah, it's... neat," Louise hesitantly and halfheartedly agrees as she eyes Matthew curiously.

Another awkward moment passes before Matthew drops the dirt and says, "We should use our entrenchment shovels in case there's any shrapnel from the explosion. I'd

463

hate for us to get our hands cut up on anything"

"Good idea," Louise nods as she reaches over to the pack that she had left on the seat that she had carved.

Matthew can tell that Louise is happy for the change in subject and this only makes him feel more foolish. Here he was, acting like a complete idiot in front of two people that had sworn their allegiance to him.

"Alright, that should do it," Alois announces after making several wide sweeps at the loose earthen wall with his shovel.

Louise takes one last scoop before she nods in agreement. Scanning the slit in the wall, she acknowledges, "Yep, that's corrugated steel alright. We should be able to bend it out of our way without too much difficulty."

"Who builds a bunker out of sheets of metal this thin?" Matthew inquires, "We don't even build boats out of stuff this thin!"

"A group on a budget," Louise shrugs, "They must have built this themselves."

"It's not bad if you think about it," Alois nods approvingly, "Think about it, a group of people that didn't get anything handed to them built this themselves as the Beets threatened them every day!"

"Yeah, it is impressive," Louise agrees, "Just not anything I'd ever go for."

"At least the roof looks pretty solid," Matthew notes, "There are some supports that I can see that are holding that up too. Not to mention it withstood the explosion that made this crater."

Rolling her eyes, Louise fires back, "Yeah, yeah, I get it. It works. I was just saying that I wouldn't want to live here."

"Me either," Matthew agrees with a chuckle, "My biggest issue is with the occupants though."

"You and me both," Louise nods.

"Enough talking," Alois grunts as he begins slowly bending some of the metal away from their hole, "Let's get in there."

Without another word, Matthew and Louise help Alois to rip into the exposed Fulcrum bunker. They work as slowly as they can in order to make as little noise as possible. As they bend and cut through the steel, Matthew can't help but notice that the sky above them is growing brighter and the shining stars are growing duller.

A half-hour passes, and Matthew stops to quietly announce, "I think that's it."

Alois examines the hole that he and the others had made before he volunteers, "I'll head in first."

Matthew considers objecting but he can see that Alois is intent on making sure that the coast was clear for the others. Alois quickly examines the small hole that they had made. A second passes and he nods approvingly before he starts working his way through it.

"Well, if Alois fit, then any of us can fit," Louise notes as she and Matthew watch the broad-shouldered man work his way to the ground from the hole.

"You want to go next?" Matthew asks Louise as Alois drops to the ground from the shelf that is butted up against the wall with the hole.

Without responding, Louise stoops down and begins crawling through the hole after her brother. Matthew thought it was strange that she didn't say anything, but he decided that he wouldn't let it bother him.

Rather than watch Louise crawl into the bunker, Matthew decides to turn around and examine his surroundings over the rim of the crater. Sure enough, the sun appears to be awakening and its light is beginning to illuminate the sad state of the Bulwark below.

Even in the faint lighting, Matthew can see the devastation all around. Small fires are still burning in every direction. Additionally, the blackened remains of that which had already burned stand like stubborn shadows that refuse to dissipate despite the presence of light. Shaking his head, Matthew notices a hollow feeling that forms at the base of his chest. The feeling makes him briefly wonder if things are just as bad off for everyone else on the planet. His lip quivers as he briefly imagines how this could be what the whole planet might look like if this war continued too much longer.

"You coming?" Louise asks after several moments.

Snapping back to reality and away from his thoughts, Matthew looks through the hole at Louise's expectant face.

"Sorry, I was making sure we were alone," Matthew apologizes before he clumsily makes his way through the hole.

"Did you see anything of note?" Louise requests.

"Nope," Matthew shakes his head once he is through. From the top shelf that he is now on, Matthew then works his way down like he is on a ladder. With his feet firmly on the ground, he frowns, "It looks terrible out there."

"What did you expect?" Louise shrugs dismissively before she turns around, "It's a war."

Matthew briefly wonders if he should ask Louise what was suddenly bothering her, but he decides against it. Instead, he turns to Alois who has his ear pressed against the sole door leading into the storage room that they are in, and asks, "Hear anything?"

Shaking his head slightly, Alois answers, "Nothing. It sounds like there is another room beyond this door. The people that were in it left as Louise snuck in."

"So, we're clear then?" Matthew requests.

"It appears so."

"Then why are we hesitating?"

"Caution is required if we're going to make it through this war."

"And taking forever is going to kill us," Matthew retorts, "If you and Louise don't want to keep going then I can."

"I can't let you do that," Alois frowns as he pulls away from the door, "I need to protect you."

"I think it might be our best course of action though," Matthew assures him, "One person would stand out less than three anyways. I think this might be our best bet."

"We can go in there just as easily as you can," Louise points out.

"No, you can't," Matthew shakes his head, "I'm the only one of us who has actually seen the inside of this place. When I told them I didn't want in, I got a glimpse of everything in here. I'm the best person for the job. Besides, I was planning on being the only one of us to sneak in here anyways."

"If this was your plan all along, then why did you have us all come down here?" Louise queries.

"In case things took a turn for the worse," Matthew answers, "If anything bad happens, you two can storm through the bunker and save me."

"But won't the people in there recognize you?" Louise asks worriedly.

"I'll try to hide my face as much as I can," Matthew shrugs as he tugs on the mud-soaked collar of the Fulcrum jacket that he had stolen earlier that night. Matthew resists the urge to shudder as he remembers why the jacket was wet and how close he had been to dying.

"Once you secure the girl, get out as

soon as you can," Alois advises, "Don't press your luck. We don't know how tight of security they have in there."

Before Matthew can respond to Alois, Louise quickly orders, "And stay safe…"

Matthew's eyes narrow slightly at Louise when he sees that she is resisting the urge to say something else. Spinning on his heels, Matthew opts to not press her to say anything else. He drops his pack and puts on his stolen hat. Looking at his outfit, he puts down the fear that his disguise wasn't good enough. He looked just like all the other Fulcrum people. Matthew takes a steadying breath and then nods to Alois who eases the door open just far enough for Matthew to squeeze out.

Looking around, Matthew thinks, *I'm on my own now… I can't mess anything up now or the twins won't ever trust me to do something like this on my own again.* As he scans the area, Matthew suddenly realizes that the lights in the room are on even though no one is in the room. Chuckling, Matthew wonders why James, the man in charge, allowed everyone to waste power and lights down here and not on the surface where it mattered. He had made turning on his flashlight sound like such an issue when he was training Matthew.

Returning his thoughts to the task at hand, Matthew begins walking ever so slowly through what he assumes is another storage room. As he walks, the glint of stainless steel catches his eye. Turning toward the object, he quickly sees that it is inside of a small bag that is situated on top of a cluttered desk.

Stopping dead in his tracks, Matthew rakes his brain for why the bag is so familiar to him and the realization causes the blood to drain from his face.

That's Marie's bag! Matthew notes as he makes his way over to it. This same bad came with all of the other medical supplies that he had given to Marie when he got back to the trench line with the gifts from Wyndover. He chuckles as he realizes that the presence of the bag should be a relief—if it was here, then Marie was too.

"I wonder if she might even come in here if I wait long enough..." Matthew whispers to himself as he casually thumbs through the contents of the bag.

Suddenly remembering the crunch for time, Matthew opens the bag up further and he purposely searches for some items to add an extra layer to his disguise. Finding a first aid symbol with a Velcro back, he hurriedly

471

attaches it to his shoulder. Delving deeper, he picks out a few of the larger medical tools and sticks them in his pocket in a way that ensures that they stick out. Hoping that these additions would make him look like he was some sort of medic, Matthew picks up the bag, fills it with the various items on the desk that he can squeeze into it, and he makes for the door that should lead into the rest of the bunker.

This is it, let's hope I can pull this off… Matthew thinks as he swings the door open.

"Woah watch it!" a man snaps as they shove on the other side of the door.

The door smacks into Matthew's forehead as it swings into him and he stumbles into the doorframe. Reaching up to his head, Matthew groans, "Ow…"

"Who do you think you are any—" the man that had slammed the door starts before he sees Matthew.

Matthew briefly wonders if his ruse is up when the man examines his face and outfit and their eyes go wide. He is about to say something that he hopes might save his cover, but the man starts talking again.

"Oh, sorry doc!" the man exclaims, "I thought you were one of the Mud Pups we let in… You're bleeding pretty bad—I'll go get the medic."

"Can you take me to her instead?" Matthew requests, hoping to get a better idea of the bunker's layout this way.

"I don't think so, you're not looking too hot…" the man shakes his head, "Why don't you take a seat and I'll be back as soon as I find the nurse lady."

Matthew is about to argue and tell the man that he had to be sure that he found the right nurse, but the throbbing in his head suddenly gets the best of him. Reaching up to his forehead, he feels the swollen bump that is firm to the touch. Not only is the lump firm, but, Matthew discovers, it's incredibly tender too. Flinching as he groans in pain, Matthew mutters, "Thanks,"

Spinning on his heels, the man starts down the hallway that they are in. Before he turns the corner to slip out of sight, he calls back, "I'll be right back, sorry for this!"

"Well, maybe this will be a bit easier than I expected," Matthew chuckles when he sees that he is alone once more. Pulling his hand away from his forehead, Matthew notes the copious amount of blood and he wonders just how bad he had been hit. As he wonders, a drip of blood works its way into his eye.

Wincing at the new stinging sensation, Matthew rubs his eye until it eases up slightly and he resolves to keep his eye shut. Frowning, he mutters, "I guess it was a lot worse than I thought."

The door in front of Matthew creaks open and Louise's head peeks through. She looks like she is about to charge through when her eyes settle on Matthew. The concerned look on her face melts away for a moment but quickly returns when her eyes settle on Matthew's forehead. Frowning, she asks, "Hey, is everything good? Is everything under control?"

"Yeah, they're bringing Marie to me," Matthew answers with a chuckle.

"Was that part of your plan?" Louise asks as she nods toward his head.

"Not at all," Matthew admits, "But it seems to have worked out pretty well."

"Indeed," Louise nods. She watches Matthew for a moment before she laughs, "Looks like you're the one that got hurt yet again."

"Just my luck," Matthew nods slightly. The action makes his head throb and he wonders once again how bad he had been hit.

"Just don't get any more hurt," Louise

requests, "And try to not make any more noise."

"Yeah, yeah," Matthew groans, "Now get back to our hole before someone sees you."

Louise looks somewhat offended at first, but the look passes, and she slips her head back out of sight without another word.

"He was just over here," Matthew hears the voice of the man that hit him say from down the hall.

"As I told you, I'm the only doctor here," Marie's familiar voice answers the man.

"He must be new then," the man says, "Because he's definitely a medic or something. He had the red and white plus thing on his shoulder like yours and he had some medical gear too."

"You didn't recognize him?" Marie asks, her voice a lot closer now.

"Umm, I don't know. I didn't look that closely."

"But you noticed that his forehead was bleeding?"

"Yeah, there was a lot of blood."

Marie rounds the corner and her eyes lock onto Matthew who is still sitting on the floor with his back against the wall. He looks back at her and hopes that she recognizes him.

Marie's face doesn't seem to register any signs of recognition as she races toward Matthew. Instead, she seems a lot more interested in simply rendering aid to someone in need.

"It looks like you'll need stitches for sure," Marie mutters, seemingly to herself as she examines Matthew's wound.

"Yeah, I got him pretty good with the door when he was using it," the man admits sheepishly as he stands awkwardly above Matthew and Marie.

"Indeed," Marie breathes as she focuses on a small pack of medical supplies that she had brought. She sighs when she seemingly fails to find what she had been looking for and then her eyes lock onto the bag that is still in one of Matthew's hands. Her eyebrows raise in surprise and she hesitantly asks Matthew, "And where did you find this?"

"He had it with him when he came through the door," the man reports before Matthew can say anything.

"Well, that's interesting because it's mine," Marie snaps, "A friend of mine gave it to me."

"Wait, so this guy was stealing?" the

man above Matthew demands, his voice growing louder as he spoke.

Before the man can say anything else, Matthew snatches a knife from Marie's bag. In one swift movement, he leaps to his feet and out of Marie's reach. As he jumps, he jabs his knife up the man's ribcage. Not wanting to sound the alarm, he covers the man's mouth with his other hand. The man looks at Matthew with a look of complete shock and he tries to let out a cry, but Matthew's grip is too strong.

Matthew closes his eyes as he realizes just how good he was getting at killing people in hand to hand combat. Grimacing, he jerks the blade inside the man to one side and then the other.

The man groans loudly through Matthew's hand on the first jerk, but he falls silent in time with the second. Now still, the man goes limp in Matthew's arms.

Opening his eyes, Matthew takes an unsteady breath and he lets gravity do its thing with the man's body. Wishing that he didn't have to do what he did, Matthew pushes down the urge to cry.

He had killed again.

Worse yet, it didn't feel as heart-wrenching this time around.

He was becoming like the twins.

"Drop the knife," Marie's voice warns from behind Matthew.

"Marie, it's me," Matthew responds as he tosses the blade away from himself with a sense of disgust. Raising his arms, he asks, "Can I turn around?"

Marie lets out a confused breath before she says, "Me? Me who? ...M—Matthew?"

"That's me," Matthew nods as he turns. He can't help but chuckle when he sees Marie holding one of her own stainless steel surgery knives like the weapon that Matthew now knew they were.

"You..." Marie trails off as she looks down at the body before her. A few brief moments pass before she tries once more, "Y—you just killed a man... In cold blood no less!"

"If I didn't, then neither of us would have much time left," Matthew assures her. Nodding toward the door that he had come through not too long ago, Matthew instructs, "Let's get out of here."

"That's a storage room," Marie tells Matthew with a chuckle.

"I know, but my friends and I dug through the room after that."

"You dug through?"

"Yeah, now let's get going!"

"What about him?" Marie asks as she points at the bloodied dead man.

Matthew looks at the body and he notices the blood on his own hand. Matthew holds his hand at a distance as he briefly wonders what to do with the blood on it. Then, seemingly without thinking, he stoops down and uses the dead man's clothes as a rag.

"Matthew?" Marie asks hesitantly.

Standing, Matthew turns to her, "Yeah?"

"Are you… alright?"

"Nope," Matthew answers honestly, "We can talk about it when we're out of this terrible place."

Harborage

The Battle for Allegra

Episode Eight

Chapter One

The Bulwark, Allegra

"Come on, it's almost daybreak," Alois urges as he drags Matthew out of the hole that they had made in the Fulcrum's bunker.

"We're going to have to run if we're going to make it to the nearest trench," Louise points out as she scans the horizon which is awash in gentle shades of orange and red.

Matthew stares at the western horizon with the others and a feeling of foreboding causes his knees to quiver slightly. Wary of the need to maintain a strong face, Matthew casts a sidelong view at his companions and he sees that none of them had noticed his tremor. Clearing his throat, Matthew announces, "Our best bet is to get to the trenches to the north. From there, we should—"

"Matthew, you're bleeding again," Marie interrupts. She quickly glances down at her bag of medical supplies that she had insisted on bringing with her.

Matthew shakes his head at Marie indicating that she shouldn't stop now to patch him up again.

"And it doesn't look good," Louise adds worriedly as she looks at Matthew's forehead.

"I'll be fine," Matthew assures the women as he wipes away a rivulet of blood that had sprung through the bandage that Marie had hastily put on his forehead. The tiny stream had threatened to slip into Matthew's eye, and he wasn't about to let that happen again. As he saw it, the stinging of blood in his eye one time was more than enough for a lifetime.

"I'm going to have to stitch that up sooner rather than later," Marie mutters, seemingly to herself.

"We can do it when we get back to Sanctuary," Matthew tells her. Nodding to the others, he gets back to telling them the original plan, "We'll have to make a run to the trenches to the north. Once we get there, we'll have to lose any tail that we might get, so we'll be taking the long way round to get back home."

"Copy," the twins say in unison as they make their way northward.

Marie and Matthew follow the twins and after a few steps, Marie asks, "What's 'Sanctuary?'"

"Our new home base," Matthew answers. He considers leaving it at that, but for Marie's sake, he adds, "You can go back to your underground hospital if you so please though."

Laughing, Louise pipes in, "Yeah, we didn't kidnap you from your kidnapers just to use you."

"Well, we will need to use your skills a little bit," Matthew says as he motions at his bloodied forehead. As he points he sees that his blood is also seeping through the bandages on his arm where Tony had slashed him as well.

"Nope, just you will," Louise declares without looking at Matthew, "You're the only one who's hurt."

"I never thought that I would be the careful one in a group," Alois boasts with a chuckle as he continues surging ahead in a crouching sprint.

"I think Matthew just missed me. He knew he couldn't get along without me." Marie quips, clearly picking up on the twins' energy. She casts a teasing look at Matthew, and she winks at him when he gives her an exasperated look in return.

"We're about there," Alois announces as he slows slightly.

Looking ahead, Matthew can now see the trench that he and the others had been running through the mud for. Glancing behind him, Matthew notes that he can't even see the crater that he had been in just a few minutes ago. As he turns back to the trench, Matthew sees the unmistakable gleam of the sun as it peeks its shimmering face above the mountains to the west.

"Daybreak!" Matthew exclaims, warning his team of the impending doom that may befall them if they stayed out in the open.

Why couldn't the mountains just hide the sun a little bit longer? We're doing all of this to protect this mountain range from the Beets and yet they stand idly. Matthew bitterly thinks as he wishes that the peaks were just a little bit higher. He knew that the mountains were lifeless and couldn't have a care in the world, but he can't help but feel like they are still doing him an injustice.

On a whim, Matthew then looks to the east toward his enemies, and the sight that greeted him cause both his heart and brain to seemingly shut off for a moment.

To the east, the Beets have been dug in for quite some time. Their countless dens and hives dot the great valley floor. Despite the Beets' initial rapid offensive, they had since stopped at the foot of the mountains at what was now the Bulwark. Since the Beets had stopped, countless raids from adventurous soldiers like the Toaz had been bringing back war trophies to the trenches. Why the Beets were waiting, Matthew didn't know. Why the Coalition didn't mount an offensive, Matthew was too afraid to ask.

"Matthew!" Louise calls out, snapping Matthew from his trance.

"Look…" Matthew moans as he points to the east.

Louise follows his stare and she nods, "Yeah, we need to go. Now."

It's too late… Matthew thinks as he shakes his head. Feeling doomed, he slowly blinks before he runs after the others who are sprinting as best they can through the mud.

To the east, the land is already awash

with the bright Allegrian sun. Small specks that Matthew can barely spot move to-and-fro and Matthew knows that they represent the Beets.

"They haven't started shooting yet!" Louise calls out excitedly as they close the distance between them and the security of the trench line ahead of them.

"Maybe they don't see us?" Marie offers.

Or they're just lining up their shots, Matthew counters Marie in his mind. He hated to admit it, but he knew they wouldn't make it to the trenches without the Beets seeing them.

Matthew takes three more steps when the first crack sounds from somewhere behind him. Matthew doesn't need to turn; he knew what it was.

The Beet snipers had seen him.

"Run!" Alois shouts as he seemingly summons the ability to run even faster than he had been a moment later.

Looking ahead, Matthew watches as Alois dives headlong into the trench that he and the others had been running toward. A moment later, Louise slides in after him.

Looking to Marie who is a few strides ahead of him, Matthew briefly wonders if one of them wasn't going to make it.

Another sniper bolt streaks through the

area between Matthew and Marie and he squints against its brightness. The bolt lets out a thunderous crack and then disappears.

Knowing that his luck was likely about to run out, Matthew scans the ground before him for some semblance of cover. Although he was very close to the trench where Louise and Alois are, Matthew isn't sure if he can make it.

"It looks like only one of them sees you!" Louise calls from the trench.

Watching where he had last seen Louise, Matthew sees her stick her head out just far enough to watch Marie and Matthew.

"Come on, Matthew, we're almost there!" Marie assures him just loud enough for Matthew to hear over the ringing in his ears from the sniper's shot.

Another sniper bolt illuminates the area between Marie and Louise.

"Looks like this one can hardly aim," Louise notes as she looks eastward in a needless effort to spot the threat. A second passes and she turns back to assure her friends, "You two will be fine!"

Tripping, Matthew falls face-first into the mud. Grunting, he picks himself up out of it and he shakes his head. As he shakes the mud off himself, he bitterly thinks, *Of course, I'm the one who falls. Out of anyone, it's always me.*

"Matthew!" Louise calls out.

Looking up, Matthew can see that Louise is trying to get over the trench to come to his aid, but something is holding her back. A moment later, Matthew watches as Marie drops to the safety of the trench's walls.

"You can still make it!" Louise assures Matthew, "Come on!"

Two additional sniper bolts flash through the air and one of them burns into the ground near Matthew's head.

"If you stay there, you'll die," Alois warns as his head joins his sister's. Now that Alois is within view, Matthew can see that he is holding his sister back with one of his arms.

"If I try to make it there, I'll die too," Matthew mutters to himself as he slips around in the mud, struggling to find something solid enough to push himself up on.

Another sniper bolt snaps somewhere behind Matthew, but he doesn't dare to look.

Finally finding something hard, Matthew kicks off from it. Propelled ahead by the action, he slithers his way through the mud to a nearby chunk of metal. This small bastion is sticking out about a meter higher than the mire, which Matthew decides is ample enough to buy him some time. Once he is behind it, Matthew allows himself an unsteady breath of relief.

He was safe, for now at least.

With his back pressed against his metal barricade, Matthew shudders every time a sniper bolt pops. Waiting several moments, he reasons that there are now five snipers firing on his position.

"Matthew, stay there!" Louise orders, "We'll find some way to get you out of there!"

Matthew looks to his right where Louise appears to be nearly hysterical with worry. He then glances over to Alois who is wearing a much more somber look.

Matthew knew what that look meant; he was on his own.

Sighing, Matthew sizes up the remaining distance between him and the trench where his team is waiting. Squinting, he judges the distance to be about five meters. He knows that this is too far for him to be guaranteed an escape without being shot in the process.

"What if I just try waiting them out?" Matthew asks his friends between the crashing of the sniper's fire.

"I don't know if they'll be stopping any time soon," Alois warns, "Not until nightfall, at least."

"And we need to get as far away as we can from the Fulcrum bunker before they find the man you killed," Marie warns.

As if Marie's words sounded the alarm, Matthew hears several shouts emanating from somewhere on his left. The people sound very angry and he can only assume that they were coming from the crater that he and the others had left. The Fulcrum people must have found the body and then discovered Matthew's entry point as they tried to find the perpetrator.

"You just had to say it," Matthew whispers to himself as he smacks the back of his head against his cover in disdain. The action causes a renewed throbbing in his head and Matthew winces as he regrets the action.

To his left, just over the noise of the weapons fire, Matthew hears a concerned voice call out, "We can't start looking for them now, James, it's daybreak! Don't you hear the snipers?"

"If we wait, then we might never find them," James's familiar voice snaps in return.

"But it isn't safe!" the first voice warns.

"If the snipers are shooting so close to us then we can be sure that the people who did this are still nearby."

"We can always track them down later!

We found how they got in and we can make the necessary repairs!"

"We will make the repairs. However, we'll make them *after* we take care of the real problem."

"But what if they already got away? We don't know if we'll even be able to find them!"

"These tracks are new, if we don't head out now then they might get away. That being said, I know that they're still close enough to catch, judging by these tracks… We have to do this. We have to set an example for everyone to see."

"Everyone here already knows not to mess with us!"

"Tell that to Khaing,"

"It was probably just some thief," the first voice begs, "Please, we don't need to lose anyone else today."

"No, we're finding the people who did this now! Get the others, we're going hunting."

Matthew takes an unsteady breath as he considers everything that he had just overheard. Fortunately, James and the other man had been speaking loudly enough that Matthew could hear them over the gunfire that was keeping him pinned down.

I wonder if James suspects me…

Matthew wonders as he looks over toward the crater where he can only assume James is still fuming. Fortunately for Matthew, the crater isn't in view which means that James can't see him. His lips quiver in worry and Matthew's thoughts progress, *If they start hunting for me then there's no way I'll be able to get away. There's no knowing how long they'll try to hunt me down. And what would they do to me if they did find me!? At least he can't see me quite yet…*

"Matthew, we found this!" Louise calls out from her trench. Evidently, she hadn't heard James and his crony conspiring.

Matthew shushes Louise loudly and she gives him a quizzical look as she cocks her head slightly. Matthew glances behind himself to make sure that no one can see him still and he tells her, "The Fulcrum guys are on to us. They're sending out a hunting party to find us."

"If we're lucky, then the Beets might shoot at them instead of us," Alois points out, "You could use that as your chance to make a run for it."

"And how long would I be running?" Matthew questions. He had already considered the opportunity to use James's search party as a distraction, but the thought left him feeling rather sick. What kind of man would use someone else's life as a sacrifice to save his own?

"Just to the trench," Alois answers simply. He had clearly overlooked Matthew's real question.

Trying to reiterate himself, Matthew explains, "I meant how long will we have to run away from the people they send out to hunt us down? There's no way that they would stop looking for us once they start."

"Ah…" Alois nods, now understanding what Matthew was talking about. Matthew can see that he is about to say something else, but Louise cuts in before he can.

"Don't worry about that, Matthew," Louise assures him, "We're good at losing a tail. They'll never track us down once we get some distance between them and us."

"All I have to do is face certain death to get to you first," Matthew mutters as he looks scornfully at the ground he had to cover. Taking another breath in an attempt to ease his nerves even slightly, Matthew asks his friends, "So, are you saying that I need to wait until the Beets start shooting at the other guys before I make a run for it"

"It sounds like it would be your safest bet," Louise replies before a sniper bolt burns a hole in the ground near her head. She drops back out of sight and Matthew can just hear her say, "Or you could use the thing we found!"

Knowing that time wasn't on his side and that he needed to get moving before the Fulcrum people could get the chance to see him, Matthew asks, "What did you find?"

"Something you can use as a shield," Louise's voice sounds in reply. There is a small sound of movement where she is followed by voices that Matthew can't make out over the snipers' barrage.

Alois suddenly peeks out from the trench and he waits a moment for Matthew to lock eyes with him. Once he is content that he has Matthew's attention, Alois ducks down.

That was weird, what was that all about? Matthew thinks as he continues looking at his friends' trench.

"The tracks lead north!" James's voice sounds as he summons his compatriots to hunt down Matthew and his friends.

"You sure about this, boss man?" someone asks worriedly.

"With the Beets out and about we shouldn't be walking up here," another warns.

"We have to find the people that killed Khaing," James answers resolutely.

Wary of the impending doom, Matthew looks back to where he had last seen Alois. He can't help but wonder and worry about why Alois hadn't come back up.

"Sanchez!" a fourth person cries out from the crater on Matthew's left.

"Leave him, he's gone!" James orders, "Don't stop moving or you'll be hit too!"

"Don't stop moving?" Matthew whispers to himself as James's words seemingly echo in his mind. Something about James's delivery made the order seem even more important. Glancing over at the trench once more, Matthew repeats himself, "Don't stop moving…"

"Come on!" James shouts to his team. By the way that their voice carries, Matthew knows that they are now facing his direction and drawing closer.

Rising to his feet, Matthew lines up to run directly to the trench where his team is waiting. He sinks slightly in the mud, but the earth around the metal barricade is a lot more firm than that of the area surrounding him. Taking a deep breath, Matthew tells himself, "Don't stop moving."

As soon as the words leave his mouth, Matthew charges forward with reckless abandon. Within just a few steps and seemingly half as many seconds, Matthew is inside of the trench laying in a puddle of mud.

"Matthew's here!" Marie calls out from just a few paces away from him.

Confused why Marie was shouting, Matthew follows her gaze to the twins. As near as Matthew can tell, the twins are engaging some sort of hostile that is around the corner of one of the trenches that leads into their own.

"About time," Alois grunts before he lets off a few wild shots and begins backing away from the bend in the trench.

"We've got gassers, so that should help to cover our tracks," Louise acknowledges before she scampers over to Matthew and Marie.

Knowing that the presence of gassers meant that their tracks would be completely trampled, Matthew briefly wonders what that would mean for the twins' plan. Before he has the chance to ask what changes might take place, Alois's booming voice sounds.

"Move!" Alois demands as he points to the east, away from where the Fulcrum people would be and where the gassers are coming from. Still pointing, Alois instructs, "That way! Come on, we don't have a lot of time!"

"Run," Louise tells Matthew and Marie, "Alois and I will be right behind you."

"Where are we running to?" Marie asks.

"Head northeast to the frontlines," Louise instructs, "That should throw off any tails pretty well. They won't suspect that we are actually their neighbors."

"Got it," Marie nods. Without another word, she rises to her feet and Matthew chases after her.

Behind them, the occasional shout and pop of weapons fire assures them that the twins are still following them. Matthew isn't certain how far away the frontmost trenches are. That being said, he can't help but assume that the Fulcrum chose to set up camp as far away from the danger as possible. They clearly had no interest in the war that they were in. There was no way that James would put his neck on the line for anything but the hope for a quick profit. Dying on the front, Matthew knew, wasn't too profitable.

"Do you know the way?" Matthew asks Marie as he chases after her. He is confident that she did, but he didn't want to risk taking any wrong turns.

"Yep," Marie answers, confirming Matthew's hunch.

"How much further is it?" Matthew asks, "Because I don't know how much running I have left in me."

Matthew reaches up to his forehead once again to wipe away a stream of blood that is threatening to get into his eye. As he does so, he sees that his bandaged arm is not doing too hot. The bandage is hanging loosely and the entire area is covered in blood and filth from at least one of his recent falls. Despite this, Matthew continues running after Marie because he is all too aware of the threat that lay behind him.

Another few minutes pass before Matthew and Marie are stopped by a loud shout from behind them, "Wait up!"

"I guess this is as far as we needed to go," Marie nods as she slows to a stop. Looking to Matthew, her eyes fill with a look of concern and she asks, "Can I take care of you now?"

"Please," Matthew groans. Nodding, he adds, "I think we should have a minute or two before the twins reach us."

"So, I can't do much…" Marie frowns as she reexamines his wounds.

"When we've lost our tail then you can fix me up right," Matthew reminds her,

"Otherwise there's no point because we'd be dead."

"I know the risks," Marie scolds, "But you're not going to be in good enough shape to run if you keep bleeding like this."

"You're telling me," Matthew says before he offers her a weak chuckle. All of the blood loss over the last few hours had left him feeling quite lightheaded. Part of him wonders if he can keep running like this at all. As he worries, Matthew quickly realizes that he must be pale and that the filth on his face is covering it.

Frowning, Marie quickly says, "I'm going to rinse your arm off and fix your bandage. Hopefully, that will slow the bleeding enough that you won't pass out on me."

No promises there, Matthew thinks as he watches Marie pull out a bottle of water. As he watches her patch him up, he briefly wonders how his injured foot is looking. Up until now, he hadn't noticed its aching. Now that he had stopped, all of the wonderful pain-numbing adrenaline is beginning to wear off.

Marie carefully washes Matthew's cut and the surrounding flesh with her water and a gloved hand. As she works to get him fixed up, she starts talking, pausing every so often as she does her thing, "Thanks to all that bleeding you probably cleared everything out of that cut... I'll have to poke around in there once we get somewhere clean though... just to be sure. Whoever wrapped this bandage did a good job... not great, but good... That looks like that should do!"

Matthew moves his arm around and he notices how much better this bandage job felt than the one that Louise had done. Everything feels a lot more secure this time around, which Matthew reasons must be a good sign. Smiling, Matthew offers Marie an appreciative nod and he is about to thank her when a sudden intruder interrupts them.

Barely winded from the run, Louise nods to Matthew and Marie before she tells them her plan, "Alright, you two are going to make your way to the front on your own. Once you get there, work your way south. Try to walk in each other's footprints and, better yet, don't leave any in the first place. Alois and I are going to leave some obvious trails to throw off anyone who might be able to track us."

The sloshing and slapping sound of additional steps precedes Alois who doesn't waste a moment before he orders, "Move! We don't know how far away your Fulcrum friends are."

"We'll cover your tracks a short way so they can't find you," Louise tells Matthew and Marie.

"Got it," Matthew nods as he starts to turn.

Stopping him, Louise anxiously looks around for a moment before she tells Matthew, "Once you go south a ways and you're sure that you don't have a tail, just wait. Wait for as long as you can. Be prepared to shoot anyone who looks like a hostile too. Kill whatever gassers you find along the way as well, just to make it seem like you're doing your job. Once you're done waiting, get back to our little safe harbor. We'll meet you guys there sooner or later."

"How long is that?" Matthew asks worriedly. He never thought he would have to be concerned about the twins' safety, but he was worrying now. They were risking their necks for him once again. Here Matthew was, on the other hand, completely helpless.

"We'll know when you do," Alois shrugs, "Losing a tail isn't a direct science."

Frowning, Louise ventures a guess, "I'd assume that we should be back there within four hours or so."

"Don't get shot without us," Alois tells

Matthew as he hides a cruel grin.

"Ha ha," Matthew rolls his eyes.

"Get moving, we probably don't have a lot of time," Louise tells Matthew.

Leading Matthew away by the hand, Marie urges, "Come on,"

Chapter Two

The Bulwark, Allegra

Matthew peeks over the lip of the trench that he and Marie are holed up in. They had been waiting for what felt like hours, but in reality, had only been about forty-five minutes. Thanks to how far south he and Marie had gone, Matthew can't even see the signs of a recent struggle here. There were plenty of craters from artillery strikes, sure, but not a whole lot beyond that.

"You thinking it's as eerie as I do?" Marie asks after a few beats.

"Yeah," Matthew nods as he climbs down the trench's high wall.

"Think we've waited long enough to go to your bunker?" Marie inquires.

Frowning, Matthew looks up and down the desolate trench. In addition to being nearly empty, the trenches this far south are a lot drier too. All in all, Matthew felt obliged to think of them as nice, at least in comparison to the swampy hellhole that he had come from.

The only thing that Matthew can think of that had actually gone his way since he split off from the twins was that there hadn't been any gassers. There were quite a few dead gassers, sure, but none that were still alive and kicking. Matthew had reasoned that the gassers had been lured north by the sounds of battle and vacated the south where seemingly no one is.

"Matthew?" Marie presses.

"The twins said wait as long as we can," Matthew shakes his head, "So we're waiting."

"But I can't treat you here," Marie reminds him yet again. She had been telling Matthew how much he needed some real medical attention for a while now, but he had waved her off every time.

"I'm fine," Matthew assures her. In reality, he knew that he was anything but fine, but he didn't want her worrying about him. All he needed now was to stay out of the twins' hair as long as he could, so he didn't mess up their efforts to lose their tail.

Sighing, Matthew takes a seat in a hole that he had carved out of the wall of the trench that he is in. Thanks to his severe blood loss he found it difficult to remain standing for long periods of time now. Even the effort of scaling the short ladder that he had just gone up had left him winded and dizzy. Blinking several times, Matthew waits for his world to fall back into focus.

"You're not fine," Marie argues, "I know you aren't."

"Yeah, but we can't head back just yet," Matthew grunts as he crosses his arms. Just about nothing that Marie could say would change his mind about heading back early at this point. He wasn't about to get talked into risking anyone else's wellbeing for his own.

"Eat something at least," Marie requests as she picks a few packages out of her bag of medical supplies. Offering the handful of packages to Matthew, she apologizes, "It's not much, but this should help at least a little bit."

"No, it's alright," Matthew shakes his head as he begins digging into his bag, "I've got some of my own food."

"Oh," Marie breathes as she slowly tucks her offerings back into her bag.

Seeing Marie's reaction, Matthew quickly offers, "Are you hungry? I've got plenty of stuff here, more than enough for both of us."

"Please," Marie weakly begs.

"Did... did they not give you anything to eat?" Matthew hesitantly asks as he hands some of his ration pouches to her.

"They said I had to wait for breakfast like everyone else," Marie frowns. Her lip quivers and a lone tear rolls down her face.

"Hey, hey, I'm sorry," Matthew promptly apologizes as he rises to his feet and wraps his arms around Marie in a protective hug. Once he is holding Marie, he momentarily freezes up and he wonders what to do from there. His first move felt so instinctual and natural and now he just felt awkward.

"Thank you," Marie whimpers once more before she hugs Matthew back, "I heard them talking…"

"Heard them talking about what?" Matthew hears himself asking as he continues hugging Marie. He can't help but begin loathing himself for putting himself in this awkward situation, but he can't help but think that he's helping.

"They weren't going to let me go after I helped all their people," Marie answers. As she tries to continue, her words are interrupted with weak sobs, "Th—they said they were going t—to kill me. I—I didn't want to let on that I knew though. I was ho—hoping… no, I was praying tha—that someone would come along and save me."

"And that we did," Matthew nods slowly as he wonders what might be his best course of action to end the prolonged hug.

505

"Thank you," Marie says in a near whisper as she pulls Matthew even tighter.

Now what do I do? Matthew asks himself as he looks down to Marie who is shuddering slightly with silent sobs. Looking around as best he can without running the risk of Marie catching on that he is doing so; Matthew hopes to see some sort of threat that might give him an excuse. Seeing none, he thinks, *So, I guess I'm just going to stand here then…*

As soon as he resigns himself to his fate, Matthew's stomach growls loudly.

Well, that's not exactly subtle, Matthew thinks as he suppresses the urge to chuckle.

Looking up to Matthew's face, Marie lets out a short laugh before she pulls away from him and sheepishly says, "You're right, we should eat now."

"Sorry, I didn't mean to have my stomach growl like that," Matthew assures her. This wasn't a lie, but he didn't want to reveal the full truth that he was happy that his stomach had ended the hug.

"No, no, that's what I needed," Marie assures him as she dries her tears with the palm of her hand. Looking down at her other hand, Marie examines the food that Matthew had given her.

"If you don't want any of that, I have other stuff too," Matthew quickly offers when Marie doesn't tear into the meal immediately.

"No, it's fine, it's just…" Marie trails off as she looks afar off. Several moments pass and Marie takes a deep breath. Turning back to Matthew, she finally says, "I'm just not cut out for this."

"I don't think anyone is cut out for war," Matthew chuckles as he takes a seat once again because of his lightheadedness. Now sitting, he quickly sips on some water in an attempt to cut through the fog in his head.

"Well, of course, but I'm talking about *all* of this."

"All of what?"

"Everything about the war. I'm sick and tired of patching people up every day because of the fighting. I'm tired of having my own life threatened without going over the top. I'm tired of being… scared."

Chuckling, Matthew tries to crack a joke, "Hey, it's not like I'm trying to get hurt every day!"

Frowning, Marie examines Matthew and her expression softens when she realizes that he was trying to lift her spirits. Sighing, Marie shakes her head, "I'm talking about everyone as a whole… I've helped so many people, and still… so many die. I'm just not cut out for this."

"As you've said."

"Well, it's true,"

"So is what I've said, no one is made for waging war."

"Well, you're adapting to it nicely," Marie points out sharply.

Wincing at her words, Matthew's lip quivers. His eyes drop to his packaged meal and he opens it clumsily before he starts eating it cold. He had hoped that he was just being overly suspicious of himself and how well he felt like he was doing, but Marie's observation sent the fact home.

Matthew *was* adapting to the war.

Like it or not, Matthew knew that he wasn't going to return home the same man.

After taking a few hesitant bites of his meal, Matthew raises his eyes and he sees that Marie is still staring into his soul. Swallowing, he answers her in a near whisper, "That's what I was afraid of."

"You were afraid of adapting?"

"I was afraid of losing myself in it, yes."

"Aren't you a little young to be worrying about things like this?" Marie chuckles awkwardly.

Matthew can tell that she didn't think that her words were particularly funny, but the chuckle still seemed to work its way out. Her words seem oddly out of place and Matthew begins examining her face to gauge how old she really was. As he does so he realizes, *She's a lot older than I originally thought.*

Marie sniffs and she wipes the remaining tears from her eyes. Straightening out her clothes she then examines Matthew. Frowning slightly, she requests, "Now, before you bleed out on me, let's get somewhere I can actually help you. I don't need to have you die on me too."

Matthew's heart races for a moment as he considers how he should argue, but his efforts quickly amount to nothing. After their conversation, Matthew can't help but realize that he would be doing this for his own sake in addition to Marie's. Unsure of how to voice his thinking, Matthew lamely stammers, "I—well… fine. Let's go."

"Good," Marie nods curtly. She doesn't make a move and Matthew quickly realizes that she is waiting for him to lead the way to Sanctuary since she didn't know where it was.

Standing, Matthew sways slightly and

he momentarily wonders if he can even make it all the way back to Sanctuary. Blinking slowly, Matthew tries to gather his strength. As he takes a deep breath, Matthew feels Marie raise his good arm over her shoulder and he looks over to her.

Nodding, Marie tells him, "You have a team now, you don't have to do everything on your own strength."

Chapter Three

The Bulwark, Allegra

Nearly delirious, Matthew points down another trench as he leads Marie through the last leg of their journey that had gone on for far too long.

He knew he was spent. He knew he was now on his last leg.

"You sure about that?" Marie asks.

Groaning in pain as Marie's words buffet his sensitive eardrums, Matthew nearly stumbles. When Marie keeps him standing upright, he finally answers, "I think so, why?"

"I was going to crack a joke and say we were lost..." Marie starts as she looks over to him in concern, "But that wouldn't be very funny right about now."

"Huh," Matthew grunts as they near their bunker.

"It sure took us a long time to get here," Marie notes as she looks to their surroundings once more.

Ever since Matthew had begun losing his wits from his state of exhaustion, Marie had been working to make sure that they didn't

511

stumble across any hostiles. In addition to that, she constantly checked Matthew's vitals which she assured him were steady.

Matthew knew that steady wasn't great though. Despite her words, Matthew couldn't help but doubt Marie as well. Nothing felt very steady right now. He can feel his heart fluttering as it works overtime to pump what little blood it can get.

But Marie said he was steady. Steady beat the alternatives. However, Matthew could see in Marie's eyes that his worries about his apparent steadiness being bad news was on point. If he stayed like this too much longer, he wouldn't make it.

Marie had offered to take Matthew to her own medical ward, but those hopes were dashed because of Matthew's deteriorating state and the fact that the hospital had been cleared out. Even if the supplies were still there, he didn't have that kind of distance left in his legs to make it. In addition to that, most of Marie's equipment and medicine was meant for the Toaz. That translated to an entirely ineffective means to treat humans.

Taking a shaky breath, Matthew shores up his remaining energy to bolster his resolve. He had to get back to Sanctuary and he knew he had to get there soon. He could feel what he can only assume was his life fading away.

Losing the strength to keep his head up, Matthew lets it drop and he looks down to the ground. His head bounces with just about every movement which causes the throbbing in his head to worsen. Despite this pain, Matthew knew that he would have to deal with it if he was going to make it home.

Would you look at that? Matthew thinks lazily as his eyes lock onto his arm. A wide swath of dried blood extends from his bandage to his hand and fingers. As he watches, thick blood continues oozing ever so slowly down his arm in a weak stream. The blood drips with every step or two and it leaves a quaint breadcrumb trail of sorts that he wonders if he might ever retrace.

"Just stay with me," Marie urges as a hint of excitement seems to sound in her voice.

That means we're on the home stretch, Matthew tells himself.

His heart yearns to look up and take in the humble earthen wall that leads into his home, but he can't. Despite the knowledge that he can't Matthew's heart continues dreaming of seeing it. In many ways, the joyous feeling in his chest that his heart is weakly trying to pump out to the rest of his body reminded him of what it felt like to return to Crail. However, it wasn't like the normal return journeys home. This feeling filled Matthew with a sense of trepidation and awe that only came after long-overdue return trips home. The kind of trips where he was certain that he wouldn't make it. The feeling was reserved for the days where people in his father's crew—his friends—had been killed right beside him as they battled the storms alongside him. Yes, there was the weighing down on his spirits from those killed, but he knew that he had defied the odds and survived. He was going to live another day and he was going to carry the memories of his friends long gone with him.

And with that thought, Matthew's world fades to black.

Chapter Four

The Bulwark, Allegra

Matthew's eyes flutter open and he sees a nondescript concrete ceiling above him. Noting that the ceiling appears to be pristine and feeling the soft mattress pad beneath him, Matthew realizes that he must be back in Sanctuary.

His brow furrows for a moment as he wonders how he might have gotten here, but that's when he hears Alois's familiar voice somewhere in the distance.

The twins must have helped Marie get me in here, Matthew surmises. Taking a deep breath, he gently rolls his head to the side to take in his surroundings and see if he can spot Alois.

Rather than see the rest of the barracks where he had spent the previous night, Matthew is greeted by another scene entirely. Confused, his eyes drift over the various objects in the room.

Matthew makes note of everything as he looks around, *Sink, cabinets, drawers, doctor tools, stainless steel everywhere... Where is this place? They've got more medical equipment in here than we have in my entire village back home!*

Once again, Matthew hears Alois's voice, but he can't make out any of the words.

"I wonder when they'll come check on me," Matthew whispers. He tries to say it louder, but the words won't form in his throat. Letting out a long breath in lieu of a groan, Matthew suddenly realizes just how sore his throat is.

Must be dehydration, Matthew reasons as he takes a tally of all the usual telltale signs of it. Nodding curtly to himself after he confirmed his suspicions, Matthew looks down at his legs and he wonders if he could make the walk to the nearby sink.

As he looks down at his toes, Matthew suddenly laughs as he makes another realization about the room, "The lights are on!"

The sudden outburst makes Matthew's throat feel like it is trying to swallow barbed wire and tears immediately well up in his eyes. Matthew lets out a breathy chuckle as he thinks about how funny it is that he can still cry despite his current need for water.

"I think Matthew's finally away," Matthew hears Marie's muffled voice sound from behind him somewhere.

For one reason or another, Matthew's instincts tell him to play dead and he does just that. He clamps his eyes shut and he returns to laying on his back just in time for Marie to open the door.

"Matthew?" Marie's voice inquisitively summons alongside the faintest sound of a door opening.

A rush of cool air hits Matthew from the door's opening and he feels goosebumps ride their way up his arm. As the cool sensation from the air spreads, Matthew can't help but shiver.

"Yeah," Matthew rasps in response as he drops his act. He still isn't sure why he felt like putting on such a childish ruse, but he had and that was that.

"Ah, water," Marie notes and Matthew hears her hurried steps pass by him and she then begins pumping some water from the sink.

Turning his head over once more, Matthew now takes in the other side of the room where Marie had entered from. She had left the door open and Matthew can now see that he is looking out at the massive room where he had found the dog, Monk.

I guess this room is attached to the room somewhere, Matthew tells himself as he makes a quick mental note.

"Let's sit you up," Marie says from Matthew's other side as one of her arms makes its way under his shoulders.

With Marie's help, Matthew is now sitting up and he briefly wonders if he even needed Marie's aid to do as much. Before another thought can cross his mind, a cup filled to the brim with water is being pressed to his lips.

"Woah, woah, gently now," Marie scolds when Matthew tried sucking more water from the cup than Marie was allowing him, "I don't want you throwing this all up."

Accepting Marie's request, Matthew allows himself to be quenched at Marie's own pace. As he swallows each sip, the cool water that tasted heavily of minerals washes down his throat and soothes its ache.

"Is he up yet?" Alois's voice booms.

"Yeah, why don't you come and see him?" Marie asks teasingly.

Matthew shoots Marie a look as he briefly wonders why she had said that like she did. A moment passes and a brief commotion precedes Alois's response.

"Maybe I will!" Alois fires back as a loud crash of metal echoes through the door.

"He didn't…" Marie mutters as she pulls the cup from Matthew's mouth and sets it down on a bedside table.

Before Matthew has the chance to protest, Alois hobbles into the room with a gleeful grin on his face. A spark in his eyes, Alois looks to Matthew and asks, "How are you feeling?"

"I've been better…" Matthew hesitantly answers as he gives Alois a confused look. He can't help but feel relieved now that talking and breathing didn't make his throat burn. Wondering if it was just a fluke, he considers talking some more just to make sure that the lack of pain was real.

"Me too," Alois tells him as he hobbles a little closer. Pointing to his foot, Alois requests, "Take a look at that! You're not the only one that's getting beat up now."

Looking down at Alois's foot, Matthew sees a thick cast that extends from just above his knee all the way to his toes. He is holding a long stainless-steel bar with a bag attached to it in order to keep his weight off of the injured foot. Matthew's eyes take in the bag and he then sees that a small clear tube is snaking its way to the crook in Alois's elbow where it disappears under a bandage.

"Looks like it hurt," Matthew nods after a beat.

Thoughtfully looking down at his leg, Alois shrugs, "I've had worse. Well, it's great to see you back at harbor, Mudskipper."

"Seems like there isn't enough water for this to be a harbor," Matthew chuckles dryly.

"Yeah, yeah," Alois makes a show of rolling his eyes.

"I told you that you couldn't walk on that for at least another few hours," Marie scolds Alois.

"I'm not walking on it," Alois fires back, "He's just hanging there. It hasn't touched the ground yet!"

Clearly unamused, Marie orders, "Get back to your bed,"

Alois flinches at Marie's tone, but he still protests, "But—"

"Out!" Marie tells him as she points to the door, "Otherwise I'll break that leg again."

"Fine," Alois grunts as his grin sinks into a frown. Casting a fleeting glance at Matthew, he solemnly requests, "Visit me when you get out of here."

"Alois," Marie warns when the large man

hesitates.

Without another word, Alois makes his retreat and he shuts the door behind him for good measure. Upon seeing this, Matthew can't help but laugh. He had never seen Alois act like this.

"What's... what's up with him?" Matthew asks.

"He broke his leg and is hyped up on glucose and painkillers," Marie answers, "He insisted the painkillers weren't helping so I gave him a double dose. Not doing that again."

"Will he be alright?" Matthew asks, still worrying for his friend.

"For sure. They'll wear off soon enough and he'll be back to himself." Marie nods confidently. She looks around for a moment before she says, "This place is amazing, by the way. It's got everything..."

"Yeah," Matthew nods as he looks around with Marie. After a beat, he inquires, "What time is it? How long was I out?"

"A while," Marie frowns.

"How long is a while?" Matthew asks nervously. As much as he hated the idea of it, he didn't like missing out on the war that was going on above him. He knew that he didn't care for the bloodshed, but he couldn't shake the feeling that things would go bad and more people would needlessly die if he wasn't up there fighting.

Marie hesitates for a few moments before she opens her mouth to speak and then stops herself. She makes a nondescript face before she finally answers, "Well, it can take several months before the human body can replace all the blood that you lost."

"I've been out for *months*?" Matthew asks in shock. Although he had no actual sense of how long he had been out he didn't think that it could have possibly been that long.

"No, I was just saying that to get a rise out of you," Marie laughs as she shakes her head. Still chuckling, she tells him, "It's only been about eight hours. It's still daytime, in fact."

"How did I wake up so fast then?" Matthew inquires, fully aware of the fact that things weren't adding up.

"Blood transfusion," Marie replies, "As I said, this bunker has everything."

"So... I have someone else's blood now?" Matthew asks hesitantly.

Shaking her head, Marie answers, "Nope, this stuff is artificial. I just put in a sample of your blood to the machine, loaded up some of the stuff it asked for and that was it! Blood tailor-made for you."

"That's… weird…" Matthew says after a few moments. He didn't have the faintest clue how to respond to that. A few more moments pass and Matthew asks, "So, what happened to Alois? Is Louise alright?"

"He broke his foot because he was being an idiot," Marie shrugs, "And Louise is fine, I can get her if you would like."

"Nah, that's alright," Matthew declines, "I'll be out and about soon anyways… right?"

"Yes,"

"So… how was Alois being an idiot?"

"He climbed a ladder faster than he should have when we were clearing away the dirt from the entrance of the garage. There was some mud on one of the rungs and he fell.

"What garage?"

"I guess it *is* more of a hangar… Regardless, the room outside of this one is a garage. There's a massive garage door at one end. Louise and Alois will be moving your mecha over here as soon as they can."

"The mech's gonna fit? Wow."

"I remind you, the hangar *is* very large."

"I knew it was, I just didn't think it was *that* big."

"Ah,"

"How long until I can get up?"

"You're free to do whatever you like now. I've stitched and patched you up and now all you need to do is be careful for the next few days to ensure that the healing salve and stitches get to do their thing. You were really banged up."

"You're telling me," Matthew chuckles as his eyes venture down to the arm that Tony had stabbed. Sure enough, there are stitches that mar the otherwise pristine-looking flesh. Wondering what the stitches were good for at this point, Matthew asks, "Why the stitches?"

"I put them in before Louise showed me the salve," Marie shrugs, "I didn't have the time to remove them between when I took care of you and now. I would have, but as it turns out, Alois is quite the needy person."

"Ah, makes sense," Matthew nods. Still looking at his arm, he asks, "So, can we get rid of them now?"

"I'd leave them just to be safe," Marie answers, "Give everything a chance to heal. I don't know if that salve is good for deep cuts like that. Just be careful and everything should be as good as new."

"Got it," Matthew nods once more.

"I mean it, Matthew," Marie chides, "If not for yourself, then for me."

Climbing off of his gurney, Matthew tests his weight underfoot and he can't help but feel refreshed. Even his injured foot felt renewed. Sure, he still had some leftover weariness, but besides that, he was like a new man. Looking to the foot of his bed he sees his boots and he quickly starts putting both them and a new pair of socks that were beside them on.

"You really cut it close this time," Marie presses before Matthew has the chance to respond to her, "According to the scans I ran, you got lucky. Blood loss like you had could cause some permanent damage. You could have even died if the twins didn't help me get you in here."

"I'll be safe," Matthew assures Marie. He waits for her to make eye contact and he nods affirmingly, "No more unnecessary risks, no more of any of that. I'm playing it safe now."

"Good," Marie nods, "Next time you're hurt, I might just let you die because you broke your promise."

"Thank you," Matthew nods to Marie before he turns for the door. He steps out and then, just before he shuts it, he sticks his head back in and adds, "Thanks for everything, I mean it. I owe you big time."

With that, Matthew slips out and he takes in the massive hangar for the second time. Now that it is illuminated with all of the overhead lights it is a lot less eerie. Looking around, Matthew sees that the room that he had come from and the room where he assumes Alois is are both in the northwestern corner of the hangar. He momentarily wonders why they were here since they would be in the way of teams that are getting ready to load up in their various vehicles, but he then realizes that there was one really good reason; if anyone was in critical condition they could immediately get moved to the med bay without having to get shuttled around anywhere.

Nodding approvingly at the layout, Matthew turns to the eastern side of the hangar and, sure enough, Matthew can see a massive garage door that appears to be large enough to accommodate the immense mech with ease. The door itself is about ten meters wide and Matthew briefly wonders why it had to be so big. Shrugging, he decides that could be a question for another day.

"I wonder how all of this got buried..." Matthew mutters to himself as he begins

526

walking toward the massive garage doors.

The walk to the east end is remarkably quick since it is now largely unobstructed. Pausing a few paces away from the door, Matthew wonders what the others might have done with all the stacks of crates that had been scattered throughout the whole area.

Frowning, Matthew looks around and he sees that the stacks of crates on the southern side nearest the entrance to the rest of the bunker are a lot higher now. Not only that, they appear to be a lot more organized as well. Meandering over to the nearest stack, Matthew sees that each crate there is full of construction materials. Moving to the next stack he sees that they are labeled munitions. He passes several other stacks and nods approvingly when he sees that someone went through the struggle of putting like things together as they reorganized the area.

Reaching the eastern wall, Matthew remembers why he had come over here and he examines the massive garage door. Off on one side are two small man doors. Curious, Matthew steps through the door furthest from the vehicle entrance and he is greeted by a dead end.

Cocking his head, Matthew eases the

door shut behind himself and he looks around. After just a few seconds, Matthew notices that the wall between this room and the next one over has a few small holes in it. Stooping over, Matthew sees that these holes likely served as some sort of arrowslit like Matthew had seen in pictures of the castles of Earth. Still looking through, Matthew examines the other room and he can see that it has a door on either side of the room making it more or less like an airlock.

"Interesting," Matthew continues nodding with approval. Exiting the room, Matthew thinks, *Whoever designed this place sure knew what they were doing.*

Matthew crosses the hangar once more and this time he climbs a few stairs and he reenters the wing that holds the barracks.

The moment the door shuts behind him, Matthew hears Jane's voice call out from the storage room whose door is still open, "Marie, is that you?"

"Nope," Matthew responds unhelpfully.

"Matthew, you're awake!" Jane squeals before a loud thump sounds. She quickly peeks out of the storage room and looks Matthew over, "You're looking a lot better now."

"He looked like death warmed over

before, so that's not saying much," Louise reminds Jane as she squeezes past the girl and enters the hallway that extends between the barracks and the hangar. Like Jane, Louise looks him up and down before she comes to a similar conclusion, "You don't look like you have one foot in the grave anymore."

"So much positivity from you," Matthew says to Louise as he chuckles, and he shakes his head. Looking over to Jane he admits, "I was afraid you were going to ditch us when we were gone."

"Nope, I'm with you guys now," Jane assures him, "If, for nothing else, you guys are the winning team."

"And…?" Louise prods.

"And I like my little Monkey," Jane shrugs, "That pup is growing on me."

"What she's trying to say is that she thinks we're great and she doesn't want to ditch us," Louise translates Jane's noncommittal responses.

After a brief pause, Jane adds, "This place is a lot more solid than the Fulcrum bunker too… not that I ever got to sleep in there."

"Seemed to me like they had plenty of room," Matthew says, "How come they didn't let you weather the night there?"

"I think it was some kind of power trip," Jane shrugs as her head drops slightly, "They were jerks."

"I'm sorry to hear that," Matthew frowns.

Looking up to Matthew, Jane smiles and tells him, "When you guys let me sleep on the cots over there, I knew that I had found my tribe. I'm with you until the end."

"That sounds a little extreme," Louise jokes, "I think I'll be ditching all of you when this is all over!"

Laughing, Matthew retorts, "That's if I don't ditch you first!"

After a laugh, the three of them fall silent. Something about their laughter had broken some unseen tension that Matthew had felt between him and the others. He isn't entirely sure why, but everyone seems so much friendlier now.

Jane and Louise slip back into the storage room and Matthew follows to help them organize. Beyond the occasional request for help with moving things and Jane's countless tips for proper organization, not a lot is said. After nearly an hour the room is completely organized to the same standard as the hangar was.

Victorious, Matthew and the others congregate around the door that had been locked at the back of the storage room earlier and they begin relaxing. Louise sips on her water and Jane passes Matthew a carton of some intensely sweet fruit juice. Opening up her own, she sighs and takes a sip.

After several minutes of silence, Jane asks, "So, what is the plan for this whole war?"

"Stay alive," Louise answers with a laugh.

Frowning, Jane shakes her head. Motioning around at everyone, she presses, "*Besides* that. What are *we* going to do?"

"I don't know," Louise shrugs before she quickly guzzles the remainder of her water. When her canteen is empty, she looks to Matthew and prompts, "It's your call, Mudskipper."

"My call?" Matthew asks, taken aback. It was one thing to ask someone's input, it was entirely another to tell them to choose to send someone against near-certain death. *A death I've just barely cheated several times now*, Matthew thinks as he shudders ever so slightly.

"Yeah, you're the one in charge around here," Louise nods.

"I'm no more in charge than the rest of

you," Matthew reminds her, "You're just saying that because you and Alois elected me to lead you. No one has any reason or obligation to follow me beyond that."

"And yet we're all still sticking around," Jane points out.

"Even your lizard girlfriend came back," Louise adds.

Surprised, Matthew can't contain his excitement. Smiling broadly, he asks, "Rav'ian's back?"

"Yep," Louise nods. Elbowing Jane, she teasingly whispers loud enough for everyone to hear, "That just shows how much he's in love."

"I am not," Matthew frowns. He knew that Louise had been kidding, but her words still hurt.

The words hurt because Matthew knew that he was thinking about Dixie less and less with every passing hour. As he thought of her less, he thought of his home less. Suddenly seemingly every thought in his world seemed to revolve around the Bulwark. His whole universe had shrunk to the single battlefront that he was on. Everything else seemed so alien and unreachable now.

Nodding, Louise tells Matthew what to expect, "Yeah, so she's in the barracks going through some gear that we found. She's also got a stack of gifts and gear from her people. She says she's not going anywhere without you now."

"Sounds like love to me!" Jane goads Matthew on some more.

Blushing slightly, Matthew sighs, "It's not like that. She taught me so much and risked her life for me on several occasions."

"Just like you've done for us," Louise says flatly.

"Matthew, there is something... strange about Rav'ian though," Jane feeds him some more information.

Wondering why the women were being so enigmatic, Matthew requests, "Can you just tell me everything already? I know you guys are hiding something that you don't want to tell me."

"Well... uh—" Louise starts before she stops to exchange a look with Jane, "Rav'ian is going on and on about owing you a debt of blood."

"So what? I owe her one as well." Matthew shrugs.

Shaking her head, Louise continues, "Well, that's not everything... evidently the Toaz take the idea a lot further than you or I would. Rav'ian is... well..."

"Rav'ian is insisting that you take her as your slave until she can save your own life like you did hers," Jane finishes.

Louise nods to Jane appreciatively before she adds, "And there's no talking her out of it either. It's servitude or death with her people. She's with you if you like it or not, Mudskipper."

"Alright, so I can just get myself into a bind and have her save me, easy as that," Matthew shrugs, not seeing the issue to be as severe as the others were making it out to be.

"It's not that simple," Louise frowns, "It has to be against certain death. Not only that, it has to be witnessed by another Toaz. Evidently one of them saw you carry Rav'ian to safety through the Beets' sniper fire, so they're expecting Rav'ian to do something comparable to that before they count her debt paid."

"I'm sure that we'll see Rav'ian save me like that soon enough then," Matthew shrugs once more.

"Well, that's the other issue," Jane sounds.

Frowning, Louise spills the worst news, "The Toaz are gone,"

Caleb Fast

Revelations

The Battle for Allegra

Episode Nine

Chapter One

The Bulwark, Allegra

"*Gone?* What do you mean 'gone?'" Matthew demands as he looks between Louise and Jane who are looking back at him with just as much worry.

A look of deep dread overshadows Louise's face as she answers, "I mean there's absolutely no sign of the Toaz anymore, Alois and I went to check things out when Rav'ian told us the news."

"Well, where did they go?" Matthew asks as he begins to shake slightly. The idea of losing such a powerful and noble fighting force like the Toaz out of nowhere concerned him deeply. In addition to this, he also wondered what that meant about the mech that Louise had left with them.

"Rav'ian says they were transferred somewhere else," Louise answers, "Evidently the higher-ups don't like them putting down roots because Rav'ian says this has happened several times now."

"Rav'ian wanted us to be sure to tell you that the mecha was secure though," Jane butts in before Matthew can respond to Louise, "She brought a few key pieces of it with her as a guarantee that no one could steal it if they found it. She brought along the thing you call a mule too."

"First off, Louise, does that mean the Toaz are safe?" Matthew asks worriedly. He hated the idea of losing any of the friends that he had made in his short time with the Toa people.

Carefully picking her words, Louise slowly answers, "Rav'ian thinks so, but I think you should be asking her these things. She only told us so much, after all. It's you that she trusts."

"Will do," Matthew nods. Turning to Jane, he asks, "Did Rav'ian say anything else about the mech?"

"She did, but I don't think I can do a

justice to what she said," Jane shrugs, "As Louise said, you should just ask her."

"Alright," Matthew nods to the two women, "Thanks for telling me everything. I don't know how long Rav'ian and I will be talking, but I would enjoy some privacy for the conversation."

Picking up on what he was getting at, Louise assures Matthew, "We'll stay out of your hair."

"And once you're done in there, we'd love to show you around!" Jane smiles broadly, "There is *so* much cool stuff in here."

"Some great equipment too," Louise adds.

"I have to admit that I am quite curious," Matthew smiles before he leaves the duo and then takes a left down the hallway. Reaching the door to the barracks, Matthew pauses long enough to collect his thoughts, *The Toaz are gone, sent on some escapade who knows where. Rav'ian thinks she owes me her life and there's no good way for her to get out of it. The mech is more or less secure and Rav'ian has some parts from it that will keep it from running. Anything else? Oh, yeah, I'm evidently in charge now and I have an empty bunker to command.*

Taking a deep breath, Matthew eases the door to the barracks area open. He is immediately greeted by Monk the moment that the door opens, and Matthew jumps slightly. He hadn't been expecting the dog to be right there.

Monk looks up to Matthew excitedly and he sniffs at Matthew's boots.

"Greetings, Matthew," Rav'ian's voice rises from the opposite end of the barracks, "Your new canine companion heard your approach."

"Yeah, I see that," Matthew chuckles as he stoops down and gives Monk a quick pet. Walking over to Rav'ian, Matthew inquires, "So, how are you feeling? Is your leg doing any better?"

"My leg is faring much better, thank you," Rav'ian nods as she looks up from her work. Scattered before her are several stacks of various odds and ends and there are a few new boxes around her as well. Frowning slightly in her Toaz way, Rav'ian solemnly reports, "However I do not believe that I will be able to join you on any hunts for another day or so. My apologies."

"Don't worry about it," Matthew shakes his head, "We shouldn't be going out a whole lot anyways since three of us are hurt."

"Yes, I was told that you were rendered unconscious from blood loss."

"Yeah, it was pretty rough,"

"I apologize for not being there to assist you,"

"Um... that's the thing. Why are you obliged to serve me? The others told me about it being a blood debt and all, but you saved my life several times now. I was only able to save you because of the stuff you did and taught me!"

"This is the way of my people."

"But your people aren't here anymore,"

"Are you implying that I should lay down my good name and honor simply because my peers are not here?"

"No, I'm saying that my people don't take slaves. Not anymore at least. We see it as—ah—dishonoring to have slaves."

"You are asking me to give up my own standing with my people for your standing with yours?"

"Well... I guess that's sort of what I'm saying..."

"If I were to do so, my people's tradition still dictates that a life can only be repaid with a life. Free or not, I am still bound to repay this debt I have to you."

"That's the other thing, how are you supposed to ever get free if there aren't any of your people left to verify it? The others were telling me how that was a rule the Toaz had."

"That is my own burden to carry, Matthew."

"It doesn't seem very fair,"

"This is not the concern."

"Well, it concerns me," Matthew frowns as he takes a seat on the bunk nearest Rav'ian and her pile of loot.

"I cannot change the dictates of my people for your concerns," Rav'ian shakes her head at Matthew.

"So, where does that leave us then?" Matthew hesitantly asks her. He is confident that he knew what her answer would be, but he hoped that he was wrong.

"I am sworn to servitude until my debt is paid," Rav'ian bows her head slightly to him, "You can choose to not refer to me as a slave to your people, but my role will remain the same."

Matthew nods wordlessly in response. He knew what she was going to say, and he hated how he couldn't change her mind. He frowns for a fraction of a second before he puts on a neutral face again. Taking a deep breath, he asks, "So, what's all this stuff?"

"Gifts from my people," Rav'ian answers as she surveys the landscape of goods around her, "Some of these items were also my own belongings."

"Very cool," Matthew nods.

"All of these items are now yours," Rav'ian informs him casually.

"Really?" Matthew asks in annoyance. The Toaz were very serious about the terms of their slavery binds and Matthew couldn't understand why.

"Yes,"

"Well, I want you to keep all of your stuff and we'll decide what to do with the rest."

"As you desire,"

"What are all of the gifts for anyways?"

"Some are from my friends as a thanks to you for saving my life. Others are simply gifts to recognize my people's friendship with you. The remainder are items that my people could not bring with them and they desired to see them delivered into your own hand. They feared that unclean and unworthy parties may try to possess them otherwise."

"Huh."

"If you are not pleased with the gifts, I

can dispose of them."

"No, they're great... I just don't know how I feel about your people getting kicked out like they were. What happened there anyways?"

"My people are forced to be sojourners everywhere we go. Nothing of what happened was due to your activities, Matthew. The Coalition simply likes to ensure that my people can never remain somewhere too long."

"And why's that?"

"This is the punishment that was bestowed upon us upon our defeat."

"You're punishment? Seems rather strange to punish people by moving them constantly."

"Upon my people's defeat at the hand of the Coalition, our monarchs were taken up along with their courts to live the lives of nomadic mercenaries for their new Coalition masters. The Coalition fears that we might stir up dissent and lead a rebellion if we are allowed to remain in one location for an extended duration of time as well. This is our lot and we await the day that we might return to the world of our ancestors."

"Royal courts?"

"Yes,"

Seeing that Rav'ian wasn't going to explain herself any further, Matthew changes gears and asks, "Where did the Coalition take your people?"

"I do not know. I can only assume that they were sent to another garrison on the frontlines, however."

"And they were okay with that?"

"We have no say in such matters,"

"No, what I'm asking is why don't they refuse?"

"We cannot refuse the beckons of our superiors."

"Why not? They clearly want to see you dead."

"We cannot refuse because doing so would give our enemies leave to take our lives. Our sole means of survival is to remain obedient until our time arises."

"And how long until that happens?"

"We expect aid to come in the near future."

"Aid? From who?" Matthew asks in surprise. Something about the change in Rav'ian's voice and wording told him that her people's hopes were not founded upon nothing.

"We have allies whom we believe we

managed to contact," Rav'ian reports, "This was only accomplished because I was able to tell my people where the derelict shuttle that carried your friend Second Lieutenant Wyndover and the mechanized warrior was."

"I'm not following."

"My people dispatched a party to salvage the wreck,"

"And?"

"Among other items, they took up a whole compliment of communications equipment. We recalibrated it as we needed and then sent our message to our allies afar off."

"Did they respond?"

"No, the distance was too great for such a message to arrive in time."

"How long until they'll get here then?"

"I cannot know such things."

"Do you have a best guess?"

"I do not," Rav'ian shakes her head.

Matthew can tell by her change in demeanor that she didn't want him to ask any more questions on the subject, so he relents. Although Rav'ian was now his slave, he refused to use that against her.

After a minute or two of silence, Matthew finally asks, "So, where's the mech?"

"Your mechanized warrior is hidden away in the cavern where you were first blooded."

"You hid it in no man's land, smart..."

"The required parts that I removed from the machine are located in the hangar. These items are small enough that you and the others should be able to transport them with you on your trek without too much difficulty.

"From what I've heard, it's midday out there," Matthew sighs, "I guess we won't be getting it tonight."

"It would be unwise to go out on such a venture, yes."

Frowning, Matthew feels like he is now risking the possibility of wasting an entire day. A moment passes before he requests, "Did your people leave the communication equipment with us?'

"They did," Rav'ian answers with another nod, "They reverted the equipment back to its original settings, however. They had to do so because the equipment would not last long otherwise. It was not designed to send messages across the galaxy."

"Across the galaxy?" Matthew asks in wonderment. Shaking his head, he remembers that Rav'ian didn't seem to like the idea of telling him too much more about her allies, so he immediately tells her, "No, it's fine. Don't tell me more if you don't want to. I was just surprised."

"I wish to say no more on the subject," Rav'ian says in a near whisper.

"Got it, thanks for answering so many of my questions."

"Such is my function."

Matthew considers saying something else, but he can't think of anything worth saying. Just about whatever he asked Rav'ian now would likely be answered only partially. Despite her pledge to serve him, her loyalties were split between him and her own people. Matthew didn't like the idea of forcing her to decide on one side or the other.

In the end, Matthew opts to simply nod once to Rav'ian, and he then takes his leave. As he steps out of the room, Matthew hears the sound of Rav'ian going through all of the gifts that her people had left once again.

Chapter Two

The Bulwark, Allegra

"Alright, what's the game plan, Mudskipper?" Jane asks.

Matthew stares blankly at Jane for a moment as he notes how she had just used the twins' name for him. He's about to sigh but opts against it. Instead, Matthew answers, "Well, that's why I gathered you all here."

Marie, Louise, Jane, Rav'ian, and Matthew are all standing around Alois in one of the bunker's operating rooms. All around them stainless steel and whitewashed walls grace the room with a less bunker-ish appeal that Matthew had taken a liking to. Something about plain concrete walls had filled Matthew with an odd sense of dread because of their dreariness.

"So… what are we supposed to do?" Alois asks flatly. He had returned to his usual reserved and businesslike demeanor about an hour ago and Matthew waited to call the meeting until he was convinced that Alois was one hundred percent back to normal.

"You guys are going to help me make a

list of the things that you'd like to see done," Matthew says with a nod. He picks up a notebook and pen that he had pulled from the storage room and he gets into position to write out his team's requests.

A few moments pass and Alois states, "I'm not following."

"Just say what you'd like us to do while we're stuck down here," Matthew instructs, "We've got time to burn, so let's make the most of it."

"Well, I'd like to make sure that everything in the barracks' kitchen works," Louise starts.

Matthew scrawls that down and nods. This was a good start.

"I need to finish taking an inventory of everything," Jane offers, "I could use a lot of help there, especially for the big stuff in the hangar."

"Good," Matthew nods as he writes down her request as well, "I can help you there."

"I'm free to help too," Marie volunteers, "I already took care of everything I wanted to as far as my inventories are concerned."

"I was thinking we could give our walls a little bit of color other than grey too," Matthew announces.

The others appreciate Matthew's idea and the ideas keep flowing for quite some time. After an hour or so, Matthew's notepad is almost entirely filled, and he can't help but feel happy with the results. They were going to turn their little Sanctuary into a home.

The conversation eventually shifts from bunker renovations to possible military campaigns and recruitments. Before long, Matthew has a long list of recommendations—especially from the twins who actually knew what they were talking about. The twins had plans to train up and equip all the newest recruits who would be left to their own devices otherwise. In addition to this, they insisted that Matthew organize the entirety of the Bulwark for everyone's sake.

"I don't think I can swing that," Matthew laughs at the thought of taking command over everyone in the Bulwark. It was one thing to give orders in Sanctuary to his own team and then bring some new people under his wing, it was entirely another to name himself the commander of the entire garrison.

Shrugging, Louise asks, "Why not? The Fulcrum gang are sure trying to do that."

"The Fulcrum seems more interested in

protecting themselves and fortifying," Matthew corrects, "They don't give a rip about anyone else."

"Then they won't oppose us," Louise smiles sinisterly.

"Ok, first off, that face is creepy," Matthew laughs. Looking to Jane, he inquires, "Do you think the Fulcrum would try to stop me if I tried that? Someone has to take command of this place sooner or later."

"I think it's worth a shot," Jane hesitantly offers, "As you said, they're so interested in themselves. I doubt they would even notice that you're taking over until you knocked on their door!"

"In addition to what has been said," Rav'ian cuts in before Matthew can respond to Jane. She had been sitting off to the side and simply observing up until now. When she sees that everyone is looking at her, she finishes, "You, Matthew, have been told by those in command that they would like to entrust the charge of the Bulwark to you already. To act on that prematurely could force their hand into promoting you."

Or it could ruin it. They might think that I'm planning some sort of rebellion. Matthew thinks pessimistically.

"They said they want you in charge?" Marie asks in surprise.

Nodding, Matthew answers, "Yeah, they said they wanted me to lead because of my experience. It's minimal experience, but they seemed to like the idea of having a minimally experience human in charge over any alien, no matter how much the alien might know."

Her eyes wide, Jane inquires, "And who said this?"

Matthew has to pause for a few beats as he tries to remember the exact ranks of those in command over him, "Master Sergeant Nelson and Captain Johnson."

"Nelson's got a lot of clout," Marie nods slowly, "If you have his backing... well, if he's behind you, then no one in their right mind would oppose you. No one wants to incur Nelson's wrath."

"I know the feeling there," Matthew shudders, "Nelson's crazy."

"What did you do that made him like you?" Jane queries.

"I beat up one of his soldiers," Matthew shrugs. The full story wasn't too glorious and telling it just seemed frivolous at this point.

"Violence," Rav'ian laughs with the laugh that Matthew had begun to miss in its absence. Nodding slowly, Rav'ian says, "Nothing attracts the admiration of Master Sergeant Nelson like the shedding of blood."

"Well, before I try taking over, how about we make sure that our bunker is as solid as it can be," Matthew tells the others. Looking around he smiles and nods at his team. After such a short amount of time they had all gained his respect and he saw them as dear friends. If the need ever arose, he could see himself trading his life for any of theirs at a moment's notice.

"Don't want the king's castle to look like a peasant's shack," Jane eventually approves.

●●●●●●●●●●●●●●

"It's looking good!" Marie happily announces from her spot up on a ladder.

Looking up where Marie is, Matthew can't help but wonder if the red 'accent line' as she called it was actually level. He had to admit that the bright red line did bring a nice color splash to the hangar, but it just seemed a little crooked. Beneath her, Louise and Jane are both painting the grey concrete wall white with some more of the paint that they had found in one of the countless crates.

"It doesn't look very straight to me," Alois calls out to her from his spot beside Matthew and Rav'ian.

"What do you mean?" Marie asks in a hollow voice that makes it sound like someone just called her talentless.

"It's higher on the left side," Alois tells her.

Marie descends from her vantage point and takes a look at her work from a few paces away. With a sigh, she admits, "Oh, I guess you're right…"

"Just make the line a bit wider," Alois recommends, "Straighter too."

Nodding, Marie responds, "Good idea… the first part, at least."

"I believe we have completed our task," Rav'ian announces.

Rav'ian's words pull Matthew's attention away from the wall that is being painted and back to the task at hand. Scattered before Rav'ian are several lines of ammo that Matthew had been helping to reorganize. For one reason or another, the previous occupants of the bunker put all of their ammunition on one shelf that wasn't bolted down to the ground or any walls. At some point that shelf had fallen to the ground, making quite the mess in the process.

"So, is that all the house cleaning now?" Alois asks after a few moments, "Because I'm going a little stir crazy in here."

"I'm ready to stretch my legs a bit outside too," Matthew agrees, "Rav'ian, you want to come?"

"I will use this time to rest," Rav'ian replies as she slowly rises to her feet and then makes for the door that leads toward the barracks.

"Do you ladies mind if Matthew and I look around outside?" Alois asks.

"Go ahead," Marie tells them, "Just keep your cast clean, Alois."

"She's treating me like a child," Alois grunts to Matthew before the two of them make for the man door beside the main garage door.

"The paint's looking great," Matthew compliments them as he walks by. He had already helped to paint the entire barracks and the hallway leading to the hangar. He had argued that the hangar didn't really need any paint, but Jane and the others had insisted.

"I'm telling you," Alois grunts as he opens the man door, "It took so long to dig this entrance out of the mud."

"Any idea why it might have gotten

buried so badly?" Matthew asks, hoping to take the necessary steps to prevent such a happening in the future.

Opening the door that leads to the outside world, Alois steps out and takes a deep breath. Looking up to the sky, he smiles. A moment passes and he returns to a more business-like tone before he answers, "I'm thinking it was some really big artillery. Nothing else could have moved that much dirt."

"It must have been huge if it collapsed the main entrance tunnel too," Matthew frowns before he follows Alois out of the bunker and into the open world.

Nodding once, Alois agrees, "Must've been,"

Matthew takes a deep breath and he immediately regrets it. Although the air felt a lot fresher than the stale recirculated air from the bunker, it carried with it a host of terrible smells. Grimacing, Matthew picks out the smells of decomposing flesh, burning chemicals, smoke, and a host of rotting things that he can't quite place.

Looking up, Matthew can't help but smile like Alois had. The sky is an absolutely beautiful shade of blue and it is completely void of any clouds. Matthew sighs as he wonders how many clouds are currently above his home that seemingly always had at least some sort of overcast that lent its rain and shade upon the land and seas below it.

"Alright, so what's the plan?" Alois asks as he looks excitedly at Matthew. He turns around as best he can with his crutch, and he eyes Matthew with a look of mischief.

"I didn't have one," Matthew shrugs, "I literally just wanted to stretch my legs out here a bit."

"Why don't we check out the abandoned Toaz bunkers?" Alois requests.

"They didn't really have that many," Matthew shakes his head, "They slept outside, usually. But their bunkers are up north a bit, we can check out Marie's old medical ward first. Maybe there's something worth bringing back for her."

•••••••••••••

"Nothing but junk," Alois complains as he and Matthew shovel through the final crate in Marie's old bunker.

"The Toaz picked it clean," Matthew agrees with a discontent sigh. He had been hoping to find something cool at the very least.

Instead, he and Alois were greeted with a bunker that almost seemed like it had been looted twenty times over already.

"I wonder how long until someone else tries to take it over," Alois muses.

"Hopefully sometime soon, I'd hate to see this place rot away."

"Think the Fulcrum guys might try to take it over?"

"I'm sure they'll try. Maybe we should find it some new occupants before then."

"We could... I'm willing to bet that there are a bunch of new recruits on their way to replace the Toaz."

"I sure hope so,"

"Do you think the Beets might try to take a run at us without them here?"

"I sure hope not... Rav'ian says that the Toaz would run patrols up and down the Bulwark to ensure that it was secure. Without them... I don't know."

"We'll have to pick up the slack."

"But there's only six of us,"

"We'll have to train up some new blood then. We've got the extra beds, might as well fill them."

"Maybe,"

"What's on your mind?"

"I just don't like this… something seems weird. Why would they just pull the Toaz away in the middle of a firefight like they were having? From what I heard, the Coalition had some shuttles that just swooped in and told the Toaz that it was time for them to leave as they were fighting off all the gassers."

"It does seem a bit odd, especially since they were the only ones that were really doing anything. Everyone else was just sitting around waiting for their orders."

"Do you think that the Coalition knew that they sent off that message that I told you and the others about?"

"The one the Toaz sent to their allies? I don't know. Maybe."

"If they did, what do you think they'd do to the Toaz?"

"They probably know that the Toaz are too useful to them, so they wouldn't just kill them. Maybe they sent them on some suicide mission or something."

"Isn't that the same as just killing them?"

"No, it would give the psychopaths that are in charge of this fight an idea of what they're really up against. They haven't been able to get a good look at what the Beets are doing well inside their lines for a while now."

"Don't they have satellites?"

"From what I heard on my trip here, the Beets have something in orbit that has destroyed anything and everything that has tried flying above the site where their first ship crashed."

"Well, that's not good…"

"What's worse is that I heard that they were preparing to send in some raids to test the enemy's defenses further in. Those teams, from what I heard, were mostly new recruits."

"How new of recruits?" Matthew asks nervously as he thinks about all of his friends from Crail who had been conscripted alongside him.

"No idea, it was all just whispers."

"At least we've got a bit of an assurance that we won't be going anywhere any time soon," Matthew frowns. He isn't sure what to think or feel now that he knew that his childhood friends could be walking into a firefight that he knew they couldn't survive. Even from his few encounters with the Beets, Matthew knew that no amount of conventional fighting tactics could dispatch them safely. They were in a war of attrition and, Lord willing, numbers would be on his side.

"What are you thinking?"

"I'm thinking about how badly I want this war to be over," Matthew answers solemnly. Shaking his head, he takes a few steps toward the exit of the bunker and he says, "Let's go, there's nothing for us here."

•••••••••••••••

Matthew and Alois stop just outside of Sanctuary and they take in their home from the outside. If one didn't know what was inside, they might just assume that the place was a filthy ruin. Despite the cleanup efforts that Alois and the others had made; the outside of the bunker still looked filthy.

Glancing over to the entryway that led into the barracks, Matthew sighs. Frowning, his shoulders slouch and he feels a pang of guilt stab through his chest as he sees how bad off everything looked. Shaking his head, Matthew thinks, *There's still a lot of work to do before this place is going to be everything that it can be. So, so, so much work.*

"Just wait until this place is fixed up," Alois announces, "It's going to be amazing."

"It's going to be a ton of work," Matthew warns.

Shrugging, Alois replies, "Everything

that's worth doing is a lot of work.

"Well, I guess we've got nothing but time," Matthew chuckles as he looks at the bunker in a new light. Alois was right, it was going to be rough, but the result would be worthwhile.

"According to Jane, we've got everything we'll need to build on some nice additions," Alois reports.

Nodding, Matthew says, "I know, she's already shown me everything. Now we just have to decide if we want to add on or maybe help patch up some other bunkers."

"We have to help ourselves first," Alois shoots Matthew's idea down, "Otherwise we won't be around long enough to help anyone else. It's just like when a shuttle gets a hull breach—you have to make sure that you're going to stay conscious and survive before you're of any use to anyone else."

"I guess you're right," Matthew nods with a half frown. As was the case with any situation—survival ones especially—he had to watch out for himself first. Once he was safe, he could help others.

"So, what kind of addition were you thinking we could do first?"

"I was thinking we could use another

barracks area. Maybe we could make the current one more of a commons area that way. I don't like the idea of having the first room that someone enters being the one we sleep in. It feels… risky."

Alois laughs and he claps Matthew on the back, "Now you're thinking like a soldier!"

"So, is that what you were thinking too?"

"Indeed it was."

"Now all we need is to figure out how to build the thing. I don't know about you, but I've never built a bunker before."

"Jane didn't show you the construction drone?"

"The what now?"

"There's an old construction drone that the builders must have left behind. We dug it out of the mud when we were clearing away the hangar's entrance."

"Does it work?"

"Not yet, but Louise and I were going to take a look at it."

"Suppose you got it working again, are you sure that it will still know how to do its thing?"

"We can only hope," Alois shrugs, "But if it doesn't, we could always program it to do stuff. Louise knows a bit of that sort of thing.

I'm more of a hardware kind of guy."

"Interesting," Matthew nods as he takes in the new information. He had never heard of a robot that could actually build a building. Sure, there were plenty of robots that he had seen and heard about that helped do menial tasks, but never something as advanced as construction. If nothing else, this robot was going to be very fun to watch.

Alois waits for several seconds before he tells Matthew, "But Louise says there's something you won't like about us fixing up the drone."

"Which is?"

"Well, we already know that there are a few parts we need that aren't in the bunker."

"So, we can't fix it then?"

"Well, Louise says she is confident that the necessary stuff is all in the smaller mechs that were damaged in the explosions and fire that we caused when we grabbed our big mech."

"And she thinks that what she needed survived all of that?"

"She is,"

"I didn't think that I would be heading back to that place any time soon…"

"Well, here we are," Alois shrugs, "Either

we go back and get everything we need to build up our bunker, or we can live with how it is and miss out on what it could be."

"You don't need to convince me to go," Matthew shakes his head, "I get it. I just didn't think we'd be heading back so soon."

"If we're lucky, we might be able to get some new gear and supplies while we're there too."

"I just hope the Fulcrum abandoned it after everything we did there."

Chapter Three

The Bulwark, Allegra

"Looks abandoned to me," Louise notes as she and Matthew lay on their stomachs on a ridge near the old Fulcrum stronghold.

Matthew had left Alois with Marie and Monk back at Sanctuary in order to launch a salvaging raid on the decrepit base. They had made it this far without any incident, which just made Matthew more suspicious. As Matthew saw it, there was no way that the Fulcrum would just stop patrolling the area around their old base just because it had seen so much action.

"I don't see why they would just abandon it though," Matthew mutters in apprehension. As much as he liked the idea that the place was apparently empty and that he wouldn't have to shoot anyone, Matthew can't help but think that this was all too good to be true.

Grunting, Louise raises herself to her knees and continues examining the structure. Shrugging, she reminds Matthew, "It's only been a few hours since we hit it, maybe they're still waiting for things to settle down."

"It still seems weird," Matthew sighs as he continues scanning the landscape before him for any signs of activity.

There are quite a few newer trails that appear to circle around the still-smoldering structure. Besides the occasional branch that breaks off from the newer trails and leads to the building, there doesn't seem to be much evidence of its use.

"We've been watching it for over an hour now and nothing has happened," Louise points out, "It's either empty or close to it. Let's go."

"How can you be so sure?" Matthew asks worriedly as he looks over to Louise.

"Well, we can't be until we get in there," Jane announces from somewhere behind Matthew.

Matthew turns and sees Jane and Rav'ian approaching from the south where he had dispatched them to keep an eye on the ex-Fulcrum stronghold from another angle.

Following several paces behind Jane, Rav'ian nods and reports, "We have failed to witness any movement within the complex."

"That means we're clear to enter," Louise happily declares as she rises the rest of the way to her feet.

Still not convinced, Matthew protests, "But—"

"Nope, you promised," Louise cuts him off, "You said that if we watched the dumb building for an hour and didn't see anything that we would go in."

"This is true," Rav'ian nods in agreement, "We must make our move presently or risk missing our opportunity."

"Jane, tell me that you're not as gung-ho as the others are," Matthew pleads with the last woman.

Shrugging, Jane sides with the others, "As they said, we need to get this done sooner rather than later. Not only that, but you did say that we would only waste an hour watching the place."

"Let's go already," Louise begs, "We'll be in and out before you'll even notice."

Matthew knew that this moment would come, but he still didn't like it. He had been wishing for any sign of hostile activity ever since he had begun watching the building. He would have taken any out that would have arisen, even if it was just the faintest sound of a gasser running amuck.

Instead, there had been absolutely nothing.

The only noises that reached Matthew's little observation post were those of the Bulwark to the east and the Beets beyond that. Everything else was completely still, somehow untouched, unaffected, and seemingly uninterested in the war raging so close to it. Even the mountains and foothills to the west had seemingly stopped echoing with the ghostly reports of battle.

"Fine," Matthew moans. He knew that the others were right, but something still was nagging at the back of his mind. He just knew that something didn't add up. Or at least he expected as much.

"Don't worry, Mudskipper," Louise says as she begins marching toward the building, "We're just going to go through what's left of the hangar. Things are going to be a lot easier this time around."

"That's not saying much," Matthew whispers to himself. He chuckles softly at his own joke as he thinks about how narrowly he and the others had made it out of this place just one Allegrian day prior.

It takes nearly a half-hour for Matthew and the others to reach the rubble and ruins that only slightly resemble the hangar that had once stood here. The mud is a lot shallower here, so walking is significantly easier. Despite the easier terrain, Matthew and the others still had to help their mule out of a few places where it still managed to get stuck. Even with the occasional struggle, Matthew knew that bringing the mule was a good choice because it would permit him and the others to load it up instead of weighing themselves down.

Looking around at the widespread damage, Matthew begins to see things from his companions' points of view. There really wasn't much left here to be worth securing for the Fulcrum. From the way Matthew saw things, it didn't even seem like it would be worth poking through the scrap and wreckage to find the parts that Louise said she needed.

Walking to the nearest pile of debris, Louise announces, "If we're lucky, I'll only need to hit one of the old mechas to find the parts we need."

"And if we're not?" Matthew queries.

Chuckling, Louise answers, "If we weren't lucky, we would have died a long time ago. Now, help me dig this thing out. I think it's under here if I'm remembering right."

"Rav'ian, keep watch while we dig," Matthew requests as he turns and starts ripping into the pile of ruined stonework and bent metal that Louise is on top of.

"Very well," Rav'ian nods as she makes her way to what remains of one of the raised platforms that had once crisscrossed the hangar area. She walks with a hint of a limp and Matthew can't help but wonder if he made the right decision in asking her to come along with him.

"Alright, that's it," Louise suddenly announces as she stops digging.

"You found it already?" Matthew asks in surprise.

Louise hops down and out of sight before she answers, "Yep, it's in a lot better shape than I was thinking it would be."

Matthew clamors up the pile and is greeted with an open hatch at the top. Peering inside, he sees Louise who is busily opening up panels and looking at their contents. He watches for a few moments before he inquires, "What are you looking for?"

"I'm thinking I might be able to fix this thing now…" Louise mutters in a weak response.

"I thought you said all of these mechs were beyond repair after the fires and whatnot?"

"They were,"

"Then why do you think you can fix them now?"

"I'm thinking if the others are even close to as good as this one, that I might be able to piece together a few of them."

"And you can do that here?"

"Yeah, it's just a few fixes, by the looks of it."

Looking around at the piles of rubble, Matthew can't help but wonder what Louise was seeing that he wasn't. Sure, she had been a salver before the Coalition took her in, but her hopes seemed to be poorly founded. Not convinced, Matthew asks, "You sure about that?"

"I'm certain of it," Louise nods as she emerges from the smaller mech. Looking around, she mutters, seemingly to herself, "I think I remember seeing some spare parts and tools over on that wall over there too…"

"So, we're going to have some new mechs now?" Matthew queries. He was still not entirely convinced that the machines could have survived the blaze.

Nodding again, Louise assures him, "Yep."

"Sounds like it will be a lot of fun!" Jane exclaims, her excitement evident.

Sounds like a lot more work than I signed up for today, Matthew thinks with a chuckle. He was more than willing to put in the work, but he hadn't been expecting to walk away with such a prize today.

"There were six of the smaller mechas, right?" Louise asks as she works her way down the pile that Matthew and Jane are still on top of.

"Yeah," Matthew answers.

"Then we've got a lot more work to do," Louise surmises.

"Indeed we do," Matthew nods as he surveys the hangar once more with a more positive outlook. Perhaps the salver mindset that Louise had was rubbing off on him.

•••••••••••••••

"That's it... that's it..." Matthew mutters mostly to himself as he guides the mechanized mule around countless obstacles that are standing between it and the final mech that Louise is finishing up with.

Louise and the others have been hard at work for the better part of ten hours. By Matthew's count, that left them just another three hours of daylight.

Matthew and the others had taken turns resting and trying to get a little bit of sleep while one person kept watch and the remaining two worked on the mechs that Louise was convinced that they could fix. Thanks to the seemingly leisurely pace, Matthew doesn't feel too tired, but he still was still ready for this escapade to be over so he could sleep in a cot instead of on the hard ground.

"How much longer, Matthew?" Louise calls from the inside of one of the mech's engine bays where she had cleared out all of the remnants of the engine that had been rendered useless from the fire and explosion that had destroyed the building.

"I'm almost there," Matthew assures her as he glances back to the mule that is towing the replacement motor.

Louise had spent a good amount of time earmarking the parts that were worth grabbing from the mechs she deemed beyond repair and giving other orders before she got to take her own midday nap. While she slept, Matthew and the others got everything in line for her to get everything into working order the moment that she woke up.

Thanks to his minimal experience working on the small motor on his father's fishing ship, Matthew discovered that he was a lot more useful than he had initially given himself credit for. Jane also seemed to have a bit of a knack for a few other things, so they were able to surprise Louise with a semi-complete trio of mechs when she woke up. After a quick examination, Louise gave their work the okay and she continued working on the three mechs that would soon be joining their ranks.

"There is movement to the east," Rav'ian announces suddenly.

Not sure if he should be worried, Matthew asks, "Are they coming our way?"

"They appear to be," Rav'ian answers, "However, they may simply be passing by as well. The group is very sizeable, I estimate there to be forty people."

"No need risking it," Matthew states, "Let's get ready for the worst. How long do you think it will be until they get here?"

Rav'ian stares eastward for a few moments before she answers, "Approximately thirty minutes."

"It would be cutting it close, but I think I can get one of these things working by then," Louise announces, "All I'll need is some fuel."

"How much will you need?" Matthew

asks worriedly. He had been thinking about the fuel issue for some time now. Thanks to the massive fire that he and the twins had stoked, there wasn't likely to be much of any fuel left sitting around. With the need for fuel in mind, Matthew had been looking around for any sign of any of the three fuels that the mech was supposed to be able to run off of. So far, he had failed to find any.

There is a brief pause as Louise assumedly runs some numbers before she answers, "Two liters should do it,"

"Two liters…" Matthew mutters as he thinks about where he might find that much fuel.

"Odds are that you'll be better off finding some alcohol in the complex's kitchen or maybe a hydrogen tank survived all the fire thanks to their various safeties," Louise tells Matthew as she pulls away from her task at hand. Frowning, she adds, "I doubt there's any diesel left after we set those tanks on fire yesterday."

I know," Matthew sighs as he suddenly regrets his decision. The regret is quickly pushed aside as he reasons that he wouldn't be alive now to regret anything if he hadn't started the fire. There were simply too many gassers at the time and he and the twins lacked the firepower and the ammo to put them all down.

"I'll look for the hydrogen," Jane volunteers, "You poke around and see if you can find any alcohol."

"Sounds like a plan," Matthew nods. He knew that their best bet was to split up and cover more ground.

"I shall continue watching for danger," Rav'ian sounds.

"And I'm still busy getting this thing fixed up enough that it might be able to help us," Louise announces.

"Alright, if worse comes to worst and we can't get the mech running, let's hide," Matthew orders as he stops the mule and helps Louise strap the engine that it had been carrying to a makeshift hoist that she had made.

"Sounds like a plan," Louise nods, "But if they try stealing my mechas, all bets are off."

A cruel grin tries working its way onto Matthew's face, but he suppresses it and opts to nod instead. As he nods, he reasons, "We'd have surprise on our side in that case, so it might be a good bet for us."

"Sounds good," Jane affirms the plan.

"Now go find me some fuel," Louise

orders, "And keep an eye out for any extra fuel too. We'll be needing a whole lot more than two liters if we're going to get these three things back home. I don't want to fix these mechas up for nothing."

Without saying another word, Matthew turns and he makes for the living section of the complex where he faintly remembered seeing signs of a kitchen.

As he marches toward the other half of the complex, Matthew lightly kicks a metallic object that quickly skitters away on its own power. His curiosity piqued, Matthew decides to follow the small object as it disappears through an open doorway that leads into the rest of the building.

As he steps through the door, Matthew quickly remembers all of the gassers from his previous adventure here and he flicks on his flashlight in order to be sure that he doesn't miss any potential hostiles. Shining the flashlight all around, Matthew sees that there is a thick layer of dust and ash on the floor. Several charred corpses are also beneath the dust and Matthew can't bring himself to look too much closer at them. Turning his attention to the ground around the bodies, Matthew notes that everything appears to be undisturbed, minus a small trail that the little metallic object had left when it scurried away from Matthew.

Matthew's eyes follow the trail and he sees that it leads into a room whose door is open. Peering into the room, he notices several shafts of sunlight that are casting spotlights onto the floor. Not far from the holes on the ceiling, Matthew sees the remains of several people that are nearly ripped apart. At first, he fears that there may be some monster lurking in the shadows, but he quickly realizes that the countless holes in the ceiling and corpses were from some large cannons. Looking through one of the holes, Matthew reasons that some airship must have done the deed and dispatched all the gassers from a safe distance.

I need to get myself one of those ships, Matthew thinks as he looks at how effective the assault had been. As he saw it, there was no better way to keep his team out of harm's way than to do their work from such a distance.

Now confident that he was alone, Matthew gets a little bit closer to the door and he sees that the room appears to have been some sort of briefing room. Thanks to the fires, however, there isn't much left besides the remnants of several charred chairs around a large burnt table.

Cutting his losses with the small metal critter, Matthew decides to look around for the kitchen. He had to find anything with alcohol in it soon if he was going to feel safe if and when the people that were approaching arrived.

"It's got to be around here somewhere..." Matthew mutters to himself as he steps into a room that appears to be a cafeteria.

This room seems untouched by the flames that ravaged the hangar and its adjoining briefing room. Besides the faint presence of smoke that is still lingering in the air and the thin layer of ash underfoot, the room is just about exactly how Matthew figured it had been left.

I wonder if there is any food in the kitchen still, Matthew wonders as he starts toward a set of double doors on the far end of the room.

Before Matthew can open the set of doors, the small metal object races between him and his destination and it smashes itself against his feet.

At first, Matthew had been startled by the sudden intrusion, but he had calmed down when he saw that it was his little friend. Looking down, Matthew notes that the thing was in fact a robot and he chuckles. The small robot is essentially just a small box that is about four centimeters wide and fifteen long. Matthew cocks his head to see the side profile of the robot and he sees that it travels on a set of tank treads.

"What do you want?" Matthew asks aloud as he stoops down and pokes at the robot with his finger.

The robot promptly backs away and it wiggles around in what Matthew can only assume is its impersonation of anger. Chuckling once again, he rises to his feet.

Before he can take another step for the door the robot runs into his toes again.

"You don't want me to go in there, huh?" Matthew asks as he looks down at his little metal companion.

The machine wiggles and beeps in response.

Wondering if the robot could understand him, Matthew quickly explains, "I have to go in there whether you like it or not, pal. I've got my gun, so I'll be fine if there are any gassers."

Pulling his rifle from his back where it was hanging by its strap, Matthew points it toward the double doors and he quickly looks around for possible escape routes in case things went bad. Once he had a few exits picked out he steps over the still-gyrating robot and forces the double doors open.

Sure enough, he had found the kitchen and Matthew's jaw drops when he sees all the food that had been left out. Before another thought can cross his mind, the scent of the spoiled food hits him and he quickly pulls up his shirt's collar to cover his nose. Taking another breath, Matthew realizes that his shirt smelled worse than the air around him and he lets it fall back into place. Making a quick mental note to wash up when he got back to Sanctuary, he then decides to continue on ahead.

Matthew steps over to the nearest table and he examines the food that is spread out on it. He can see that the vegetables were already rotting, and the meat was grey and had mold growing on it as well.

Grimacing at the ghastly sight, Matthew turns and begins rifling through the various cabinets and cupboards around him. When he finally finds a pantry full of canned goods he pauses and briefly wonders if it was worth gathering.

Before he can decide, Matthew hears the muffled cry of a gasser.

Spinning around Matthew looks for its source and his eyes settle on a large metal door at the other end of the kitchen area. He looks at the door for several moments as he prays that it was sealed shut. As he stares, a brief thud sounds from the door and is followed by another lonely wail.

The small robot skids to a stop between Matthew and the metal door and it waggles its body at him once more in its pathetic threatening way.

Chuckling, Matthew shakes his head and sighs as he looks at the food once more. Reasoning that he could always pick it up later, Matthew gently shuts the door and he resumes his search for anything with alcohol in it.

After far too many failures, Matthew finally checks under the large sink and he finds what he can only assume was someone's secret stash. Smiling broadly, Matthew pulls out an assortment of large and small bottles of everything ranging from wine to vodka. Nodding approvingly, he carefully stows the various bottles in his pockets and pack.

With his mission accomplished, Matthew returns to the destroyed hangar and he sees that Jane is still poking around in the rubble in search of some hydrogen tanks. Not wanting to stop her because he hoped that she would find some, Matthew silently makes his way to Louise who is still hard at work restoring the small mechs.

"Welcome back," Louise grunts as Matthew draws near. She had evidently heard his feet crunching in the gravel underfoot. Without pulling her head out of the mech's engine bay, Louise asks, "Did you find anything?"

"I found a lot," Matthew answers as he begins pulling out his treasure trove and lays them out one by one.

"How much did you get?" Louise asks as she pulls her head away from her work. Watching Matthew unload for a few seconds she exclaims, "That's a ton!"

"There's a lot more than just this," Matthew answers as he pulls the final small bottle from his pocket and places it beside all the others. Pulling off his bag, Matthew sets it down and he pulls out the larger jugs which he sets beside the smaller containers.

"Well, that looks like it will be enough to get all the mechas to Sanctuary with ease," Louise notes as she nods approvingly at the haul. Laughing, she adds, "If I were a drinker, I would even say that there was enough for other uses as well!"

"I know, right?" Matthew joins in on the laughter, "It was quite the stash that I found."

Louise's laughter suddenly stops and Louise casts an odd look at the bottles of alcohol. Matthew is about to ask what was wrong when she looks Matthew in the eyes and tells him, "We can't let Alois know about this stuff—especially if you decide to save any of it."

"Why not?" Matthew pries before he can stop himself. He could figure why, but he still asked for some dumb reason.

Maintaining her new somber demeanor, Louise answers, "Alois has done some… things in his life that he would rather forget. He did a lot of them to save me from the worst of it… I owe a lot to him for that."

"I'm sorry to hear that," Matthew apologizes, his voice sounding rather hollow and distant. He had heard of people drowning away their sorrows but, where he was from, those people weren't around long enough to get to know and love.

"He's not an alcoholic or anything," Louise quickly assures Matthew, "He just takes whatever out he can to get his hands on stuff that can ease the pain... He's not some heartless monster like he tries to pretend he is. That's why he had Marie give him those extra painkillers today. It's all in an effort to... escape from the world he's made for himself."

His heart breaking slightly, Matthew starts, "I'm—"

Louise cuts him off and Matthew sees that Jane was coming within earshot. As she draws near, Louise quickly reports, "Jane says she found some hydrogen tanks as well, but she couldn't pull them out on her own."

"Great," Matthew nods as he tries to snap out of the subdued mood that Louise had sent him into. Offering a smile that doesn't extend past his lips, he declares with mock happiness, "We're set for a whole war now!"

"Not quite," Louise shakes her head, "These mechas burn through their fuel a lot faster than you would think. We're going to have to use them sparingly if we don't find anything else to refuel with soon."

"Oh," Matthew breathes, his disappointment evident.

"Well, once we get everything going, we shouldn't have to worry too much," Louise assures him, "We can assign other people to scrounge up fuel for us."

"I hope you're right," Matthew nods apprehensively. He didn't mind the idea of ordering people to do busywork, since so much of the work on his father's ship was mindless and required a lot of grunt labor, but he didn't like the idea of running out of fuel in the middle of a fight either.

"I must recommend that you refuel one of your machines," Rav'ian suddenly calls, "The others are drawing near."

"Does it look like they are actually coming for us now?" Matthew asks.

There is a brief pause before Rav'ian warily answers, "Yes."

•••••••••••••

"I'm all set!" Louise calls from the mech that she had been focusing on for so long.

Louise's efforts to get it running took longer than expected but Rav'ian reported that the intruders had stopped and that gave Louise enough time to finish up. According to Rav'ian, the new group was now about fifteen minutes out.

"Not a moment too soon," Matthew whispers to himself before he lets out a breath that he didn't realize he had been holding. His nerves ease up slightly, but he is still very worried about the battle to be.

"I'm going to pilot this one," Louise announces, "I'm the only one who will be able to troubleshoot any issues if they arise in the middle of a firefight.

Matthew nods in understanding and he then motions for the others to hide behind their various entrenchments that they had made for themselves as Louise finished up. Matthew had initially thought that he would be piloting the mech, but he wasn't too worried that he wasn't going to. If anything, he was relieved that he shouldn't have to shoot at anyone.

Before Louise can climb into the hatch to the mech, Matthew orders her, "Play dead in there until we're ready. We don't want them to know that we got that thing working!"

"Got it," Louise nods as she enters the mech. Although it is a lot smaller than the large one that Matthew and the twins had taken on their first visit here, this mech was still quite big. Before she shuts the hatch, Louise tells Matthew, "I'll wait for you guys to start shooting. If you don't shoot, then I'll assume that they are either not hostiles or they are just passing by."

With that, Louise disappears and the mech roars to life. She quickly lays the mech onto its back and she does her best to partially bury it so it doesn't stand out.

"How many did you say there were?" Matthew asks Rav'ian, speaking only as loudly as he dared.

Peeking out from her fortification, Rav'ian answers, "Fifty-seven,"

"Fifty-seven…" Matthew mutters to himself as he considers the odds. He had yet to see any mech in action, but the high regard that the twins help them in was enough to make him think that they must be quite fearsome.

"Did you get a good look at their uniforms?" Jane asks hesitantly from her position not too far from Matthew.

"They appear to be Fulcrum agents," Rav'ian replies in an emotionless tone.

"You all set, little buddy?" Matthew whispers to the small robot that had taken a liking to him.

The robot wiggles around and lets out a few quieted beeps at Matthew's foot.

"Tell that thing to keep quiet!" Jane urges.

Jane and the others had taken an

immediate liking to the robot despite their short-lived initial concerns about where it had come from or who its original owner was. Whoever it once belonged to was most likely dead and the robot seemed to be sentient enough to pick a new master.

Before Matthew can say anything, the robot skids away from him and then nudges against Jane as it happily beeps.

"Now he's your problem," Matthew laughs as Jane tries pushing the robot away from her leg while it tries to climb up it.

"They are near!" Rav'ian warns.

Looking up to Rav'ian's fortified observation point, Matthew sees her shrink down even further. She slowly checks her weapons and then lines up her sights on the breach in the wall that Matthew and the others had come through.

"I'm just glad that I won't have to end up shooting at Tony," Jane whispers just loud enough for Matthew to hear.

"I'm sorry about that," Matthew apologizes once again. He had taken part in the killing of Tony and he couldn't help but feel bad for it. Time and time again he had played scenarios through his head that could have left the man alive. Shuddering, Matthew remembers the horde of maggots and he quickly shuts the door on that memory.

"He did it to himself," Jane assures Matthew with the same words she had every time.

"I still feel bad about it," Matthew mutters.

"There's no point in that," Jane declares, "Tony knew the risks when he tried to knife you. Besides, you weren't even the one who killed him."

Sighing loudly, Matthew allows the conversation to end there. Everyone around him seemed so much more comfortable with death than he was. The only other person who seemed averse to killing was Marie, but Matthew had yet to see her in combat. For all he knew, she could be just as twisted as the others.

Shuddering, Matthew remembers how casual he had been when he killed that man who was about to blow his cover when he was saving Marie. A look of concern washes over his face when he thinks for the millionth time how he might just be becoming the killer that the others were.

"I see them!" Jane hisses before she flattens herself against the ground and falls still.

Looking to the hole in the wall, Matthew watches as the first person steps into the hangar area. Sure enough, they are dressed in the Fulcrum uniform and Matthew realizes that he had seen this man's face somewhere before. The man looks around and his eyes narrow in suspicion as they do so. They take a few steps forward and they begin examining some of the tracks that Matthew and the others had left when they entered.

Another man slips into the hangar followed by another and another. Before long, Matthew counted a total of twenty people. At that, the flow of soldiers stops as the others assumedly wait outside to stand watch.

These are the people who stole the mech and killed all those Coalition soldiers! Matthew realizes as he suddenly recognizes the face of the first man. At this revelation, Matthew looks around at the others and he picks out the remaining two from the image that Louise had pulled up of the killers.

For a moment, Matthew mentally draws up the same image and he frowns as he remembers the victorious faces of the five people who had sabotaged the Coalition troop transport in order to steal just one mech. Alois had said that they had already killed two of them and that left the three that are now standing in front of him.

Matthew knew that he had to act now. If he failed to do so, then he might never get the chance to take revenge for Wyndover's people. He knew that he wouldn't have this good of an opportunity to fulfill the Second Lieutenant's special assignment again—it wasn't often that this many Fulcrum people were outside of their bunker all at once. Cocking his head in thought, Matthew reasons that this could very well be the entirety of the Fulcrum fighting force.

This might just be the fight of Matthew's life.

Knowing that he had no way out of this, Matthew allows a brief bitter thought to cross his mind, *Rav'ian just had to tell Wyndover that I would take care of everything.*

"Someone has been here," the first man announces menacingly.

Nodding, the sole woman from the group that Matthew would have to kill points at a nearby mech and announces, "It looks like they did the hard work for us, look! They already dug up the mechas."

"They might have just been stealing

parts," the first man shakes his head, "This isn't good."

"Joe, it looks like they might still be here," the final member of the team that Matthew had in his sights warns as he points at the tracks on the ground that the first man, Joe, had been examining.

"I know, Bill," Joe grunts, "That means that they either ran out some other way or they're hiding."

"Well, we've got them outnumbered," the woman points out, "It looks like there was only three or four of them."

"Would you two stop pointing out things that I already know?" Joe snaps as he stares down his compatriots. Turning to the remainder of those who had followed him into the hangar area, Joe orders, "Search the area. I don't want these thieves getting away with our parts."

The group lets out a chorus of affirmations, but they don't get the chance to start moving before Matthew interrupts.

"If you leave now, I won't kill all of you!" Matthew shouts from his hiding spot as he dips out of sight. He knew that he would be giving up his position, but he hoped that the Fulcrum team wouldn't find the others quite so quickly because of that. Matthew was also mindful to only say 'I' instead of 'we' to ensure that the hostiles didn't suspect that he had friends.

Joe laughs mockingly before he counters, "If you leave now, I won't kill your friends."

Matthew peeks out from his barricade and he sees that Joe is looking for him. He continues watching for a few seconds as Joe frantically flashes a handful of seemingly random motions to his team. The group begins to disperse as they all start looking around for Matthew and the others.

Knowing that he was now out of time, Matthew reaches into his pack that is lying beside him and he pulls out two grenades. He pulls the pins out of both and he holds them. Alois had told him that the grenades had a ten-second fuse, so he decides to hold them for six of those seconds. Thanks to his time as a fisherman, Matthew knew just how long it took for things to fly and hit their targets when you threw them. He also was a very good throw.

Without even standing, Matthew finally lobs the grenades and he smiles cruelly as they fly and land a meter to either side of his adversary as he had intended. He takes a sharp breath and calls out, "Bad choice, Joe!"

Joe's head snaps around and his eyes

settle on Matthew. A fraction of a second passes before his eyes widen as he assumedly takes note of the grenades.

Joe shoves his two companions to the side, assumedly in an effort to save them, before he dives to the ground.

"Take cover!" Joe cries out when his body hits the ground.

Unfortunately for him, no amount of taking cover could help him. Matthew made a living throwing lines out to land directly on bobbing buoys from an unsteady deck. Throwing small grenades that were the perfect weight to throw and being on solid ground made this child's play for Matthew.

As Joe's companions hit the ground, the two grenades that Matthew had thrown land just about exactly between them and their courageous leader who is cowering on the ground. Before they have the time to warn each other, the grenades explode in a dazzling display of light, smoke, and fire.

At this, Matthew brings his rifle to bear and he makes quick work of seven of the Fulcrum soldiers. He mows down three who had been approaching from his left and four on his right.

On cue, Rav'ian and Jane join in on the

shooting. As they do so, the small mech roars back to life as Louise prepares to join the battle in her war machine.

Matthew, Jane, and Rav'ian finish off the remaining soldiers that had intruded on them just as the rest of the Fulcrum team begins rushing in.

As soon as the first Fulcrum replacement enters the hangar, Louise's mech dies. A second later, the man that had stepped through is shot and follows the mech's example.

"Oh no!" Jane cries out when the mech falls silent.

"She'll get it running again," Matthew assures her as he opens fire on one of the people that are rushing in through the gaps in the hangar's wall. So far they are all coming in from the same direction, but Matthew is certain that that would not be the case for long.

Ducking down, Matthew gasps as a few well-placed bullets smack into his barricade from his right where the rest of the complex is. Grit and dust shower over him and he slowly reaches up to his face to pick some of the gravel out of his eye. It seemed the Fulcrum had saved the best for last in this incursion.

"Matthew, I know it's you!" James's

voice calls out threateningly from the direction of the shots, "I heard your voice!"

"So what if it is me?" Matthew shouts back. He was surprised that James had worked his way through the building and lined up his shot so quickly.

"I know you're the one who killed my man in my bunker too," James goes on as he opens fire on Jane's position.

Jane rolls out of harm's way and she continues firing at the main group that is forcing their way over their fallen allies. For one reason or another, she seemed content in leaving Matthew to finish off James on his own.

"I liked you, kid," James drones on. He fires at random intervals at Matthew and Jane's entrenchments to ensure that neither of them could get a shot off. A moment passes and he takes note of Rav'ian's outpost as well and he adds her to his gun's route.

"Well, I'm not too fond of you either," Matthew calls back to the man, "I think you're a jerk, actually."

Once he finishes talking, Matthew carves a hole through the pile of rubble that he is hiding behind so he can shoot at James's Fulcrum allies. Despite James's presence, Matthew doesn't feel like the man is his main concern right now. Such a thought strikes Matthew as odd, but he continues firing at the main force of enemies anyway.

"Look at me when I'm talking to you!" James cries out. It seemed that he had noticed that Matthew wasn't paying him the heed that he thought he deserved.

"Who does this guy think he is?" Jane asks just loud enough for Matthew to hear over the steady stream of gunfire.

Looking over in Jane's direction, Matthew sees her looking at him expectantly. As she looks at him, she fires several random shots toward the bulk of the enemies.

"I don't know," Matthew answers with a shrug, "He wasn't like this before."

"What are you two saying?" James demands. When Matthew doesn't immediately answer, James's verbal assault turns to Jane, "I know you turned your back on us too, Jane Sloane! You're a traitor!"

"Back off!" Matthew warns James, "You know you've lost this round!"

Matthew suddenly sees Jane throw something in James's direction and he quickly realizes that it is a grenade. It soars and Matthew hears it land somewhere near the man.

James lets out a laugh before he announces, "Not even close, treasonous Jane! I'm glad we never let you in our bunker! Now I know why your team never came back, you probably killed them!"

"Your forces have been defeated," Rav'ian announces as her gun falls silent, "Leave now or join their ranks in death."

"Is that a Toaz I hear?" James scoffs. Before he can continue, an explosion sounds.

Matthew peeks over his defenses toward James and he sees that the man is wearing an evil grin. Behind him, several fires are blazing where the grenade had gone off. The entrance that James had entered through had been reduced to a pile of rubble. Without this exit, James would have to now run past his fallen team if he was going to try to escape.

Upon seeing Matthew's face, James's eyes take on another layer of deep darkness and he fires wildly at Matthew.

Matthew drops back behind his cover, his eyes still wide. Bullets are still smacking against his foxhole but that isn't what was scaring him.

Something about the look in James's eyes made his heart race and sent a coldness throughout his body. If there were any doubts that something was terribly wrong with James, Matthew knew they were now dashed. For one reason or another, James looked like he had been possessed by the devil himself.

"It's a shame your people were all sent to the slaughter!" James finally calls out. For a moment, Matthew wonders if James knew something about the others from his homeworld, but he then remembers that James had turned his attention to Rav'ian.

"Matthew! He's trying to get into our heads!" Jane warns this time she speaks softly enough that Matthew is certain that James couldn't hear her.

"*You're* the one who had his people slaughtered!" Matthew derides James as he picks up a rock and blindly lobs it over his barricade in the man's direction. Matthew hears the stone crash against the rubble, and he presses his verbal assault, "Just look at what happened to them under your leadership! Each and every one of them is dead. Just wait until I'm put in charge of the Bulwark, I'll have every one of your people hunted down!"

Jane looks at Matthew with a confused and concerned face and Matthew shakes his head at her in an effort to show her that he didn't mean anything that he was saying. She nods once and the look of worry lessens but doesn't fully disappear as she slips back behind her cover.

"Face me like a real man, hero!" James beckons as his gun finally falls silent.

Realizing that James was likely out of ammo, Matthew quickly peeks over his cover and sees that James is standing just a few meters away from the base of the pile of rubble that Matthew is dug in at the top of.

Without a second thought, Matthew raises his rifle and he unloads the entirety of his mag in the blood-crazed man. Even when his magazine is empty, he finds himself still tugging on his trigger.

Click! Click! Click! Matthew's gun sounds as the hammer finds itself without a bullet to smack against.

"Matthew!" Jane calls out from behind him.

Click! Click! Click! Matthew continues tugging on his trigger as he stares at James's bloodied and mangled body. He had never seen a man lose it like James had. Just a matter of a few days ago he had spoken to the man and he seemed perfectly normal... *Click! Click! Click!*

"Matthew!" Jane sounds again, this time

she is a lot closer.

Matthew can't tear his eyes away from James's corpse. *What happened to him!?* Matthew thinks as a sense of terror washes over him, *No one that was as put together as James had been could have gone this crazy… Did someone drug him? What happened? If* he *went nuts, are any of us truly safe?*

The rifle is ripped out of Matthew's hands and Jane's hand slaps hard against his face.

Matthew falls to the ground and he snaps out of his trance. His hands dig into the rubble as he stops himself and one of his hands starts bleeding as the edge of one of the pieces of stonework dig into it. Looking up to Jane, Matthew asks in a hollow voice, "What happened to James?"

"You… shot him?" Jane answers hesitantly. She finishes her response with more of a questioning tone as she sees the terrified look on Matthew's face. Cocking her head slightly, she tosses both her and Matthew's guns a few paces away and she crouches in front of him.

Taking this as her permission to continue, the words begin spilling out of Matthew's mouth in a frantic effort to voice his thoughts, "James wasn't crazy. He was totally normal, just like us. I talked to him! We talked! He was completely normal! This doesn't make sense—how does someone just go crazy? That can't just happen! It doesn't *just* happen! How did—why did... I—I don't—"

Jane places a hand on Matthew's knee and she gently shushes him.

Matthew can see a sadness in her eyes which worries him at first, but then he realizes that this look beat the one that it had replaced. He can see that her look is one of sympathy or even empathy. No longer was Jane looking at him with scared eyes that showed that she thought that Matthew was going off the deep end alongside James.

"It doesn't make sense," Matthew finally whispers. His whole body feels stiff and cold and he can't shake the feeling that the hangar is now holding some kind of evil.

"Ma—Matthew!" Rav'ian stammers from the direction of James's body.

"What?" Matthew asks as he and Jane look toward her. Suddenly Matthew's preoccupation with his own terror was replaced—if only momentarily—by his duty. He had to be present for his team. He had never heard Rav'ian stammer before, so this grabbed his attention in a way he knew few things could.

"Look," Rav'ian grunts as she prods at James's mangled body with her foot.

Confused, Matthew looks closer and he sees that the toe of Rav'ian's boot is lifting a small necklace from James's cratered chest. Matthew squints as he tries to make out what the objects are.

Unable to make heads or tails of what is strung on the necklace, Matthew and Jane climb over the little wall that Matthew had made. They approach James and Rav'ian and take a closer look at the band around the dead man's neck.

As soon as Matthew sees what is around James's neck, he bends over and throws up. He vomits so hard that he wonders if his eyes might pop out.

Around James's neck are an assortment of tongues. Human tongues, alien tongues, Beet tongues. All likely war trophies of a mentally ill man.

James was not as together as Matthew had assumed.

All it took was a gruesome fight for James to reveal the true horrors of war and what war could do to someone to Matthew.

Promotion

The Battle for Allegra

Episode Ten

Chapter One

The Bulwark, Allegra

Matthew casts a quick glance behind himself at the hangar and wonders once more about what could have sent James off the deep end. He had no way of knowing how long the man had been psychotic and part of him didn't want to dig too much deeper into the whole situation. As he saw it, what mattered was that James wouldn't be bothering him again.

Odds were that no one would be.

"Matthew, we're all done in there," Louise informs him as she slips out of the ruined building and approaches Matthew, Rav'ian and Jane.

Matthew and the others had been

607

waiting for Louise on the rocky hillside that overlooked the Fulcrum's old base from the east for quite some time. The sun is sinking behind the eastern enemy lines, but its heat and light are still washing Matthew and his companions. Matthew hadn't realized how bone-cold he had gotten, and he relishes the sun's warmth. In addition to enjoying the heat, Matthew and the others were using their time on the dry hillside to let their boots and outer shells of clothing air out. With the fighting done for the day, moisture was their sole remaining threat.

While Matthew and the others enjoyed the sun, Louise is wrapping up her final exploration of the hangar. All of them had wanted to be out of the dreadful place sooner rather than later and Louise was the only one who could stomach the idea of heading back in and sticking around long enough to get a good look at everything. Matthew, Rav'ian, and Marie, on the other hand, simply went in and out as fast as they could to grab what they knew they would need.

This was just another mark against Louise, in Matthew's eyes. He never wanted to get to the point where that level of gore and that level of evil could be overlooked.

"So, who's walking?" Louise asks casually as she stops a few paces away from the others.

Matthew looks behind him to the three mechs that are all squatting on the ground. Without a ladder, it would be just about impossible to get inside of the mechs if they weren't close to the ground thanks to their height.

Sighing, Matthew says, "I was thinking I could ride on top or something."

"That works too," Louise nods as she looks at the three mechs.

Two of the mechs are hauling all of the gear, supplies, and scrap metal that Louise and the others could load up on them in the shortest amount of time.

A lot of the gear that the machine nearest Matthew was carrying had been stripped from the fallen Fulcrum people— everyone but James at least. On top of that, Louise had strapped the large hydrogen storage tank that Jane had found in addition to several toolboxes and sacks onto its underbelly and sides to allow it to carry even more useful items and supplies.

The other mech that was hauling stuff was brimming with scrap and other potential construction materials. In addition to that, it would also be hauling a lot of spare parts that Louise had insisted that they strip from the other mechs that she couldn't get up and running.

"We ready to go then?" Jane asks with a hollow voice.

Like Matthew, Jane had thrown up profusely when she saw James's horde of war trophies. He couldn't help but think that this was partially his own fault because he threw up first, but he didn't like dwelling on those moments. He knew that he was now scarred for life. Not even the passage of time could lessen the clarity and horror of those moments that marked the end of James's life.

"Yeah," Matthew breathes, "Let's never come back here."

"Matthew, I burned James's body with one of our bottles of alcohol," Louise whispers as she covertly points toward a faint new column of smoke, "I figured you wouldn't want anyone else stumbling across that."

"I was thinking you could just rain some artillery on the building so no one ever comes back here," Matthew says quietly as he looks at the third mech—the one that wasn't carrying anything. Louise had insisted that one of the machines remain unhindered by the salvage of their trip so it could fight if the need arose. Matthew understood her reasoning and, spurred on by the fear of another Fulcrum attack, he encouraged the idea. He doubted that the Fulcrum had the numbers to mount another attack at this point, but he still felt the need to be cautious.

"That sounds even better," Louise nods approvingly.

"Are you sure that we grabbed everything that we needed?" Jane asks with a hint of concern in her voice, "There's no going back if we blow it all up now."

"We can get more stuff from somewhere else," Matthew answers, "I don't want anyone ever going back in there."

Clearly unwilling to throw away any potential prizes that might be sitting in the abandoned building, Jane presses, "What if there's something else worth finding though? Some secret Fulcrum plans or something?"

"Now you sound like a true salver!" Louise exclaims with a laugh. She shakes her head once before she assures Jane and the others, "There's nothing in there worth looting—I went through everything. Lots of bodies, but it seems someone already grabbed most everything that was loose."

"Let's blow it up now, then," Matthew orders.

"You want to pull the trigger?" Louise asks.

Matthew freezes at Louise's words. Something about the way she asked it makes Matthew feel like he was covering up some heinous crime. He shudders slightly as he considers his part in the slaughter that had occurred.

He and his team had killed fifty-seven human beings. These were people that were supposed to be on his side.

All dead.

Dead because of his orders.

Killed by his own gun.

"Matthew?" Louise summons him back from his living nightmare.

"All yours," Matthew quickly answers as he turns his back on the building. He couldn't bear to look at it any longer. Some part of him had been lost in there and he didn't want to look at it to think about what it might have been.

Behind him, Matthew hears Louise grunt a few times as she climbs up the mech that would do the deed. The hatch opens and shuts behind Louise with two respective squeaks. After a few more seconds the mech rumbles to life. Matthew chuckles as he remembers how Louise had explained how just a few more parts on the machine reduced the noise level to the current rumble over the roar that it had earlier.

"It's good to see that the stinking things actually work now," Jane chuckles, "Things would have been a lot easier if that thing worked during our firefight."

"Indeed, it would have been," Rav'ian agrees, "We were quite fortunate to survive that."

Frowning, Matthew can't help but feel guilty about putting his team in harm's way. As he saw it, he should have had Louise ensure that the mech worked long before the fight started. Feeling defeated, Matthew says, "I'm sorry we cut it so close,"

"Do not concern yourself with this, Matthew," Rav'ian sounds. With the crunch of gravel underfoot, Rav'ian pulls up alongside Matthew and she continues, "Battle has its way of... throwing curveballs... at you—as your people say."

"We should have been better prepared though," Matthew grunts, "That was way too close. James could have killed all of us if we weren't so lucky."

"Well, not all of us were so lucky," Jane reminds him as she holds up the small robot that Matthew had found inside the Fulcrum compound. Thanks to James's mad shooting, the small robot had been hit and it lost one of its tank treads. Rather than leave it behind, Jane decided to bring her new friend with her.

Behind Matthew, the sound of electronic motors hum to life. Knowing that these noises were coming from the mech as it lined up its shot, Matthew covers his ears and crouches down. Out of the corner of his eye, Matthew can see Jane and Rav'ian doing the same.

A few seconds pass and Louise's voice sounds over the mech's loudspeakers, "Cover your ears, I'm firing in three, two, one."

At this, the mech's cannons roar to life and Matthew counts five shots with brief pauses in between as Louise locks on to her next target.

About thirty seconds pass and Matthew finally removes his hands from his ears. Despite the noise, the area around him seems perfectly unaware of anything outside of the usual. Turning, Matthew surveys Louise's handiwork.

I won't have to worry about this place ever again, Matthew thinks as his eyes dart across the piles of rubble for any signs of hostiles. Sure enough, nothing is moving, save the occasional chunk of stone or metal that topples from an unsteady pile. Taking a deep breath, Matthew whispers, "It's over."

"So… are we set to head back to Sanctuary?" Jane asks after several more beats.

"I don't see why not," Matthew shrugs as he tears his attention away from the old Fulcrum hideout. As much as he appreciated its being reduced to rubble, he can't help but wish that he could remove its presence entirely. He didn't want to even look at the gravel that was left behind anymore.

"Looks like Louise is ready for you to climb up," Jane notes as she points toward the mech that Louise is in. The mech is now crouching to make it easier for Matthew to climb up.

"Travel safely," Rav'ian nods to Matthew as she climbs into another one of the mechs.

"Don't fall off!" Jane laughs as she closes the door on her own machine.

"This is going to be so much fun," Matthew mutters to himself sarcastically as he climbs onto the roof of Louise's mech. He takes a firm hold of several bars that were supposed to serve as tie-downs and then he knocks on the machine's roof with his heel.

A moment later, the mech rises to its feet and the three mechanized war machines begin the trek back to their bunker.

Chapter Two

The Bulwark, Allegra

I never want to do that again, Matthew thinks with a dissatisfied grumble as he climbs down from the mech with shaky legs. Dropping to the mud, Matthew notes that no amount of time on the sea could have prepared him for the jostling about and jerky motions of riding on top of a mech.

"Looks like we made it in one piece," Jane announces as she emerges from her mech and stretches.

"Don't get out quite yet," Matthew instructs, "We need to park these things inside."

"Ah, right," Jane nods before she slips back into her mech and fires it back up.

Matthew makes his way over to the man port on the side of the garage door and he quickly makes his way through the airlock-like room. Emerging on the other side, he then hits a toggle and the door begins opening ever so slowly.

"How was it out there?" Alois's booming voice calls from somewhere within the hangar.

617

Turning, Matthew sees that Alois is sitting not too far from the garage door and he is whittling away at a piece of wood.

Not wanting to answer the question, Matthew says, "We got three new mechs. Louise was able to fix them up."

"Interesting," Alois nods as he puts down his blade and the piece of wood. Now that the object isn't in Alois's hand, Matthew can see that it is a small figurine.

"What's that?" Matthew asks as he points at the wooden person.

"Nothing," Alois replies as he stands and approaches the garage door.

A few seconds pass and the three mechs begin moving toward the opening. Nearly an additional ten minutes pass before Alois and Matthew finally manage to get the final mech parked where they wanted it.

Nodding approvingly at the sight of the three massive machines, Matthew chuckles, "These things make this place look a lot cooler."

"A lot more threatening too," Alois adds as he also surveys the scene.

Louise drops from where her mech is squatting and she announces, "It's going to look a lot cooler when we get *Firefly* back."

"What's *Firefly*?" Jane asks as she shimmies her way down her own mech.

"She's our big mech," Alois answers, "Our really big one."

Nodding slowly, Jane looks over the three mechs and breathes, "Oh, nice,"

"We still need to name these three," Louise reminds the others.

"I'm always open to suggestions," Matthew nods as he looks at the machines before him.

Every machine looked like it had been through the fight of its life already thanks to the dozens of dents and scratches that absolutely cover their bodies. In addition to those, their paint jobs are all severely discolored thanks to the fires that they had withstood. Matthew was surprised that they survived the fire that he and the others had made in the first place. The fact that they were operating now left him nearly speechless.

"I've got an idea," Louise informs the others after several beats, "But I was thinking you guys should take this one."

"Alright," Matthew nods to Louise. She had named quite a few things already, so he could see where she was coming from by wanting someone else to have a turn. Looking to the others, Matthew requests, "Any ideas?"

"I believe I know the proper names for these machines," Rav'ian says as her black on blue eyes dart between the mechs.

"Which is?" Alois prompts.

"Your people have a story where three emerge from a fire, do you not?" Rav'ian asks.

Seeing where Rav'ian is going, Matthew looks at the machines and smiles, "I like it."

"You agree that their names should be Shadrach, Meshach, and Abednego?" Rav'ian asks Matthew and the others.

"I love it," Matthew nods approvingly. Chuckling, he adds, "But I do think that we should think of some nicknames for them."

"Shad, Mesh, and Abe?" Louise offers.

"Sounds good to me!" Jane declares.

Everyone else sounds their approval of the names and they then decide to clean the mechs up a bit. Once the machines are clean, Jane volunteers to paint the caricatures for them. Matthew and the others leave her to it, and they make their way back to the barracks area.

"So, what's the plan now, boss?" Alois requests as he takes a seat on one of the bunks.

"I was thinking we should get our *Firefly*

back now," Matthew answers, "After some quick naps and some dinner, at least."

"Sounds like a plan," Alois nods, "Will I be able to come along?"

Looking down at Alois's leg that is still in a cast, Matthew briefly considers denying the man's request. He didn't think it would be right to put him into harm's way for no reason.

Before Matthew can say anything, Louise butts in, "He can take one of the mechas! He wouldn't have to walk on his leg that way."

Nodding slowly, Matthew agrees, "Alright, but you can't exit your mech when we get to *Firefly*. That still sound good to you, Alois?"

"Yes," Alois nods excitedly, "I can't wait to get out of here."

"You haven't even been stuck in here for a whole day yet!" Matthew points out with a laugh.

"Doesn't mean I don't want out," Alois shrugs, "When do we leave?"

"Let's get some sleep and then decide," Matthew shrugs, "I'm thinking I need a good shower in there too."

"We got all of them working now, so you should have all the hot water you need," Alois reports, "Marie says the water pressure is great in the lady's, I can't say the same for ours, Mudskipper."

"I'll make do," Matthew shrugs. He hadn't considered that there would be hot water for the showers down here anyways, so, as he saw it, things were already a lot better than they could have been.

"What's the plan of attack to get *Firefly*?" Louise asks before Matthew can stand to leave.

"Oh, uh…" Matthew starts, caught off guard. He hadn't thought of anything besides how Alois was going to get there. Nodding in thought, he eventually answers, "The three of us can take *Shad*, *Mesh*, and *Abe* in… Someone else will have to either ride on top of one of the mechs or walk so they can pilot *Firefly* back here. Riding on top of those things isn't great, so they might be better off walking—that will add a lot of time to our trip though."

"I think *Firefly* could carry one of the mechs pretty easily," Louise reports after a brief silence, "It might be a bit of work to hook the other mecha up to it, but I think it's doable."

"Well, that works," Matthew nods. He had to admit that he liked the idea of not forcing anyone to ride on top of a mech on the way to *Firefly*.

Frowning, Louise shakes her head and points out, "But sending out three units *would* burn up a lot of fuel,"

"And we don't have much to spare," Matthew recalls as he thinks about the limited supply that they had. Until they had the means to produce their own fuel, Matthew knew that it would be best to ration it.

Likely picking up on Matthew's thoughts, Louise asks, "So, are you sure you want to send in three mechas still?"

"I guess not," Matthew frowns, "Maybe it would be better if we just went on foot and had Alois cover us in one."

"Sounds like a plan," Louise nods.

Nodding slowly, Matthew puts together his new game plan. A few seconds pass before he finally announces, "But let's just have it be the three of us and Rav'ian. No need to waste Jane and Marie's time, the four of us should be more than enough to get everything done."

"You sure we need Rav'ian?" Alois asks.

"She knows the land and she knows the threats," Matthew shrugs. He knew that he was just being extra cautious by bringing her along, but he liked the idea of having an extra set of eyes. The twins had yet to go over the top yet, so Matthew didn't like the idea of keeping the two of them safe all on his own.

"But her leg is still healing," Alois reminds Matthew.

"Right…" Matthew breathes as the realization hits him. Frowning, he cedes, "I guess it will just be us then."

Letting out a sudden laugh, Louise gives her brother a shove and chides, "Your leg is hurt too, genius,"

"But I won't be walking," Alois shrugs dumbly.

A thoughtful look on her face, Louise nods and offers, "I'm with Alois though, we shouldn't force her to come along."

"Sorry, Mudskipper," Alois apologizes, "I just could see that she looked rather spent when you all got back here. She wouldn't say no if you asked her to come along, but I wouldn't want to see her do that to herself."

"No, I just forgot," Matthew assures Alois, "I've got a lot on my mind is all."

"Well, now that we've got a plan, let's stick to it," Louise announces as she grabs a bundle of clothing from a nearby sack.

•••••••••••••••

Matthew yawns into his fist as he contemplates scrubbing the mission to get the *Firefly*. As he saw it, they mech would still be stuck in the same hole in a few hours after he got a full eight hours of sleep. The four-hour nap that he had just didn't seem to cut it.

"Are you certain that you do not require my assistance?" Rav'ian asks Matthew for the tenth time since he woke up.

"Yes, I'm sure," Matthew tells her, "I know the way and I'll keep an eye out for the Latchers."

"There are additional threats beyond the Latchers," Rav'ian reminds Matthew.

Lacing up his fresh boots, Matthew looks up to Rav'ian and chuckles softly. If he didn't know better, he would think that she was just worrying about him because she had sworn her life to him. In reality, he knew that this was just her nature. She cared deeply for everyone that she fought beside.

Sighing, he looks around the locker room where Louise had directed him. In here, he had found a new—and dry—pair of boots that fit in addition to a wide array of armor. He had smiled when he found that there was just as much armor made from dead Beets as there was traditional bulletproof gear. Rav'ian had done a lot to store and incorporate the gifts from her people with everything in the bunker.

On Matthew's right, someone knocks on a locker and he looks over to see Louise looking at him. A brief moment passes before she asks, "You set? Alois and I are all geared up."

"Just about," Matthew assures her as he fixes his Beet breastplate into place with Rav'ian's help. He had considered wearing a bulletproof vest like the twins, but he couldn't help but be drawn to the piece that the Toaz had gifted him after his first hunt. Sure, there was the hint of disgust that Matthew felt over wearing what was essentially a war trophy like those that James had, but something about the Toaz's fashioning the armor for him seemed to nullify those feelings.

"Do not forget these," Rav'ian says with her toothy Toaz smile as she holds two bracers near Matthew's forearms, "Another gift from my people."

"Great," Matthew nods as he takes the pieces and laces them into place one at a time. When he finishes, Rav'ian presents some guards for his legs which he also puts on. With everything in place, Matthew stands, and he realizes how light the armor felt for how much it covered. If he hadn't seen the Beet carapace in action, he would feel very exposed right now. But he had seen just what kind of punishment the shell that this armor was formed from could take. Walking over to a nearby mirror with ease, he examines himself.

"My people would approve," Rav'ian sounds from somewhere out of sight, "However, there is one last piece that you require."

"What's that?" Matthew inquires as he tears his attention away from his polished black armor. The glittering shells were sure to attract attention, but Matthew wasn't sure if he cared at this point. He was in love with them.

Rav'ian holds up a disk that is made up of a dozen or so Beet legs. The legs branch out from the center where they are the thinnest and then grow wider near the edge of the ovoidal shield. The shield itself is about one meter tall and a half meter wide.

"Wow," Matthew breathes as he gawks at the shield. He faintly remembered wanting a shield, but he had forgotten this desire as the days dragged on. Now that he was looking at one, the dreams returned.

"Because of the tales of your exploits,

my people deemed you worthy of such a tool," Rav'ian explains as she helps Matthew to strap the shield into place on his left arm, "Any warrior who faces an adversary in hand to hand combat, as you have done, must have adequate protection. This is quite the honor."

"Thanks," Matthew nods as he tests the shield's weight. As was the case with the rest of the armor, the shield is also surprisingly light, and Matthew can't help but think how he would be better protected with this light stuff than the twins would be with their heavy vests and other gear.

"Come on, let's go already!" Louise calls from the hangar.

"I'm coming," Matthew laughs as he excuses himself. He leaves Rav'ian in the locker room area as he slips into the adjacent armory just long enough to grab his pack and rifle that he had prepped before suiting up. Content that he had everything that he would need, Matthew then marches into the hangar.

Louise whistles and says, "Love the armor, Mudskipper."

"Very pretty stuff," Jane nods approvingly.

"Looks like it'd stand out from several kilometers away," Alois grunts from the mech that he had chosen for their outing, "Way too shiny."

Looking over at Alois, Matthew sees that he had chosen the mech *Shad*, the mech that looked the most fearsome due to all of the damage it had taken in the fire. Without skipping a beat, Matthew points out, "Even if this sticks out, I'll still be perfectly safe. This stuff is just about impenetrable."

"Indeed it is," Rav'ian agrees from behind him, "Matthew was struck by a sniper bolt in the head and the helmet did not fail."

"Let's not try getting shot in the head again," Marie advises, "No need pressing our luck."

"Wasn't planning on it," Matthew agrees with a weak chuckle as he recalls the pain of the hit. Although he was still alive thanks to the helmet, he couldn't help but wish that it could have stopped at least a little bit of the blow.

"Don't mess up my paint job!" Jane warns Alois as he climbs through the hatch on the *Shad*.

"Don't worry, I won't smear it," Alois grunts before he slams the door shut behind himself.

"I was meaning to ask," Matthew sounds as he looks at Jane, "How come you never shared your last name with us?"

"My last name?" Jane asks, surprised. Shrugging, she answers, "I didn't think it mattered. Sloane isn't too exciting. I wasn't meaning to hide anything, it just didn't come up."

"Huh," Matthew grunts in thought, "So, what's it mean?"

"Fighter… or something along those lines," Jane shrugs, "I always thought it was dumb until I got stuck here. Now I'm a soldier, so I guess I can live up to my name."

"You never asked what my last name was either," Marie reminds Matthew as she steps away from the *Shad*. A moment later, the mech rises to its full height as Alois waits for the hangar door to open.

"You're right," Matthew nods, "What is it?"

"I'll tell you when you get back," Marie smirks.

"Let's get a move on!" Louise calls out in a menacing voice as she shifts her grip on her rifle and starts toward the garage door.

"Remain vigilant," Rav'ian urges Matthew.

"Don't get shot," Jane winks.

"And if you do get shot, I'll be sure to kill

you," Marie adds as she gives him a playful shove toward the hangar's door that is now opening.

"Great, I've got three moms telling me what to do," Matthew chuckles as he walks away from the trio that were in charge of holding down the fort.

Something hits Matthew's exposed shoulder from behind and is followed by Jane's voice, "I ain't anyone's mom!"

"Yeah, yeah," Matthew laughs as he shakes his head. Looking down he sees that Jane had thrown a good-sized bolt at him from who knows where. Shaking his head, he teases, "Whatever you say, *mom*."

This is met with a frustrated sigh from Jane who doesn't say anything else.

Louise waits for Matthew to follow the *Shad* out of the hangar before she hits the toggle to shut the door behind them. After walking a few more steps she stops and announces, "If we're lucky, then we'll be able to fix the *Firefly* and get back here without anyone missing us."

"It's quite a long way to where the Toaz left it," Matthew warns.

"Yeah, but we'll manage," Alois pledges over the *Shad's* loudspeakers.

"We have all the parts we need, right?" Matthew requests as he looks up to the *Shad's* underbelly where a makeshift bag is hanging.

Nodding, Louise answers, "Yep, I checked myself and double-checked with Rav'ian. We're all set."

Well, time to go then," Matthew sighs. As much as he hated to admit it, he was excited to be going over the top once more. After getting shot at and having his life threatened by people that should have been on his side for so long, he liked the idea of taking on the real enemy. Not only that, but he liked the idea of knowing exactly who the enemy was at first glance.

"Lead the way," Louise requests, "You're the one that knows where that hole is."

Chapter Three

The Bulwark, Allegra

After quite the long walk, Matthew can just make out the hole that he had killed his first Beet in just a few Allegrian days prior. Over the course of the hours-long trudge, Matthew had only found a handful of Latchers that were buried in the mud waiting for an unfortunate soul to stir up their wrath. After showing the twins what to look out for and how to kill them, Matthew had dispatched them and left their bodies. He was done collecting bodies from the battlefield; James's collection had seen to that.

"You said it's just a little further ahead?" Louise requests as she slowly scans their surroundings.

Besides the occasional Latcher, there weren't any other hostiles from the Beets. Despite their massive offensive with the artillery strikes, the Beets seemed to be content waiting for the Coalition counterattack.

When that attack was supposed to come, Matthew didn't know. All he did know was that Beets were here and they wouldn't be going anywhere without some very compelling arguments to leave—arguments in the form of lead.

"Just a little bit further?" Louise repeats when Matthew fails to say anything.

"It's just over there," Matthew assures her as he points at the entrance into the hole, "Alois can probably see it from his vantage point."

"I sure can," Alois sounds over the *Shad's* speakers, "It looks pretty big."

"The Toaz probably widened the hold to get the *Firefly* down there," Matthew reasons as he stops to scan the dark landscape.

Wary of the Beets' response to lights, Matthew had ensured that the mech's lights were all dimmed or off and that everyone kept their flashlights put away. He didn't want to risk getting attacked by any Beets that mistook the light from their flashlights as daylight. One near-death encounter from that mistake was more than enough for him.

"The Toaz sure did a great job at covering their tracks," Alois notes, "You can't even tell that a mech went through here."

"It's probably for the best," Matthew shrugs, "If they left tracks then James might have tried to take it back."

Louise shudders in front of Matthew before she whispers, "I would have hated to see how that would have ended up for us."

Frowning, Matthew tries to stir up some sort of emotional response, but he can't. For one reason or another, his emotional tanks are empty, and he can't help but feel like that might be because of the firefight that James had started. Something was off with him now and he knew it. Despite this knowledge, Matthew still feels scared. He knew something was different, but he isn't quite sure how to fix it, if it was permanent, or how he could stop it.

"Let's stop here," Matthew announces as he holds up a hand for Alois to see.

The *Shad* stops but its engine continues humming contently. As far as Matthew can tell, the rumble is the only sound in the valley.

"You want me to wait here?" Alois asks after a beat.

"Yeah, keep watch," Matthew answers, "Louise and I are going to go the rest of the way on foot. I don't want the *Shad* falling into the hold or getting stuck."

"Copy," Alois's voice buzzes over the speakers. A moment passes and the machine begins slowly turning from one side to the other as Alois looks for any sign of hostiles.

Matthew marches over to the Shad and he pulls the bag full of the *Firefly's* parts down. Glancing inside, he confirms that everything is still present, and he sighs. Tying the bag onto his backpack, Matthew returns to Louise.

"After you," Louise says as she motions ahead, "I don't want to step on any of those Latcher things. You've got a better eye for them."

Chuckling, Matthew admits, "I'm surprised I've seen as many as I have. Rav'ian is the one who's good at finding them."

"We'll have to be sure that she teaches the new recruits down the road," Louise muses.

"Yeah we do," Matthew agrees as he slowly begins heading toward the hole.

With every step, a deeper sense of hollowness rises in Matthew's chest. Something about returning to the place where he shed his first blood felt wrong. It felt like he was desecrating a grave.

"You've been pretty quiet this whole trip, what's up?" Louise prods as they slog through the mud.

Matthew tries to stop in order to look around, but he slips instead. The mud out here is a lot slimier than the stuff in the trenches and

Matthew can't help but wonder why. Catching himself before he falls all the way to the ground, Matthew sighs. *I don't like this place,* he thinks with a sense of disgust.

"I'm seeing some movement to the north," Alois warns, "Not sure what it is though."

Shaking his head, Matthew finally answers Louise's question, "I'm not feeling like myself lately."

"That fight with James getting to you?"

"Yeah,"

"Was it just that, or was it his trophy necklace too?"

"A bit of both, actually. It all just feels so… wrong."

"War does that to people."

"Think it could happen to us?"

"It might be our job to fight the fight here," Louise says as she motions around them. Pointing at her head, she finishes, "But we can't forget that we also have to fight the same fight here. So long as we win the fight in our heads, we'll be fine."

"But James seemed so normal before. I mean, sure, he wasn't a good guy, but I didn't think he was crazy."

"People snap sometimes. My bet is that

637

he was always a little crazy and really went over the edge when we—"

"When we what?" Matthew asks worriedly. The thought of his own actions pushing James over the edge made his stomach churn.

Louise waits a few moments, assumedly trying to select the best response before she mutters, "When we attacked his bunker. I'm guessing we shattered his sense of security and that was the only thing keeping him sane."

An ache at the pit of Matthew's stomach quickly spreads throughout his abdomen as a feeling of guilt rears its ugly head. Swallowing, Matthew whimpers with a dry mouth, "So it was our fault."

Louise chuckles weakly before she assures Matthew, "There's no point in blaming yourself for a madman snapping. Anything could do it."

"But—"

"Let's get the *Firefly* and we can discuss this further when we're inside it," Louise interrupts. She quickly looks around before she adds, "I don't like it out here. We're far too exposed."

"Feels like we're being watched," Matthew agrees as he starts toward the hole again.

"I'm glad I'm not the only one thinking it."

"Think it's that thing that Alois saw?"

"Probably not, he would have warned us if it stopped to watch us."

"So it's got a friend…"

"Why did you have to say that?" Louise asks with a tremor in her voice.

"I know you were thinking it too," Matthew breathes as he sneaks a quick look at the stout hills and berms that are surrounding him and the twins on all sides. Everything was set up for the perfect trap.

"Can we hurry it up a bit?" Louise requests in a whisper.

At Louise's whisper, Matthew suddenly realizes that he had slowed down to the point that he was hardly moving in an effort to make as little sound as possible. Something about the eeriness just made silence seem like the only correct route.

"Think we should have Alois kill the engines on his mech?" Matthew whispers back as he increases his pace ever so slightly.

"No," Louise quickly answers, "The noise might be just enough to cover our advance."

"I hope you're right," Matthew mumbles

as his eyes lock onto the hole ahead of him.

Trying his best to soothe his nerves, Matthew assures himself. *We just have to get in, plug in a few things, and get out. Totally easy.*

"We're here," Matthew sounds as he slows to a stop about two meters from the entrance to the burrow. Looking back to Louise, he explains, "It can be super slick around the hole. Not only that, the ground might give way."

"Then what's the plan?"

"Got any rope?"

Louise nods and Matthew secures both his and Louise's ropes to two pegs that he sinks firmly into the ground. After handing one to Louise, Matthew slowly works his way to the lip of the hole.

Sure enough, Matthew can see the roof of the *Firefly* clear as day. Its smooth hull is only a meter or so below where Matthew is crouching.

Looking back to Louise, Matthew motions for her to wait and he jumps.

The mud underfoot gives way and his feet slide out from under him. With that, Matthew enters the hole much in the same way as he had on his first time—an uncontrolled fall. As he falls, he loses hold of his rope and he has nothing to slow the ground's advance with. Taking a quick breath, he reaches out with his arms to try and soften his landing.

Matthew's attempt to catch himself is rather futile as his hands slip into the mud which may as well have been water. The fall and his own weight causes him to sink and the mud rises up his outstretched arms to his shoulders. As suddenly as he fell, Matthew stops. Now motionless, he suddenly realizes how much it hurt when his full body slapped against the mud. Groaning, he takes an unsteady breath.

Pulling himself out of the mud at the base of the hole, Matthew sighs. Reaching up to his face, he gently wipes the filth away from his eyes, nose, and mouth.

"Are you alright?" Louise asks from above.

Spitting out some of the mud that had gotten into his mouth, Matthew sarcastically answers, "I'm absolutely great."

"That sounded like it hurt," Louise says as her footsteps make loud sloshing sounds and she approaches the lip of the hole.

"It did," Matthew grunts at her as he presses his hand against his sternum. Part of him wonders if the presence of the armor did more harm than good as it spread the entire impact over his whole front. Shaking his head, Matthew refocuses himself. Looking up, he asks, "Think you can make the jump?"

"I know I can," Louise's voice answers confidently. A moment later, Matthew hears several hurried steps and then he sees Louise's silhouetted body flash overhead. Several thumps on top of the *Firefly* betray the results of her leap before Louise triumphantly announces, "Yep, I made it."

Outside of the hole, Matthew hears Alois's voice say something, but he can't make out the words. He waits for Alois to fall silent before he asks Louise, "What was that? I couldn't hear him."

"He says that he finally got a good look at the thing to the north," Louise answers with a hint of worry.

"And?" Matthew presses.

Sighing, Louise answers, "It's coming this way,"

"Any idea what it is?" Matthew asks. A few days ago, he would have been worried sick by the idea of something coming straight for him, now the idea felt natural. As Matthew saw it, this was just the way things were now.

"He says he's never seen anything like it. It's definitely one of the Beets, but it isn't like anything that he's heard about. Evidently, it's rather small too."

Shuddering, Matthew immediately thinks about the maggots from the crater that he had nearly drowned in. Shaking his head to clear the memory, his thoughts then turn to the thing that he had felt moving below the mud shortly before that.

"Whatever this thing is, I don't want to be down here to face it," Matthew whispers as he looks at the walls of the cave that he is in.

Louise looks over the edge of the *Firefly* down to Matthew and she worriedly asks, "Did you drop any of the parts we needed?"

"No, I…" Matthew starts to answer as he grabs at the bag of the *Firefly's* parts. As he pulls on it, he realizes that the bag is a lot lighter now. Whipping the bag around, Matthew sees that the bag had opened and dumped out about half of the parts that he and Louise needed. He quickly counts the parts and he notes that he is missing seven of them.

"You lost some parts," Louise surmises with a disgruntled groan.

"I had them a few minutes ago," Matthew assures her as he looks at the ground, "They just fell out when I fell…"

"Well, toss me what you have," Louise requests, "I'll start putting the Firefly back together."

"Got it," Matthew nods as he gives the half-empty bag a good toss to ensure that it made it all the way to Louise. Once he sees that Louise caught the parts, he turns and starts sifting through the mud around where he fell.

Matthew quickly finds five of the seven missing items and he breathes a sigh of relief. Brushing the mud off them, he quickly sees that they are undamaged. Looking up to where he had last seen Louise, he briefly considers tossing the parts to her, but he decides against it. He needed to let her work and she would call down to him when she was ready for the other parts.

Cleaning away the remaining mud, Matthew quickly sets the parts aside using one of the *Firefly's* feet as a shelf to keep them off the mud. While standing beside the *Firefly's* foot, Matthew sheds his pack as well, but he is careful to keep his rifle on him. He had no intention of being caught down here again without a weapon at the ready.

"Where are the other two parts?"

Matthew breathes as he crouches down and takes a look at where he had fallen from further away. From this new vantage point, he sees a mound of mud that appears to be newer.

Reasoning that he had found one of the missing parts, Matthew marches over to the mound and he slips his hand in.

Rather than feeling a cool piece of metal, Matthew feels something else entirely. The blood drains from his face when he realizes that he is touching another Beet-like creature.

Before he can whip his hand away, the creature shoots out of Matthew's grip and its shell slices his hand in its retreat.

"Louise!" Matthew calls, "There's something down here!"

"Then hurry up and get out of there," Louise instructs simply before she grunts and mutters something under her breath.

"No really?" Matthew grumbles as he looks at his bleeding and muddied hand. Shaking his head, Matthew decides that he doesn't have the time to clean or bandage himself up. Despite this, he also knew that he couldn't risk getting his new wound any dirtier, so he opts to use the butt of his rifle to poke around in the slime in search of his missing two parts. Knowing that the gun's stock wouldn't cover enough ground, Matthew shuffles his feet through the mud as well as he blindly searches.

Overhead, Matthew hears Alois's muffled voice once more. His voice sounds a lot more frantic this time.

Before Matthew can ask, Louise relays the message, "There's a lot of those creatures coming our way now. Alois says that they're coming faster too."

"Do you think he can shoot at them to scare them off?" Matthew asks as he tenses up.

There is a grunt and a metallic clank before Louise answers, "I don't think we should try that just yet; it might wake up some more hostiles. Once we get the *Firefly* out of here, we should be clear to open fire though."

"Then I'd better hurry," Matthew frowns as he quickens his pace. Despite his best efforts, his movements are a lot jerkier now and he is convinced that he is going to miss something. As this thought crosses his mind, his rifle strikes something hard.

Reaching down with his good hand, Matthew takes a deep breath before sending it into the unknown.

His fingers touch a sharp edge which initially makes Matthew flinch and pull back. When the object doesn't move, Matthew reasons that it is inanimate, and his fingers explore deeper into the mire. After a brief search, Matthew grasps a small box-like object which he pulls out of the mud. Smiling, he sees that the object is one of the *Firefly's* parts.

"Just one more part to go!" Matthew calls up to Louise. He can't help but hope that she might join in on his celebration, but she doesn't. Instead, there are a few more clanks and thuds and grunts from where Louise is.

"Bring them up here," Louise finally orders with a hint of disapproval, "I just need one last part for my work up here, then everything else should be inside of the cockpit."

"What about the last part that I need?" Matthew asks as he gathers his gear and the parts. After ensuring that he had everything, he begins scaling the *Firefly's* stout ladder. The ladder would be unreachable if the mech wasn't crouching and Matthew can't help but feel thankful for its presence. Without it, he would have to climb back up his rope with his injured hand.

Doing his best to keep the wounded part

of his palm off of the rungs, Matthew struggles up the ladder. Between the weight of his pack and the poor grip that his bad hand offered, things are far from ideal.

"You got the master fuse?" Louise calls down to Matthew as she peeks down at him from her perch.

His brows furrow as he tries to think about what the master fuse was before he answers, "I don't know."

"It's a cylinder," Louise explains. She holds her hands apart a short way and continues, "About this big?"

"Then yeah, I got it," Matthew nods as he remembers the first part that he had grabbed from the mud.

Smiling, Louise exclaims, "Perfect! That's the last one I need up here, by the looks of it. As I said a bit ago, the rest of the parts should belong inside of the cockpit."

"I still need that last part," Matthew reminds her as he finally crests the ladder.

"It's over where you tried to jump from," Louise tells him, "We'll have to figure out a way to get back up there. I noticed it just a few seconds ago."

"Any idea what it is?"

"I'm not certain, but I think it's some sort

of computer board. We'll probably need it before we can start this thing back up."

"And I take it that it's my job to get it?"

"You guessed it, hotshot," Louise winks and offers Matthew an exaggerated nod.

"Lovely," Matthew breathes as thoughts of an easy trek go out the window.

"Matthew…" Louise trails off as she looks behind him.

Looking down, Matthew sees that the ground beneath him is moving. More accurately, he can see that something just under the surface is seemingly waking up.

"Nope!" Matthew calls as he scales the last step on the ladder and spins around so his back is against the *Firefly's* entrance hatch. Shuddering at the thought of being eaten by the unseen creatures below, Matthew grabs his rifle and clicks off its safety.

"Give me the fuse," Louise instructs, "We can't stay here."

Passing the cylindrical item up to Louise, Matthew uses his other hand to open the *Firefly's* hatch. He opens it just wide enough to put in the parts that he had in addition to his heavy pack. Before shutting the door, he pulls out most of his spare mags and two of his grenades.

"No pressure," Matthew mutters as he shuts the door and approaches the ledge.

Looking down once more, Matthew sees that the sea of mud beneath him is churning. Several small black creatures leap out of the mud in an effort to reach him, but they fail to get too close. Matthew can't help but chuckle as the sight before him reminds him of what the water looked like as he pulled in nets full of fish. Just as the catch would break the surface the water would seemingly boil, and fish would try to escape the net's hold.

Cutting his memory short, Matthew tugs sharply on his gun's operating rod and he chambers the first round from his mag. Feeling oddly indifferent about what he was about to do, Matthew sighs.

Taking a sharp breath, he thinks, *This is war.*

Pulling the trigger, Matthew opens fire. He rakes his weapon side to side in an effort to ensure that every monster beneath him found the same amount of attention wherever it hid. Without many other options, Matthew reasoned that he had to kill every one of the fishlike Beets before he could move along. Matthew knew that he would face an unsightly demise if he fell when he was trying to get the final part that Louise had told him was at the mouth of their cave. In an effort to rig the odds in his favor, Matthew hoped to kill most, if not all, of the fish-Beets.

"I'm all set!" Louise calls from the roof. Her voice is just loud enough to be heard over Matthew's firing in the semi-confined space. Thankfully for both of them, the mud seems to be a good sound absorber and prevents too much of an echo.

"Get in the *Firefly*!" Matthew orders as he lets his gun dangle by its strap. Gathering his munitions, he starts up the ladder to the mech's roof and he requests, "And get me your rope!"

Louise meets Matthew at the lip of the mech's roof and she helps him up. Once he is standing beside her, Louise hands him her rope and then drops her pack to the small landing just in front of the *Firefly's* hatch. Looking back to Matthew for a second, she nods and then hops down after her pack.

"Shut the hatch after you!" Matthew demands harshly when he notices that the writhing mud is now reaching the walls of the cavern. He knew that the creatures would use the higher elevation to try to jump at him and he wasn't about to have Louise needlessly die from the creatures.

Gritting his teeth, Matthew unloads the remaining bullets of his fifth magazine into the stream of movement that had gotten the furthest up the wall.

The movement stops, but Matthew can see at least a dozen other spots where the strange Beet mutants are ascending.

Knowing that time was anything but on his side, Matthew looks at the rope that Louise had handed him. Letting his rifle hang once more, Matthew gives the rope a few sharp tugs in an attempt to dislodge it. When it refuses to budge, he realizes that his hopes to lasso the out of reach part was no longer an option.

"They're coming closer!" Alois's voice warns over the loudspeakers on the *Shad*.

"Shoot them!" Matthew shouts for all that he is worth. He momentarily wonders if Alois had heard him, but the heavy machinegun fire that ensues cuts those doubts short. A moment later, Alois engages the heavier cannons on his mech as well and, even at this distance, Matthew can feel the gun reports in the base of his gut.

I'm going to have to climb… Matthew thinks in concern as he looks down at his hand. Upon closer inspection, he can see that the cut that the strange creature had left him with is both deep and jagged. Frowning, Matthew notes that it would take some time to heal on its own and it wouldn't stop bleeding without some proper attention.

Shaking his head, Matthew decides that he didn't have time to slow down. Death was climbing up on all sides and inactivity would doom him and Louise both. Wrapping his torn hand in the rope that he would use to climb, Matthew winces and takes in a sharp breath. The rope's fibers dig into his sensitive exposed flesh, but they aren't nearly as course as some of the rope that he had worked with before.

Swallowing, Matthew pushes down the pain and he walks to the edge of the *Firefly* that is nearest the ledge he jumped from earlier. Looking up, he sees the small box-like part that Louise had said she needed. If the *Firefly* was just a little bit taller, he would have been able to grab the part without having to climb. The ledge that the computer chip is on is dripping with mud and what Matthew hopes is water. Even as he looks at it, several chunks of waterlogged earth tumble to the writhing ground below.

"They're not stopping!" Alois's voice cries from where he and the *Shad* are as he momentarily stops firing. The reprieve is very short-lived and Matthew quickly sees the world overhead flash with yellows, oranges, and reds as tracers from the *Shad's* guns begin streaking by once again.

"This is going to hurt," Matthew grunts to himself as he tightens his grip on the rope. He drops his rifle and pack on the roof beneath him and takes another long breath. A moment later, he is climbing up the line.

With every gain up the rope. Matthew's wounded hand burns more and more. The pain rises to the point that Matthew's arm begins to feel almost numb until the pain is just a dull ache. By now, Matthew is within reach of the lip of the hole by the time that his arm seemingly fell asleep.

He tries a few times to pull one of his arms from the rope, but he can't manage. Every time he tries, the strain on the remaining hand is too much. Frowning, Matthew realizes that his wound must be zapping away his energy.

Taking a deep breath, Matthew considers his options. Knowing that he can't risk falling, he decides to climb even further up the rope.

After six long pulls, Matthew is eye level

with the surface world. Not too far away he can see Alois opening fire and the bullets whiz over his head. By now, Matthew's side is burning in his body's attempt to tell his brain that it is time to call it quits. Grimacing, Matthew whispers to his body, "Not… yet…"

Knowing that he couldn't make it all the way up, Matthew opts to do the next best thing. Pulling himself a few centimeters higher, Matthew opens his mouth and grabs the edge of the circuit board with his teeth. Letting out several celebratory grunts, Matthew quickly descends his rope. His muscles give out on him several times, but he doesn't fall thanks to the fact that he has the rope wrapped around his mangled hand. With each fall, Matthew can feel the flesh on his hand rip further despite the numbness and he flinches as every drop of blood falls from it.

After a good three minutes, Matthew is finally back to the level that the *Firefly's* roof is at and he begins peddling his legs in an effort to swing over to it. With each swing, more and more of Matthew's world becomes focused on one thing: the *Firefly's* top. His salvation.

After his sixth swing, Matthew feels something slap against his side. Looking over to it, he sees one of the fishlike Beets clamoring for hold before it falls to the ground. Looking around, Matthew sees that there are hundreds of the Beets leaping from the muddied walls of the cave toward him.

Without so much as a thought, Matthew releases the rope and he finds himself flying through the air. As he flies, one thought slowly passes through his head, *Please don't land in the mud... I don't want these things to eat me alive.*

Before he can concoct another thought he slams into the ground. Bouncing against the hard surface twice, Matthew rolls over and he lets out a relieved sigh as he stares at a steel panel beneath him.

Taking a deep breath, Matthew then spits out the computer component and it clatters on the steel surface. Rolling onto his front he slowly picks himself up and his world begins to draw back into focus. As he rises to his feet the pain in his hand comes back to the forefront and he dizzily sways for a few seconds.

A fish-Beet suddenly smacks into Matthew's foot and it bounces off and comes to a stop a half meter away. Once it stops, the creature starts worming its way back to Matthew. Matthew's eyes dart toward where the Beet had come from as he kicks it away and he remembers the dire straits that he is in.

"Do or die time," Matthew whispers to himself.

Spurred on by the countless fish-Beets that are leaping at him and the *Firefly*, Matthew quickly picks up his gear and the chip that he had just risked his life for. Looking around for a brief moment, he confirms that he has everything, and he quickly makes his way back down the ladder to the *Firefly's* hatch.

He stops just short of the landing and frowns as he looks at all the fish-Beets that are squirming around on the small platform. He couldn't take another step down without putting his ankles at risk of getting nicked by one of the fish's barbs.

Thinking quickly, Matthew takes an inventory of his supplies and he remembers the shield that he had strapped to the side of his pack. Pulling it free, he reaches down and begins swatting the fish-Beets away. Once he clears enough area, drops down and slips into the mech's cockpit.

The moment that Matthew is through, Louise asks, "You get the part?"

Looking over to where the voice had come from, Matthew sees that Louise is buried in a slew of wiring and other stuff. She must have had to yank it all out to get to where the Toaz had removed one of the parts from. Matthew stares for a moment before he dumbly answers, "Uh, yeah."

"Hand it here," Louise requests as her hand emerges from the wiring.

Matthew walks over to her and he hands her the chip. Once he does so, his focus turns to the cockpit window where dozens upon dozens of the fish-Beets are slapping against the thick glass. They don't make too much of a sound through the glass beyond a dull thud. If Matthew wasn't listening carefully, he was sure that he wouldn't be able to even hear them. The even duller smack of the fish-Beets hitting the mech's hull is even harder to pick out, but Matthew can still detect them.

"Alright, that's all set now," Louise announces as she begins emerging from the mess of wiring. Once she's out she invites Matthew to clean things up after her and she then informs him, "I'll have to boot everything up now, that'll take a bit."

"How long is a bit?" Matthew asks nervously as he casts a worried look at the mech's windscreen. Outside, the fish-Beets' assault has seemingly tripled and now Matthew can't hear the gun reports from Alois's shooting over the noise.

"A lot longer than you'd like it to be," Louise grunts as she fires up one of the computers. She examines the readouts for a few moments before she sadly reports, "I don't know how long it will take. This thing wasn't built to have so many of its systems taken offline like the Toaz did."

"Is it still safe?" Matthew worriedly asks as he pauses long enough to ensure that he didn't feel anything too far out of the norm. Beyond his hand and the odd numbness on that side of his body, nothing seemed too far off.

Before Matthew can get back to the task at hand, he freezes and remembers the last time that a spike on a Beet had cut into him like this. The same numbness had ensued, and he remembered later finding out that it was poison. With a gasp, his jaw drops at the realization and he thinks, *Not again…*

"What is it?" Louise asks as she finally turns from her work to take a good look at Matthew. Her eyes drop to his bleeding hand and they grow wide. Her voice cracks with worry as she asks, "Are you alright? That looks pretty bad."

"I… I think I might have gotten poisoned again," Matthew tells her after a second. Looking down at his dangling arm he watches a few drops of blood drip from his fingers to the ground. Swallowing, Matthew adds, "We'll have to pick up one of those Latchers that I killed. Marie used one last time to make an antivenom or something."

"Alright, I'll radio Alois," Louise volunteers, "How long will you be able to hold out?"

"I don't know," Matthew shrugs as he shakes his head. Looking back to the mess of wires, he adds, "I'm going to clean this up and then I think I'll have to sit down."

"Fix up your hand first," Louise orders, "I can't have you bleed out before you finish. The medkit is on the wall behind you."

Nodding slowly, Matthew turns to the kit and he begins patching himself up. As he does so, he can't help but feel bad for his getting hurt yet again. He had just promised Marie that he would play it safe and here he was. As he wraps up his hand, he hears Louise informing Alois of his predicament over the mech's radios.

"Do you think we have enough time to get both him and the mech out?" Alois's voice buzzes quietly.

Frowning, Matthew considers butting into the twins' conversation. The thought quickly passes as Matthew considers Alois's words. He knew that Alois was onto something, there was no knowing just how dangerous the fish-Beet's toxins were.

"I don't know," Louise whispers back in response, "All I know is that we need to get him back to Marie sooner rather than later."

The twins continue talking for some time and Matthew loses interest. Instead, he focuses on reorganizing the slew of wiring. Matthew isn't sure how much longer he had before he passed out, but he had noticed that staying focused helped keep the fogginess in his brain at bay.

Fifteen minutes pass and Louise finally announces, "I've got it!"

"Good," Matthew nods as he casually continues sorting and securing wires.

"Are you feeling alright?" Louise asks hesitantly.

"I think so," Matthew nods without taking his eyes off of his work. He had been fiddling with the same wire for a while now because the tiny strand kept slipping away from his calloused fingers. When he manages to tie it down at long last he turns to Louise and says, "I think I'm actually feeling better, believe it or not."

"Some venoms give you a fever, do you have one?" Louise asks, clearly not convinced that Matthew was suddenly doing better.

Reaching up to his forehead, Matthew holds the back of his hand there for a few beats. Feeling nothing out of the ordinary, he answers, "Nope, I feel fine. My hand hurts and that side of my body aches, but that's about it.

"Interesting..." Louise breathes as she looks Matthew over with an inquisitive look. Her brows furrow and she offers, "Maybe there wasn't any venom this time."

"Maybe," Matthew shrugs as he turns back to his work.

Flipping a few switches, Louise announces, "Well, hang on, I'm getting this thing moving. Hopefully, we'll be able to get out of here without too much difficulty."

Looking out of the mech's viewport, Matthew strains to see any signs of the outside world through the seemingly solid sheet of the fish-Beets. He sighs and says, "We don't have many other options if we can't..."

"Yeah..." Louise agrees as she casts a wary look toward the horde outside. Frowning, she flatly says, "I don't think either of us will want to go out there any time soon."

"Nope,"

"If we're lucky, Alois will be able to get all of those things off of us."

"Speaking of Alois, we should probably warn him that we're coming up."

"Already done, he's ready to get moving."

"No need to keep him waiting then."

At that, Louise nods and then pulls sharply on the *Firefly's* controls. Matthew takes a firm hold of a nearby handle with his good hand and he uses his other arm to hook around another one. With a few more sudden lurches the mech pauses and Matthew looks over to Louise expectantly.

"I think I might be able to shake a good amount of these things off," Louise announces.

"Sounds good," Matthew nods as he tightens his grip even further.

"I will as soon as you close up that hatch and strap in. It'll be a wild ride."

Sighing, Matthew casts one last glance at his nearly complete wiring work. He replaces the panel over it and carefully secures it into place. With that done, Matthew stows his gear and shield away, and takes a seat beside

Louise and puts on his various harnesses.

The moment that his last harness clicks into place, Louise begins jerking wildly on the *Firefly's* controls. With every sudden movement, Matthew sees large swaths of the fish-Beets slide off of the sleek windscreen while even more topple off from above. After a minute or so of lurching around Louise stops and gives Matthew a triumphant nod.

"That helped a lot," Matthew acknowledges as he looks out to the cave that they are still in. As he looks, he can see even more of the fish-Beets jumping toward him and the mech. Looking up to the outside world, Matthew asks, "Think it's time to get out of here?"

"Yep," Louise says right before she tugs on the controls before her and flips a switch or two.

Matthew sinks deep into his seat as the *Firefly* suddenly jumps and is airborne. The machine peaks and Matthew momentarily feels like he is weightless before gravity has its way with the massive machine once more. Chuckling, Matthew notes how similar it felt to riding over the crest of a large wave on rough seas.

Matthew is caught by surprise when the

mech slams into the ground and he lets out a loud grunt of pain. He rubs his newly aching gut as Louise directs the mech to rise back to its feet.

"Sorry, I should have warned you about the impact," Louise says when she sees that Matthew is in pain.

Reaching to his lower back, Matthew groans and lets out a sigh. Shaking his head, he chuckles and assures her, "Nah, I should have expected it."

"Looks like Alois is keeping busy," Louise notes as she points ahead of them.

Sure enough, Alois and the *Shad* are fighting for their lives against a seemingly endless horde of the fish-Beets that are splashing about in the mud beneath them. All around the *Shad*, bullets and explosions work ceaselessly to put an end to the swarm of hostiles.

"If we don't get moving, I'm willing to bet that we won't be doing so hot either," Matthew points out as he turns his attention to the display before him.

"What's the plan, Mudskipper?" Louise asks as she begins guiding the *Firefly* forward.

"Let's clear a path for Alois and then we'll take the long way home."

"The long way?"

"Yeah, let's go parallel to the trenches until we lose these fish-Beets. I don't want to lead them straight to the Bulwark."

"Fish-Beets, I like the sound of that."

"It made sense to me,"

"Alois and I were just calling them larva. Fish-Beets is a lot more fun though."

"Oh…" Matthew breathes as Louise's words get the gears turning in his head. Suddenly everything made a lot more sense. The 'fish-Beets' were clearly just the larvae of the invaders but he had overlooked that in his brief and frightening encounter with them. Chuckling, Matthew finally admits, "I didn't put that together."

"No worries there, Mudskipper. I like calling them fish more anyways." Louise assures him, "Now man the cannons. Those things aren't going to fire themselves."

Matthew quickly looses himself from his harness and he jumps over to the gunner's chair. He fires everything up and, after some quick computer troubleshooting, he brings his weapons to bear on the fish-Beets that are harassing Alois. Peering at the screens in front of him, Matthew lines up his first shots and he releases a volley of death from his larger cannons.

Matthew allows himself a sadistic grin as he watches the ground ahead of the *Shad* explode. Mud and burnt fish-Beets rain down all around the newly formed crater and Matthew doesn't waste a second before he fires again.

"About time you two joined me!" Alois's voice calls over the *Firefly's* interior speakers, "These things have been harassing me for too long!"

"Welcome to the club," Louise fires back.

"What's the plan?" Alois asks.

Glancing back to Matthew for a second, Louise then answers, "Mudskipper says we're taking the long way home. Let's head south a ways—at least until we lose these things."

"Think we'll have to take these things on back at the Bulwark soon?"

"Hopefully not," Matthew says between shots, "I don't think we'd be able to last too long against them without these mechs... everyone else would get slaughtered too."

"Let's hope it doesn't come to that," Louise agrees.

"Onward and southward!" Alois excitedly announces as his mech slowly begins moving.

Gritting his teeth, Matthew tries his best to clear the way for Alois without shooting anything too close to him.

Chapter Four

Somewhere on the Front, Allegra

"The crash site is just over there a ways," Matthew reports as he scans the semi-familiar hills ahead of him.

After making a shooting retreat for about two kilometers the fish-Beets had finally relented. The creatures' retreat was possibly more alarming than their initial attack because they disappeared entirely. Not only that, but they vanished at the same time as well. Alois had pointed out that this meant they were organized, and such a thought made Matthew even more wary of the Beets.

As Matthew saw things, if the Beets were that well organized then there was a reason why they were holding back. Any living creature could see that the Bulwark was an easy target right now—especially with the Toaz gone—so there had to be a reason why the Beets weren't pressing their attack.

"Think we'll find anything worthwhile in there?" Louise asks as the Coalition transport's wreck finally comes into view.

"I hope so," Matthew says as he slowly

nods and looks the area over, "The Toaz already salvaged a lot of stuff, according to Rav'ian, but it looks like there's still plenty of things that we can sift through."

The crash site has clearly seen a lot of foot traffic since Matthew left it. Dozens of trails lead westward toward the Bulwark and one or two continue on eastward past the wreckage. Quite a few new dead Beets are also scattered across the impact crater. Some are stacked in piles while others appear to have been left where they fell. Their presence is a clear testament that there had been a lot more action here than Matthew would have expected after all this time.

The speakers in the *Firefly* buzz before Alois's voice muses, "Looks like the Toaz made quite a few friends during their visit."

"We'll have to keep our eyes open for any hostiles while we're looking around," Louise states, "If the Toaz came across this many Beets then there's no knowing what we might see."

"At least the fish are gone," Alois reminds everyone.

"For now," Matthew mutters pessimistically as he slowly scans the surrounding hills.

"Well, we can always hold off on salvaging until we have more manpower," Louise points out, "That way we'll have more people who can keep a lookout for hostiles."

"That means we'd have more people helping us pull stuff out too," Alois adds.

"So you guys aren't feeling up to it now?" Matthew frowns. He had hoped to do a bit more than just survey the wreckage on his way back to Sanctuary.

"*You're* the one who got poisoned here," Louise points out, "Alois and I don't want to be the ones to tell the others that you died. We can head back once Marie gives you the all-clear, I doubt anyone will be taking too much of anything out of the wreck any time soon. With all those Beets hanging around anyone who's crazy enough to try it probably wouldn't get too far."

The speakers crackle once more before Alois adds, "And all those fish too. My bet is that no one will be going out on any adventures until those things are taken back a notch."

Shifting awkwardly in his seat, Matthew inquires, "So we're just going to leave everything out like this?"

"There's no point in risking it if most everything will still be here later," Louise reminds him, "Besides, Alois and I are the veteran salvers here. When we say that no one will be taking anything out of here we mean it. With the Toaz gone, no one is crazy enough to come out here."

"No one besides us," Alois clarifies with a laugh.

"Indeed," Louise chuckles. Looking back to Matthew who is still in the gunner's seat, Louise queries, "So, can we head back now?"

Matthew purses his lips as he looks over the vast quarry before him. On the one hand, he could totally see where the twins were coming from. No one in their right minds would be coming all the way out here to salvage a derelict wreck. Not only that, the various trails leading to the site were likely left by the Toaz when they launched their own salvage op. No one else would be either courageous or stupid enough to head out here to visit the still-smoldering remains.

Nearly a minute passes without Matthew answering and Louise presses, "Matthew?"

Shrugging, Matthew sighs and starts, "I guess we can if—"

Matthew is cut off when the roar of a ship's thrusters suddenly thunders overhead. The noise is so loud that Matthew has to cover his ears. As suddenly as the noise started seemingly a million searchlights lock onto the *Firefly* and illuminate its cockpit.

The speakers on the *Firefly* crackle loudly and several beeps and chirps sound before an unfamiliar voice calls, "Attention occupants of the hijacked mechanized marine units! Under direct order of Commander Jones, you are to turn off and exit your machines."

"What's the plan, Mudskipper?" Louise hisses as she looks upward at their unexpected—and bossy—guest.

"Uh… maybe I can try talking us out of this?" Matthew answers, saying it as more of a question than anything. Before Louise can offer a response, Matthew flicks on his radio and responds to the person who had passed along the order, "That's a negative, we are not turning these mechs over. We didn't hijack them either."

The speakers crackle and some white noise from the aircraft overhead comes through. A few moments pass as there is a brief commotion on their end before a man on the other end finally demands, "Provide us your name, rank, birth date, and serial number immediately, soldier."

"Think you made yourself a new friend?"

Louise whispers after flinching at the voice's harshness.

"Ha ha," Matthew lets out the most sarcastic laugh that he can make. Swallowing nervously, Matthew clears his throat and answers the man, "My name is Matthew Campbell. Birthdate Earth Standard December thirteenth, twenty-two sixty-three. I... wasn't ever assigned a rank or serial number."

"No serial, eh? Please standby..." the voice sounds before the transmission cuts out.

"What's the plan, Mudskipper?" Alois repeats his twin's question, "I think we could blast their ship out of the sky if we needed to, it looks like it's just a little recon vessel."

"We're not blowing anyone up," Matthew snaps, "These people are supposed to be on our side and they're just checking things out."

The *Firefly's* speakers buzz to life with a few more chirps before the other man's voice cuts through the faint static, "According to our records, you should be in the Bulwark, Matthew Campbell. What reason do you have to be out here?"

"I—um... We're running a recovery op out here. The Beets are usually dormant at night, so we're making the most of our time."

"On who's authority? We were

dispatched to the site to recover sensitive materials from the wreck."

"Under my own?"

"According to the little records we have on you, you don't seem to have the clearance to be making operational calls."

"According to the records *I've* seen, no one up here has the authority to stop me," Matthew fires back before he can stop himself. His hand flashes over his mouth and his eyes go wide as he wonders what overcame him there.

Chuckling softly, Louise looks back to him and gives him a look that appears to be both pleasantly surprised and impressed. Smirking, she jokingly asks, "You trying to get us killed?"

Before Matthew can answer Louise, the man in the ship overhead requests, "Standby, we're contacting General Nelson."

"*General* Nelson?" Matthew repeats with a hint of shock. Last time he had seen Nelson the man was only a Master Sergeant. Matthew knew that he didn't know all the ranks in the military, but he was confident that a jump to General was quite the leap for someone with Nelson's previous rank.

"Affirmative," the man on the other end

of the radio confirms, "The General was recently promoted after the previous leadership was ousted by the top brass."

Matthew is momentarily struck with disbelief when he realizes that he had spoken into the radio and not directly to Louise, as he had intended. Fortunately, he hadn't said anything negative about the new general because he knew that doing so would land him into even hotter water than he was already in. Stifling a chuckle, he assures himself that there wasn't a whole lot more that anyone could do to him in the way of punishment though, which he found oddly reassuring.

"This the same Nelson that stuck you on the front?" Louise asks after a few beats.

Nodding, Matthew answers with a hollow voice, "Yeah,"

"This a good thing or a bad thing? I thought he liked you?"

"He does, but…" Matthew pauses long enough to ensure that he isn't broadcasting this time, "But he's a little crazy."

"You have to be at least a little crazy to be a career soldier. Crazier than Alois and me, at least."

"He told me that he wants me to be in charge of the whole Bulwark. Says I'll be a captain."

"A captain in charge of a whole garrison of troops? Seems like your rank doesn't measure up to what you're supposed to be doing."

"Captain Johnson is currently in charge of the Bulwark, so I guess it's pretty standard."

"Probably just because they don't care what we do so long as we sit around and play soldier until they're ready to execute their plan."

"Think they won't like the idea of us *not* 'playing soldier?' We're a ways away from our post."

"Better to ask forgiveness than permission," Louise shrugs.

"Hmm," Matthew sounds as he crosses his arms and presses himself further into his chair's protective grasp. He didn't like the idea of being in the gun sights of the ship overhead, but he hated the thought of blowing them out of the sky as well. Closing his eyes, he offers up a quick prayer that things would end peaceably. When his prayer ends, he reaches over to the Beet carapace shield beside him, something about the shield made him feel safer, even though it would likely do nothing against the overhead threat.

"Nelson wants to speak to you, Campbell," the radio man sounds, "Good luck."

Before Matthew can thank the man, several clicks sound. Deciding that caution would best suit him now, Matthew decides to keep quiet until someone else speaks to him.

"Campbell!" Nelson's voice calls over the *Firefly's* speakers. Despite his loudness, Nelson doesn't seem to be angry this time around, which Matthew takes as a good sign.

"Yes, sir," Matthew acknowledges, trying to sound as formal as he can.

"Not only do you survive your first few days on the front, but now you go and lead assaults into no-man's-land! I'm impressed, boy."

"Thank you, sir,"

"Tell me, how did you get that mech that I'm told you're using? It was assigned to the ship that you're interrupting a recovery on. Did you steal it? My teams say that it was sabotaged—was that you?"

"I… No, sir. We tracked down the party responsible for the sabotage and… commandeered these two mechs from them once they were dealt with."

"So, you're policing my Bulwark, then? Very nice for a Mudder."

"I'm just making the most of my time here, sir," Matthew assures the man, trying to make his efforts sound far less impressive. Matthew glances over to Louise and he offers her a shrug in response to her astonished look.

"If you're so into policing your new home, then I've got a special mission for you,"

"Yes?"

"There's a Fulcrum hideout over there. The man who trained you heads it up. They're not the kindest crew out there, I'm sure you've already been acquainted with at least a few of them—"

"They've been dealt with, General," Matthew interrupts, "Down to the last man."

"Why, aren't you the industrious one?" Nelson chuckles, "Well, that leaves a definite void in command there, as James was the ranking soldier that we had stationed up there…"

When Nelson fails to go on, Matthew can't help but wonder if the man was still on the other end, "Sir?"

"I'm promoting you, Campbell."

Not entirely sure what that entailed, Matthew tries to sound as excited and thankful as he can, "Oh. Thank you, sir."

"I'll be in touch, Campbell," Nelson

sounds before a click and some static.

DESPERATE PLEA!

Thank you for exploring the future alongside me!

I'd love to hear what you think about my book!

Please drop an honest review of what you thought about it on Amazon or Goodreads!

Thank you so much!

Caleb Fast

P.S. Sign up to my newsletter to get updates on future book releases, other book news, and some fun, free short stories!

https://calebfast.com/newsletter/

The Story Continues,

Season two of The Battle for Allegra is being released in 2021 piece by piece, so be sure to stick with Matthew as he fights to save Allegra!

The Battle for Allegra Episode Eleven:

https://www.amazon.com/dp/B094ZLQCGL

Want to read my full-length novels?

Start out with book one of The Limit of Infinity!

Renaissance: The Limit of Infinity

https://www.amazon.com/dp/B07QXKFDV9

Printed in Great Britain
by Amazon

23932597R00383